C. J. G

CW00516874

NEVER CAME HOME

A DI Max Byrd &
DI Orion Tanzy Thriller
Book 2

C. J. GRAYSON

1

C. J. Grayson

ISBN: 9798564027731
Print Edition May 2020
Version: First Edition

Never Came Home

Books by C. J. Grayson

Standalones –
Someone's There

DI Max Byrd & DI Orion Tanzy –
That Night (book 1)
Never Came Home (book 2)

C. J. Grayson

'Often the best conversations happen in silence.'
– Unknown

Prologue
Darlington
2019

DI Max Byrd pulled up in his BMW X5 and turned off the engine. Noticing the Golf parked in front of him, Byrd knew DI Orion Tanzy was already here, but he couldn't see him inside the car.

Byrd yawned, then opened the door and stepped out into the bitter cold. The ground was dry but a thin layer of frost was starting to develop. It wasn't expected to rain, which made a change because it had been awful for days now. Rivers overflowing, drains clogging up, not being able to withstand the relentless downpours that looked like they'd never end. But finally, a dry day for Darlington albeit still freezing.

Byrd, dressed in his long black coat, black jeans, and black shoes, stepped around the back of his car, up onto the path, and through the entrance of Stanhope Park. Up ahead, he saw them.

From the small crowd, although it was dark, he could make out Tanzy, standing beside Jacob Tallow, the Senior Forensic Officer. He was accompanied by the other Senior Forensic Officer, Emily Hope. Both of them were dressed in their familiar white disposable overalls and white face masks.

As he got closer, Tanzy heard his footsteps and glanced his way.

'You made it?' he asked Byrd. 'Sorry I woke you.'

Byrd nodded, then caught the overshoes Tanzy threw at him, and tiredly put them on. He bowed under the tape and joined Tanzy.

Moments before Byrd had turned up, Amy Weaver, a small, slim, blonde Police Constable, along with PC Phillip Cornty, a tall, thin guy with glasses and a pointy nose, had already set up a perimeter. At 4 a.m., it was unlikely that there would be many people around, but they had to do things right, had to make sure they didn't disturb any potential evidence.

Byrd watched the senior forensic, Tallow, and grabbed his attention. 'How long do you think she's been there?'

'A good few hours, Max, she's stone cold,' he replied, crouching down near the body.

Byrd, from a few feet away, looked down on her. She was laid on her right side with her left leg over her right, and her left arm down in front of her face. She looked peaceful in a strange way, as if she was sleeping.

'What do you think happened?' Byrd asked, noticing the cloudy saliva around her mouth, under her chin, and around the floor under her face. Whatever happened, she'd been violently sick; that much was obvious.

'I wouldn't like to say for definite but most likely a drug overdose, Max,' Tallow replied.

Byrd nodded. 'Who called it in?'

Tanzy pointed behind them towards a male, bordering the age of late teens to early twenties, who was standing with PC Weaver. From what Tanzy and Byrd could see, he couldn't seem to keep still, constantly fidgeting and shivering in the early morning frost.

'He called it in, said she'd gone missing from the party,' Tanzy said, who'd already spoken with him. 'Everyone assumed she was somewhere in the house. After a while, people started to get worried. Eventually, they started looking on the streets for her. He came across her and rang an ambulance.'

'Where was the party?'

'Few streets from here.' Tanzy pointed south. 'Swinburn Road.'

'Where are the paramedics?'

Tanzy pointed up to their right, where an ambulance was parked at the side of the road. 'She was dead when they arrived. They did what they could but...' He fell silent for a moment. 'We need to contact the undertaker.'

'Do they think a drug overdose, too?' Byrd asked.

Tanzy nodded. 'They think it's possible but aren't ruling out other possibilities.'

'We're taking the samples we need and will take her to the morgue,' Tallow informed him, overhearing their conversation. 'We'll do further tests back at the lab and give you a better picture soon enough.'

'Okay...' Byrd drifted off and had a good look around. A red taxi flying down Stanhope Road caught his attention for a moment, taking a customer to their house no doubt after a wild Friday night in town. Byrd remembered those days, the days of no responsibility and worries. When the biggest choice he had to make was what outfit to wear.

'First impressions, Max?' Tanzy asked him.

Byrd curled his lip but stayed silent in thought. He then glanced towards the young lad who was still with Weaver, then returned his focus on the dead girl. 'It could be anything, Orion, it really could.'

'You know what our biggest question is though?'

Byrd nodded. 'Yes, I do... why is she naked - where are her clothes?'

1

Waiting patiently in the car, the man watched the teenage boy standing on the corner of Salisbury Terrace, just along from where he was parked. The teenager, who could have been anywhere between fifteen and twenty, might have been one of the familiars, but the man couldn't be sure; there were so many of them and it was too dark to tell.

He'd been parked up for ten minutes and so far, he'd —

His phone rang in his pocket, making him tense until he realised what it was. He looked down, plucked it out, pressed ANSWER and put it to his ear.

'Hey,' he said, sheepishly.

'Hey yourself, where are you?' asked his wife.

'I'm – I'm just going into the shop now. Need anything?'

'No, I'm okay,' she said. 'Just thought I'd call. How's Jake?'

'He's okay. It was good to catch up with him. I haven't seen him in a long time.'

'How's Elaine doing?' she asked. Elaine was Jake's wife. But because he hadn't actually been to see Jake, he lied again.

'She's good - are you sure you don't need anything; I'm just getting out of the car now...'

'No, I'm good, I'll see you soon.' She hung up, none the wiser as to what he was actually doing. He put the phone back into his pocket and glanced up through the frost covered windscreen.

Three people approached the teenager and had handed over the money in exchange for something small. The operation was quick, efficient. If you didn't know what was happening, you'd miss it.

Like a magician's trick.

In the last month or so, it had been the police's biggest problem. The growth of its use, and consequently, the parallel effects it had on the rise in crime, which was now a noticeable statistic for local police. It was certainly something they'd have to try and control. But they never would, despite the excess efforts and new plans they seemed to consistently put in place.

Drugs. A growing game in Darlington in recent times, and there was nothing that could be done to prevent it. If one of them was arrested, the dealers would send out another desperate soul, who'd do anything for a bit of money. What the dealers made in profits compared to what the teenagers were paid was ridiculous. The teenagers didn't know any different, being paid nearly two-hundred pound a night to stand somewhere handing out bags of cocaine and heroin to equally desperate souls who needed their fix, wasn't a bad gig. Dangerous, of course, but it beat working nine till five for less than minimum wage which was the other miserable option.

The game had its perks; it made them feel powerful, too. One of the *players* around the town. Their friends, when they heard who they were working for, feared them as well as respected them, giving them an air of arrogance and importance in their young naivety.

The man in the car continued to watch, knowing he'd have his chance soon. To him, it was risky. He didn't want to be seen. But it had to be done.

The boy on the corner glanced left and right every couple of seconds, keeping his eyes on the street. To his left, just around the corner of the betting shop, he watched a man appear, his eyes clearly scanning the area, until they landed and stayed on him. The man, who appeared scrawny, wearing a dark coloured cheap-looking track-suit with holes in random places, sauntered over the road towards him desperate for his daily fix. The teenager nod-ded and said something to him as they met on the corner. The man put his hand in his pocket and handed him something in exchange for a bag of white powder.

A few minutes later, the teenager decided he'd been there long enough and pulled his hood over his head, then left the corner and crossed the road.

The man watched the teenager walk towards him, step-ping up onto the path near his car. After he passed the car, the man watched him in the wing mirror as the teenager moved along the side of the park's metal railings and take a right through the archway entrance into the Denes park.

He knew he wouldn't get a better chance, so decided it was time. He opened the door and stepped out into the cold. The air hit his skin like a thousand tiny pins. Locking the car, he rounded it and stepped up onto the path, mak-ing his way along to the entrance. Through the fence rail-ings, he watched the teenager carefully pad down the hill near the play area and disappear into the darkness.

It could be too risky, the man kept saying over and over in his head.

Passing the gates, he peered into the park, then slowed a little, unsure if it was really worth it. He'd been going through a tough time recently; did he really need to buy drugs? Was his life really at that point where drugs would fix his problems? Fair enough, they helped the minority but for most it was the start of a spiralling hell. And of course, it would only be a temporary fix, he knew.

He sighed, continued deeper into the darkness. Some-where in front, although he couldn't see, he faintly heard the teenager's footsteps and knew he'd have to speed up to catch him. His heart was thumping through his chest as he cautiously made his way down the ramp. For a moment, he thought about using the torch app on his phone but he'd risk being seen, which could scare the teenager away and that's something he didn't want.

The play area was in darkness to his left. He heard a murmur of voices and stopped dead, glaring into the night.

The voices suddenly hushed.

'Hello,' he said in the direction of the noise.

Silence answered him.

To his right, he could still hear the footsteps of the teenager, each step getting quieter as it moved away from him. He needed to catch him, otherwise he'd miss his chance, and his wife would be expecting him home soon. The last thing he wanted was for her to ring him again.

He moved forward, crossing over the shallow beck, and stopped at the base of the grassy hill, glancing left and right.

Nothing.

'Shit,' he whispered.

He decided to take a right, focusing on any movement but it was too dark. He heard the slow flow of the shallow stream at the base of the gentle slope but he couldn't see a thing. Maybe this wasn't such a good —

'Why are you following me?' a voice said from behind him.

He physically jumped and gasped, turning one-eighty, raising his hands up in defence. Under the very dim conditions of the park he saw the faintest outline of the teenager standing there. His hood was up over his head. The space where his face should be was black.

'Why are you following me?' the teenager said again, this time firmer.

'I – I was hoping to – to… erm… get some…'

'Blow? Smack?'

The man nodded, then realised the boy probably couldn't see him, and said, 'Yeah... something. Anything.'

'You a cop?' the boy asked without hesitation.

'No, no cop. I'm feeling down,' the man explained. 'I need something to... to pick me up. Can – can you help me?'

'You were watching me from the car up there, weren't you?' the teenager asked. 'The dark blue Kia Sportage?'

'I... was,' he admitted.

'Why?'

He wasn't sure if it was the darkness, but the teenager appeared to move closer to him, so he stepped back, feeling the incline of the damp grass bank near the stream under his heels. He was cornered. There was no one around. The only sounds were the hum of passing engines up on Northcote Terrace, and the steady flowing water a few metres behind him. His heart beat faster, and as each second passed, he wondered why he'd put himself in this situation with this stranger.

Anything could happen.

He glanced around to see if anyone was nearby, in case they could help if the teenager decided to attack him. 'I - I didn't know if I wanted to go through with it...' the man explained, softly.

'Through with what?' the teenager asked.

Very quickly, with the knife he'd been holding behind his back, the man lunged forward and drove the knife into the teenager's throat. The teenager gagged, throwing his hands up to his chin, stumbling back several wobbly paces, gargling on the excess blood in his throat. A moment passed, then the teenager lurched forward, collapsing to his knees and clutching at his own throat.

The man took a step back watching him struggle and smiled when the teenager fell forward and tumbled down the grassy incline into the stream.

The man casually placed the knife back into his coat and quickly checked around him. With no one in sight he made his way back across the short bridge and up to Widdowfield Street. He unlocked his car, opened the door and climbed in.

In the rear view mirror, he smiled at himself.

It was the first time he'd ever done that.

And he knew it wouldn't be the last.

2

Mandy Spencer sighed heavily sitting at the low desk in the corner of the spacious office. It had been a long day, longer than usual, filled with meetings and phone calls, leaving her so little time, she'd forgotten to eat. Silence surrounded her, a polar opposite of the activity during the day but she was glad of the solitary time. The peace allowed her to focus better, but the office felt a little eerie at this time with no one else around.

Henry and Tracy had already left a few hours ago, as well as most of the other people in the building and adjoining offices. After the usual four-thirty finish, a handful of managers and maintenance personnel were the only council members around, apart from the cleaner, who'd do her round to make the place presentable for the following day.

Mandy told Henry and Tracy she'd stay back to look over some of the plans for upcoming enquiries and would set aside the important ones for tomorrow. The enquiries, most of the time, were basic, and included typical housing developments, conservatories, single and double storey extensions. It would be up to Mandy, Henry, and Tracy to decide whether these plans based on the current laws and legislations, would be accepted. It wasn't just the laws they needed to adhere to, it was the public, too. For example, if an occupier wanted to build a double storey extension and lived in a semi-detached house, Mandy had to decide if the plans would affect their next-door neighbours. Would the new extension block the sunlight? Would it restrict their view? Everything had to be considered. She always remembered years ago she dealt with an awkward old lady in Yoredale Avenue who'd complained about a neighbour putting up an extension because she wouldn't be able to see the chimney tops a few streets away. Still made her giggle now, thinking about it.

The biggest planning enquiry recently had come from a wealthy property developer who made an offer for the old building that used to be Cactus Jacks night club, or if you remembered before then, the Plastered Parrot. Located just behind Queen Street, it was a spacious plot with a lot of potential, and most importantly to the buyer, a prime location. Not only did the buyer want the building, but he wanted the car parks next to them. This was an issue, as the car parks were owned by the council and the council had, on several unpleasant occasions, clearly stated that it wasn't up for debate and that under no circumstances, would the land be sold to him. It was then Mandy's job to explain the enquiry and the restriction of plans to the buyer to make him understand why this couldn't happen.

She leaned to her right, picked up her orange mug that Henry had bought for her birthday and finished the rest of the lukewarm coffee, then placed it back down and opened another email. Before she started reading the first line, the phone to her right started ringing. She frowned, glanced down at her watch. It was nearly eight p.m..

'Who's this?' she whispered to herself, wondering who it could be. She picked it up, and hesitantly said, 'Hello?'

'Mrs Spencer?'

Her frown deepened. 'Yeah...?'

'Have you changed your mind?' the voice asked.

She recognised it. It was the buyer who wanted the old Cactus Jacks building and nearby car parks.

'About the sale of the building and planning permission of the car parks?'

'Yes.'

'Mr Cairn, we've spoken about this. I'm sorry to tell you that what I'd explained last week is still the same this week. The owners of the club are willing to sell you their plot, but the car parks are council property. They have nothing to do with the building. The council have relayed back to me – on several occasions now – that they won't sell you the land.'

'I need the car parks,' he said, sternly.

Mandy sighed, her shoulders dipping. 'I know you do. You've made that clear. But there's nothing I can do. I really wish there was. I'm so very sorry.'

Mr Cairn didn't answer.

'Do you understand?' Mandy asked.

'It must be lonely?'

'I'm sorry?'

'Working in that large office by yourself?'

'By myself – I work in a team of three. You know Henry and Susan?'

'I know them well, yes,' he replied, 'but I mean right now. Sitting at that desk in that black dress you've worn all day. Isn't your husband getting worried about you? Won't he be expecting you home soon?'

She quickly scanned the office but she couldn't see anyone. It was very quiet. The last time she'd heard the cleaner was almost an hour ago, and she remembered her saying 'Bye' as she left.

'Mrs Spencer?'

'I'm here…' she whispered, her eyes still flitting around nervously. The glass windows at the edge of the massive room were black, reflecting the office space under the bright lights from the ceiling, preventing her seeing through them, not that she would see much being on the second floor.

'It's a nice dress,' the voice said. 'Does your husband like it?'

Her words got stuck in her throat.

'Does he?' the man said.

'Yeah.'

'I'm sorry?'

'Yes,' she said, louder.

'I like it, too.'

'Can – can you see me?' She looked around the room wearily.

'I'm always watching...'

She tried to stay calm and professional. 'Listen, I need to ask you to stop ringing about the planning permission. We have made it abundantly clear that the council are not granting you the car parks, therefore there is nothing left to discuss. And to be honest, you're making me feel uncomfortable.'

'I'm very fond of what you, Henry, and Susan have done for us in the past. You've been great. If this planning permission doesn't go through, I wouldn't want anything bad to happen to you.'

'Goodbye, Mr Cairn!' she shouted, slamming the phone down into the receiver.

Over the next few minutes, she couldn't concentrate. The comments about her black dress were playing over and over in her mind. Had he been in earlier and seen her wearing it? If so, how did he know she was there alone now? She didn't like it one bit and decided to log off her computer and deal with the emails tomorrow with the help of Susan and Henry. They could wait, that's for sure. And her son, Damien, and husband, Paul, would be waiting for her getting home. She'd promised them a game of monopoly tonight.

She stood up, used her fingers to curl her blonde hair behind her ears and grabbed her jacket from the back of the chair, and put it on. She wasn't looking forward to leaving. It was freezing outside. It had been like that for days. No doubt driving would be dangerous again on the way home. She had almost skid off the road yesterday due to some stupid driver who'd broke harshly in front of her for no apparent reason.

At the exit door to the office, she hit the switch, causing the room behind her to plummet into darkness. She closed the door and locked it, then put the key in her pocket. Each worker had their own key in case they stayed back, which was often the case depending on workloads. She made her way along the wide corridor to the lifts, and when she got there, she pressed the button. She was only up two flights, but she always used the lift. It was easier. There was a mechanical sound behind the thick, silver doors then the lift doors opened with a ping.

She glared into the dark lift for a moment, then, bending at her knees low enough to see the ceiling of the lift, she noticed the lights were out.

In two minds whether to take a pitch-black lift down two levels or just use the stairs, she decided to take the stairs instead. After a couple of moments, the doors pinged closed, and she moved to the right and pushed open the stairwell door, then started to descend them.

The words of Mr Cairn played heavily on her mind.

The black dress.

Working alone.

She'd dealt with him in the past, but she'd never had the pleasure – if that's what you'd call it – of meeting him. Everything was done over emails and phone calls. How the past week had turned out, with him phoning everyday asking them to reconsider the planning permission, she was glad she'd never met him. But it was strange he knew she was married and about the black dress she was currently wearing.

She'd almost reached the first floor when it happened.

The lights in the stairwell went off, leaving her in total darkness.

'God, what now?' she muttered, freezing for a second. Then very slowly and cautiously she descended the remaining three steps with the help of the handrail to her right, edged the doors open onto the first floor, and peered down the corridor. Pitch black. To the left, through the floor-to-ceiling glass window, she could see the side of the Dolphin Centre across the road.

'Hello?' she said loudly, more so for the benefit of hearing her own voice so she wouldn't feel alone. 'Is anyone there?' she said, this time almost shouting down the corridor. A shadowy silence answered her back.

From her bag, she grabbed her phone quickly, her hands shaking, and scrolled through her contact list until she found the right number, then pressed CALL.

'Hello,' said the voice after a few rings.

'Hi, this is Mandy Spencer of Planning Permission. I'm in the office alone, and the lights have gone out. The whole building is in darkness.'

'Hi, Mandy,' said the voice of Tony Mclean, the maintenance man. 'Just hold tight. I'm near the power supply now. Give me two seconds, just stay where you are.'

'Okay, I'm just in the stairwell at the Dolphin Centre end, first floor level.'

'I'm the opposite end, just going into the Utilities room now.'

She heard a click through the phone, then after a few moments of fiddling around, he said, 'Right okay, looks like it's tripped for some reason. Hold on.'

'Okay, I'm holding…'

'Oh, by the way, did he come up and see you?' Tony asked.

'Who?' Mandy said, scowling in the darkness.

'The man – don't know his name. Saw him only a few minutes ago. I asked him what he was doing, and he told me he was collecting something from your office on the second floor. Told me he'd checked in with Roger, the security guard.'

'Who – who was he?'

'I don't know, he… oh, hold on, think I've found the problem,' Tony said, looking at the Town Hall's complicated electrical distribution board. He went quiet for a while until the silence became uncomfortable.

'Tony?' she said softly.

After a long moment of silence, she pulled the phone away from her head, noticing the call had been disconnected. 'Shit.'

When she heard the quiet footsteps behind her she felt something grab her shoulder.

3

Tuesday Night
Town Hall

In reaction, she jumped forward, falling to the floor and screamed. With her body twisted, she turned but could barely see the figure standing on the stairs staring down at her.

'What the fuck?' she shouted. 'Who – who's there?'

The figure didn't say anything, nor was there any sound in the whole building. She shuffled back towards the double doors on her backside into the corridor of the first floor, almost hyperventilating. Somewhere ahead of her, she heard footsteps pacing towards her. Her heart rate doubled as she frantically tapped the button on her phone, desperate for some light. When the phone erupted with a bright white light, she shone it into the pitch black stairwell.

Then she saw him.

'Jesus, Henry... you fucking... God... you scared me... Jesus Christ.' She sighed heavily and dropped her face into her hands with relief. 'Never, and I mean never... do that again!'

Henry moved closer, erupting in laughter. 'I – I couldn't miss the opportunity. I'm sorry.' He placed a hand on the outside of her arm. 'Are you okay, Mand?'

'I think I've died and come back to life. Honestly, I've never been so scared.'

'What's happened with the electric – why's it off?'

'I don't know, it just went off, I was coming down the stairs and it just—

The staircase filled with light. It took a few seconds for her eyes to adjust and there in front of her, was her colleague, Henry, dressed in a dark hoody and jogging bottoms.

'Why are you here?' she said.

'I left my laptop here. The missus wanted to have a look at holidays for the summer. I was going to Sainsburys anyway, so thought I'd pop in. I told her she could have just checked on her phone, but you know what she's like.'

She raised her eyebrows in humour. 'From what you've told me, yes I do.'

Henry's wife was very particular. Choosey. High maintenance. Anything else you'd describe a woman with the ability to take a strop if something didn't go her way, would probably fit the bill.

'Have you got a key for the office?'

He used a palm to pad the outside of his hoody. After there was a ping of keys, he nodded. 'I'll lock up when I leave. See you in the morning. Watch those roads by the way, it's icy out there.'

'See you in the morning,' she said with a nod, then moved around him and descended the stairs.

When she reached the ground floor, she took a right after she went through the doors, making her way along the long corridor to the opposite end. When she reached it, she pushed hard on the exit door and stepped out into the cold car park. Her car was about twenty metres ahead of her. Shivering as she rounded the bonnet of the car, she pulled her keys from her pocket, climbed in and shut the door, the sound echoing around her.

'What a day it's been.' She sighed, placing her bag onto the passenger seat and turning on the engine. As she put the car in reverse she turned her head to face the rear windscreen then stopped, glaring at the piece of paper tucked under her rear wiper.

'What the…'

She put the gear back into neutral and got out of the car. She plucked the paper from the faint grip of the wiper's rubber and looked at it. There was writing on it.

Frowning, she read it: *Something bad is going to happen if that planning permission isn't approved.*

4

Wednesday Morning
Denes Park

Six-year-old Ethan had been ill last night. Stomach cramps his mother thought, but she wasn't sure, so she'd taken him to Moorland's surgery to have him checked out by their family doctor, who they'd been seeing as far back as when *she* was a child. Apparently, he'd eaten something that hadn't agreed with his stomach, according to the Doctor's analysis when he pressed firmly on the different areas of Ethan's stomach. Calpol was the advised cure.

They took a right onto Hollyhurst road, walked nearly a minute then went left into the park and made their way down the steady decline.

'How you feeling, Ethan?'

He placed his palm tiredly over his stomach and looked up at her with glassy eyes. 'Tummy hurts, Mummy.' His saddened expression broke her heart.

'Aww baby, we'll give you some medicine when we get home, okay?' She wrapped her padded arm around him, pulled him gently into her. 'We'll be home soon, okay?'

Nodding, he embraced her hug, then turned away and looked back at the path. The park was wet, a smell of damp leaves and moisture hung in the air from the rain last night, between them going to bed and waking up.

As the path levelled out, a man walking a dog came towards them, a short lead wrapped around his hand. Ethan loved dogs. They used to have a black Lab, but this was a dog that Ethan had never seen before. Anna, his mother, was checking something on the phone which was never out of her hands.

'Mammy... doggy,' Ethan said, pointing.

'Huh?' She kept her concentration down on her phone and never noticed, closing in on the man.

The man had long blonde hair, a short but unkept beard, and was in his sixties, maybe seventies, dressed completely in blue denim that was ripped in places and black boots that had seen better days. He glanced up to meet Ethan's gaze for a moment and smiled at the boy with a mouthful of missing teeth, and said, 'Good morning.'

Anna glanced up, slightly taken aback by his greeting, but managed to return his politeness with a shy smile. When they were past the man, Ethan turned and watched the dog.

'Ethan, come on,' Anna snapped, 'stop staring.'

They continued to walk on, could see the play area over the other side of the beck. It was empty, which wasn't a surprise as most children would be in school. Anna couldn't wait to get home and get the kettle on. She'd already spoken to the school about keeping Ethan off, so she could make sure he was okay. They told her to keep the doctor's note to hand in the following day. Truancy was through the roof nowadays simply because some parents couldn't be bothered to get out of their dressing gowns and take them.

'I'm cold...' he told her.

'I know, Eath, we'll be home soon.'

They took a right and started to cross the small bridge when Ethan stopped, noticing something down in the beck. 'Mammy...'

'Yeah?' she said, feeling his hand dragging her back slightly.

'What's that?' He pointed down into the beck, a little further up, near the low, narrow tunnel that went under Surtees Street.

She stopped and frowned. 'I – I don't know. Could be rubbish. Probably just a bin bag, Ethan. Come on, let's —'

'I wanna go see,' he begged.

'Ethan, it'll be a bin bag or something. We need to get you home, you're not very well.'

He looked up at her with sad, puppy-dog eyes that said everything without him saying a word.

'Okay, we'll walk that way, and go up there then. It won't be much longer anyway.'

'Thanks,' he shouted, excitedly.

He was always the curious type ever since he'd been able to speak. She'd say to her friends she was sick of him asking every question under the sun but she knew one day he'd grow up and shut himself off through the teenage years, which was what her other son, Mark, did when he went through them.

They turned and continued along the path towards the bin bag. He was so excited.

'Mammy, what do we do if it's gold? Can we keep it?'

She smiled widely. 'If it's gold, we can keep it. But you have to promise me something?'

He looked up at her, waiting.

'That you can't tell anyone if it's gold. Then we can buy a nice big house and a big car and go on sunny holidays.'

'Yeeeaaaah. I promise.'

'Good boy.'

As they approached the shape in the beck, Anna figured out it wasn't a binbag. It didn't have that shiny, light-reflective appearance you assume a bag would have. It was black though, longer than a bag, the shape of it becoming clearer as they grew nearer. Then it dawned on her. She didn't want to believe it.

'Mammy?' Ethan asked, frowning.

'Is that man poorly? Has he fallen over?'

Her heart raised a few notches when she saw the soles of some black Nike Air trainers, then the legs of the body.

'Jesus…' she whispered, pulling him back, so he couldn't see.

'Mammy!' he gasped. 'I want to see, I want to see.'

She turned and put her palms on the outside of each of his shoulders, keeping him back. 'Listen, Ethan, you need to stay here okay? I need to see what it is…'

Nodding under her instruction, he waited, watching her get closer to the beck. She carefully made her way down the muddy decline, fully aware of what she was looking at. She needed to see if the person was alive. There was a chance they'd just lost balance and fallen in.

But she knew the truth.

She knew the person was dead.

And she knew it was a male. Not because it was obvious but because her eldest son, Mark, wore the exact same trainers and tracksuit bottoms yesterday.

And he never came home last night.

C. J. Grayson

5
Wednesday Morning
Denes Park

Tanzy was advised by DC Leonard to park up on Willow-field Road. It was easier for access but, unfortunately, he couldn't get parked along the path parallel to the railings because not only were there several police cars, people had got wind of what had happened and had decided to interrupt their busy schedules to check it out. Nothing would beat taking that perfect photo and uploading it to their social media profiles with news like this. Unless their camera phones had an 40x optical zoom, they wouldn't get very far though because PC Donny Grearer and PC Eric Timms were manning the gate, only allowing police officers and forensic teams in and out of the entrance at the top of the hill.

Tanzy closed his door, stepped up onto the path and made his way down to Willowfield Road. He'd got a space roughly six houses up Greenbank Road and left his Golf there, so it wasn't too far. It gave him time to get his stomach ready for what he was about to walk into. He felt them. The butterflies. Flitting around his stomach relent-lessly.

The rusty old metal railings along the side of the park were almost hidden by the plethora of eager people watching. A murmur of excitement and anxiety filled the air.

'What is going on here?' Tanzy asked himself, stepping off the path, joining the back of the two-deep crowd. PC Andrews trailed him, trying to peer over the heads but couldn't see much of what was happening down in the park. Tanzy moved to the left and didn't need to flash his credentials to Grearer and Timms to pass through the gate they were standing at, then started down the bank with Andrews trailing slightly behind him.

'Why do you think it happened?' Andrews asked.

'I don't know – could be anything.'

Andrews got the feeling that Tanzy wasn't up for much conversation so said nothing more as they went down the damp decline. Just over the small bridge, Tanzy clocked DC Leonard and PC Amy Weaver speaking to a woman. Tanzy noticed she moved with energy and anger, her arms constantly raising and lowering, her mouth moving rapidly but he couldn't hear what she was saying. DC Leonard had mentioned that the body had been found by a woman claiming to be the mother of the victim, so Tanzy assumed the woman could be her.

They ambled slowly over the bridge and stopped behind DC Leonard. Beyond him, sitting on a bench by himself, was a little blonde-haired boy, no older than the age of seven or eight, who Tanzy could see had been crying.

The closer they got, the conversation with the apparent mother came into ear shot.

'… don't you dare fucking tell me that!' the woman shouted at Leonard. 'How can you stand there while my son is lying in that cold, dirty stream?'

Leonard attempted to raise a calming palm, but she moved closer and swatted it out the way, her eyes wide and body trembling.

'Hey, hey!' PC Weaver shouted, stepping forward and grabbing her wrists. 'Mrs Greenwell, that's enough. We need you to calm down, or we will arrest you.'

Anna Greenwell tried to shrug her grip, but Weaver held on tight. 'I wouldn't do that if I was you. Listen, I know you're upset, but all we are doing is trying to help you here.'

Instead of becoming aggressive again, she nodded, dropped her shoulders an inch and started to cry. Weaver let go of her wrists and watched her raise them to her face. 'Why... why him? I don't understand!'

'Hey,' Tanzy said softly, just behind Leonard and Weaver. 'What do we have?'

'Teenager is over there'—he turned and pointed—'and this is his mother, Anna, and her son, Ethan.'

Tanzy briefly glanced at Anna, then beyond her to Ethan for a moment longer, seeing the sadness in his small face.

'Hi, Anna, I'm Detective Inspector Orion Tanzy with Durham Constabulary.' He edged forward but didn't invade her personal space. 'I can understand you're upset but you must believe us when we say we are doing our very best in this situation.' He glanced to the right for a moment, thinking about his words carefully. 'The forensic team will do their best to determine what happened and, from there, we can hopefully gather enough evidence to uncover the reason why this awful thing has happened. I've witnessed dozens of these situations and what you're feeling is absolutely normal. What I ask is could you try and be patient and have faith we can do our job?'

Anna's tears stopped falling from her eyes as she nodded at Tanzy.

He turned to PC Weaver. 'Would you mind waiting here with Mrs Greenwell while I go speak with the team?'

'No problem.' Weaver switched her focus to Anna, who bobbed her head implying she'd cause her no trouble.

Tanzy turned with Andrews and they headed along the path. Although the sun had crept out behind a cloud, it was freezing and didn't seem to be getting any warmer. In his long grey Parker coat Tanzy didn't feel it but the PCs in uniform were almost visibly shaking.

Underfoot the ground was wet, the grass tinkered with dew. Up ahead, dressed in their white disposable suits, were Amanda Forrest, Jacob Tallow, and Emily Hope, standing a few metres down the bank. They were staring down at the teenager, whose legs and stomach were resting on the grass but whose face and shoulders were under the water of the gently flowing stream.

Along the path as it inclined up to Surtees Street the park entrance under the archway was manned by two officers stopping members of the public getting in. It was a similar crowd to the one up on Willowfield Road. Up on the left, up the grass bank, standing at the metal railings, were a number of people with phones in their hands interested in why the police were there too. From where they were, no doubt they could see the teenager lying on his front with his face submerged in the water and Tanzy would put a month's wage on pictures being uploaded to social media soon, if they hadn't already.

'All we need, isn't it... those people watching,' Tanzy muttered to Andrews.

Amanda noticed them approach, looked away from the display screen of the black camera in her hand, and said, 'Morning.' Not only looking exhausted, she sounded it too, her voice dull and flat, as if all the energy had been drained from her.

'Hey, Amanda,' Tanzy said, noticing her tired appearance but didn't mention it. 'What do we have?'

'Male teenager. Aged somewhere I think between fifteen and eighteen in my opinion. No ID but DC Leonard has spoken to the woman down there who claims to be his mother.'

Tanzy nodded, briefly glanced back at the woman who was standing next to Weaver and Leonard. 'Yeah, she says she's the mother. He's called Mark, aged seventeen. Has anyone contacted Peter yet?'

'Yeah.'

'Is he coming over?'

'No, he said due to the position of the body, and what Tallow had told him, he's happy to meet us at the hospital later this afternoon,' she replied.

'Okay, good,' Tanzy said, looking past her.

When a body is found dead, it isn't even within the capability of a police officer to pronounce the individual as dead, even if the person's head is separated from the body in a sea of blood. Local laws and legislations state that only a paramedic, doctor or coroner can officially pronounce someone as dead. Peter Gibbs, the local coroner, with his professional background of being a doctor, was on his way. Peter had a couple of technicians working under him and when he needed assistance, he'd use them, but he liked to do a lot of the work himself. If there was ever a body found under circumstances which implied something malicious, he'd be there as soon as he could.

Tanzy rubbed his cold, bald head.

'When's Max back?'

'Tomorrow I think. I haven't spoken with him much.'

'How's he doing?' Forrest asked, genuinely concerned about a friend.

'He's – he's okay. Just takes a little getting used to with what happened. Would be hard for anyone.'

Forrest replied with a sympathetic nod and close-lipped smile.

'So, what's happened here?' he asked, nodding towards the riverbank. 'You had a good look?'

She turned. 'We know that Mrs Greenwell found him earlier. She told us she lifted his face up to have a look at him, then dropped him again and started screaming. We've spoken to'—she pointed along the path, then seemed to lose what she was looking for—'don't know where he is, but a local man who lives in one of the streets. He was walking past and heard her screaming then ran down to see what all the commotion was about. Think DC Leonard spoke with him and took down some notes.'

'How was he killed? Tripped and fell, or something more sinister…'

'Knife to the throat unfortunately,' she said, briefly wincing. 'We lifted his head up to observe and take photos of the cut. Standard incision with a clean knife, nothing special about it really. But after checking his pockets, we found a load of money and a plastic bag filled with a number of smaller bags. White and brown substance.'

'Cocaine and Heroin?'

Amanda half nodded. 'It's possible.'

'Nice,' Tanzy commented. 'So potential dealer. Gang war? Buyer not happy with the product? With the price?'

'Maybe,' Forrest replied, this time shrugging. 'That's why you're the detective.'

'Does there seem to be any other injuries?'

'Not that we can see, not yet. It looks like there's a significant amount of blood on his clothes and hands'—she indicated around her own chest area—'so whatever happened, he attempted to stop the bleeding quickly.' She shivered for a moment, suddenly feeling the cold even though she was well padded under her thin white suit.

'Did he have a phone?' Tanzy asked.

She nodded. 'In his left pocket.'

'Good. Bag it up. Take it back for analysis. We need to see his recent calls and text messages. And anything on his social media profiles that could help us.'

'Understood,' she replied.

'I'll come back, I need to speak with his mother,' said Tanzy. Then they both glanced in her direction. DC Leonard's palm was on the side of her shoulder attempting to soothe her. 'Get a better idea of the kind of lad he was. It might give us a possible idea who could have done this.'

Forrest nodded, turned away and joined Tallow at the side of the stream, who greeted Tanzy with a nod. He too appeared exhausted, his body and posture out of the norm.

DC Leonard seemed to have Anna Greenwell under control. She appeared calmer now, although upset, occasionally wiping her eyes. Tanzy went over to Leonard while PC Andrews waited with forensics to take some notes on the teenage body.

'Hey,' Tanzy said to Leonard, then faced Anna. 'It's an awful time, Anna, I can appreciate that, but we're here to help. And for you to help us. Would you mind answering a few questions?'

She stared vacantly at him, as if she was too tired to stand.

'We'd be ever so grateful,' he added. 'It won't take long.'

'What's going to happen to my son?'

Tanzy kept his voice low, so Ethan, who was sitting on the bench behind, couldn't hear. 'He'll be taken to the hospital for a post-mortem by a pathologist, then we can make arrangements for the rest of the process.'

She nodded slowly, taking it all in, then more tears came. Tanzy had never lost a child and couldn't understand what she was going through, but if anything ever happened to his own, Eric or Jasmine, the weight of that loss would be devastating.

'It was his birthday last week. Seventeen. God... we were planning on going away next weekend with the family. Somewhere in the Lakes.' She paused a beat, lowered her gaze to the floor. 'He - he was looking forward to it.'

Tanzy nodded. 'Where was he yesterday?'

'He said he was going out with friends. Said he'd be back last night.'

'At what time did you get worried that he wasn't home?'

She sighed, glanced back to the floor, as if something was bothering her.

Tanzy waited a few seconds then asked the question again.

'I – I fell' —she looked away from the detective towards the stream where her eldest son was lying with sad eyes — 'asleep.'

'You fell asleep?' Tanzy asked softly, not intending for his words to sound judgemental.

She gave him a small, almost unnoticeable nod.

'So, when you woke up this morning, and he wasn't there, what did you do?'

'I rang and rang him. I sent him messages and left a few voicemails, but he never replied. I assumed he stayed at one of his friends but I didn't have any of their numbers. You know what kids are like?'

Tanzy nodded as if he understood but his own children were only ten and six so in reality he had no idea.

She was going to say something but stopped, so Tanzy said, 'Was Mark involved with some bad people?'

She frowned. 'What do you mean… bad people?'

'What are his friends like?'

She tilted her head, thinking hard. 'They're… nice. He knocks around with a couple of them. Mainly the lads from school. They're no trouble, really.'

Tanzy paused a beat before he said the next part.

'Have you known Mark to ever take any form of drugs?'

Her eyes widened and face straightened as if he'd slapped her hard in the face. 'Excuse me? Mark, my son?'

'Yes?'

'I absolutely have no idea why you would say that,' she gasped, physically shaking at the accusation. 'How dare you, how dare you think —'

Tanzy elevated a quick palm to try and settle the situation. To his right DC Leonard straightened his posture in case he was needed to restrain her but, after a few seconds, she seemed to calm down. 'Please listen to me, Mrs Greenwell. The reason I'm asking is because the forensic team found a lot of money and a bag full of drugs in his pocket. Now, to me, it seems he was involved in something that you weren't aware of. I needed to ask you first in case you knew anything.'

She opened her mouth but stopped herself, her words falling back down her throat.

'Would you and your son, Ethan, mind going to the station and give a formal statement. I think we could all agree it's too cold to be standing here. Let my colleague' — he motioned towards PC Weaver — 'take you to the station. We can get you warmed up, get you a coffee, and see if we can get to the bottom of this.'

Her sigh implied she wasn't keen on the idea.

Tanzy personally didn't see her as a suspect and she certainly wasn't acting like one. Guilty people tended to go over the top and lose all sense of emotion, as if they were trying too hard. Tanzy had seen it a hundred times. If his gut feeling was right Anna had nothing to do with it, so he wouldn't have to arrest and take her to the station. He decided to try a different approach.

'Or, if you'd prefer, Mrs Greenwell,' Tanzy said, 'we could go to your house and we can ask you a few questions there. No need in trailing to the station if we don't need to.'

She agreed.

Tanzy turned to Weaver. 'Amy, could you and James' — he glanced at Leonard too — 'take Mrs Greenwell and her son, Ethan, to their house and get a witness statement?'

Weaver took a step forward. 'No problem.'

Anna waved Ethan off the bench. He came to her side and tucked himself into her, as if the cold world around him was too much to bear. PC Weaver smiled at them and asked them where they lived. It wasn't far. Other side of the park, and up Greenbank Road. As Weaver led the way Anna and Ethan slowly trailed her, their eyes fixated on Mark who was less than forty metres away.

'Hey, Jim,' Tanzy whispered, pulling on DC Leonard's hand. 'Have a look around Mark's bedroom. Tell Anna it's important we get a feel for who he was. You know the drill... look for anything. Let me know.'

'Will do,' Leonard said, turning—

'Oh, by the way... Have you seen DS Stockdale this morning?'

Leonard stopped. 'No I haven't. Didn't see him at the station. What's up?'

Tanzy waved the comment away. 'Just need to speak to him about a report he did a few days ago, that's all.'

'If I see him I'll tell him you need him.' With that Leonard turned and followed Weaver.

Tanzy watched them crossed the small bridge and amble tiredly up the path towards the top exit. He smiled sadly, wondering what was going through Anna's head. After he took a breath of cold, fresh air, he turned back to where the forensics were and walked towards them.

A loud noise attracted his attention somewhere up the path beyond Tallow and Forrest.

A man charging down towards him, face full of thunder.

'For God's sake,' Tanzy whispered, watching him closely.

It was the last person he wanted to see.

6

Wednesday Morning
Denes Park

'What the hell is going on, Tanzy?' DCI Fuller shouted.

Tanzy sighed and shrugged, getting severely annoyed with the man's attitude. 'What does it look like?'

'It looks like this fucking town is falling apart. And it looks like my DI is doing nothing about it.' Fuller came to a halt in front of him and stared deep into his eyes, leaving the question hanging in the air. A common power tactic that managers often used in situations with lower ranked individuals. DCI Martin Fuller had taken over the role two months ago.

Tanzy, who never felt threatened or bullied by anyone, held his ground and said nothing. Fuller, although the DCI and usually a scary character to some, realised that Tanzy's stare was unbreakable and consequently was the first one to look away for a moment. 'Tanzy, what's happened?'

Tanzy really wanted to punch him square in the face. He imagined it in his head for a split second: lunging forward, fist tight, knuckles colliding with Fuller's nose. The sound of bone on bone. The way he'd fall back and cry out in pain—

'A teenager, aged seventeen, has been stabbed, Sir. He was found by his mother and younger brother less than an hour ago. Chances are he's been here overnight.'

Fuller nodded. 'Why do you suggest that?'

'Suggest what?'

Fuller gave an are-you-thick expression. 'That he's been here overnight?'

Tanzy's patience was growing very thin with this new guy. 'Because, according to his mother, he never came home. She assumed he was sleeping at a friend's house. But earlier, she'd gone to the doctors with her youngest child because he was unwell and walked back through on her way home and spotted him lying there in the beck. Forensics found a lot of money and multiple bags of white and brown substance. Possible gang conflict over drugs.' Tanzy pointed past him to where Tallow and Forrest were. Fuller had actually walked past them and not even realised what was going on because he was filled with so much anger, he needed to vent to Tanzy. He'd been warned by Superintendent Barry Eckles it was his job to clean up the streets. Each individual case put more weight on Fuller's shoulders, and he needed to keep a lid on this town.

Tanzy, in general, had a cool head, but when he got sick of someone he wasn't Mr Nice Guy anymore. Hopefully Fuller wouldn't see that side of Tanzy, for everyone's sake.

Fuller glanced away, turned, and stared at Forrest and Tallow, who were standing roughly ten metres from him and Tanzy. 'Seventeen years old, eh?'

'Yeah,' Tanzy said.

'No age is it?' he said, turning back.

Tanzy shook his head. 'Not at all.'

'We need to get this shit figured out, Tanzy.'

'I couldn't agree more,' he said, forcing a half-smile for Fuller's benefit.

'Why are you smiling?' Fuller asked, frowning.

'I'm smiling because you seem to like blaming everyone else for what's going on in this town.'

Fuller was taken aback by Tanzy's response and narrowed his eyes. 'What do you mean?'

Tanzy wished he hadn't said anything but he couldn't help it. 'You seem to blame me and Max for a lot of things. I understand that Barry is on your back about what's going on and what cases we are knee-deep in but as a DCI, in my opinion, you should recognise that we are valuable members of this force and treat us with respect. After all, we are all a team who do our best and work together for the benefit of this town. People tend to work more efficiently as a team when they feel appreciated. I feel like I need to tell you that, Martin.'

Fuller took a lung full of cold air and expelled it quickly. 'That sounds like a lovely story. And thank you, I'll take your opinions on board, think about them for a few seconds, then forget about them. You need to understand that it isn't my job to make you happy at work. Or are you under the illusion that it is?'

Tanzy stared, holding his gaze, but said nothing, feeling his blood start to warm.

Fuller went on: 'Didn't think so. It's my job to manage everyone under me, including you and Max. So, I guess you'll just have to get used to the way things are from now on.'

Tanzy smiled widely but said nothing. It was either that or lunge forward and head butt him. The DCI couldn't care less about what anyone thought of him, that much was clear. It was something that Tanzy would have to grin and bare.

'Any other nice little stories you want to share before I go?' Fuller enquired, glancing down at his wristwatch with wide, impatient eyes. 'I have things to do.'

'I'm sure you do, being a DCI is a very responsible position.'

'Yes, it is…'

'Then no, that's all the lovely stories for today, boss. I might pop my head in your office tomorrow. I have a few more.'

Fuller gave a sarcastic grin and turned. 'Look forward to it. Now get this shit tidied up. I want your report at the end of the day.'

He turned away, making his way past Tallow and Forrest without saying a word, who, in their defence, were occupied over the body of the teenager so didn't see him go by, not that they liked him any better than Tanzy did. Just before Fuller reached the gate manned by two PCs, a familiar face appeared, who ducked under the temporary tape, making his way down the path.

'Good afternoon, Sir.'

Fuller stopped dead. 'You shouldn't be here. You need to go home and come back when you're on duty.'

'Nice to see you, too.'

'Go home.'

'But, Sir, I—'

'I don't want to hear it. Go home. Come back tomorrow.'

The man stood his ground. 'I've already cleared this with HR, so I'm within my rights to be here. If there's an issue, you can phone Judith at the office.'

Fuller sighed heavily. 'Fine.' He moved around him and left, disappearing through the small crowd of people back to his car.

'Arsehole,' the man whispered to himself.

Tanzy recognised the familiar face coming towards him. He also noticed Fuller say something to him, something which didn't seem very friendly. They met near where the forensics were, and both glanced towards them and the body of the teenager in the beck for a moment before looking back at each other.

'You haven't chosen the best day to come back,' Tanzy commented.

'I've heard. That's why I'm here. You know what I'm like? I don't want to miss out on the action.'

'That's true, mate.' Tanzy moved closer, shook his hand firmly. It was warm, welcoming, despite the freezing morning temperature.

'Fuller told me to go home and come back tomorrow.'

'Fuller is a prick who has no respect for anything or anyone,' Tanzy replied.

He agreed with a nod. 'So, have you missed me, Ori?'

'Of course, I have, Max, the whole town has. Welcome back, DI Byrd.'

7

Wednesday Morning
Denes Park

Tanzy and Byrd stood at the top of the steady incline, watching Tallow, Hope, and Forrest at the stream near the body.

'Have I missed much?' Byrd asked.

'Not really, mate. Usual shit. But you're just in time for all the action.' Tanzy fell silent for a moment, then said, 'You look well, by the way.'

Byrd nodded in thanks.

'Seriously,' Tanzy went on, 'the diet you're on is really working. How much weight have you shifted – must be a stone?'

'Nearly two actually.' A proud smile ran across Byrd's face.

Tanzy patted him on the back. He could see it in his complexion, his cheeks more prominent, less excess fat under his chin. 'Well done. You'll be getting a six pack soon.'

Byrd puffed air from his mouth humorously before he turned back to the forensics. 'Story here then, Ori?'

Tallow looked up at the bank and gave Byrd a wave, who courteously returned it.

'Mark Greenwell. Seventeen. Knife cut to the throat,' Tanzy started. 'They found a handful of money and bags full of drugs in his pockets. It could be a deal gone wrong or it could be gang wars, hard to say.' Tanzy paused a beat. 'His mother found him when she was walking back through here from the doctors'—Tanzy pointed to their right—'Moorlands surgery, just along the road.'

Byrd knew where it was. It was actually his own doctors and had been most of his life. 'Must have been difficult. Especially with his younger brother there as well.'

'She said he never came home last night and just assumed he'd stopped out. Stayed at a friend's house. You know what seventeen year olds are like. At least I know what I was like at that age.'

Byrd nodded. 'Where is the mother now?'

'Weaver and Leonard have gone back to their house. They just live up the road. I told them to get a statement. Told Leonard to have a quick look in his bedroom to see if he could see anything suspicious.'

Another nod from Byrd. 'Peter been yet?'

'No, he's happy to meet us at the hospital.'

Byrd let out a sigh.

'You alright? Seem quiet?'

'I'm okay mate. Nice to get back but at the same time, we're greeted with this.' He pointed down at the beck.

'How was the holiday?'

'Nice to get away to be honest. We needed it. Think things are on the up. Got that old flame back that I was on about a few weeks ago. She's moving in as it happens. Going to put her house on the market. Just makes sense, you know.'

'When?'

'When what?'

'She moving in?'

'Today.'

Tanzy smiled. 'Glad to hear it.'

'How's Pip and the kids doing?' Byrd asked, glancing his way. 'Hey, what's this?' He raised his fingers to Tanzy's chin.

Tanzy swatted it away playfully. Since Byrd had been away, Tanzy had tidied up his goatee, thinning it out very neatly. 'It's fashion, that's what it is. Something you wouldn't understand, Max.' They both smiled before Tanzy continued: 'Yeah... she's good mate,' Tanzy went on, 'she's been sober for two months now, so things are looking good. I hope she can keep it up, for all of our sakes. The kids are good too. Pip's mother, Elaine, pops over frequently to keep an eye on her and they spend a couple of nights a week around there, which Elaine loves as well as the kids.'

'Good. Glad things are getting back to normal.'

Their conversation came to a stop when Tallow slowly made his way up the bank towards the detectives. 'Hey, boys, bloody cold one today.'

'You'll be moaning in the summer when it's too hot,' Tanzy replied, grinning.

'What you make of this?' Byrd asked, although Tanzy had filled him in moments ago. 'Seen anything new in the last ten minutes or so?'

Tallow took a lung full of air and gave a small shake of his head. He was tall and thin, roughly six foot, four inches, almost making Tanzy, who was six, two, look small. Byrd was a midget next them both standing at a mere, although respectable, six foot.

'Simple knife cut really. Seems to be the only cut on him from what I can see. We'll let the pathologists have a closer look at the hospital.'

'You're looking well, Max,' Emily Hope noted, pointing to his gut, smiling, as she sauntered up the bank towards them.

'Was just saying that before,' Tanzy said. 'Nearly two stone,' he said, pointing to Byrd's stomach too.

'You can tell, well done,' she said. Then to Tallow. 'We have all the pictures we need, Jacob. The video looks good too, so we can analyse that later. When the pathologists are done I'll request the clothing to see if I can get anything off them.'

Both detectives nodded.

She went on. 'I also see two sets of footprints here. One of them matches with the male's trainers. But the other is different. You see?'

Byrd and Tanzy edged forward. There was a footprint in a small area of mud at the edge of the path.

'Good spot,' Byrd said, nodding.

'And,' Hope added, moving over to the right where she'd placed a couple of yellow counters. 'See here?'

The detectives followed her finger.

'Blood droplets. I've taken samples already. Swept the area. Looks like the victim was attacked up here on the path, stumbled forward and fell down into the stream.'

Byrd and Tanzy both nodded.

'We okay for the undertakers to come down and handle it?' Byrd enquired.

Tallow looked up at Byrd and gave the thumbs up.

Byrd backed up a few steps and, to his left, he waved at the PCs standing up at the entrance near Surtees Street.

Grearer waved and headed towards the ambulance which was parked half-way along the fence.

'Let's see what we find in the post-mortem this afternoon,' Byrd said to Tanzy. 'In the meantime, we'll get Grearer and Timms knocking on doors. Someone might have seen something last night. Slim chance, but you never know.'

8

Wednesday Afternoon
Stonedale Crescent, Cleveland Avenue

Alex Richards was sitting in his office, leaning over his chair, focusing on the laptop screen in front of him. He was working. Studying how local businesses were performing compared to the same time last year. As it was February, it was common to see the January dip. It happened every year, and this year was no exception. He worked as a business analyst comparing and formulating trends in the local markets. These calculations hopefully would explain why one company was doing better than another. Usually, a company hired him for a certain length of time, for example, two to three months, depending on the level of analysis they required. Some companies wanted a basic comparison so the length of his contract was determined by what they required. Gross turnovers, net profits, material costs, employee expenditure such as wages, pensions, and sickness benefits.

He'd completed a Business Management Diploma a few years back and decided this was the route he'd like to go down. Before he hit the laptop screens, he was in the army. Although he worked from home, upstairs in the small front bedroom that he'd converted into an office, he still wore a shirt, tie, and trousers. A pointless activity, but he felt it helped him get in the zone and focus better. He knew other people who did that, and a lot that didn't. It was personal preference.

His office was a rectangular shape, approximately fifteen feet by ten, housing a desk on the right-hand side, with a shelving unit, packed with files, folders, and paperwork to the right of it. The opposite wall contained photos from his army days with some of the troops. Straight ahead, there was a window and to the left of it, fixed on the wall with a swivel bracket, a twenty-two inch flat screen television. ITV News was set on a low volume as the quiet background noise helped him concentrate.

Most of it was nonsense but something distracted him so he stopped what he was doing and turned his head. On the screen, the reporter, a man in a grey suit and blue tie, with an overgrown mop of dark hair swept to the side of his plain serious face, was talking about the latest updates in Darlington.

Richards frowned after hearing the name of his hometown being mentioned and swivelled fully towards the television.

'We go live now to Greenbank Road,' the news desk reporter said, 'where this awful, awful event has occurred.' The man gave a short sympathetic nod before the screen switched to a live feed from Greenbank Road.

In front of a handheld camera was a woman, probably in her mid-twenties, looking apprehensive about the news she was about to tell the world. She was positioned at the entrance of the park just under a metal archway.

'Hi, this is Lisa Walker from ITV News. Today, in the Denes Park behind me'—she angled her body and pointed behind her—'the police discovered the body of Mark Greenwell, a seventeen-year-old male. According to sources he'd been violently attacked and, in consequence, lost his life. A team of police have been here earlier and forensics have examined the scene to find out exactly what happened. Once we know more we'll be in touch with any updates. This is Lisa Walker from ITV News.'

The camera cut off.

Alex Richards stood up quickly. He was a tall, slim man, standing at six foot one but, underneath his shirt and tie, he was lined with a layer of muscle from working out three times a week at the local gym combined with a healthy diet regime. After the Army he wanted to keep fit. Not for any particular reason but for his own self-happiness.

He raced out of his office, dashed down the stairs, along the hall and into the large kitchen, where his wife, Alice, was standing at the worktop preparing food with a black apron wrapped around her waist.

'Alice, you seen the—'

'Jesus, Alex!' she sighed heavily, placing her left hand on her chest. 'You scared me...'

'Sorry... you seen the news?' He walked to the table, picked up the remote and turned it on. 'Look at this.'

She placed the knife down next to the pile of chopped carrots and shifted over, stopping near him. 'What?'

'Just look.'

As the television flashed to life he found the correct channel and they both focused on the screen but the report had finished and the man in the grey suit and blue tie was talking about something else now. Sighing, he pulled his phone from his pocket and unlocked it.

'Shouldn't you be working?' she asked.

'Yeah... just have a look at this then I'll go.' He searched for 'Darlington Murder' and pressed GO. He clicked on the first result that came up, quickly scanned the content, and handed his phone to her. 'Read this.'

With furrowed brows, she took the phone and read the article, putting her hand to her mouth in disbelief when she'd finished. 'God, that's awful. One of my mam's friends lives near there.'

She handed the phone back to Alex and went over to the worktop, picked up her own and found a number she needed to ring.

'Who you phoning?'

'Claire,' she replied. 'Max will probably know all about it.'

'Haven't they just got back from their week away?' Alex asked. 'Might be best not bothering her with it just yet.'

'Yeah, but you know what Max is like? He'll have gone straight there. I'll just mention it. Need to know the gossip.'

'You women, eh,' Richards sighed. 'Well if she ends up popping over for a coffee, make sure my office door is closed.'

9

DI Max Byrd had been home and changed into something more professional. A pair of smart black trousers, a white shirt under a thick black jumper, and his usual long black coat that brushed the side of his knees as he walked.

He was the last one to arrive, and as he closed the door behind him, Tanzy nodded in his direction. Already in the dim-lit room, was the coroner Peter Gibbs, the Pathologist Arnold Hemsley, Hemsley's assistant, Laura Thompson, the senior forensics Tallow and Hope, and of course, his colleague, DI Tanzy.

'Welcome, Max,' Arnold said, holding his gaze in Byrd's direction.

'Good afternoon,' Byrd replied to Hemsley, then greeted everyone else with a slight nod before he focused on the paperwork down in the pathologist's hands.

'Let's begin,' Hemsley started, then over the next few minutes, gave a summary of Mark Greenwell and the circumstances in which he was found. He hadn't seen the body when it was at the park, so when he mentioned certain points, he looked at Tallow and Hope for confirmation. Because of the nature of the killing, which in Tallow and Hope's opinion, was a slice to his neck, there was only need for a visual post-mortem at this stage, instead of a limited or full post-mortem.

During a full post-mortem, the victim's body parts, such as the heart, liver, lungs, blood vessels, intestines, brain etc. would be carefully removed and samples would be taken for each of these. A limited post-mortem would be suggested if the victim had had lung cancer and that was the cause of death, so if agreed by closest family members and to benefit research and development, the lungs would be extracted and analysed for tissue damage and cell deterioration. For a knife cut to the throat there was no need to start removing the victim's body parts to get samples which, Hemsley and Gibbs, after they'd spoken to his mother, Anna Greenwell, had both agreed. She just needed to know why this had happened and told the police to do something.

Usually, a post-mortem happens between two to three days after a person dying and it's common practise for the body itself to be identified by at least two people before the post-mortem takes place. However, under the circumstances where Anna found Mark in the park, it was obvious to her, and her other son, Ethan, that this was Mark. Because of the nature of his death DI Byrd and DI Tanzy, along with Peter Gibbs, had pushed the post-mortem forward. In similar cases, the pathology department will prioritise their workloads to aid the police for investigation purposes.

Anna Greenwell had requested to come in and see Mark. She said she wouldn't be able to settle without seeing her son in a peaceful state. The pathologist, Hemsley, had informed her that because the forensics only needed to carry out a visual inspection, not requiring to cut his body open to access anything, she could come in later. Often, family members requested to see the victim before they are sliced open for a little comfort and not have that one last image of their loved one as a piece of meat with stitches from chest to stomach. Anna was reassured this wouldn't be the case so had given consent to the forensics and police to carry out the post-mortem.

Once they'd finished speaking Hemsley led them all into a square-shaped room with a low ceiling and bright white walls. There was a rectangular-shaped metal trolley in the centre of it under a singular bright light where the body of Mark Greenwell lay. To the right, the detectives noticed an array of instruments sitting on the top of a thin, narrow trolley pushed against the wall. The room itself was no doubt the cleanest room they'd been in and smelled so clinical it hit the back of their throat.

With plenty of room for the seven of them they all circled the table, standing back a couple of feet to allow the pathologist, Hemsley, and his female assistant, Thompson, to step forward.

Mark Greenwell was completely naked. His clothes had been removed by Thompson shortly before and placed neatly in a brown paper evidence bag in a different room. Earlier at the park, Tallow and Hope had taken samples of fibres from Mark's tracksuit, a hair sample, and blood samples from the cut to his throat and were happy for the clothes to be removed for the post-mortem.

After he let out a short sigh Hemsley focused on the body. DI Tanzy and DI Byrd watched him closely. Hemsley was a short, slim man with thinning hair that he kept short. He was clean shaven but the crow's feet around his eyes and around his mouth told them he was likely a smoker and close to fifty years of age. The detectives hadn't seen him before but knew he'd been working here for a while.

Using the camera hanging around her neck Hope took a few snaps of Greenwell.

Whilst looking at Mark's throat Hemsley said, 'Sorry guys, I never introduced you to Laura.' He glanced in her direction, then back at the body. 'She's my new assistant. Completed her degree in bio-medical science with a focus on Haematology. She's doing her training and I hope, from what I've seen so far, that she'll be with me for as long as I can keep her.'

'Hi, Laura,' Byrd said.

'Hi,' Tanzy added.

The senior forensics, Tallow and Hope, and the coroner Gibbs said nothing, indicating to the detectives that they'd already been introduced at some point in the recent past.

'As we can see it's a violent knife attack,' Hemsley said, leaning over the table, observing the cut with the aid of a large magnifying glass. 'The way the skin has separated tells me'—he paused a beat, his eyes in severe concentration—'the blade used was inserted quickly. It was definitely something malicious. One-hundred percent.'

Byrd nodded at the pathologist's comment. 'Good enough for me.'

Tanzy said, 'Any other marks on the body, besides to the throat?'

The forensics focused on Hemsley, as the last time they saw the body, he was fully clothed.

Hemsley slowly nodded and looked to his assistant. 'Laura, would you like to tell them?'

Laura, who looked to be in her early twenties with long black hair nodded several times and coughed quietly, as if readying herself. 'Yeah, I – When I removed the clothes I saw something on his back. Something we need to have a good look at.'

Byrd and Tanzy frowned.

'We'll turn him over, let them see,' Hemsley said to Thompson. 'You take his legs, Laura.' She moved to her right, level with his knees. 'Pull him slightly towards you then we'll very slowly turn him over.'

'Need a hand?' Tallow asked, standing on the opposite side but willing to move around if needed.

'We're okay, thanks,' Hemsley said.

Hemsley and Thompson carefully turned over Mark Greenwell's body until he was on his front. Hemsley then placed both of the victim's arms down by his side and stepped back, allowing the detectives, the coroner, and forensics to have a look.

Byrd leaned over with wide eyes focusing on Mark's back. 'What the hell is that?'

10

Wednesday Late Afternoon
Darlington

On the table in front of Jonny Darchem there was nearly twenty thousand pound in cash. Most of it was in twenties, the rest in tens and fives. It had been counted by one of the boys, Jamie, who'd worked for him for many, many years. Jamie, now twenty-two, was probably his most loyal servant, and his eyes and ears out on the streets. The one he could trust. He'd proved it time and time again.

Darchem had picked Jamie up off the streets when he was only twelve years old. Apparently, according to Jamie, his parents had thrown him out and he had nowhere to stay. Darchem could recall the memory, as it had always stuck in his mind. He was driving along Neasham Road and saw Jamie sitting inside the bus stop outside The Copper Beach pub.

The following day he went past and saw the boy again and decided to pull over to speak to him. Jamie had told Darchem that his father relentlessly hit him and that his mother repeatedly spat at him. They'd told him to go, to live somewhere else. Darchem couldn't believe that parents could do that to their own. As the rain pelted down on top of the bus shelter Darchem had told Jamie to get in the car and that he could come and live with him. Once Jamie got into the car and explained his situation further, telling him all the bad things his father had done to him, Darchem had asked him where his parents lived. Five minutes after he'd told him he pulled up outside a house at the end of Neasham Road and got out of the car, telling

Jamie to stay put and keep his head down, and that he'd only be two minutes.

After Darchem knocked on the door and it opened, he kicked the door as hard as he could, causing it to slam into the woman's face who was behind it. She balled in pain and stumbled backwards into the hallway. Darchem, who was six foot two, and nearly as wide as he was tall, stepped inside, and punched her six times in the face. From somewhere upstairs, he heard someone shout: 'What the fuck is going on?' Then Jamie's father appeared, roaring down the stairs, covered head to toe in tattoos dressed in his pants and a grubby white ill-fitting vest that was covered in stains.

Jamie's dad swung at Darchem but Darchem jabbed him in the nose, causing a blood vessel to rupture, before falling back onto the floor near his wife. Before he could get up Darchem straddled the man and beat his face until his knuckles were bloody and his arm started to tire.

Letting out a sigh, Darchem stood up, stepped outside, and casually closed the door, then returned to the car. Jamie had asked him what happened when he saw the blood on his hands but Darchem told him not to worry and that everything would be okay now. That was ten years ago.

'How much exactly?' Darchem said, needing the details.

Jamie glanced up. 'Nineteen thousand, six hundred.'

Darchem frowned, pivoted on his heels, and went over to the huge living room bay window. The grass outside was cut like a golf green and the flowers running down either side to the front wall wouldn't have looked out of place at the Chelsea Flower Show.

He turned back to Jamie who was looking down at something on his phone.

'It seems we are short, Jamie.'

Jamie glanced up, lowered his phone to give him his full attention. When it came to business and money, Jamie knew Darchem was very serious. If he thought his men weren't listening to him and not taking things as seriously as he was there'd be unpleasant consequences.

Jamie had seen it first-hand two years ago when Darchem questioned one of his men about money. It wasn't difficult to see the man had been skimming the takings. It didn't take long for a thick glass ashtray to collide with the man's face, taking out three of his front teeth. There was blood all over the carpet. Then Darchem had ordered him at gun point to clean up his own blood. It had taken him hours to get the stains off the white carpet.

Frowning at Darchem, Jamie noticed dark eyes burning holes into his skin. 'We're… short?'

Darchem nodded twice. 'Yes, we are. Why?'

'I – I think… we—'

'Spit it out, Jamie, I haven't got all day.'

Jamie coughed, then forced some saliva down his throat before he spoke. 'I think something happened last night with one of the boys.'

'Go on…'

'He didn't turn up at meeting time.'

'Which one?'

'Mark Greenwell. He was doing the Denes. I kept ringing and ringing. Even sent him loads of texts but nothing back. When I turned up for the money he wasn't there. None of the other lads have seen him either.'

'Done a runner?' Darchem asked, tilting his head to one side.

'No, I highly doubt it, I mean why—'

'Why?'

'Why what, Boss?'

'Why do you highly doubt it?' Darchem asked.

'He's loyal to me. He's loyal to you. I know he's been punished in the past but he's a good lad now. I trust him.

He knows what would happen if he tried anything. All of the lads do. They've heard the stories.'

Reluctantly, Darchem managed a nod. 'Okay. Do me a favour. Find him. Go to his house if you have to. Ask around. We're a few grand short here and, to be honest, there's more money missing than from just one lad. Did anyone else not turn up?'

'Not that I know of. Only Mark from my crew. I'll ask Andy and Leeroy about their lads.'

'Good. Let me know,' Darchem instructed.

Jamie stood there for a moment, his gaze falling to the floor.

'What's the matter, young man?' Darchem asked from the window, noticing his hesitation.

'Just thinking. Could it be a local firm cleaning up? Pissed off about us selling in their area?'

Anger flashed in Darchem's eyes. 'No one would dare do that, Jamie. You know that. No rival gang have the balls to do that to me. So, go ask around about Mark. He must be somewhere.'

Jamie, with a nod, stood immediately and left the room with an urgency about him. His number one priority was to find Mark Greenwell, the seventeen-year-old who was doing the Denes last night.

Darchem watched him leave, then went over to his chair in the corner of the huge living room and sat down. He stared into the fire crackling under the mantel piece, the orange flames almost out as they hissed and spat tiredly.

From the other side of the room, there was a knock on the door. Darchem turned and saw the tall, thin man enter. At nearly six foot six, he had very short dark hair, thick eyebrows and the darkest eyes Darchem had ever seen.

'Arthur,' Darchem said with a nod. 'Come in.'

'Any news on Mark's whereabouts?'

'Not yet. Jamie is going out to find him.'

Arthur ambled over the dark blue carpet and stopped on the thick white rug in the centre of the room. 'That's not good, Jonny.'

'Yes… I'm aware.' Darchem sighed and closed his eyes, turning back to the bay window again.

Arthur moved over to the leather sofa positioned in front of the bay window and lowered himself into it. 'Is there anything you want me to do about it?'

'Wait till Jamie asks around, then we'll see.'

'Just let me know,' Arthur said. Arthur was his go-to guy. He'd been working for Darchem from before they started slicing bread. Okay, maybe a slight exaggeration as that was 1928, but Arthur had been by his side for a long time. When things got tricky, instead of sorting it himself, he let Arthur deal with it. That's what he paid him for.

Nearly a decade ago, there was a family that had moved up from Manchester. The Peacocks. They were big players in the drug game back in Manchester, but after a few disagreements with some other dangerous families they'd moved up north, choosing Darlington as their new location. It didn't take long for Darchem to hear about them. What happened on the streets made the rounds fast, and when the Peacocks, a big family consisting of a handful of brothers and cousins, started supplying the town with cocaine at a lower price than Darchem did, users stopped getting in touch with Darchem's dealers and started buying from the Peacocks.

Darchem had to put this to an end.

With Arthur, they came up with a plan to remove the family from the town so things could go back to the way they were. It was a tricky operation, but they targeted them all one by one. Arthur, after speaking to a handful of Darchem's boys and doing the rounds in town on Friday and Saturday nights, mingling with the so-called town boys, came up with a list of men. For weeks he watched them carefully, finding out where they lived and the places they liked to go. Arthur took the list of the unlucky thirteen back to Darchem who gave Arthur the nod to do his thing.

With his expertise training in martial arts, Arthur took them out over the course of a month. He'd break into their houses at night and deal with it however he saw fit.

Cold blooded.

Not a care in the world.

He was like that, Arthur. When things returned to normal and Darchem's enterprise was back up and running, it didn't take long for word to get around that Darchem was responsible for the disappearance of the thirteen men, but no one could prove it, no one would testify, not that anyone would be stupid enough to testify. In ten years, no one from outside – and definitely not inside – the town has attempted to cross him. His name was known by everyone but spoken by no one.

In recent times, he'd got into property and planning. With high intelligence and careful studying he saw the potential in developing properties and how to make money in the markets. Selling drugs and beating people up was getting boring. He wanted to expand. So far he owned several shops on High Row and three pubs. With money being almost no object he was always looking for ways to expand.

'Did you speak to the council?' Arthur asked.

Darchem snapped out of his daydream, looking over to him. 'Yes. They won't budge at all. I've given them so many chances. What happens next is down to them. It's their own fault. I'll tell you the plan later.'

'Very well,' Arthur said, getting to his feet. 'Phone me when you need me.'

After Arthur left the room Darchem stood up and went to the slightly open window, feeling the cold air seep in through the small gap. He glared at the passing cars out on the road for a long moment until his phone rang in his pocket. He plucked it out.

For the select few that actually knew him, he was known as Jonny Darchem, but for years, he'd carried several different passports and driving licenses with other identities to keep his businesses separate. For the incoming phone call, he was the man in charge of Cairnfield Property Developments.

He answered the phone. 'Yes, Mr Cairn speaking.'

11

'What is that?' Tanzy whispered, leaning closer to the body of Mark Greenwell. The senior forensics, Tallow and Hope, leaned closer, squinting, absorbing the marks on his back.

Along the length of his back, from the rear of his right shoulder down to his left hip, there were nine long, thin scars, roughly three to four millimetres thick, varying from twelve to eighteen inches in length. Some of the scars appeared fainter and lighter in colour than the others, as if they'd happened a while ago and had healed.

Hemsley, pointing to the back, indicating four of them one at a time, said, 'Usually scars like these would be older than two years old. That's how long it would take the body to heal for scars like this.'

Several of the scars looked quite new, the appearance of them a darker red colour and slightly raised. Hemsley's finger hovered over these. 'Scars like these look newer, maybe a few months old. Would you agree, Laura?' His gaze fell on his assistant.

'Yes, I'd agree with you,' she replied with a nod, carefully studying them.

'But this one' — he indicated to the longest one, roughly eighteen inches long — 'looks a few weeks old at the most.' The red, sore tissue, displaying a deeper cut, told the pathologist that whatever had done this had torn through the epidermis, the outer layer of skin made up by four layers. These layers are known as the thin skin and contain no blood vessels. For the palms and soles of the feet, this 'thin' skin is slightly thicker, containing a fifth layer called the stratum lucidum. Its appearance told them it happened recently.

'What has caused this?' Tanzy said with a frown. 'He looks like he's been whipped over a long period of time.'

Hemsley stayed silent, nodding. 'I would have to agree with you, Detective.'

'I'm no whipping expert,' Byrd added, 'but I've seen enough films to also agree.'

Hemsley ran his palm over the top of the scars, hovering above them about two inches. 'It's like some old ritual punishment. I've seen a lot of strange things over the years, but nothing really like this.'

The room suddenly got cold for the detectives. 'A ritual?' Tanzy asked. 'We're not in the eighteen hundreds anymore.'

Hemsley half-nodded, as if it was merely a thought. 'That's true. Thing is, I can see a similarity in these marks and the way they've healed.' He looked to the right towards his assistant, who craned her neck in his direction and nodded. He went on: 'Whoever has done this has known Mark for a while, at least two years.'

'Why only two years?' Byrd asked.

'As I mentioned before'—Hemsley pointed to the older, flatter scars—'these are at least two years old. They could be older, I simply can't tell, but I do know a scar like this is a process of the skin healing. That process can take up to two years.'

Tanzy and Byrd nodded at him, then focused back down on the body.

'So, we need to find out what he's been doing for at least two years,' Byrd suggested. 'Who he's been knocking around with, his friends, his associates. We need to speak to his mother too. It's possible she could be involved in this... or...'

'Or?' Tallow enquired.

'Or she may not know at all. Often teenagers hide things from their parents. Some lead hidden lives and have their own secrets that only their friends know. Some secrets, they keep to themselves. Doctor, could this be self-inflicted?'

All eyes fell on the pathologist Hemsley.

He pushed his tongue to the side of his cheek, deep in thought. 'I highly doubt it…'

'I would also say no,' Hope chipped in. She stepped back a little, raising her left arm high across her body and clenching her own fist, as if holding the handle of a whip. Then she slowly did the motion as if she was whipping herself on the back over her right shoulder. 'Even if this was possible, he wouldn't generate enough speed or power to cause that much damage.'

Tanzy squinted a little. 'The speed of a whip can be lethal though, Emily. Not saying you're wrong with what you're saying but the speed of the whip itself can be up to thirty times faster than the speed of the handle. Not to mention the mini sonic boom it creates when it breaks the sound barrier.'

Byrd frowned at him curiously.

'Watched a few Westerns growing up with my Dad,' Tanzy explained.

Byrd smiled. 'Fair enough.' He glanced back to the body. 'So apart from the scars on his back, there's nothing else?'

Hemsley slowly shook his head, then glanced toward the coroner, Peter Gibbs. 'Peter, as this is only a visual, do you require the need for a limited or full post-mortem to be carried out on the victim?'

Gibbs studied the body for a moment, then said, 'No. I think regarding the nature of this crime, it's clear to me how he died. The scars on his back indicate something more sinister, but there'd be no pleasure in cutting him open to search for anything else. Keep the body intact. I'll contact his mother with our findings.'

'We need to speak to her too,' Tanzy said. 'I need to ask her about the scars to see how she reacts.'

'Orion, let's get going,' Byrd said. 'We have a fun-packed day. No doubt, along with everything else, the media will demand a press conference once they get wind of this.'

Tanzy rubbed his nicely trimmed beard and sighed. 'Yeah, no doubt.'

Byrd looked up at Hemsley and his assistant, Thompson. 'Thank you for your time.' Then to Tallow and Hope: 'We'll catch up with you later back at the station once we see what comes back from the blood samples and fibres.'

12

Back at the station, the detectives were more than happy to get out of the rain. On their way there, the heavens had opened, causing the road drains to fill quickly and over-flow. Both of them were saturated and couldn't wait to get out of their coats and hang them in the locker room to dry.

On his way back to his desk Tanzy stopped at DC Leonard's workspace.

'Jim, hey man.'

Leonard glanced up. Then a smile ran across his face. 'Look a little damp there, Boss.'

Tanzy looked to his right through the window. 'Tell me about it. What did you find at Mark Greenwell's house?' Tanzy shuffled around the back of him, grabbed a chair and took a seat.

Swivelling in his direction, Leonard said, 'Anna gave us a statement about seeing him yesterday before he went out. She said he hadn't mentioned about what he was do-ing or who he was seeing, just that he was going out and would be back later. She confirmed the phone calls she'd made to him. Even showed me on her phone.'

'Did you go to his room?'

Leonard nodded. 'Yes, after noticing there wasn't a toi-let downstairs, I asked if I could use one. She pointed up-stairs. The first room was covered in toy cars and shark wallpaper, so I moved onto the next one, which was dec-orated for someone older.' He plucked the phone from his right pocket, unlocked it, and found the image. 'Here, Boss.'

Tanzy took the phone off him and analysed it. On the screen, in the bottom of what seemed like a wardrobe, there were three shoe boxes stacked on top of each other. The lid of the top box had been removed, and, inside, Tanzy could see a large amount of small white bags stacked closely together.'

'What was in the boxes below?' Tanzy said.

'The same. Each box was filled with... Cocaine, I'd guess.'

'Okay, good work,' Tanzy said. 'Looks like an operation this one.'

Tanzy knew that Leonard, without a warrant, shouldn't have been up in Mark Greenwell's room, so he'd get a warrant issued to search his house because of what they'd found in his pockets earlier.

'What did you find at the post-mortem?' Leonard inquired.

'Something interesting. We're going to have a meeting very soon, so you'll find out then. In the meantime I'll contact the magistrate for the warrant. Don't mention to anyone about the drugs. Obviously, Weaver will know but tell no one else. You haven't mentioned it to anyone have you?'

Leonard shook his head several times. 'I knew I shouldn't have been there so no I've kept that under wraps.'

'Good man,' Tanzy said, patting his shoulder. 'Right, catch up soon.' Tanzy returned to his desk, where a lukewarm coffee was waiting for him on the desk.

'Where've you been?' Byrd said, watching him approach. 'Your coffee's there.'

'Thanks, Max.' After pulling the chair out, he took a seat. 'Talking with Leonard. I need to get a search warrant issued to search the Greenwell's house.'

Byrd knew exactly why and nodded, then focused his attention to his computer screen. Behind them, the door to DCI Fuller's office opened.

'You two. In here. I need an update pronto.'

As Tanzy let out a tired sigh, he found Byrd squinting at him. He didn't need to say anything as they both stood up and pushed their chairs in. Tanzy said, 'Yes boss.' Then to Byrd, Tanzy whispered, 'This'll be fun.'

13

Wednesday Late Afternoon
Police Station

'Close the door, please,' Fuller said to them.

Byrd and Tanzy took a seat in front of the large, wide desk in front of DCI Fuller. Nothing about the room had changed since DCI Thornton was in charge. The position of the desk, the drawers to the left corner, the shelving to the right. The window on the left wall still possessed the ageing grey pull-down blind that had seen better days. It was half open, allowing enough light into the room for Fuller not to use the lamp on his desk or the light above his head. The only noticeable change were the certificates Thornton used to have hanging on the wall behind her had gone. There were very faint, but hardly noticeable outlines of where they used to be. Fuller had not put any credentials up yet. Neither Tanzy nor Byrd really knew a lot about him, so didn't really know what credentials he really had.

Fuller was not tall, not short, but a respectable six foot. Approximately two inches under Tanzy and a similar height to Byrd. But Fuller's thick head of hair almost levelled the playing field compared with Tanzy's bald head. Fuller had wide shoulders and a strong accent. He'd transferred from the West Midlands after the replacement of DCI Thornton. According to a rumour, he'd spent a lot of time with the martial arts instructors in his previous role of DCI at West Midlands. Tanzy, although he'd been doing Judo since he was six years old, had never felt threatened, or that his 'manliness' was questioned in any way. They were both aware of each other's abilities and that, without question, prompted a level of respect for each other. Although that didn't stop Fuller being an arsehole when he wanted to be.

From taking over two months ago, Fuller had rattled a few cages and hadn't been bothered about upsetting his colleagues and many of the lower ranks. He was old school. Tanzy had discussed his management style with Byrd in the first few days but Byrd told him it is what it is. 'He's our boss, it's his way or no way,' Byrd had said.

'So what's the score? I had to shoot off for a meeting with Eckles. He was asking me every question under the sun.'

'We went to the hospital with Tallow and Hope,' Tanzy started, 'along with Peter Gibbs. There we met with the pathologist, Arnold Hemsley, and his assistant, Laura Thompson. They confirmed it was a malicious attack from the way the knife had torn the skin.'

Fuller nodded, waiting.

'But they showed us something else,' Tanzy said, adjusting his position on the chair. 'They turned him over and we saw nine whip marks on his back. Some of them were old, some of them recent, according to their analysis.'

Fuller nodded again. 'Interesting. Some kind of punishment?'

'It's possible,' Tanzy replied.

Then Fuller looked at Byrd. 'I want to apologise for earlier, Max. I was harsh with you when you turned up. I didn't expect you until tomorrow. After you told me that you'd cleared it with Judith in HR, I accepted it, although I know I didn't come across best pleased. Eckles is really on my case at the moment. I think what happened to DCI Thornton has put him under some extreme pressure and he needs me to pull through and keep this town safe. So, I apologise to you, Max.'

Byrd held up a palm and gave a small smile in acceptance.

'So, what's next?' Fuller asked. He knew what was next. He wanted his DI's to tell him.

'We need to get a search warrant for Mark Greenwell's house,' Byrd said. 'Finding the drugs and money in his pocket and the possibility this was gang-related gives us enough ammunition to search his bedroom as a minimum.'

'Good shout...' Fuller commented, then fell silent.

Tanzy's turn. 'We need to speak with his mother too. It's important we find out about the scars on his back. There's a possibility that she's aware of them, and also a possibility that she isn't. We won't know until we ask her.'

'Also, we need to find out who he's been knocking around with,' Byrd added. 'For at least two years. The scars that we saw, in the pathologist's opinion, could go back that far. The person responsible for the scars might be the person responsible for his murder.'

Fuller leaned back a few inches then nodded twice. 'Good. Get on it. I've just had word that the media are wanting a press release and Barry Eckles has agreed that for tonight.'

'Tonight?' Byrd frowned.

'He's putting us under as much pressure as possible. He wants to see me crumble. Seven p.m. at Darlington Business Centre up Yarm Road.'

Tanzy sighed at his response. He knew, as much as Byrd and the rest of the team, that Barry Eckles was an arsehole.

When Fuller said no more, Byrd and Tanzy found their feet and made their way to the door.

'Oh, by the way...'

The detectives turned back.

'Which one of you likes public speaking? Whichever is the best can do the press conference.'

Byrd craned his neck towards Tanzy. 'I did the last one, pal. It's your turn.'

'Great…'

14

Wednesday Late Afternoon
Police Station, Conference Room

In the large rectangular conference room on the first floor of the station, Byrd and Tanzy were standing at the front near the door. Seated on the chairs in the centre of the room, were DC James Leonard, DC Anne Tiffin, DC Phil Cornty, DS Phil Stockdale, PC Amy Weaver, PC Josh Andrews, PC Donny Grearer and PC Eric Timms, all positioned in a semi-circle. The tables were tucked against the wall to the left. To the right, Tanzy looked out of the window. He noticed it had finally stopped raining but could see the roads and pathways on St. Cuthbert's Way were saturated.

'The boss not sitting in for this one?' DC Cornty asked.

'Not this time… unfortunately,' Tanzy replied. 'Fuller is tied up in his office.'

Everyone smiled for a moment. It appeared DCI Fuller's old-school type management techniques had annoyed more than only Byrd and Tanzy.

'Right,' Byrd said, 'let's make a start.' He took a breath and, using the small black remote in his hand, he half turned to the screen on the wall behind him. He'd spent the last twenty minutes putting a brief presentation together about the events of the day so far, and as he pressed the button on the remote, the first slide came up, telling everyone the day and date. 'This morning,' he began, 'Anna Greenwell was walking through the park when she came across a teenage male lying dead in the beck. Not a shadow of a doubt went through her mind that he wasn't her son, Mark. She said he went out last night and never came home. Tallow and Hope found a stash of money and a handsome collection of what looked to be Cocaine, a Class-A drug that many in this town seems to be a little partial to.'

'Not me, Sir, I'm a good boy,' DC Cornty chipped in, grinning.

Tanzy briefly smiled but didn't comment on it.

Byrd ignored it and carried on: 'So we've sent a number of samples off to the lab to determine which drug it actually is.' He paused a beat, turned back to the screen and pressed the button on the remote. On the screen, there was a photo. 'At the scene Hope found a footprint on the grass which she believes doesn't belong to Mark. She also found several blood droplets too, which she's taken samples of. Chances are that it could belong to the person who did this.'

'How – how did the post-mortem go?' asked PC Josh Andrews over to the right.

Byrd clicked the remote again. An image of the knife wound came up, which gathered a couple of sighs from Weaver and Cornty. 'When Orion and I went to the hospital for the visual,' Byrd went on, 'the pathologist was confident this was a vicious intended attack, judging by the way the knife had torn the skin on Mark's throat. Judging by the items in his pocket, we'd say it could be a gang-related attack. Maybe some pissed off local dealers not happy. We don't know yet.'

'Has anyone been to his house, his bedroom?' DS Stockdale asked.

Tanzy exchanged a very brief glance with DC Leonard, then focused on Stockdale. 'Leonard and Weaver went to speak with his mother, Anna, to obtain a statement. Due to the items found in his pocket I've requested a warrant to search the house.'

'When will we get it?' Weaver asked.

'Spoken with the magistrates just before this meeting, so I'm hoping quite soon,' Tanzy said.

'Okay.'

Byrd nodded after the question had been answered and pressed the button.

'What the hell is that?' Cornty blurted, pointing.

'I'm about to tell you. When Orion and I were at the hospital the pathologist wanted to show us something else, something unusual.' He glimpsed at Tanzy for a moment, then back to the small crowd. 'These marks were on his back'—Byrd indicated several diagonal lines through the air with his finger—'they seem to have come from a whip.'

'He's been watching Fifty Shades, then?' Cornty commented, but no one acknowledged his childish humour.

Byrd looked unamused. 'Strange thing is, they all happened at different times. Some, according to the pathologist, are over two years old. Some are fresh, could have happened last week.' His focus fell on DC Cornty. 'Phil, I need you to do some digging on Mark Greenwell. Go back a minimum of two years. Previous jobs, colleges, even his school. Check all of his social media profiles. We need to know who he's been knocking around with.'

Cornty nodded, accepting the challenge. 'I'll make a start straight away.'

'Good. Thanks, Phil. Whoever caused this damage to his back could be the person responsible for this.'

'Okay, that's all folk—'

The door opened suddenly to the detective's left. It was Tallow, the senior forensic, with a serious look on his face.

'Jacob?' Byrd asked, taking a few steps towards him. 'What is it?'

'Results are back from the blood found on the grass at the park. Max, you need to see this.'

15

Wednesday Late Afternoon
Forensics Lab

Byrd exchanged worried glances with Tanzy on their way down the corridor towards the lab. It was impossible not to see that Tallow was distressed about something. They stepped through the door. The room was cool, a couple of degrees below being comfortable.

'Come and see,' Tallow said, pointing towards Emily Hope, who was sitting at her desk, her focus on the computer in front of her. Tallow pulled the chair out next to her and took a seat, then dropped his face into his hands.

'Hey, guys,' she said, a little urgency in her voice. She was wearing tight fitting blue jeans with an equally tight-fitting black t-shirt. Her lab coat was hanging over the other side of the room on a set of hooks near the window.

'Hey, Emily,' Tanzy replied stopping near her. 'What do we have?'

She looked up, smiled at him, then her focus fell on Byrd. 'Max, the results have come back. Have a seat.'

Frowning, Byrd took a few steps over to his right, grabbed a chair, dragged it towards the computer and dropped into it, wondering why she'd singled him out more than Tanzy. 'What is it, Emily?'

'DNA from the blood droplets found at the park. We have two sets. Obviously, one is Mark Greenwell's.'

'The other?' Byrd enquired.

'Lyle Wilson,' she said quietly.

Byrd took a lung full of cool air, sighed heavily and brought his palms up to his face. 'Jesus.'

'Who's Lyle Wilson?' Tanzy asked, not familiar with the name.

Byrd tilted his head back in Tanzy's direction. 'You know my friend, Keith?'

'Guy you've known since school. One of your closest mates?'

Byrd nodded. 'Yeah. Well, Lyle is his son. About a year ago, Cornty and Weaver caught him shop lifting in town, attempting to walk out of Binns with a handful of t-shirts. He was stopped by Cornty who had been notified by the security guard that there was someone inside acting suspiciously. Cornty and Weaver followed him around the shop, then casually, Lyle walked out with the stuff. Nearly three-hundred pounds worth. Anyway, they searched him and found cocaine on him, along with a load of money. They brought him in. He'd actually requested to see me to explain himself. He told me that he was sorry for taking the clothes, but the drugs weren't his. He was looking after them for a "friend".'

'Never heard that excuse before…' Tanzy humoured.

Byrd nodded. 'I did my best for him, but he got four months inside for it.'

'Lucky,' Tanzy said, 'could have got longer.'

'Yeah, I know. Since that happened I haven't spoken with Keith about it. He said I should have done better and got him off. I tried to explain vouching for him as an individual was the reason he only got four months and not a day more. But like the stubborn old fool he is he was having none of it.'

'So, Lyle has been out around eight months?'

'Yeah, roughly eight months.'

'Keith not been in touch in that time?'

Byrd shrugged. 'The odd text here and there but nothing more,' Byrd explained, rubbing his chin, 'I haven't seen him in over a year.'

The forensics absorbed his heart-felt words and bobbed their heads.

'Just thought I'd let you know first, Max,' Tallow said. 'Only the people in this room know about this. I've taken it no further. I wasn't sure how you wanted to handle this one.'

'Appreciate that,' Byrd said. 'I'll go speak with Keith. See if Lyle is at home, because at the moment, and it's an awful thought, Lyle Wilson is our number one suspect.' Byrd glanced down at his watch. 'Orion, you better be making a move for the conference. You head over there. Go do your thing.'

'I'll give you a ring after it's finished,' Tanzy replied. 'You taking one of the PCs with you?'

Byrd thought for a moment. 'No, I'll be okay. I need to hear what Keith has to say first and, of course, what Lyle has to say. I need to know why he was at the park last night.'

With that Byrd stood up, thanked Tallow and Hope for their discretion and left the room.

16

Wednesday Early Evening
Willow Road, The Denes

Byrd stepped out of his X5 and used the fob to lock it. As the sidelights flashed twice, the almost inaudible drone of the mechanism closing wing mirrors hummed as they narrowed towards the centre of the car.

Stepping up onto the pavement he paused for a moment, looking at the house. Even in the dark he could see it still needed a fresh coat of paint to hide the rising mould just above the damp proof coursing. The cracked paintwork on the red door needed scraping off and needed a fresh coat. The windows looked older than Byrd did and the light coming from behind the curtains highlighted traces of mould and excessive condensation in the lower corners of the glass. The garden was full of weeds and the grass was nearly a foot tall.

Keith had always been the same. Not very house proud. Ever since his wife died three years ago things hadn't been the same. As a self-employed plumber Keith spent the majority of his time working, often out of town, which meant he needed to set off early and often returned home late. For three years, his son Lyle, had pretty much, to an extent, been on his own. He'd make his own tea and sort himself out. At nineteen you would expect no less but, since Janice had been diagnosed with breast cancer and died soon after, things between Keith and Lyle had been different. If was clear to most, especially to Byrd, that they'd grown apart.

Taking a lungful of cold, winter air, Byrd knocked three times on the door. The sound echoed around the silent street. After waiting a minute he tried again. No answer.

Although there was a dim light coming from the living room, it was possible he could be in the kitchen or upstairs. He pulled his phone out of his black trousers and rang him. The automated voice told Byrd that the number was no longer in use. He either didn't have the same number or Keith had blocked him which, at the time of dealing with Lyle's sentencing, he'd told Byrd he was going to do.

Lifting his arm again to the door, he tried the handle, which was locked.

From his right jacket pocket he grabbed his mini torch and stepped down away from the door, switching it on and moving around the side of the house. At the end of the torch's light, along the narrow space between the house and the fence, stood the gate, painted in the same red that Byrd remembered and, similar to the front door and rest of the house, needed some TLC.

Very quietly Byrd pressed the latch down and applied a little pressure against the gate, edging it open. Under the light of the torch, Byrd thought the back garden seemed the same as it was a year ago, although the grass was higher and he realised there was a bad smell coming from the rubbish over to the left against the fence.

He took a right, slowly cornering the brick work of the utility extension, his torch sweeping across the concrete behind the house, briefly highlighting a chair and table set which looked old and stained, several of the chairs only having three legs. As strange as it was, and as relaxed as he felt in familiar surroundings, he was there because Lyle Wilson's blood was found at the scene of a crime. That made him the number one suspect, so he needed to forget about his friendship with Keith Wilson and concentrate on finding Lyle.

Trying the handle of the back door, although a little stiff, Byrd was shocked when it opened with a low thud. As slowly and lightly as possible he stepped up into the dark utility room and closed the door behind him. He felt the warmth of the central heating and could smell curry coming from the kitchen. He peered around the doorframe but no one was there. The under-cupboard lights were on, shining down on the clustered items on the black worktops. Through the long kitchen he could see the light in the dining room was on with the table underneath it. A mug was positioned next to some paperwork. He turned his torch off and moved forward towards the dining room.

Before he reached the door he paused, turning his head to the side, listening carefully. Not a sound from anywhere, not even a television or a whispered murmur of conversation from the dining room, living room or upstairs.

The gargle of the washing machine draining made him tense coming as it did from the utility behind him, but he recognised the sound and composed himself, then carefully padded forward into the dining room where —

By the time he saw the object coming towards his head it was too late. His legs buckled from under him and he blacked out.

17

Wednesday Early Evening
Darlington Business Centre, Yarm Road

Before he got out of the car Tanzy picked up his phone from the passenger seat and found his wife's number.

'Hey, Ori,' she answered softly.

'Hey, Pip. You okay?' He nonchalantly scanned the car park, eyeing up the handful of people making their way towards the doors of the building's entrance in idle conversation. Several of them had cameras hanging from their necks and a few had note pads in their hands. Bloody reporters.

'Yeah, just sorting the kids,' she said. 'My mam has just left. She bathed them whilst I made tea. Just finishing the dishes now. Saves you a job for when you get in.'

'Thank you, that's kind…' he trailed off.

'Everything okay, Ori?' she said, picking up on something.

'I'm about to stand in front of the press about the body we found this morning.'

'Oh my God. What happened?'

'Found a seventeen year old this morning at Denes Park. You probably won't know it very well?'

'No, never heard of it. How old did you say? Seventeen?'

'Yeah…'

'My God.' She fell silent for a few seconds. 'Are you coming home straight after?'

'Yeah, my stomach is rumbling. What's for tea?' He took his eyes off the building's entrance and checked the time on the dashboard. 6.48 p.m..

'Your favourite.'

'Say no more. Hey, listen Pip, I need to go. I'll see you soon.'

He hung up the phone before she replied and looked forward to the spaghetti Bolognese that would be waiting when he got home. He unclipped his seat belt, opened the car door, and stepped out into the cold. It wasn't raining but there was moisture in the air that certainly threatened it. As he passed through the sliding entrance doors a man appeared from his right wearing a bland, faded blue uniform and black shoes, raising his right palm towards Tanzy's chest.

'Can I see some identification please, Sir?' His voice was deep, as if he smoked forty a day.

'Sure.' Tanzy reached into the inside pocket of his long, grey Parker coat and pulled out his credentials. The security guard, if that's what he was meant to be, eyed it for a while, as if making the most of the power card he possessed allowing people in the building. Finally, he nodded.

'Thanks,' Tanzy said, placing his badge back into his pocket and stepping around him.

'Just go through there, it's starting soon,' the man in blue told him.

Tanzy glanced down at his watch and passed a couple of people scattered in the lobby area. He overheard a young-looking woman speaking with an older man about Mark's murder as he approached the door, where he was stopped by Barbara, a forty-something blonde haired classy individual dressed in a tight-fitting blue suit, who recognised him and told him to go straight in.

Things got underway and Tanzy was called up to the podium. His heart was thumping through his chest as he heard the clicking of the cameras. He took a long breath, absorbing it all, trying to remain calm. A conference about a murder was different to a missing person's appeal. He remembered standing in the same position with Ray and Jane Jones when their daughter, Evelyn, went missing over two months ago. Luckily, they found her, thank God. But when it was about a murder the damage was done, the hurt had already been caused. And now it was down to the police to not only find out why, but to catch and arrest the person responsible for it.

'Hello, everyone,' Tanzy started, his voice a little shaky. 'Welcome. My name is Detective Inspector Orion Tanzy of Durham Constabulary. This morning—'

'Sounds like Onion,' said a voice from near the back, followed by a couple of humoured murmurs.

Ignoring the stupid comment, Tanzy continued: 'This morning the body of a seventeen year old, Mark Green-well, was found in Denes Park, near the Greenbank Road area of Darlington.' He paused for breath, noticing he was calmer now. 'The cause of his death was a violent knife attack. His body was found in the beck.'

'Any idea who did this?' The question came from a woman in the second row.

Tanzy focused in. 'At this moment, we don't know. We have our suspicions, but we can't comment until we have the evidence to back those suspicions up. With the help of our forensic team we're hoping to come up with some new findings very soon and are currently running DNA tests on some samples of blood we obtained. Once we know we'll move forward with this investigation.'

'What about cameras?' another reporter asked. Tanzy shifted his focus over to the left, where a grey-haired man was sitting in a black suit, a pen in his hand and a notepad resting on his lap.

'After checking the cameras in the nearby area, it appears they are of no use unfortunately.'

'Isn't it your job to keep us safe?' A different voice this time. Tanzy scowled over to the familiar face of Amy Tilton, a twenty-something eager reporter from the Northern Echo Newspaper with jet black perfect hair and legs to die for. Even though it was Winter, her bottom half was always dressed for a night out in the height of summer.

Tanzy gave her a small smile. 'Yes, Amy, it certainly is.'

'So, what's the police going to do then, Detective Inspector?'

'We have made enquiries in the local area, asking people if they saw anything between last night and this morning. We need to speak to his mother again as there's a few issues we need to clear up before moving forward.'

'What issues?' a voice asked near the back. 'Do you think his mother has something to do with this?'

Tanzy shook his head. 'Issues that won't be discussed during this conference. However our biggest lead is the blood we found near Mark's body. As soon as we know who it belongs to, we can move forward.'

18

Wednesday Early Evening
Willow Road, The Denes

Byrd tried to open his eyes but he couldn't. It was as if his eye lids had been glued shut with the strongest adhesive in the world. Attempting to move his body, he realised he was unable to. His body felt frozen, his muscles wouldn't respond. A few moments passed until his hearing returned. Although almost a drone, his heartbeat quickened when he heard someone panting lightly to his left. The feeling of his body was starting to return, but all he managed was a twitch, nothing more.

Then he let out an inaudible grunt, making no sense to even himself.

'Max...en tee...' the voice faded out.

The words were distorted, muffled in his head, as if spoken in another language. Then a severe pain came to the side of his head, pounding throbs coming in waves.

'Max?' More clarity. 'Max, is that you?'

Byrd grunted a few times, could feel his body becoming one with him as he slowly lifted his left hand to the side of his head, tenderly touching the bruise that was swelling rapidly.

'Jesus...' Byrd whispered.

'Max, is that you? God, Max, what are you doing here?'

'Keith?' Byrd asked, his eyes still closed.

'Yeah mate, it's me. Let – let me help you.' Byrd heard footsteps come closer, then felt firm hands grab his left arm and slowly pull him up.

'Jesus, my head…' Byrd sighed heavily, the throbs worsening.

Keith helped Byrd up to his feet. 'You steady?' Byrd nodded. 'Sorry, Max, I – I didn't know it was you. I wouldn't have done that if I'd known.' Keith still kept hold of him.

Finally opening his eyes, he saw Keith standing in front of him, wearing a black t-shirt and red shorts. He had no socks on. 'What did you hit me with, a bloody baseball bat?'

'A cricket bat actually.'

'Thanks…'

'Here, come and sit down.' Keith helped him over to one of the chairs at the table and lowered him carefully into it. A few awkward moments passed, then Keith moved around the other side of the low rectangular table and pulled out a chair. 'Listen, I'm sorry about that, I noticed someone's outline through the blinds here' — he pointed to his right at the window — 'and instinct took over. I didn't recognise you.'

Byrd smiled briefly, still touching the side of his head.

'Just a bruise, Max, nothing a tough copper like you can't shake off,' Keith said, then looked at him up and down. 'You've lost a few pounds haven't you?'

Byrd angled his focus towards him across the table, his face wincing in pain. 'Two stone. Well, almost two stone.'

'You look great, mate, you really do.' Keith stood up and went to the sink, poured a glass of water, then brought it over to Byrd. 'Drink this, might help.'

'Thanks,' he said, but never reached for it.

'How come you're here?' Keith asked.

'It's a tough one,' Byrd started, 'I need to speak with Lyle. Is he in?'

The frown on Keith's face deepened. 'Lyle? No, he isn't, I haven't seen him all day. What – why do you need to speak with him?'

Byrd waited a few seconds, managed to lower his hand from his head and turned towards his friend. 'You hear about the murder down in the Denes this morning?'

Keith nodded several times, leaning back on his chair. 'I... did.'

'Well, there were traces of Lyle's blood at the scene, Keith. My forensic team came to me first with it. No one else knows about it. Out of respect to you and him, I needed to speak with him first before reporting it. I need to know why his blood is there.'

Keith let out a long sigh which Byrd picked up on. 'What is it?'

'He didn't come home last night, Max,' Keith explained. 'We had an argument about something stupid and he stormed out around eight o'clock. It was eleven before I went to bed, but I figured he'd get home later than that anyway, so I didn't wait up for him. I sent him a text telling him I loved him. When I woke up this morning, he wasn't here. He's probably pissed off at me.'

Byrd hesitated for a moment. 'What – what was the argument about?'

'About his mother. I told him he needed to clean up his act, start doing his bit around the house. We started swearing at each other and he left, slamming the door on his way out. On the text, I told him I was sorry and that I loved him. My fault really, it started over his dirty underwear on the stairs. Then, as things normally do, they escalated.'

Byrd hummed in understanding but didn't want to comment on the areas of the house that needed a bit of TLC. 'And he hasn't been back today?'

Shaking his head, Keith said, 'No.'

'Is he still working for that builder?'

'Yeah, yeah, he's still on with him. Just coming out of his time so he's looking forward to the pay increase.'

'I bet.' Byrd paused a brief moment. 'Listen Keith, I think Lyle could be in some serious trouble here. The blood sample is an exact match to his DNA. Same as when we took it a year ago. I really need to talk to him.'

'I could ring him?'

Byrd nodded. 'Please.'

'I've tried earlier but I'll try again.' Keith grabbed his phone from his pocket, unlocked it and found his son's number. After putting it to his ear, he slouched a little in the chair, waiting.

'Straight to voicemail. I'll try again.' Silence passed, then: 'Voicemail again.'

'Who does he knock around with?'

'His friends?'

Byrd nodded.

'He has a few. One of them is called Simmo… or Simon, don't know how he says it. Lives somewhere on Greenbank Road. Another lad is called Liam H. Don't know his second name, or where he lives. They often hang around the park. Drinking, smoking, that kinda thing.'

'Okay. Does Lyle use any drugs, Keith?'

Keith's face formed as if he'd been slapped, then he shook his head. 'Not under this roof he doesn't, Max. What are you saying?'

Byrd raised a quick palm. 'I'm trying to understand what's going on,' explained Byrd. 'Your son is missing and could be linked to something very serious. Now I know you don't think I did anything when he was caught shoplifting but believe me when I say the four months he got was the best possible outcome for the situation. I did my best. I know you don't believe me but trust me when I say I did. I've known him since he was this big' — Byrd moved his hand out and indicated the height Lyle used to be when he was a toddler — 'and would do anything to help you guys.'

Keith inhaled slowly. 'I know, Max.'

Moving on, Byrd asked, 'Is there anything that could help me find him?'

It was a difficult situation, but he realised that all Byrd was doing was his job. 'I'll ring him again but if you're asking me where he is, I don't know, Max, I'm sorry.'

Keith found Lyle's number again and pressed CALL. Just as before, he didn't answer, taking Keith to his voicemail.

'If you wouldn't mind, could I have his number? It's so important I speak to him. If not, Keith, forensics will have to report it tomorrow at the latest and he'll be our number one suspect in this murder enquiry.'

Keith sighed slowly and reluctantly told Byrd the number.

Byrd stood, feeling the effects of the cricket bat on his head minutes earlier. 'I'll look for him. He can't be far. Let me know when he comes home or if he contacts you. He doesn't have long, Keith, until the whole of the station knows.'

Keith bobbed his head.

'You understand?'

'Yes, yes, I understand.'

Byrd turned, made his way through the kitchen towards the back door.

'Max?'

Byrd backed up a little and glanced his way.

'Sorry about the head,' Keith said, sincerely.

Nodding, Byrd stepped into the cold night and closed the door. Once he was back inside the car, he mentally calculated where in the park Keith was referring to, then put his gear in first and edged out into the road.

Almost a minute later, Byrd stopped the X5 on Surtees Street, close to where the body of Mark Greenwell had been found earlier that morning. He opened the door, got out, and briefly looked through the metal railings down into the pitch-black park. He couldn't see anyone or hear anything, but there was a faint smell of cannabis coming from somewhere.

From inside his coat, he grabbed his phone and his mini Maglite, then dialled the number Keith had given him. It rang and rang and rang until he ended the call and lowered it in frustration. To his left he approached the part of the stream where Mark Greenwell had been found, face down earlier.

Somewhere up ahead he heard quiet footsteps and inaudible whispers he couldn't make out. Knowing the park, he knew teenagers hung around on the play area where the swings and climbing apparatus were on the other side just over the stream, so assumed they were coming from over there.

Up to the right the traffic was light. Every so often cars passed up on Northcote Terrace, their engine sounds increasing then fading after a few seconds, leaving Byrd by himself and the murmurs somewhere across the beck. Disregarding them for a moment he pressed CALL on Lyle's number again and held it to his head, gingerly making his way down the path.

He stopped dead when he heard it.

'What...' he said.

The sound of a song was coming from somewhere. Closing his eyes to listen he picked up the music louder in his left ear, telling him it was coming from the direction of the beck. He pulled the phone away from his head and listened carefully. Some kind of pop song he realised. Something which he'd heard before.

The call went to voicemail. He disconnected and phoned again. As he reached the green bank where he'd stood earlier in the day with Tanzy, he stared down into the stream, hearing the tranquil, gently flowing water moving along. Slowly padding down the bank he dug the soles of his shoes hard into the grass to reduce the chance of slipping and scanned the area with wide eyes. The music was getting louder the closer he got to the water.

'Where is it coming from?' he whispered, feeling like he was on to something.

He reached the water's edge and shone his powerful light into the stream, the brilliant beam highlighting a handful of tiny fish swimming in multiple directions. Moving the focus of the light across the water, he pointed at lengthy tufts of grass at the opposite side. When he saw movement he stiffened a little, hearing something scurry off into the grass. His heart was racing. The music was very close, the song now something he recognised. A remix version of Dancing In The Moonlight. Hated the original but didn't mind this version. He moved to the left —

Crack. The sound of something under his foot. He bent down, picked up the ringing phone, saw his number on the screen with an option to answer or end the call.

'Shit,' he said. It was good he'd found the phone but not good that Lyle wasn't with it.

He ended the call and placed his own phone away, then noticed there'd been umpteen missed calls and countless messages. On the lock screen, he saw a text message from his Dad, Keith. It read: **I'm sorry Lyle. I love you man** x

The text message appeared unopened, as if he had parted with the phone before he'd had the chance to read it or before Keith had sent it. In Byrd's mind, Lyle had either murdered Mark Greenwell and fled the scene, making him the prime suspect, or Lyle was another victim.

'Where the hell are you Lyle?' he said into the darkness.

19

Wednesday Night
Edward Street, Albert Hill Industrial Estate,
Darlington

Sitting in the car by himself, the man checked the time on the dashboard. 8.46 p.m.. His wife wouldn't be getting worried because he'd told her he was going round a friend's house for a catch up. He had, in fact, already been to his friend's house but said he wasn't feeling great early on so could they rearrange. Quite simple really. He had a few hours before she'd expect him home.

The video playing on his phone had just come to an end. It was the sixth time he'd watched it on The Northern Echo website and thought about watching it again, but he was satisfied he was safe. The detective standing at the podium, Orion Tanzy, didn't seem to know much about what was happening. So far, the police had nothing on him. The only thing that possibly worried him was if he had cut his lip when he attacked Mark Greenwell. Racking his brains over and over, he couldn't remember doing it when he stabbed the teenager in the throat, but it all happened so fast – anything was possible. It was sore, slightly raised. This morning, his wife had asked how it happened and he said he couldn't remember. Then he saw the blood on his pillow and said he must've bitten it during the night. Lies.

He sighed, locked the phone, threw it down on the passenger seat, and stared out across the small road, eagerly watching an old-looking man at unit seventeen tinkering on with something inside his unit. The unit itself never had a sign on, so he didn't know if it was a business, but the man was dressed in red overalls which were covered in black stuff, probably oil by the looks of it. The harsh, cold light inside the unit shone down on an array of car parts: exhaust pipes, car batteries, wires, and God knows whatever else he had in boxes.

Minutes later, the man in the overalls, with a struggle, pulled down the shutters, the sound of it ripping through the silent surrounding, causing the area to suddenly become dark. After locking the padlock, the old man padded over to a brown truck that looked like it should have been scrapped in the 80's. The truck took three attempts to start, before the rear lights finally stayed on. The truck reversed, then painfully crept away from unit seventeen towards Cleveland Street, leaving the space to plummet into darkness.

This was a good place.

It was out of the way. No streetlights or cameras.

'At last,' the man whispered. He tipped his head back, thinking about his daughter. He felt like it got him into character. He wasn't a mean person. He was a kind, gentle, individual who'd do anything for anyone. And now he knew who to blame, no one was going to stand in his way.

After weeks of research he'd come up with a list. It wasn't at random. The individuals unlucky enough to be on the list were there because they deserved to be.

He'd feel no remorse in doing this. And he'd do it until he got the man who was really responsible for what happened. Until then, he'd make him suffer.

Sitting up, he smiled, then turned his head to the teenager on the back seat, who was lying down with duct tape over his mouth, his hands and legs both tied, glaring up at him with an unknown fear of not knowing what was to come. It was time to play.

'Let's have some fun should we, Lyle?' the man whispered.

20

Wednesday Night
Newton Aycliffe

Tanzy applied the handbrake and switched off the engine outside his semi-detached house. The front of the house was covered in a thin film of frost which glistened from a nearby streetlight, making it almost look magical. A castle from one of Jasmine's reading books. The living room curtains were closed but a light was on. Upstairs, he noticed both Eric's and Jasmine's bedroom lights were on, meaning they were still up.

Grabbing his phone, he found Byrd's number and pressed CALL.

'Ori,' Byrd answered.

'Hey, Max.'

'How'd it go?'

'Not the best,' Tanzy noted. 'Got hounded by the press. Some awkward people out there, you know.' He sounded tired.

'You know what people are like, just doing their job. Hopefully, someone comes forward with something.' Byrd fell silent for a moment, then: 'Went to see Keith about Lyle ...'

'Speak with Lyle?'

'I wish I had, would've saved the cricket bat to the side of the head.'

'What?'

Byrd filled him in, telling Tanzy that Keith had knocked him out and then told him he hadn't seen Lyle until some point the night before.

'Could get him for assault you know?' Tanzy suggested, half-joking.

'If I hadn't known him for as long as I have, he'd be in a cell now, trust me,' Byrd replied.

'No doubt. What happened then?'

'After I left Keith's, I headed to the Denes Park. According to Keith, he said Lyle liked to hang around there drinking with his mates.'

'Same place as Mark was found?'

'Yeah,' Byrd replied. 'I figured I'd go check it out. Anyway, he gave me Lyle's number, which I rang over and over, but no one answered. When I got close to the stream where Mark's body was found, I heard something. A ringtone…'

'Lyle's phone?' Tanzy said, putting it together.

'Yeah, it was his phone, Ori. I don't know how Tallow or Hope missed it to be honest. So, what I'm assuming here is one of two things. One: Lyle was involved in Mark's murder. I don't know, maybe they had a fight, and he dropped his phone whilst they fought. After that, he panicked and fled. Maybe later he realised he'd lost the phone but didn't want to go back because of what'd happened.'

'Second thing?'

'Mark was with Lyle at the time and someone attacked them both. The suspect killed Mark, leaving him in the stream and took Lyle …'

Tanzy thought for a moment. 'Interesting theory. Would have been the work of a couple of suspects I'd guess.'

Byrd said, 'Possible.'

'Have you got the phone? Lyle's phone?'

'Yeah, it's in my hand. I'm back in the car now. The phone is locked though. I've tried unlocking it but it's blocked me for another ten minutes because I keep getting it wrong.'

'Take it to Keith. He might know the pin?'

'Yeah… but I don't want to panic him just yet,' Byrd confessed. 'It's early stages.'

'Teenagers don't just leave their phones anywhere. Trust me, it's not there out of choice,' Tanzy said.

Byrd had to agree with him.

'I'll go back to Keith's house, see if he knows. Oh, hold on, I can try again. It's been ten minutes.'

'Try one one one one,' Tanzy suggested.

'Ori, I don't think'—Byrd pressed the number one four times and pressed ENTER—'What… How did—'

'You in?'

'Yeah yeah, I'm in.'

'See if there's a Mark Greenwell in his contacts?'

Byrd went quiet for a moment. 'Hold on… there's a Mark G but no Greenwell at the end of it.'

'Good start. Now click on that number and it should show the recent communications between them. Phone calls and text messages. Usually.'

'Both,' Byrd said. 'Last phone call was seven p.m. last night, Ori.'

'What did the last text say?'

'Hold on… I can barely work this thing.'

'Old people and technology…'

After a long moment, Byrd told him the last message had been sent yesterday just before six p.m..

'What did it say?'

'It says - On the green tonight?'

'The green,' Tanzy repeated, deep in thought. 'By the green, he could mean the park. Is he selling on the green. Sounds like they could be a part of a little operation here. Did Lyle reply to that?'

'He texted back saying, Yeah.'

Silence grew between them and Tanzy knew Byrd well enough to know what he was thinking. 'I know you don't want to hear this, Max, but I think he was a part of something big.'

'I'll ring DFU,' Byrd said abruptly. DFU was the Digital Forensics Unit. 'I heard Mac saying he was staying late tonight so I'll see if he's had a look at Mark's phone. What if Mark G isn't Mark Greenwell?'

'Only one way to find out, Max.'

'Let you know what I find,' Byrd said, then hung up.

21

Wednesday Night
Low Coniscliffe, Outskirts of Darlington

Byrd hung his long black coat on the bottom of the stairs and took off his shoes, placing them in the new shoe rack that Claire had bought last week. Usually, Byrd left his shoes wherever he liked but things had changed now. The place needed a woman's touch and that's exactly what Claire was going to give it. After placing them underneath a pair of his black running shoes, he stood up and stretched, relieved he was home, and his first long day back was finally over.

'Hey, you!' she said as he entered the kitchen.

Smiling, he made his way over to her and kissed her. 'Missed you today,' he said.

'You too,' she replied, hugging him. 'Thanks for abandoning me and letting me unpack the clothes and do all the washing.'

Byrd picked up on the humour in her tone, gave her a smile, and moved over to the right, reached up to one of the high cupboards, grabbing one of his favourite mugs – the one that Tanzy bought him last year, saying 'I'm never wrong…' and asked her if she wanted a coffee.

She nodded. 'How was your day? Happy to be back?'

'Phenomenal to be back…'

They shared a laugh. Then Byrd told her briefly what'd happened at the park earlier that morning after the body of Mark Greenwell had been found.

'Yeah, Alice rang me asking if I knew anything about it?'

C. J. Grayson

Byrd smiled. 'Women and gossip, eh.'

Claire shrugged and noticed the mark on the side of his head.

'What on earth is that?' she said worriedly, placing the basket of damp clothes on the worktop and going over to him. He then explained about the blood results coming back from the murder scene. How it matched up with his friend's son, Lyle Wilson, and that he'd gone to his house and his father, Keith, had used his head as a cricket ball.

'Your own fault for sneaking around in other people's houses,' she mused, then frowned at it. 'It does look bad.'

'It's throbbing, but I'll live.'

'How come you're so late, anyway?'

After explaining he'd gone to the park where the body of the teenager was found this morning, he told her he'd found Lyle's phone.

'Have you spoken to Keith about what you've found?'

Byrd moved over to the table and dropped into a chair. 'It's too soon. I don't want to panic him just yet.'

'Maybe he has a right to know. It's his son.' She curled her lip in thought. 'Where's the phone?'

'At the station,' he said, 'I went there before coming home. The DFU guy, Mac, was working so I asked him to have a good look at it. There's loads of messages and phone calls on it. There's communication between Lyle and the teenager who was found dead too. Could have been friends.'

She gave a sad smile and padded over to him. He leaned in and held her for a few moments, saying nothing. From her pocket, her phone vibrated.

'Oh, that'll be Alice,' she said, reaching for it. She unlocked the phone and read the message.

'What's she wanting?'

'To come over tomorrow for a few glasses of wine.' Claire's eyes fell on Byrd's stare. 'That is okay, isn't it – Jesus, sorry, I never asked you—'

'Hey, you live here too now. This is your house,' he re-assured her.

'We'll stay in the living room, out the way,' she said.

'You can do as you please.'

Smiling, she leaned over and kissed him. 'Thanks.' Pushing the phone back into the pocket of her jeans, she grabbed the basket of clothes.

Byrd nodded at her. Claire had met Alice at her Zumba classes which she'd gone to for nearly a year now. They'd hit it off straight away, sharing interests in TV shows, fashion, political views etc.. Claire had been out with her a few times around the town in the last six months and they'd been to each other's houses for coffee. Alice worked in town at Barclays Bank as a customer support assistant. Things had changed in the banking world with upgraded technology and machines and most of the cashiers were trained in other areas, such as mortgages and debt management. According to Claire, Alice's job varied from day-to-day, but she seemed happy and was looking at a promotion sometime in the future.

Although Byrd had seen the pictures of them both on social media, he'd never officially met her yet. Most of his time was spent working and occasionally playing football, so for her to see her friends often when he was busy was perfectly natural. It was healthy. Something people needed to do. Maybe Byrd needed more of that, to go out for a meal and unwind. Over two months had passed since Byrd, Claire, Tanzy and Pip had been out for a meal, but it had felt longer for Byrd.

'Your tea is on there,' she said, noticing his searching look, knowing he'd be hungry. As she reached the door, she turned back. 'Max, we should all do something together. Me, you, Alice and Alex. She says he gets bored on a night and doesn't really do a lot. In fact, I think he plays football, you know, for fun.'

Byrd raised his eyebrows. 'Does he?'

She nodded. 'Think so. Apart from that though, he doesn't get out a lot. It'll be good for us to do something. Alice is telling me he wants to meet you. Hey, they went walking in the Lakes last year, so I suggested maybe us four going together at some point. What you think?'

Byrd had seen the pictures of Alex on social media too. Claire said he's nice but does seem a little lonely. She'd said since he left the army last year, his life had changed and working from home doing his Business Analysis stuff was okay, but it wasn't fulfilling him like the army days did. According to Alice anyway.

'What do you think?' Claire asked again, tilting her head to one side, her straight black hair falling over her right shoulder.

Byrd nodded. 'Sounds good. We'll sort out a meal or something.'

'Good, because I've planned to do something this weekend,' she said, smiling as she left the kitchen. 'Saturday night at Uno Momento in town.'

'I'll be there.'

'I know,' she mused and left the kitchen.

Standing, he went over to the plate of cheesy pasta and put it in the microwave, closed the door, set a timer and stood as it whirred away. As he stared at nothing, his gaze focused on the photograph on the opposite wall, just next to the door. He edged away from the worktop and went to it. It was A4-sized, the colours vivid and bright. The two people on it were both smiling, their teeth perfectly white and bright, even if he knew they were false.

As the microwave pinged behind him, he held his gaze, looking into their eyes as they stared back with happiness into the lens of the camera that had taken it, then finally said, 'I miss you guys so much. Love you Mam and Dad.'

22
Wednesday Night
Brougham Street

Mandy Spencer spent a few minutes standing at her son's bedroom door watching him as he drifted off to sleep. Everything about tonight had been great and, most importantly, Damien had really enjoyed himself. During his parents' evening, his teacher at school, Mrs Cornforth, had told her that Damien had been doing very well, nearly topping the class in most of the subjects. For a treat he had chosen Ham and Pineapple pizza, which wasn't Mandy's favourite, but that didn't matter.

Smiling as he drifted off to sleep, she left the room and closed the door, leaving it open an inch to allow the light on the landing to get in. She paused just outside his room as a worrying thought came back to her. Deciding she needed to tell someone, she took out her phone and dialled the number.

After four rings, Tracy Clarke picked up. 'Mand, you alright?'

'Hey, Tracy,' she said, slowly descending the stairs. 'I'm okay. Listen I forgot to tell you something earlier, but when I came back to my desk, you'd gone home.'

'What?'

'Mr Cairn rang again today.'

'Again?'

'Yeah.'

'I don't see why he keeps ringing.'

'I know,' Mandy said, 'I've told him we've done all we can to persuade the council to sell him the car parks, but he won't have it. I think because we've helped him out in the past, he's expecting us to do it again.'

'We can only do what we can do, Mandy…'

'I know.' Mandy paused a beat, reaching the kitchen. 'I just think things are getting… out of control.'

'Why?'

'When I got back to my car there was another note on the back window. Same as the one from yesterday. It said if it doesn't go ahead, something bad will happen.'

Tracy sighed heavily. 'Did you check the cameras when you found the first note yesterday?'

'Yeah, when I went in this morning, I spoke with Roger, the security guard. Before he left he checked the cameras. I was parked in a blind spot. We saw no one.'

'Must have seen someone nearby from the other cameras?'

'There was a woman walking a dog along the river. That's about it,' Mandy told her.

Tracy didn't respond for a few seconds. 'Think we should ring the police?'

'I don't know. That's two notes within two days now. I'm assuming it's coming directly from Mr Cairn but there's no way of proving it. I suppose if we told the police and explained what was going on, then they could go and speak with him.'

Tracy mulled over her words. 'I suppose.'

'Henry seemed a little off today I thought.'

'How do you mean?'

'Seemed quiet, not quite himself, as if there was something on his mind. He's usually quite talkative and smiley but today was the first time, in however long I've known him, he's been a little… strangely subdued. And he left a few hours early too.'

'Told me he was taking his son to the doctors. Thinks he has a problem with his heart. Says when he sleeps at night, he watches him, and sometimes, Eddy doesn't breathe for up to a minute.'

'God, I hope he doesn't have what Damien has, it's awful,' Mandy admitted.

'Remind me of Damien's condition, Mandy?'

'Paediatric Coronary Artery disease. He takes tablets twice a day to thin his blood so it can reach his heart properly. Even with them, running around can be a struggle. It'll be like that forever. But hey, that's life.'

'Bless him,' Tracy said, softly. 'Melissa loves Damien. They sit next to each other, don't they? Mel says he's very clever. She's even admitted to copying some of his work, the cheeky little thing.'

'I bet Damien lets her. Think he has a crush on her.'

They shared a laugh, then Tracy said, 'Think Eddy and Damien will have to fight it out. Henry says Eddy follows her around all day.'

'The three of them are cute together, aren't they?'

'They are,' Tracy replied. 'So, what are you going to do about the notes?'

'I'm - I'm not sure… he's - he's a property developer.'

'A very keen, can't-take-no-for-an-answer property developer?' Tracy added.

'Tell me about it. If he rings again tomorrow, I'll explain that the next stage is contacting the police about the letters. Maybe he'll understand I feel threatened and leave it at that. Then hopefully the letters on the car window will stop.'

'Yeah, sounds fair enough. Hey, I was thinking…'

'Yeah?' Mandy asked.

'What if it's a wind up?'

'The notes on my car?'

'Yeah. Who else knows about it? Me, you, Henry, Mr Cairn…'

'Roger, the security guard,' Mandy added. 'Don't see why anyone would be so mean to do it as a joke.'

'Maybe… hold on,' Tracy said quietly.

'What is it, Trace?'

'I've just heard the letterbox. Weird.' Tracy pulled the phone away from her ear a few inches. 'Melissa, is that you? Melissa?'

'What's happening?' Mandy asked.

Tracy brought the phone closer. 'I've just heard the letterbox go. Melissa is upstairs in bed. Jack is working. Why would someone be at the door at this time?'

Mandy checked the kitchen clock on the wall to her right. Nearly ten-thirty. 'You at your door?'

There was a rustling sound.

'It's a note,' Tracy said.

'A note?'

'Yeah – hold on.' Tracy unfolded it and gasped when she read the words: *You're too late. Time to face the consequences.*

'What does it say?' Mandy asked.

Tracy told her.

'Pretty sick if this is a wind up.'

23

Wednesday Night
Darlington

Arthur's tall, slim frame stepped into Jonny Darchem's living room and, instantly, he could feel the heat from the open fire to the left. Darchem sat comfortably on the three-seater sofa in the centre of the room, his focus on the huge flat screen television in the corner resting on an expensive-looking wooden cabinet, a few metres past the fire. To his right, through the large bay window, he could see the outline of the long garden and the road at the end of it, empty of cars and well-lit from the bright street lamps scattered along it.

On the screen there was the news report about the death of Mark Greenwell. A local detective, Detective Inspector Orion Tanzy, was being hounded by reporters, asking him what the police are going to do. For once Darchem felt like he was on the same side as the police, as he too, more than anyone, would love to know what happened to Mark. The DI on the screen explained to the cameras that forensics have found a few clues which he was confident would offer them some assistance in understanding exactly what happened.

'That's all they ever say,' Darchem laughed. 'But they have nothing, as usual. That's why there's people like me in the world because the police are shit. They never do anything.'

Arthur stopped at the sofa, dropped down near Darchem, and focused on the screen. 'He's not a bad looking bloke,' Arthur said, pointing to DI Tanzy.

'Yeah… he's your type isn't he?'

Arthur, in his usual serious manner, nodded somberly. Rarely a smile found his lips and Darchem could probably count on one hand how many times he'd heard Arthur laugh in the years he'd employed him.

'Have you finalised the plan?' Arthur asked, eagerly.

'Ah, straight to business, Arthur, I like that,' Darchem whispered, grinning in his direction. Arthur never smiled or messed around. Standing up, Darchem went over to a large, wide dark oak unit that was positioned between the right alcove of the chimney breast and the television. From one of the higher shelves Darchem pulled out a file, then went back to the sofa and dropped it on Arthur's lap.

For a few minutes, Arthur, with dark-focused eyes, studied the three separate pages.

'Who are these people?'

'These, my friend, are people that haven't done their job properly, and will now be punished. These people will learn from their mistakes and will face the consequence of their actions, or in this case, their inactions.'

Arthur nodded but said nothing.

'Can you do it?'

'Of course.' His eyes narrowed for a moment, then he looked up. 'Have you spoken with Jamie or Andy about what happened with Mark yet?' Arthur asked.

Just as Darchem was about to reply he heard something out in the hallway. Then Jamie appeared carrying three shoeboxes.

'Speak of the devil!' Darchem shouted. 'Hey, Jamie, what you got there?'

Jamie came over to the sofa and placed the shoeboxes on the spare seat next to Darchem. 'Mark Greenwell's cocaine. I've been over to his place to get it.'

Darchem's eyes narrowed. 'You didn't go hurting anyone did you?'

'I put something in his Mam's wine, waited a while till it knocked her out. Then went in, got the gear.'

'Impressive.' He glanced down at the boxes. 'All full?'

Jamie nodded towards him, in a see-for-yourself kind of way. Darchem lifted the lid from the top box and saw the small bags of white powder. 'Good lad.'

Jamie nodded, happy Darchem was pleased with him, then moved on. 'I spoke with Andy earlier. He said that Lyle Wilson never turned up last night either. Said he didn't go to the house on Craig Street.'

'He didn't?' Darchem frowned again.

Jamie shook his head. 'No, he didn't. I'll go to his place and—'

Darchem held up a palm. 'Leave it for now, we have bigger things going on.' He nodded towards the file of Arthur's lap and, immediately, Jamie understood.

'Need any help with it?' Jamie asked Arthur.

Arthur shook his head and said, 'I'll be just fine.' With that, he stood up and walked out of the room with the file in his hand.

C. J. Grayson

24

Wednesday Midnight
Edward Street, Albert Hill Industrial Estate

It had been over twenty four hours since Lyle Wilson had been seen by his father Keith or any of his friends.

From the ceiling of the small rectangular shaped unit there was a rope hanging down from a securely fixed hook, tied around his wrists, holding the majority of his weight up. Although he still had the ability to stand on his tiptoes, his legs were tired, causing him to bend every so often, putting massive pressure on the rope gouging into the skin on his wrists.

They had started to bleed.

'What the fuck do you want with me?' he cried.

'Isn't it strange?' the man said, almost as quiet as a whisper, 'that when you put people in vulnerable positions, they see things differently don't they?'

Lyle frowned at him, distracted by the pain coming from his bloody wrists. He could feel a slither of crimson liquid slowly dripping down his forearm. 'Wha…?'

'Oh, you know? You see these people strutting around so confidently like they own everything, like they possess this magical ability to be invincible?'

Lyle didn't answer him.

The man burst into laughter. 'That surprises me, because you'—the man prodded his chest so hard his finger nearly pierced the skin—'are one of them.' Lyle cried out in agony. 'You, Lyle fucking Wilson,' the man went on, his voice stern and filled with a calm, frightening anger, 'walk around that park like you own it. You pick on

113

young, vulnerable teenagers, almost forcing them to buy your drugs. No, no, don't shake your head. I've watched you. You pick on them, then they keep coming back for more, don't they?'

Lyle didn't say a word. Instead, he looked away. The smell inside the unit was musty, the air was still. From the two strip lights above his head, one either side of where the hook was fixed supporting the rope his hands were tied to, he could see the space around him. Four brick walls. The wall to his right had shelving, but through his glassy, tear-filled eyes, he couldn't make out the objects.

'Hey,' the man shouted, 'look at me when I'm speaking. You're not dealing with kids at the park tonight. You're here with me, hung up from a rope. And depending on how you answer the next question will determine if you leave here walking or dead. It's your choice.'

There seemed to be a level of focus appear in Lyle's face that the man hadn't seen since he first hung him up. 'I – I don't understand?'

The man came within an inch of Lyle's face, feeling his warm breath on his skin. He could smell something he vaguely recognised as spearmint chewing gum. Holding his breath, he stared into the man's serious eyes.

'You want to know what the question is?'

Lyle, after several unsure seconds, nodded twice. Maybe if the question was asked, and he got the answer right, he could go. Anything to get rid of the pain in his wrists. It was unlike anything he'd ever felt.

'Okay,' the man said, turning away from Lyle. From the shelving unit over to the right he picked up a pair of scissors, opened and closed them a few times, so Lyle could hear clearly what they were. When he saw the blades reflect the light on the ceiling his eyes widened, and his heart rate multiplied.

'What are you—'

'Shh, Lyle, it's not time to answer the question just yet.'

114

The man brought the scissors up to his face, holding them there for Lyle to have a good look at. Then he opened the blade and snapped them shut so quickly, Lyle edged back, causing the man to burst out in laughter once again.

'Hey,' the man said, 'it's warm in here, isn't it?'

Lyle frowned. It wasn't warm at all. It was two degrees outside. Probably felt colder inside the brick-walled unit they were in. Wearing a dark tracksuit, trainers and a thin t-shirt, Lyle watched the scissors carefully, wondering what the hell the man was going to do with them.

'Yes, it's warm in here,' the man said without waiting for a response. He moved the scissors closer to Lyle's face then lowered them to his stomach. He leaned forward and took hold of the bottom of the hoody then, using the scissors, he started slicing into the material cutting upwards until he reached his throat. The hoodie fell open.

'Are you a little cooler now?'

Lyle was too afraid to answer, not knowing where this was going. He thought about trying to kick him, but his feet were tied together. If he brought both feet up in an attempt to kick the man, the horrendous searing pain would multiply in his cut wrists and that would be un-bearable.

'Good,' the man replied to Lyle's silence. Pulling the material of the sleeve to one side, he cut a line down his arm and pulled off one of the sleeves, then repeated it on the opposite side. Lyle felt the bitter cold attack his bare skin and started to shiver.

Almost two minutes later, the man pulled off Lyle's torn boxers and launched them across the garage, topping the small mound of cut-up fabric from the other items of clothing.

Standing naked from the rope, Lyle started to cry. He'd never felt so defenceless in his whole life.

'Aw, what's the matter, little Lyle?' The man leaned closer, whispering in his ear, 'It isn't nice, is it?'

'Can you imagine taking so many drugs that it messed with your brain and made you take off all your clothes and then go outside at two in the morning? Then, when your friends are looking for you, they find your body in a park, dead?'

Lyle's eyes became lost, as if he wasn't following the scenario the man had told him.

'Lyle! Focus!'

His harsh words sent a shudder through Lyle. He saw the anger in the man's eyes and, down in his hand, he noticed the scissors. The space around him was becoming unbearable. Freezing. Damp. His bare feet were sore on the cold concrete and his skin was aching.

'You know what makes it worse?' the man said. 'It's that you don't even know what I'm talking about, do you?'

Quivering, Lyle shook his head a few times, then his eyes rolled back into his head for a moment. The thin slugs of blood had reached his arm pits. He was losing blood quicker now, the cuts on his wrists becoming deeper and wider.

'Stay with me, young man,' the man told him firmly. 'Wake up.'

For a short intense moment, his attention came back suddenly after the man slapped his face a few times. Then he gave him one final slap and asked him a very particular question.

'If you had the choice to start again, which one would you choose? I'll give you an option A and an option B. Drum roll please… Option A, you get drawn into drugs by your mates and think, do you know what, this isn't for me. You walk away from it and lead a hard-working innocent life. Or option B, you get drawn into the life of drugs and selling it and think, hey I'm making so much money here, I'm going to continue to do it, not caring if you hurt others along the way, as long as you have the fancy watches and the nice cars.'

Lyle, unsteady on his feet, tried his best to understand the question.

'I'll repeat myself,' the man told him, then did so.

Lyle's eyes narrowed and, finally, he managed to say, 'Option A - A. I choose A.'

The man tilted his head and smiled. 'Good answer. Because of your answer Lyle I'm going to let you go. Good boy.'

Sighing with relief, Lyle closed his eyes for a few seconds, exhausted but ecstatic it was over.

The man went over to the shutters and flicked the light off, the cold garage becoming pitch black. Lyle, unable to see a thing, grunted in fear.

'Calm down, hold on,' the man said softly.

Then a loud continuous mechanical sound erupted to Lyle's left, followed by a slither of moonlight that entered, allowing the teenager to see his feet. The garage door opened fully and for a moment he felt exposed, standing with his hands tied above his head, naked.

'I'm going to release your wrists, Lyle. If you try anything I'll stab you in the throat. Do you understand?'

Quietly, Lyle said he did.

The man pulled a folded pair of steps from somewhere, opened them and stepped up. Lyle felt his wrists being pulled from side to side until they became loose and he tumbled to the damp, icy floor in a heap. The freezing ground hit his skin, but he didn't care. He was happy to be free, and not hung up like some helpless pig.

'Okay, young man,' the man said, although Lyle couldn't really see where he was in the shadows. 'You can go.'

Without even looking for his clothes he dashed out onto the street. From the dim moonlight above he followed the road until he made it to Cleveland Street. Somewhere behind him he heard the mechanical hum of the garage door chatter away but the road was too dark to see anything.

Then he heard another sound.

A door closing. A car door.

Cleveland Street looked familiar to him and he realised where he was. Naked and desperate to get away he took a left, his bare feet slapping off the concrete, in a hope he'd see a passing car soon.

Nearly fifty metres down the road, he heard a car somewhere behind him.

Fast, sharp breaths left his lungs as he turned, waving his hands up in the air, beyond caring that he was naked and was covered in blood.

The car coming from the direction of the railway bridge appeared to be coming fast, then slowed on its approach, the driver behind the dark glass obviously spotting him from a distance. Seconds later, with his hands waving in the air, a relieved smile grew on his face as he observed the vehicle slowing down a little. It looked to be a 4x4 type, quite high and wide, but he wasn't sure of the make, but the colour could have been blue.

'Thank God,' he panted. His body trembled so much, even breathing was difficult.

The 4x4 slowed. Then very suddenly there was the roar of its engine and the vehicle surged forward, picking up speed as the driver manoeuvred onto the path towards Lyle.

With wide terrified eyes Lyle watched the vehicle speed towards him. Then, with a sickening thud, his body bounced off the fast-moving bonnet, forcing him up high into the air. He landed on the road a few metres beyond the car with a sickening crunch.

The driver casually got out of the car and closed his door. Glancing around to make sure there was no one watching, he walked briskly to the front of the car and observed the lifeless body down on the ground. Lyle's body was mangled, almost distorted. There was a new pool of blood appearing between his head and the road. The man grinned widely.

'You chose the right option, but I don't believe you meant it, Lyle,' the man whispered, his cold words almost fading in the gentle winds. He leaned over, picked up Lyle's bloody, naked body like he weighed a bag of sugar, hauled him over his shoulder and put him in the boot of his car. After closing the boot, he quickly glanced around, then got back in through the driver's door and drove away.

25

Thursday Early Morning
Darlington

Byrd stopped at the door and took a long, slow breath.

He hated doing this.

Pushing down the handle, he edged the door open a few inches. The dim glow from the lamp positioned on the other side of the room gave him enough light to see. He closed the door gently and respectfully, feeling the warmth inside the space, and turned to see the small, thin man at the other side of it, who was as still as a glass lake on a windless day, facing away from him.

As Byrd quietly made his way down the centre of the room, he noticed the two black coffins the man was looking at. Both of them were open, their polished lids raised just past ninety degrees held in place with small, mechanical, brass arms.

'Welcome, Max,' the man said, without turning towards him.

'Hi,' Byrd replied, slowly approaching him. Once he was level, Byrd stared down into the coffins too.

The man angled his focus towards Byrd and said, 'Are you happy, Max?'

Sighing, Byrd glared back at the coffins. At the two people lying inside them. They looked so peaceful and content, their faces pale and lifeless.

'Yes, thank you.'

'Speak with them if you like, Max. Take all the time you need,' the man said. 'I'll be in there'—he pointed through an open door to their right—'so just let me know when you're done, okay.' His tone genuinely implied there was no pressure and Byrd could take as long as he needed.

Byrd gave him a thankful nod, waited until he'd walked through the doorway before moving over to his father. He was in the coffin on the right. Byrd had chosen a suit for him to wear. One of his favourites which he seemed to wear at every suit-worthy event they went to. Down by his side, Byrd had positioned a folded-up Newcastle shirt, which meant the world to his father. Every chance his father had, he went to the home games, and some of the away games if he could, depending on the distance. His favourite player was Alan Shearer. After speaking with his father for a few moments, he told him he loved him and leaned down, kissing his forehead.

A few paces to the left, just as peaceful, was his mother. 'Hi, Mam,' he began, then spoke with her for a while, telling her how much he loved her and thanked her for everything she'd ever done for him and dad.

He bent down to kiss—

She opened her eyes and glared up at him.

Byrd froze, his heart thumping rapidly in his chest, half-bent over the coffin.

She then whispered, 'Find the killer, Max…'

Byrd woke up quickly, panting heavily, his vision blurry for a moment. Then the dark ceiling of his bedroom came into focus. Realising he was in his own bed, he noticed a slither of light coming through the blinds from a nearby streetlight, and a hazy glare coming from the landing to his left. Claire liked having the landing light on for comfort. To his right she lightly snored, her bare chest gently rising and falling.

He wiped the remaining sweat from his forehead, swung his legs off the side of the bed, picked up his phone, and made his way through to the en-suite bathroom as silently as he could. He lifted the toilet seat and sat down, unlocking his phone. There was an email from

Mac, the IT guy at work. He'd sent him a list of phone numbers and text messages that were on Lyle Wilson's phone.

'You okay, Max?' a muffled voice asked from the bedroom.

Byrd stiffened at the sound, then replied with a simple, 'Yeah.'

Claire knew Byrd never slept very well, even before they'd spent their first full night together, Byrd had thought it would be a good idea to mention it to her before she woke up in the middle of the night and wondered where he was, assuming he'd done a runner. For Claire it was normal to wake up to an empty bed.

At the bottom of the email Mac confirmed the phone's location settings had been on over the past two weeks and, as well as spending time on Willow Road where he lived with his dad, Keith, there was another frequently visited address on Craig Street. Byrd made a mental note to look into that tomorrow. What he needed now was sleep.

Because tomorrow he'd be getting no rest at all.

.

26

Thursday Morning
Brougham Street, North Road

Parked up at the side of the road Arthur sat patiently in his car. He'd been there for nearly twenty-six minutes and had checked his watch three times. His focus had been on the red door of the house about a third of the way up the street. He'd checked over the file that Darchem had given him last night and been through it so many times, he'd memorised every word.

It would only be a matter of time.

He knew he hadn't missed him, so he assumed the boy was running later than usual today. Probably getting his school bag ready and his packed lunch which, considering his age, was no doubt done by his mother.

The road was covered in a fine coating of ice from the sub-zero temperatures that Darlington had endured overnight. Although the sun was trying it's best to rise, a cluster of thick black clouds covered it, preventing the day from really waking up, leaving the street in a chilly grey mist.

The time on the dashboard was 8.23 a.m..

Down on the passenger seat his phone buzzed. He took his eyes away from the red door, glanced down, and picked up the phone. *Do you have the package?*

Not yet.

He started to type something in reply but his long, thin fingers froze when he heard a young boy's voice across the street. His short, blonde-haired mother waved him off and closed the red door as the boy pulled his rucksack higher onto his back and stepped down onto the path.

The only difference with this particular morning was that it would be the last time his mother would ever get to do that. It was a shame she didn't know. The boy took hold of the straps of his bag and casually started trotting up the street in the direction of North Park, the small key-rings attached to his zip clinking each small stride he took.

The man sat for a few moments and took a breath. He put the car into first gear and edged out slowly, then crawled along at a steady seven miles an hour.

Through the windscreen he saw the boy take a left down the alley between Brougham Street and Zetland Street.

Arthur increased the speed of the car until he reached the alley, then slowed, taking the left. The boy was daw-dling ahead, half-way down the alley between Brougham street and Zetland Street and turned when he heard the car's tyres on the cobbles behind him. After seeing the car, he kept to the left so the car could pass safely.

But the car never passed.

Instead, it stopped next to the boy. The passenger side window lowered, and Arthur said, 'Hey, Damien.'

The boy frowned at him, his young brain trying to work out where he'd seen the man before, but nothing seemed familiar.

'It's cold today, isn't it, mate. Hey, listen, Mrs Cornforth has asked me to pick you up.'

'My teacher?' A heavy scowl ran across the top of the boy's eyes.

'Yeah. You want to jump in, and I'll take you from here?'

'I – it's just up there, I'm okay to walk,' he replied, pointing towards the school.

'It's no trouble, honestly. I'm going that way anyway. We have a lot of fun things planned for the class today.'

A puzzled look came on the boy's face. He studied Arthur with caution. Damien was highly intelligent for his age and observed everything about the man. Short black hair. Skin which looked like it had been bronzed by a few days in the sun. Thick, black eyebrows over the top of dark brown eyes.

'Who – who are you? I've never seen you before,' Damien said.

'I'm the assistant teacher today. My name is Mr Simms. I've just actually knocked on your door, but your mother said you'd started walking and that it would be okay to catch you up.'

'You spoke to my mum?'

Arthur nodded confidently. 'Yeah.'

'What does my mum look like?' he asked.

'She has blonde hair and today she's wearing a white blouse and black skirt,' Arthur replied, hoping that would be enough. It wasn't.

'What accent does she speak with?'

Arthur sighed, feeling anger growing inside. 'I don't know, I couldn't quite place it. Now come on, get in, we're just around the corner.'

'I don't know,' Damien said sheepishly, almost folding into himself. 'I don't really know you. I shouldn't really be getting into a stranger's car.' He took a few steps back until his rucksack hit the brick wall behind him.

'Hey, don't be afraid'—he leaned over, opening the passenger door for him—'I'm the assistant teacher today. Like I said my name is Mr Simms. I'll be helping you with your Maths and English. Come on, get in.'

Damien kept his focus on the man's large hands, how his fingers looked abnormally too big for a human hand.

'Come on, Damien, nothing to be scared of. Get in,' he pressured, keeping his big brown eyes on him.

Damien didn't move and slowly shook his head. 'I – I don't thin—'

'Damien, get in the fucking car now!' Arthur shouted through gritted teeth, his face drastically changing.

After witnessing his anger, Damien edged back a little and shuffled to the right, his bag scraping off the wall until he rounded the corner and stepped back into the alley that ran parallel with Brougham Street and Zetland Street.

'Damien, get in!'

His body started to shake, but it didn't take nine-year-old Damien long to realise there was a threat, so he turned and ran as fast as his little legs could carry him.

Arthur jumped out of the car, and with a surging anger in his face, bolted after him down the alley.

27

Thursday Morning
Brougham Street, North Road

Damien's little legs burned as he galloped down the cold alley away from the car. His little heart pounded so hard, he could feel it coming through his chest, like a continuous drumroll of frantic panic radiating from him. The weight of the bag collided into his back every stride he took, and he could feel his back starting to ache and the straps of the bag were rubbing against his bony shoulders.

Over the frantic echoes of his small school shoes pounding on the frosty cobbles he could hear large, heavy, quicker strides behind him, growing louder by the second.

Suddenly there was a metallic ping behind him, but he didn't turn to see what it was.

Keeping his focus ahead he knew he had a choice to make once he hit the end of the alley. He could go left, or he could go right. If he went left he could run back into Brougham Street and try make it home and shout for help. Alternatively, turning right would take him onto Zetland Street, away from his home but closer to his school.

'Damien! Stop!' the man shouted, sounding so close to Damien. He was only metres behind him.

As he approached the T-junction of the alley he slowed a fraction and angled his body, deciding to take the left. The blood pounding in his ears was the only thing he heard, the absolute desperation of getting away from this stranger setting his nerves on fire. He took the left, but his heavy bag kept going forward and the momentum of the external weight pulled him around further than he needed to go, swinging him around one-hundred and eighty degrees.

In a split second he felt himself flying through the air and landing down hard onto the cobbles with a sickening thud. Luckily, his bag took most of the impact when he landed on his back but he'd fallen awkwardly, trapping his arm underneath him and scraping his right knee off the icy cobbles.

'Ahhhh…' he cried out, feeling a sudden wave of white heat in his wrist, and a general pain all over his body.

Near him, the heavy footsteps slowed then eventually stopped. The air around him was silent, except for the sound of the morning traffic tinkering along North Road over the row of houses behind him.

'Damien… why didn't you just get in the car?' Arthur said, panting from running the length of the alley.

Damien wearily glanced up at him. He looked like a giant and looked taller because he was so thin.

'What do you want from me?' Damien asked, wincing in pain from his sore wrist.

'It doesn't matt—'

'Is he okay?' they both heard a concerned voice say from the opening of the alley at Brougham Street.

Arthur looked to the left, seeing an elderly lady standing there with a walking stick. She was wearing a long red coat and wore glasses that resembled jam jar bottoms. She was short and was hunched over a touch, implying her better years were behind her.

'He's fine, don't worry about him.'

'Is that – is that you, Damien?' she said, squinting a little.

Damien looked up. It was Sheena from three doors down. She lived at the house with the black door and spoke with his mother often. She occasionally baked them cakes which Damien wasn't too fussed about but ate them to be kind.

'Sheena,' Damien begged, 'you nee—'

'Damien is fine,' Arthur said, cutting him off, holding a soft palm out towards her. She didn't seem convinced. 'Isn't that right, Damien?' he asked him.

Damien didn't say a word. Instead, he glared at the cobbles below her.

'Damien, what's wrong?' Sheena asked, waddling into the alley with the aid of her stick. She'd had a hip replacement the previous year and, according to the doctor's appointment she'd attended, she needed the other hip doing soon.

'The boy is fine!' Arthur claimed, agitation creeping into his voice.

'Well from where I'm standing mister, he doesn't look fine to me.' She was a few metres away now, then stopped near him. 'Have you fallen, Damien?'

Damien nodded several times but never looked up. He liked Sheena. She used to look after him when his parents went out for meals. She was almost like another grandmother to him.

'Come on, let's get you up,' she said, bending down slightly, extending her arm.

'The boy is coming with me,' Arthur said, coldly.

Sheena paused and frowned, angling her focus up at him. 'I'm sorry – hey, aren't you the guy who was sat in the red Mondeo? You were parked across the road earlier?'

Arthur frowned and tilted his head slightly, surprised about her perceptions.

'Yes, you are,' she said without a reply, 'I knew you looked familiar.' She turned away from him and lowered again to Damien.

Arthur leaned forward and grabbed her wrist, then pulled her close to him with so much ease it frightened her.

'I really wish you had minded your own business,' he whispered in her ear.

'Hey, let go of me, you can't—'

She stopped talking and gasped loudly when the knife pierced her frail, wrinkly throat, just above the collar of her red coat. Blood fell over the blade and soaked the front of her jacket. She dropped her silver walking stick and threw both hands up to her face in an attempt to stop it but she started gargling uncontrollably, Arthur let go of her and watched her wobble a couple of steps before she collapsed to the cold cobbles below.

Damien, with wide terrified eyes, watched his life-long neighbour wriggling in agony, clutching at her throat with frantic hands. It seemed like hours to him, but it took only seconds for the life to drain from her. When her eyes and body became still, the reality of witnessing what'd just happened hit him hard.

The man pushed the knife back inside his jacket and zipped it back up. Then he looked down at Damien and smiled.

'If you don't get in the car, the same will happen to you. Understand?'

Damien quickly nodded up at him, then glared back down at the pooling blood as it glistened in the morning frost.

'Come on, let's go,' Arthur said, turning and walking back up the alley towards his car.

Damien, his body trembling, slowly found his feet, and followed Arthur back to the red Mondeo.

C. J. Grayson

28

Thursday Morning
Police Station

'Morning, Ori,' Byrd said, approaching his desk with a coffee in his hand.

Tanzy looked up and smiled. 'Morning.' He'd already been in the office nearly half-an-hour. In fact, he'd left his house nearly two hours ago. They'd changed one of his Judo classes to a Thursday morning instead of a Sunday, so that he had to do Monday nights and Thursday mornings now.

'Hey, Max, how you doing? You've lost more weight haven't you?'

Byrd was wearing a different coat today. It was shorter than his usual black one but it was woven with a similar material and looked like the same colour. It seemed to narrow his shoulder width and pull in his stomach. He took a seat next to him and told Tanzy he was fine, it was probably only the jacket that made him appear that way, which he'd taken off and hung on the back of his chair.

Tanzy noticed the paper in his hand and enquired about it.

'Numbers and texts from Lyle's phone,' Byrd informed him. 'Mac printed it out and left it on his desk.' Tanzy slid over on his desk chair and studied it for a moment. 'What's that at the bottom?'

Byrd ran a palm through his hair. 'These are the places the phone has been the most over the last two weeks. He mentioned something about the location settings on it and being able to see them. See here' —Byrd placed his finger

131

on the largest dot—'Mac explained this was his most frequently visited spot.'

Tanzy frowned, unsure where it was, or how big the area that the map covered. There were no street names. 'Is it… somewhere in the Denes?'

Byrd nodded twice. 'Craig street. See here, there's Hollyhurst Road and along there is Greenbank Road.'

Tanzy followed his finger and bobbed his head. 'And he lives… on Willow Road?'

'He does, but from this it seems he's spent more time at Craig Street than his own home.'

'Could be a friend of his,' Tanzy said. 'That's probably why Keith wasn't too worried about his whereabouts. He probably comes and goes. If Keith's busy working all the time, sometimes out of town, he probably just lets Lyle get on with it.' Tanzy looked for a few moments. 'Do we know what number on Craig Street?'

Shaking his head, Byrd said they didn't and that they have to find that out for themselves. 'We'll set up surveillance soon, see if there's any activity going on somewhere.'

Tanzy nodded in agreement.

'You two!' blurted DCI Fuller.

Frowning, Byrd and Tanzy both turned. 'What?' Byrd asked.

'Get to Brougham Street off North Road. A woman has been stabbed in the throat.'

Byrd and Tanzy turned, logged off their computers and put their chairs under their desks with urgency. Within minutes, they were inside Tanzy's Golf, heading for Brougham Street.

29

ursday Late Morning
Brougham Street

DI Tanzy pulled up to the side of the road and switched off the engine. They'd been on the phone to DCI Fuller who'd briefly updated them both on the situation. Fuller told them he'd be down very soon, once he'd finished an important meeting, and that Tanzy and Byrd were to get things under control.

Tanzy took a breath, opened the car door then, as he stood, had a quick look around Brougham Street. Up the street were residents standing on their doorsteps peeking along the street to see what all the commotion was about. Down the road, there were a number of PCs standing inside a temporary barrier stopping people from getting in. DC Leonard was speaking to a woman who was standing on her doorstep, dressed in a pink dressing gown, the expression on her face showing she was both upset and appalled at what'd happened in the alley behind. Leonard was holding a notepad in his hand and was intently nodding as she answered his questions.

Byrd and Tanzy started walking down the street towards the tape.

'Morning, Sir,' DC Leonard said, as the woman he was speaking to backed into her house and closed the door. He folded his small notepad and placed it back into the inside pocket of his coat. He said the same to Byrd and gave him a nod.

'Good Morning,' Tanzy replied. 'What's the score?'

'Forensics are in the alley. Cornty and Weaver are manning this tape'—he nodded to his right at the tape twenty-five metres away from them—'and Grearer and Timms are on the opposite side manning the other tape.'

'Forensics – Tallow and Hope?'

DC Leonard nodded. 'And Amanda, too.'

'Okay, what are you doing?'

'Knocking on doors, seeing if anyone had seen anything that could be useful. So far, nothing at all—'

'Wait, sir, you can't be in here!' cried a voice down the street.

Tanzy, Byrd, and Leonard turned to the voice. An elderly gentleman had stepped under the tape and was charging up the alley as DC Cornty trailed behind him.

'Wait, Sir, you can't—'

'Get the fuck off me,' the man shouted, flaying his arms at Cornty. Weaver watched the minor commotion from the tape to prevent anyone else trying the same thing.

'Never a dull moment in this town,' Tanzy said as they approached the temporary tape. Weaver lifted up the tape to allow the three of them under and, as they rounded the brickwork of the last house, they saw Cornty restraining the old man, preventing him going any further.

'Please, sir,' Cornty said, 'you need to calm down. You can't be in here. This is a crime scene.'

'I know, I – it's my wife,' he pleaded. 'Please, I need to see if it's my wife. She hasn't come home yet.'

A sick feeling grew in the pit of Tanzy's stomach. He joined level with Cornty and placed a soft hand on the man's back. Byrd and Leonard were a few steps behind. 'Excuse me, sir.' He felt the man trembling, almost vibrating, even through the thick feather-filled coat he was wearing. 'Listen, you can't be in here, this is a crime scene and for the purpose of not contaminating it, I need to ask you to move back behind the tape.'

'You don't understand, I think—'

'Sir, what's your name?'

'Huh?' The man shuffled his feet.

'Your name, what's your name?' Tanzy asked calmly.

'Malcolm.'

'Malcolm?'

'Malcolm Edwards.' He had a thick, long nose resting under heavy-framed glasses which magnified his brown eyes almost to the point of it becoming comical. His skin was a little blotchy and his hair was so thin Tanzy could see his scalp through the fine strands that remained.

'I understand your concern, Mr Edwards. But for the moment, could I ask my colleague'—he looked at DC Cornty—'to take you to one side and speak with you. We can't risk altering any evidence that could help us with this investigation. I'll personally come and speak with you very, very soon. You have my word, sir.' He turned to Cornty and said, 'Phil, can you go and speak with Malcolm on the other side of the tape?'

Malcolm let out a heavy sigh and realised he wouldn't out muscle both Cornty and Tanzy. He reluctantly turned, almost knocking into Byrd as he ambled down the cobbles back to Brougham Street, muttering to himself how ridiculous it all was.

'I think he's pissed off,' Leonard said to Tanzy, now by his side.

'He will be if he thinks we're not letting him see his wife.'

'I'd be the same,' Byrd said, eyeing the crowds in front and behind them.

'No...' Leonard said, smiling. 'I mean Cornty. I don't think he's happy with me. I need to speak to you about something later. It's draining me.'

'Okay, remind me later on, Jim, because I'll forget,' Tanzy told him.

Leonard nodded and walked with Byrd and Tanzy until they reached DS Stockdale, who was standing at the corner of the cobbled T-junction. So far, the body wasn't visible to them. They assumed it would be to the right, up the alley joining Zetland and Brougham.

'Morning,' Stockdale said, glancing up. There was a notepad and a pen in his hand. He was first responder signing people in and out of the area.

Tanzy glanced past him up the alley, noticing Tallow and Hope leaning down to the floor over a body. They were both wearing their white overalls, but they looked padded, as if they had jumpers and extra layers on underneath. No surprise really. The suits were paper thin and would be no use in a month like February.

Amanda Forrest was standing a few metres back with a camera in her hand, also wearing the compulsory whites, taking pictures of the blood spatter on the faded brick wall behind the body of the old lady. With no wind in the alley the air was cold and still. A faint visible mist hung around them, adding to the terrifying effect of another crime scene.

'Were you the first responder?' Tanzy asked him.

'Yeah, call came in on the radio,' Stockdale replied, 'I was on North Road at the time. I parked down there'—he pointed behind him towards Zetland Street—'and came down to see two young boys crying. They'd made the phone call to Dispatch and were asked to wait until someone showed.'

'Where are they now?'

'On Zetland Street. We phoned their parents to come and collect them. But they're still speaking with PC Andrews.'

Tanzy stayed silent but nodded.

'You going in?' Stockdale asked, ready with his notepad and pen.

'I'd like to speak with the boys first,' he replied, angling his focus towards Zetland Street. 'Just round there?'

'Yeah to the right,' Stockdale confirmed.

'Let's go see.'

Tanzy and Leonard approached the tape fixed across the Zetland street alley entrance which was manned by PC Donny Grearer and PC Eric Timms. They both smiled at their superiors – although, technically, a DC, wasn't a higher rank than a PC – and made sure the interested members of the public stepped back, leaving enough room for them to bend down under the tape.

On Zetland Street, towards the right, they saw PC Josh Andrews kneeling down on the floor speaking with a small group of people. Two of them were small boys, who were stood but at the same level as Andrews kneeling. The tactic was never to speak down to a child who was frightened because they'd never open up.

If Tanzy had to guess he'd say the two boys were around the age of ten or eleven. The others in the group, judging by the positions, were the childs' parents.

'Hey,' Tanzy said, interrupting them for a moment.

Andrews, from his kneeling position, glanced up at Tanzy. 'Hey, boss.'

'I'm Detective Inspector Orion Tanzy,' the DI said, introducing himself to the two boys and their parents.

They all looked at Tanzy for a moment.

'And this is DC Leonard,' Tanzy added.

They shifted their focus to Leonard, then back to Tanzy. Byrd, a few steps behind, stayed quiet, allowing Tanzy and Leonard to lead.

'Would you mind if we joined in?' Tanzy asked Andrews.

'Not at all,' Andrews replied, smiling, then looking back at the two boys and motioned to the boy on the left. 'This is Mitchell.' To the boy on the right. 'And this is Rory.'

'Hi, Mitchell and Rory,' Tanzy said, then slowly lowered to his knees to listen. DI Leonard did the same.

'So, when you came around the corner, what did you see?'

It appeared that Andrews had just started the conversation.

The boys stayed silent. One of them was shaking, but his mother lowered herself to him and whispered something in his ear. This seemed to soothe him, no doubt comforting him in a way and letting him know he wasn't in trouble for what he saw.

'The old lady was just lying there still,' Mitchell started. 'We went to help her. We thought she'd fallen down but then we saw all the blood…' The young boy trailed off and started to cry, turning and throwing himself into his mother's comfort. The man next to them, presumably the boy's father, who was wearing a DeWalt storm jacket and work trousers with excess pockets overhanging down either side of his legs, sighed heavily. 'Is this really necessary? Can you not see they are distraught?'

'I'm sorry, Sir,' Tanzy explained, 'but we need to find out what happened. Any little piece of information could assist us in finding out how this terrible thing happened.'

The man bobbed his head in understanding but clearly wasn't happy about the situation.

PC Josh Andrews glanced towards the other boy, who had been very quiet.

'I pushed her arm to see if she was alive, but she didn't move. Then I phoned the police after I saw the blood. The lady on the phone told us to stay here but not too close until someone came. Then I saw a policeman turn the corner and he said his name was DS Stockdale. That's when he phoned my mum—' he angled his head and smiled at his mother, who gave him a tight smile, a sense of pride for their bravery.

'Did you see anyone else in the alley?' Andrews asked, softly.

Mitchell shook his head. Rory did the same.

'Okay, that's brilliant. Did any of you see anything on the floor, anything that stood out?'

Again, both boys shook their heads.

Andrews paused for a moment, knowing Tanzy and Byrd were both listening to him, and tried to think of anything else he may have missed regarding the questioning. Then he said, 'You've done brilliant, Mitchell and Rory. Thank you very much for your time.'

Their parents sighed in relief as Andrews stood and took a few steps towards the alley.

'Good work, Josh, well done.'

Andrews smiled at Byrd.

'Come on, let's go see how forensics are doing,' Tanzy suggested.

They all turned back to the alley, squeezing through the plethora of nosey people, and ducked under the tape. At the next tape DS Stockdale signed Byrd, Tanzy, and Leonard in on the register as they passed him, then they slowly made their way up to the heart of the scene. Andrews stopped at the tape and looked over his notes so far.

The body of an elderly lady was up on the right, two feet from the wall. She lay on her right side, her arms tucked into herself, with her feet pointing towards Tanzy. From his position he could see a trail of blood from under her body to where DS Stockdale was standing.

'Morning,' Tanzy said to Tallow and Hope. Leonard hung back a stride, allowing Tanzy and Byrd to lead the conversation.

Tallow, in his white disposable overalls, stood back from the body, his eyes and fingers fixed on his tablet. Forrest was on the other side of him showing him the photos which she'd taken so far. He nodded his approval, stepped away, and glanced at Tanzy as he approached.

Tanzy said, 'What's happened?'

He looked up from his tablet and lowered it by his side, then switched his focus to the lifeless body on the floor near the wall. 'Knife wound to her throat. Judging by the cut, and the skin around the cut, there wasn't much force taken to do it, which means it was a very sharp knife. Probably not one you could get from any local DIY supplier.'

'Hunting knife?'

'Maybe. It was very finely sharpened. From the blood spatter'— he moved a few steps down towards the direction of the tape and pointed further down the alley where the trail of blood was thinner—'it looks like she was attacked there, then judging by the colour of her hands, she'd tried to stop the blood and made it a few steps before her body couldn't stand any longer.'

'She did well to make it that far, considering she had a walking stick.'

'I had a quick look at the rest of her neck and throat, and even her wrists. There's no immediate bruising. Whoever did this, must have grabbed her by the coat.'

Tanzy nodded, then spent a moment looking at the blood around her. 'So much blood. Have you checked her pockets for ID, or do we know who she is?' Tanzy asked.

'The only items in her pockets were a packet of cigarettes, a lighter and a handful of change. She was more than likely coming back from a local shop.'

'How long has she been dead?'

'Not long at all, Ori,' Tallow replied. 'Maybe two hours. She's cold but that's because it's February. It will have slowed the rate of decomposition, but that would only be an issue or more obvious if she was left much longer.'

Tanzy nodded. Apart from the blood, the elderly lady could appear to be sleeping peacefully.

Footsteps came from their left. It was Emily Hope with an unusual look on her face.

'Hey,' Tanzy said, frowning at her.

'I've found something. It could be nothing, but...'

In her gloved hand she was holding two items. One was a small yellow smiley face keyring. The other was a rectangular metal pencil case with something written on it.

'Where'd you find them?' Tanzy asked, looking down at them. Byrd stepped closer, leaned in to have a look.

'Just up there, about halfway up. Against the wall.'

'What does it say on the pencil case?'

'It's looks like a name – Damien.'

'Who's Damien?'

30

Thursday Afternoon
Police Station

Tanzy sipped on his hot coffee at his desk. It had been an eventful day so far and little did he know, it would get busier.

Peter Gibbs had turned up to see the body of Sheena Edwards before she was taken to Darlington Memorial where he'd be a part of the autopsy. According to forensics it appeared she died from the knife to the throat, but to conclude that as the only cause of death, they'd need to remove her clothes and decide after the examination.

Tallow, Hope, and Forrest had wrapped everything up before they left. Tallow had taken a video, which he normally did, so they could watch that during further analysis. The original assumption of Sheena being stabbed then stumbling a few steps before she fell seemed the likely event that occurred, but the blood spatter analysis would later settle that.

Tanzy and Byrd spoke with Malcolm Edwards, who confirmed it was his wife who'd been killed. He knew by her red coat and her shoes, which he could see from the end of the alley. When he collapsed to the cold floor the silence was broken by his helpless sobs, filling the hearts of nearby people with sadness and sympathy.

From speaking with Malcolm, Byrd and Tanzy had learnt that he and Sheena lived further up the street. He confirmed that she'd popped out to the shop and would normally take ten minutes. When it reached nearly an hour, Malcolm had got his coat on and done out looking for her. Then he saw the crowds at the alley, overhearing someone say it was an old lady. He knew straight away it was his wife, Sheena.

Tanzy had asked Malcolm to come to the station but he didn't want to so, instead, DC Leonard had walked him back home with PC Weaver and, together, they'd taken a statement from him before they left him with a family liaison officer.

As Tanzy looked at his computer screen with intense concentration, placing his coffee back down beside his monitor, the door behind him opened.

'Orion, in here please.' DCI Fuller's tone was stern, a tinge of apprehension about it.

Tanzy angled himself around, nodded at DCI Fuller, and found his feet.

'What happened? Fill me in,' Fuller said as Tanzy dropped into the seat on the opposite side of his desk. Tanzy explained what had happened earlier that morning.

'Did anyone see anything?'

'We've knocked on most of the houses on Zetland Street and Brougham Street. No one saw anything.'

Superintendent Barry Eckles had been on the phone earlier to Fuller, telling him to get shit under control as soon as possible, or Fuller wouldn't like the consequences. He'd promised the Chief Superintendent, Garry Best, and the Assistant Chief Constable, Edward Johnson, that he would get things sorted, that Darlington would be a safe place for the people living in it.

Of course, it was inevitable that crime was going to happen. It's only a natural process for some people. Some don't know any different. Petty crime, tax evasion, theft, companies not obeying correct procedures in relation to how they should treat their workforce. Shit happens. People are envious, people are angry, people are greedy and don't like to see the hard-working, often labelled so called 'fortunate', doing well.

'Okay, Orion, good work. Have forensics found anything unusual?'

'Tallow claims there wasn't much of a struggle, that the wound implied she was taken by surprise – oh, we found something else down the alley too.'

Fuller raised his eyebrows.

'We found a small keyring and a pencil case with a name on it. It could be something innocent like a kid dropping it in the alley.'

'What was the name on the pencil case?'

'Damien,' Tanzy said.

'Okay, could have been left with the—'

There were several sharp knocks at the door.

Tanzy turned. Fuller looked beyond him, shouting, 'Come in!'

DC Cornty opened the door, panting a little, a look of worry in his eye. 'Orion, I need to speak with you?'

'Go on.'

'There's been a call from a woman who lives on Brougham Street. She said her son had left for school but has listened to a voice message from the school saying he didn't turn up this morning. He wasn't in the class.'

'What's her son's name?'

'Damien Spencer.'

31

Thursday Afternoon
Cleveland Street

Jack Liddle sighed at the customer in front of him, trying to explain the policy at HSS Hire. The angry man was attempting to get a refund on the hire of a chainsaw he'd used for the full week, then claimed it didn't work properly. Jack told the customer they wouldn't offer the refund as he should've complained about it when he realised it never worked. The chainsaw itself had clearly been used, the blade damaged from its use over the past week. The man shook his head, telling Jack he'd never use them again and stormed out.

Moments later Jack told his assistant, Frank, that he was popping out for a while, and that he'd be back later. Jack opened the door and stepped out into the cold. After zipping up his jacket just under his beard, he noticed something on the road which stopped him in his stride. Frowning, he moved closer to the road and squinted at it. It appeared to be a red substance on the road.

'What is that?'

Roughly two feet in diameter, circular, it appeared to be paint but slightly different, thinner, darker in colour. The texture different to paint.

If the faint red pool was there the day before he'd have seen it, no doubt. Whatever had caused it had happened earlier that day, or overnight, he was sure. He turned around, looked up at the camera above the door, and decided, whatever it was, the footage recorded on the camera would show him when he returned.

Roughly thirty minutes later he stepped in through the door and passed Frank, who was standing at the counter, looking at something on the computer screen. The room at the back was small, roughly ten feet deep, six feet wide. A small desk was pushed against the right that housed a box that resembled an ancient VHS video player. In fact it was an electrical box with a multitude of wires hanging down the back of it against the wall and trailing off in various directions.

Taking a seat he switched on the monitor and waited till it came to life. There was a musty smell hanging in the air coming from, he guessed, a pile of cardboard boxes that had been there a while.

On the computer he found the CCTV folder and double-clicked. The files in the folder were automatically organised into date order and the most recent files were positioned at the top of the list. Each file contained a recording for twelve hours, then the system saved the file, labelling the file with the date, followed by the number one or two, depending on if it was morning or afternoon, one being morning and two being the afternoon.

He clicked on yesterday's date with the number two next to it.

On the video he could see the road outside the shop. Despite yesterday's cold temperature the road appeared bright, the low sun shining from the left of the screen, causing the damp tarmac to glisten slightly.

After watching it for a few minutes in real time, he realised this could take twelve hours to watch the whole thing, so tapped on fast forward. Minutes passed and he realised he'd hit one p.m.. After an impatient sigh he tapped the fast forward button again and squinted as he watched it. At six-thirty on the moving clock, a few hours after darkness had set in, under the illumination of nearby streetlights, he watched himself lock the front door and pull down the shutter, then walk away off to the right.

Keeping his eye on the area where he'd noticed the faint red patch, he flicked his attention to the continuous moving time in the right top corner, then back down on the road.

As the time was fast approaching midnight he was ready to exit the screen —

'Jesus!' he gasped, not believing what he'd just seen.

He rewound the footage a few minutes and pressed play, watching it now in real time. The dark road was still in the staggered streetlights until a naked man appeared from the right. He stopped suddenly and turned, gazed at something coming from the right. Twenty seconds later a car collided into him, forcing him back a few metres until he crashed onto the floor in a mangled heap.

Under the light of the vehicle's headlights he saw the blood pooling around the man's head as he lay still on the road, his body tangled, his right arm bent the opposite way to his elbow.

Jack Liddle winced, raising a clenched fist to his mouth in despair, imagining the pain that he'd have felt.

Seconds later, coming from the top of the screen, a man appeared calmly, stepping around the front of the dark-coloured vehicle's bonnet, and stood there watching the naked man on the ground.

After he glanced around, he leaned down and lifted him up with ease, hauling him over his shoulder, then disappeared towards the top of the screen out of the camera view. The vehicle rocked slightly, then it edged forward slowly, crawling across the screen until it vanished out of sight.

Jack pulled out his phone and unlocked it, then dialled 999.

The call was connected after two rings. 'Emergency, which service?' asked a young-sounding female operator.

'Police. I need the police. I've just witnessed a murder.'

32

Thursday Afternoon
Brougham Street

PC Amy Weaver knocked on the white door three times and took a step back, standing next to Tanzy. It wasn't long before they heard the key turn and the door open. Standing there was a woman in her forties, dressed in a white blouse and black trousers. She had short blonde hair and bright green eyes. The smell seeping from the hallway and the wrinkles around her mouth were evidence she was likely a smoker.

'Mrs Spencer?' Tanzy asked.

She bobbed her head and stepped back. 'Yes. Please come in.' It was warm in the hallway, heat blasting from a radiator to their left. The faint smell of lavender coming from a plug-in near the small table at the base of the stairs was an admirable effort but came second place to the stale lingering smoke.

Tanzy hated the stuff.

'Just take a right, we'll sit in there,' she said, indicating with her hand towards the living room. 'Sorry the house is a mess, I really —'

'Don't worry about a thing, Mrs Spencer,' Weaver reassured her, stepping into the small living room. It was nicely decorated; colours of creams and browns combined, giving it a modern feel. The room was occupied by two large white leather sofas, a large flat screen television that was fixed to the wall space above the fireplace, and a coffee table in the centre of the room.

'Can I get you a coffee?' she asked.

Tanzy raised a palm. Although he wanted one he remembered the stale smoke hanging in the kitchen. 'Not for me, thank you. I've just had one,' he lied.

She glanced at Weaver.

'Ahh, no thanks. I've had one, not long ago but thank you.'

Mandy Spencer half-smiled and dropped down on the opposite sofa, her eyes falling on the carrier bag that Tanzy had brought in with him.

'Mrs Spencer, let—'

'Please, call me Mandy,' she said, smiling nervously, flicking her attention between them.

'Mandy, let me start by asking about the phone call from the school earlier.'

She nodded, as if readying herself for the explanation she was about to give. 'The receptionist phoned me, but I was at work. When I checked my phone, I listened to the message and rang straight back. She said that Damien wasn't in class, and that after looking around the school, no one could find him...' she trailed off, tears forming. 'They said he hadn't turned up. I told my supervisor I had to leave and came home.'

Weaver gave a heart-felt smile. 'Where do you work, Mandy?'

'At the town hall. In the planning office. We decide on which planning designs and projects are accepted.'

'Mandy'—Tanzy paused for a second and lowered his hand into the carrier bag, bringing out the pencil case and broken key ring—'we found these in the alley when forensics were at the crime scene.'

She studied them for a second, but it didn't take long to realise they belonged to her son and she began to cry.

'Can you confirm these belong to your son, Damien?'

She bobbed her head several times, tears streaming down her face. 'Where were they?'

'The forensic team found them on the ground.'

She frowned at him, wiping her eyes. 'Has anyone seen him?'

Tanzy shook his head. 'No, no, not yet. We—'

There were loud, quick knocks at the front door, frantic bursts of energy colliding against the wood, echoing through the terraced house.

They all frowned, angling their focus to the hallway.

'I'm sorry, I better answer that.' With a frown, Mandy rose to her feet and went to the front door. Opening it, she found Jackie, a neighbour from just up the street, standing there with wide eyes.

'Jackie? What's the matter?'

Jackie seemed alert and upset. 'Mandy, Mandy, I've just spoken to Jerry up the street.'

Jerry lived further up the road, almost opposite the alley that Damien usually walked along to access Zetland Street on his walk to school.

She continued quickly: 'I heard the news about Damien, that he never turned up at school and that he's missing?'

'Yeah, he is…' Mandy said, sadly.

'Jerry said he saw a red car parked down the alley. He said he was unsure what to do.'

Tanzy and Weaver came to the door, their inquisitive eyes falling on Jackie, dressed in old clothes and a blue cleaning apron wrapped around her.

'A man that Jerry said was really tall, maybe six and a half feet – came back to the car with Damien following him. Damien then got into the passenger seat and the car left onto Zetland Street.'

'What colour was the car?'

Jackie switched her attention to Tanzy. 'It was red according to Jerry.'

'Why has he just told you now?' Tanzy asked.

'He's on tablets, he doesn't know what day it is half the time. I clean for him. I was dusting the skirting boards when I heard him say to himself that he hopes the boy is okay, so I looked up asking him what boy. I assumed he was seeing things, or imagining things but, when I looked up, he was stood at the window looking out. He told me what he'd seen earlier, but then he said he thought it might have been a dream.'

Weaver sighed, not convinced at all.

Mandy raised her hands to her mouth, her eyes growing with fear about who this man could be. 'A man has taken my boy?'

Jackie nodded. 'According to Jerry, yes. He said Damien just casually got in the car and off they went.'

'We need to go speak with Jerry, immediately,' Tanzy said. 'Can you take us to him?'

Jackie nodded quickly.

33

Thursday Afternoon
Brougham Street

After four knocks, Jerry opened his old white front door. Jackie smiled at him, then asked if it would be okay for Tanzy and Weaver to ask him about what he'd seen in the alley earlier that morning.

Instead of allowing them in, he stood there, his face blank, as if he didn't know who Jackie was. There was a slight recognition in his face when his eyes fell on Mandy Spencer.

'Jerry, can we come in?' Jackie asked again, dragging his fading attention back to her.

He pointed at Tanzy. 'Who is that bald man?'

'He's from the police,' she explained slowly. 'Can they come in and ask you a few questions?'

He didn't reply, still weighing up the strangers standing on his doorstep.

'She's a pretty one,' he said, nodding at Weaver, who almost blushed. Then his face became serious. 'I've paid my taxes you know. I pay them every time I receive my money. You don't have to worry ab—'

'Sir,' Tanzy said, cutting him off, not wanting to waste any unnecessary time. 'My name is Orion Tanzy. I'm with the police. If it's okay with you, could we ask you a few questions about what you saw earlier. It's very important.'

'Orion? I used to have an Orion. A Ford Orion. It was red. Fast. The girls loved it.'

Tanzy let out a small, frustrated sigh, doing his best not to let it show. In one way, Jerry reminded Tanzy of his grandad. Awkward. 'I bet they did. They were nice cars. Can we come in?'

Jerry surprisingly nodded and shuffled back, taking a left into the living room.

Jackie half-smiled at Tanzy, rolling her eyes. 'Come on, this'll be fun.'

The four of them stepped up into the house. The central heating had been on all day and it gently slapped them in the face as they padded down the hallway. The creaking floor beneath them was carpeted with a hideous, ancient flower design that was only popular before Tanzy was alive. The walls were lined with a thick, padded cream pattern, and the ceiling was heavily filled with a swirling pattern design that was evidently only desirable to someone like Jerry.

They took a left into the living room and, adding to the humidity in the house, the gas fire was blasting away at the base of the chimney breast, dancing orange flames wavering in the brass coloured surround. Jerry was standing at the window, staring out on to the street.

Tanzy and Weaver stopped side by side in the centre of the room, watching him, waiting for him to turn. Jackie, in her stained blue apron, moved around them and went to the window. 'Jerry?' She placed a hand on his back. 'Can the police ask you a few questions? It's very important.'

'Oh… yeah, of course.' He slowly turned, looked down at his watch, then lifted his head and stared at Tanzy. 'Ask away.'

Tanzy smiled. 'Jackie tells me that you saw a red car parked'—Tanzy moved a few paces towards him and pointed out of the window in the direction of the alley— 'just over there in the alley. And you saw a tall man, walking back to it with a young boy?'

For a moment, and no surprise to Tanzy, Jerry looked puzzled, his eyebrows furrowing to the centre of his forehead. He then turned to the window, gazed out for a few seconds. 'A red car?'

Tanzy physically sighed, knowing valuable time was being wasted here.

But if the story that Jackie had told him was true, and the information was correct, it could be vital. He knew he'd have to be patient with him.

'Yes, a red car. You told Jackie'—he pointed back to Jackie—'that you saw a red car parked in the alley. Do you remember? It happened this morning.'

He suddenly seemed alert, as if a switch had been flicked. 'Of course, it happened this morning, I was sitting on the chair over there and saw it.'

Finally getting somewhere.

'What did you see?' Tanzy probed.

'The red car was parked there for a while. I thought it was a strange place to park, so I stood up and waited to see if the driver came back, otherwise I would have reported it. I don't drive myself, but I know you're not allowed to park in an alley, in case of emergency vehicle access.'

'That's right,' Tanzy agreed, trying to hurry the story along. 'Then what happened?'

'A man appeared. He was tall. Very thin. He had a brown jacket on, the zip high up to his pointy chin. He walked in a strange way. Huge strides. Weird. He came around the car and got in the driver's door. Then Damien got into the passenger seat.'

It was a long shot. 'Can you remember what model of car it was?'

'Yes. A Mondeo Titanium.'

Tanzy realised he was frowning, surprised at how confident Jerry seemed. 'You sure?'

'Yes. It was a newer model, ST Line. I've always liked my cars.'

Tanzy felt like this was going somewhere, but unsure if he believed how confident he was. 'By any chance – no worries if you don't – but you don't happen to remember the registration plate?'

'NA66 CFD.'

Tanzy was taken aback for a moment, tilting his head. 'Are you sure?'

Jerry nodded confidently. 'Absolutely.'

'Did you write it down?'

'No, I memorized it. I only have to look at something once. Numbers and letters. My son calls it a photographic memory. I used to be better than I am now, but I'm sure.'

Without being obvious, Tanzy gazed over towards Jackie, who nodded in agreement that chances are he would be right. He returned his focus to Jerry.

'Wow, thank you, Jerry. Well that's all.' Tanzy turned to Weaver. 'You got that?'

Weaver finished typing the registration plate of the Mondeo into her phone, then peered up and nodded. 'Got it.'

'We'll run the plate, see who it belongs to.' Tanzy turned back to Jerry. 'Thank you again, you've been a very big help.'

'Please find my boy,' pleaded Mandy, who was standing near the door. 'He has a medical condition.'

'Which condition does he have?' Tanzy asked her.

'Paediatric Coronary Artery disease.'

'His heart?' Weaver asked.

Mandy nodded. 'Yeah. If he doesn't take his tablets twice a day, he'll get very sick. I gave him one before he left this morning. He gets his second dose when he comes in from school. They thin his blood, so it can get to his heart properly.'

'What happens if he doesn't take the second dose?' Tanzy asked, becoming more worried than he already was.

'His heart will eventually fail, sooner or later.'

Tanzy and Weaver understood the magnitude of her words and nodded slowly. Then they both headed for the hallway, passing Jackie.

'What about the other children?' Jerry asked, still standing at the window.

Tanzy paused and swivelled before he reached the door. 'I'm sorry?'

'What about the other children?'

'I don't understand.' Tanzy appeared puzzled. 'Which other children?'

'The boy and girl sitting in the back of the red Mondeo.'

34

Thursday Late Afternoon
Police Station

Before Tanzy managed to reach his desk he was stopped halfway down the office by DC Leonard. He informed him that a call had come in moments after Tanzy and Weaver had left the station from a worried mother, who lived on Westmoreland Street, a couple of streets away from Brougham Street. She said her daughter hadn't turned up at school and that she didn't know where she was.

'Okay,' Tanzy said, his head swimming with this new information. 'Did you go to the house?'

'Cornty and I went round to speak with her. The school receptionist had said that Melissa Clarke was nowhere to be seen. We took a witness statement and a recent photograph of Melissa.'

'Not good,' Tanzy muttered. 'Thanks for letting me know. File the report. I need to speak to Fuller.' Tanzy briefly smiled and turned away from Leonard, who edged back to his desk, sat down, and started typing away on his keyboard.

'Orion?' he heard a voice coming from the right this time. It was DS Stockdale.

'Hey,' Tanzy said, padding towards him. Stockdale remained seated, looking up to his superior.

'Thought you should know. Just after you left, a call came in from a woman who lives on Zetland Street about her missing—'

'Son?' Tanzy said, finishing the sentence.

Stockdale's eyebrows furrowed. 'Yeah, Eddy Long. How did you know?'

He remembered what Jerry had said about the boy and girl in the back of the Mondeo. 'Did you go to the house?'

Stockdale nodded. 'Yeah, took Andrews with me. We haven't been back long.'

'Did you get a photo of him?'

'Yes.'

'Good,' Tanzy said. 'File the report, I need to speak to Fuller. We need a meeting as soon as possible about what's happened this morning. Never a dull day in this town.'

Tanzy wrapped his knuckles on Fuller's door and waited.

'Come in,' a drowned-out voice said. Tanzy entered the warm office. There was a heater to the left in the corner, a white tall unit fixed to a still base that slowly swivelled in a small arc. The DCI was on a phone call but it wasn't too long before he ended the call and told Tanzy to take a seat.

'We have a witness who said he saw Damien Spencer get into a car. He also claimed he saw a boy and a girl in the back of the car.'

Fuller nodded. 'Hence the two calls whilst you were out?'

'Yeah.'

'What about the car, did the witness…'

'We have a registration plate on the car that took Damien Spencer. But, unfortunately, the plates are fake. They don't exist.'

Fuller sighed, picked up his half-drunk cup of coffee and took a swig, then placed it back down on the desk.

'So, we have three children missing. Likely the same man responsible for taking them?'

'We need to find this guy ASAP,' countered Tanzy.

'If it's true what my witness said, I find it strange that Damien just went with him so easily,' Fuller noted.

'Or maybe he'd just witnessed the man kill Sheena Edwards and was told to go with him. Maybe he was threatened?'

'What about the other children?'

'Could have had the knife and used that to scare them. Perhaps when he tried to get Damien, Sheena was in the wrong place at the wrong time.'

'We have a list of the children?' Fuller took another long sip of coffee.

Tanzy nodded. 'Damien Spencer, Melissa Clarke, and Eddy Long.'

'Photos?'

Another nod from Tanzy. Although they knew the identities of the missing children, the scary thing was was that no one had seen what happened further down that alley. No one could confirm what exactly had happened to Sheena or really define the true events about the disappearance of Damien, or the other two children. Apart from a man in his eighties on a daily high dose of medication.

'Did you speak to other people in the street about Damien?'

'Yeah, we knocked on most of the doors on Brougham Street. No one had seen anything. We have nothing to go on, especially with the plate being fake.'

'Would you say he was a reliable source?'

'The witness?'

Fuller nodded.

'Yes and no. He told me the make and model of the car, including the registration in a heartbeat, as if he had some kind of photographic memory, but then the next second, he looked at me blank, not knowing where he was or why I was standing in his living room.'

'So... say his story is true, it be wise assuming the other missing children reported by the school and parents were in the same car. Next step is checking the CCTV camera in that area. You have a contact at the control room, don't you?'

Tanzy nodded. 'I do. Her name is Jennifer Lucas.'

'Speak with Jennifer right after you leave here, see if she can pick up the red Mondeo. It's a long shot, but we know the time, and we know the place and, although the reg is fake, the plate that's on can identify it and hopefully track its movements. From my limited experience in Darlington, I know there isn't a lot of coverage in that area, but I've heard good things about her so, hopefully, she can find something.'

'I'll get straight on it,' Tanzy said, standing. 'I'll go to the school as well. I need to speak to their headteacher. I need to know why these specific three children have been taken.'

'Good. Take one of the PCs or DCs. Let me know if there's any developments regarding the forensics report on Sheena Edwards. I know the basics but, if they find anything else or anything unusual that the Pathologist finds, please let me know as soon as possible. Eckles has been on my case all day. You know what he's like.'

'Will do.'

Back at his desk Tanzy picked up the phone but, before he made the phone call, he noticed there was a text from his wife, Pip, who was at home cooking another one of his favourite meals. Lasagne. He replied, thanking her, then found Jennifer Lucas' number, and pressed CALL.

35

Thursday Afternoon
Ventress Hall Care Home, Trinity Road

Byrd, after calling the twenty-something care assistant, Emma, to tell her he was outside, hung up the phone and dropped it onto the passenger seat. A heavy sigh left his mouth as he tipped his head back and closed his eyes. As if he didn't have enough shit going on.

Emma had phoned him to tell him he needed to come in. Usually they could handle the situation. But, his mother Jackie, was convinced that one of the male residents was Byrd's father, Alan, and she'd physically tried to drag him out of a chair in the living area so he could go back to *their* room. The man, who Byrd was told was an elderly man in his eighties, called Phillip, had landed hard on the floor and was being treated by one of the first aiders for a cut to his eyebrow.

Byrd told Tanzy he wouldn't be long and to ring if something drastic came up. Based on what'd happened in the past few days nothing wouldn't come as a surprise. They were both knee-deep in work and didn't have time to take a breath, but this needed sorting. It was the fourth time she'd done this since his father failed to wake up from his coma.

Byrd locked his X5, stepping up onto the path and making his way across the small carpark towards the main door. The building itself was huge. Several houses that been knocked together and an additional building work carried out for its needs. Inside the care home had one-hundred and four rooms, most of them with en-suite facilities. It catered for residential care, dementia care, and had nursing facilities too. At a costly seven hundred pounds a week, Byrd had set up dementia care for his mother, Jackie. Ever since she'd woken up from the coma resulting from the crash on the A1 over two months ago, she hadn't been right. It took Byrd just over a week to accept her brain had been too permanently damaged for her to stay at home and look after herself. Evidently, she kept scolding herself on the kettle and kept leaving the bath running too long so it overflowed.

Through the main door, Byrd felt a sheet of warmth hit him. He unzipped his jacket and glanced round the empty reception area for a familiar face but failed to find one, so went straight through to the living area where the residents normally sat.

'Oh… it's my favourite son!' he heard from the right.

Sighing lightly, he glanced at Marjorie, one of the dementia residents, and gave her a wave. Byrd had made it clear on several occasions that he wasn't her son but had decided to play along when he visited.

'Hi, Max,' said a voice from the right. Emma, the twenty-something assistant padded towards him with her hands in her pockets. 'How you doing?' She was dressed in a smart purple uniform.

'Hi, Emma, thanks for the call,' Byrd started, 'sorry she's at it again.'

'It's honestly fine, it's a part and the parcel of the job,' she admitted. Byrd could tell her comments were genuine and that she wasn't lying. Care work wasn't done for money. It never had been because the money was very poor for what you had to do. Carers did it to care, to make a difference, to help others and ease their living in the restricted lives they now had to live. 'Follow me.'

Byrd followed Emma out of the living area into a narrow corridor. 'How's she been then, apart from the incident earlier?'

'Erm...' she hesitated, 'she—'

'Doesn't sound very good,' Byrd countered.

'She's deteriorating if I'm honest, Max. I was going to speak with you about full-time care. Maybe worth a thought.'

Byrd smiled sadly but said nothing.

Emma stopped at room twenty-seven and knocked on the door.

'Jackie dear, it's Emma, I'm coming in,' she said delicately, slowly opening the door. Inside the room, the bed was to the right against the wall. Jackie was laid down, with the covers pulled up to her chin. 'Jackie, your son Max is here to see you,' she said, stepping out of the way and allowing Byrd to see her.

As he drew nearer, he noticed she'd dramatically lost weight, the shape of her skull almost visible, her eyes had sunk deeper than before.

He turned to Emma. 'Is she eating?'

'Not as much as she should be.'

Byrd took a seat next to her and took her hand. It felt weak, the bones more prominent.

'How've you been, Mum?'

In a split second, her grin seemed to fade, and she suddenly looked worried, as if Byrd was there to cause her harm. She glared beyond Byrd towards Emma and said, 'Who's this strange man in my room?'

36

Thursday Afternoon
Darlington

The red Mondeo slowly came to a halt at the end of the long driveway, just in front of the white double garage behind the back of the house. Arthur applied the hand-brake and turned off the engine. He glanced down at Damien, who met his stare with wide, terrified eyes, then glared into the back of the car towards Melissa and Eddy, who were both physically shaking.

Arthur saw a wet patch on the seat under her.

'You haven't wet yourself, have you?'

Melissa, instead of answering, started to cry.

The man sighed, looking forward towards the double garage, then started humming a tune out loud which suddenly silenced Melissa.

When Damien had got into the car earlier, he noticed his class friends in the back, but before he had the chance to speak, the tall man told them all to be silent and not to make a sound. He told them if they wanted to cry, they could, but if it was louder than the classical music he was playing on his car CD, the consequences would be severe.

Arthur opened the door, stepped out into the cold air, then closed it, the sound echoing around the quiet grounds of the house. Standing at the back door of the mansion, he saw Jonny Darchem watching them.

Arthur turned back to the car, leaning into the open driver's door.

'You three wait here, I'll be back soon.' He closed the door, pressed the button on the fob to lock them in, and made his way across the gravel towards his boss.

'Damien,' Melissa whispered from the back of the car. He turned around. 'Why are we here? What is this place? Where are we?'

'I don't know,' he replied. He lifted his head, watched the tall man walking towards the house through the rear windscreen. 'He has a knife. I watched him kill someone. A woman. Sheena. My mum's friend.'

Melissa threw her hands to her mouth as her eyes filled with more tears. 'Really?'

'He – he killed someone?' Eddy asked, his voice almost sticking in his throat.

Damien nodded, and told them what had happened.

'Oh, God,' Eddy said, pure terror on his face.

'We need to do what he says,' Damien said. 'He's very dangerous.'

'But why has he taken us?'

Damien shrugged. 'I don't know, but we need to do something soon.'

'How was it?' Darchem asked Arthur. 'Everything go to plan?'

'We ran into a problem.'

Darchem tilted his head, narrowing his eyes. 'A problem?'

'Yes. When I grabbed Damien, a neighbour saw us in the alley. I had to kill her.'

'You had to what?'

'I grabbed my knife from my jacket and pushed it into her throat,' he said, without any remorse or consideration for human life. But that's why they picked him for the job.

'For fuck's sake.'

'I had no other choice. There was no way she was letting me just walk off with him.'

'That is a problem. Unless no one saw you?'

'No one was around.'

'You sure?'

Arthur nodded convincingly. 'I'm sure.'

'Okay, well the room is ready for them. Take them up there. The others are waiting.'

'Understood.' He turned, heading back to the car.

As Arthur returned to the car, Darchem's phone rang in his pocket. He didn't recognise the number but he knew, in this game, you didn't have many numbers saved. He answered it.

'Is this Darchem?'

'Speaking.'

'I was told you're the man to supply me what I'm after,' the voice said.

'And what is it you're after?'

The man on the other end explained his needs.

'Yes… we have something which I think you'll like,' Darchem said. 'Funny enough, one of them has just arrived here.'

37

Thursday Afternoon
Darlington Town Hall

Tanzy and PC Josh Andrews entered through the sliding glass doors of the Town Hall and made their way to the reception desk, where a small, plumped woman was focused on the computer screen in front of her.

'Can I help?' she said, peeling her attention away from it.

'Here to see Jennifer Lucas. She knows we're coming.'

'Hold on a second,' the woman said, picking up the phone to her right.

Tanzy smiled, turned a full one-eighty, and glanced outside through the glass doors. 'Miserable day, eh.'

Andrews turned, watched the dark, grey clouds above, and agreed. 'Meant to be like this for a few days, boss. You never know though. Might brighten up. They're known to be wrong sometimes.'

'*Only* sometimes?' Tanzy said.

'Just go right up.' The receptionist behind them said. 'She's on the—'

'First floor, just along the corridor, halfway down on the left?' Tanzy said, turning to face her.

'Lift or stairs, take your pick.'

'Thanks.'

They took the stairs and stepped out onto the first floor, then took a right. The carpet still smelt new, the white paint on the walls still giving off a faint smell, but Tanzy knew it had been over two months since they were last painted, unless they'd been done again.

167

He knocked three times on the door labelled 'Control Room' and waited for a response.

'Come in,' a muffled voice said from behind the closed door.

Sitting at the table in the centre of the dark room facing the computer screens to the left, was Jennifer Lucas. Tanzy almost paused for a second when he laid eyes on her. Wearing a tight, black shirt, a red-checkered pencil skirt and black tights with black ankle boots, she looked absolutely amazing. Her black, shiny hair was tightly tied up into a ponytail, then trailed halfway down her back. The gentle glow from the screens in front of her did what they always did when she was sitting there: highlighted her beauty.

'Hello, Orion,' she said softly, her accent indicating she was born somewhere between Durham and Newcastle. Her voice alone made him go weak at the knees.

'Hi, Jennifer,' he said, sauntering in towards her.

Andrews trailed Tanzy, glancing around the room, absorbing the screens to the left, the desks in the middle and some on the right. It was the first time he'd been here. There was a shelving arrangement positioned behind the desk fixed to the right wall, mainly filled with old boxes and A4 ring binders. On the ceiling, there were roughly ten spotlights scattered around the room, making sure it was adequately lit but dark enough so the computer screens could be easily monitored without having to strain your eyes.

'How you doing?' Tanzy asked her, pulling out the chair next to her and dropping into it. It took less than a second for him to smell her perfume. It wasn't familiar, but it was so nice, he could have leaned forward and sniffed her neck, then—

Focus, he told himself. 'Did you find it?' he then asked, referring to the red Mondeo.

She nodded. 'Eventually. But then...' She winced. 'I kind of lost it again. The cameras around there are not very good at all.'

'I know,' Tanzy replied. 'So...'

'You say the car left Brougham Street and headed in the direction of town, according to the witness, the elderly gent who was watching through the window.' Tanzy nodded. She went on. 'I checked North Road. North and South. Nothing. I then looked at the map and drew out several alternate routes to where, if I was driving, I would be heading. It took a while.'

Tanzy kept still, watching her, inhaling the sweet scent of her perfume, her—

'What did you find?' Andrews said behind him.

Tanzy almost forgot he was there. He needed to get a grip. He'd just started sorting things out with Pip; they were falling back in love. The kids were happy. But despite this, there was something about Jennifer. She seemed perfect in every way.

'I mapped out the route that would take me down Whessoe Road, up Brinkburn Road, through Cockerton. The first camera that picked me up was in Cockerton.'

'There's no cameras from Zetland street to Cockerton?' Tanzy frowned, not believing what he was hearing.

'There is, except two of them don't work.'

'Typical,' Andrews countered with a sigh.

Jennifer glanced up at him and smiled. 'Don't worry, I've told maintenance about them. I've even put repair tickets in for them, but the council seem to want to spend money on flowerbeds. Nothing wrong with that as it freshens the town up, and I'm all for that, but when the basics aren't being fixed, that's when it becomes a problem and should be addressed. Unfortunately, I'm not in charge of how we spend the money, I can only advise and point out what works and what doesn't. It used to aggravate me in the past, but I just accept it now,' she said with a heavy shrug.

Andrews nodded. He was a tallish thin man, had a similar body shape to Tanzy, but he wasn't lined with as much muscle, and stood maybe two inches shorter. His posture was recognisable almost anywhere, the way he moved, the way he carried himself. Straight back, rigid neck, very correct. His hair was well kept, swept neatly to the side. It was obvious to others he took pride in his appearance, but both Tanzy and Byrd knew why. In the few years he'd been a PC they had learned about his background: his father was military and he spent much of his time growing up moving around, home to home, in and out of education but his father had ensured he received the best private tuition available wherever they went. His father was a man of principle and had clearly passed that down to Josh Andrews.

'Yeah, definitely,' Tanzy agreed, stealing a look.

She fiddled with the mouse on the desk. 'Look at this.'

The red Mondeo turned left on West Auckland Road and headed down past the Co-op into Cockerton. The camera then lost it, but the car was picked up by the next camera further down. It was clear to them that the car then took a left, towards the small roundabout at the end of Woodland Road, passing Cockerton club on the left-hand side.

'Where is he going?' Andrews asked no one in particular.

As the Mondeo reached the roundabout, it took a right, towards the next mini-roundabout then disappeared.

'Where's he gone?' Tanzy said, flicking his concentration to the other screens, hoping to pick up the Mondeo without success.

'This is where I lose him,' Jennifer explained. She clicked the mouse a few times. 'There should be, last time

I checked, a camera somewhere up here.' She paused the frame and used the cursor to point to the right top corner.

'Is it not working?' Tanzy asked, turning to her.

'I don't know. It's the first time I've noticed it hasn't been. I'll need to contact maintenance about that one, too.' She rolled her eyes.

'So...' Tanzy tilted his head. 'We have him going left up Carmel Road or right onto...'

'Staindrop Road,' Jennifer said, finishing his trail of thought.

'Yeah. So, they either went left or right?'

'That's true, but there's a camera roughly two-hundred metres further up on Carmel Road. Maybe a little more. And there's a camera near the Mowden Pub along Staindrop Road. Neither camera sees the Mondeo.'

'Which means the car didn't make it that far in either direction,' Tanzy replied. 'Meaning the car is somewhere in that area.'

Jennifer looked up, nodded. 'I'd say so, yeah.'

'Okay. Do you have a map handy?'

'Yeah, sure, hold on.' She pushed her chair out, stood up and made her way over to the shelving units behind them. He did his best but Tanzy couldn't help watching her move in that red patterned skirt. She pulled out a large, folded piece of paper from one of the units and returned to the desk.

Jennifer placed it down and located the area with her finger. The map itself didn't show the whole of Darlington. It was the west end of Darlington, starting from Duke Street near the town centre all the way up to Mowden. Although it covered a large area, the A3 size of the page made every street visible.

'Here,' she said, her finger stopping at the small roundabout where they last saw the Mondeo on the camera.

'So, where roughly do you think the other cameras are? The ones that didn't pick it up?'

She studied the map for a moment, her eyes concentrating on the array of roads, streets, and cul-de-sacs. 'The camera on Carmel road is here.' She pointed to a spot close to Nunnery Lane. 'And... the other is... here.' She indicated the position of The Mowden Pub.

'Leaves a lot of choices for a driver to make,' Tanzy commented.

'All those houses, too,' Andrews added with a beaten look on his face.

'I'll ring the station, get a search going around that area for the red Mondeo. We might spot something.' He stood and glanced down at Jennifer. 'Thanks. Let me know if you find anything else.'

'Anything for you, Orion.'

Tanzy and Andrews left the large, dark room and stepped into the brightly lit, white painted hallway. As they waited for the lift, Andrews angled his gaze on Tanzy for a moment.

'What?' Tanzy said, noticing his sudden interest in him.

'Nothing, Sir.' Andrews had picked up on the way they'd exchanged looks, could physically feel the tension between him and Jennifer, but decided not to ask about it. Whatever it was, harmless or not, it wasn't his business.

38

DC Leonard and PC Weaver entered the shop, letting the door close by the spring mechanism at the top. It was warm and stuffy inside the rectangular reception area but beat the cold outside. A smell of coffee hit them as they approached the counter.

Standing behind it was a tall thin man who was looking at them over the top of narrow glasses. 'You guys from the police?'

'We are,' Leonard said. 'I'm DC Leonard, and this is PC Weaver. We're here to speak to Jack Liddle. Is he available?'

Just as the words left his mouth, a man rushed through an open door behind the desk. 'I'm Jack Liddle.' He was almost panting. 'Please, please, come through, you need to see this,' he told them, lifting up the hatch. 'This way.'

Jack Liddle clicked several times on the computer and opened the video he'd watched earlier. 'The video records twelve hours' worth, then a new file starts. This was from last night.'

'Okay.' Leonard lowered his posture a fraction, focusing on the screen.

'I'll fast forward it.' All of them watched the time speed up rapidly. 'I almost got to midnight then this happened. Are you ready?' he asked, looking up at them both one by one.

They nodded in unison.

He pressed play. Over the next few minutes they uncovered what had happened the previous night outside the shop they were currently standing in.

'Jesus,' Weaver gasped.

'Take it back. I need to see it again,' Leonard said.

'Sure.' He scrolled it back.

After watching it again, Weaver frowned. 'So, whoever did this, just picked him up and…'

'It looks like, judging by how the cars dips slightly a moment before he drives off, that he must have put the person into the back or the boot of the car.'

Weaver nodded in agreement.

For the fourth time, they all watched the dark blue 4x4 pass the screen and disappear to the left.

Jack turned to Leonard, who was peering over his shoulder, and said, 'Who is he? There must be someone missing, or someone must've filed a missing person's report?'

Leonard, instead of replying, held his gaze, then looked back at the screen. 'Play it again, please.'

The manager did as he was told and the three of them watched it for the fifth time.

Weaver pulled a memory stick from her pocket and held it up. 'We need to copy that video file on to here, then take it back to the station to analyse it.'

'Of course, of course,' Jack replied, more than happy to help.

Back out in the car, Leonard sighed heavily.

'What's up, Jim?' Weaver asked, settling into the driver's seat and putting on her seatbelt. She looked over at him, noticing his defeated body posture.

'It never ends, does it?'

She frowned. 'What doesn't?'

'This...' He opened his palms, indicating either the situation they were in or something else. Weaver wasn't really sure. 'It's non-stop all the time.' He glanced away, focused out the window, watching a green Renault Clio drive past.

Silence filled the car for a few moments. 'It's relentless, I know with everything that's gone on in the past few days, then this. But that's what we signed up for, Jim, you know that.'

'I know...' he turned his head towards her and held her gaze a second too long. In the time he'd been working with her, he'd never really noticed how attractive she was. Was it the angle of her face, or the perfect fall of her straight blonde hair, or the faint afternoon light that had slipped through a crack in the clouds above? He wasn't sure. He also didn't understand why she and DC Cornty had stopped seeing each other. After hearing a story about them arguing too much, they had decided to call it a day. Leonard didn't really know her, but he couldn't see how she'd be the argumentative type.

'Come on, chin up,' she said, smiling. 'This isn't like you.' She patted him on the thigh twice then pulled her hand back slowly, taking hold of the gear stick. 'Or is there something else?'

His eyebrows furrowed towards the centre of his forehead. 'What do you mean?'

'Is there anything on your mind? Anything you want to talk about? After all, we are work colleagues. We're all here for one another.'

He pondered her comment for a moment, looking straight through the dim windscreen down Cleveland Street. Two teenagers walked towards the car, their focus on the marked Astra. Leonard watched them approach from North Road with their youthful, defiant, confident swagger. As they passed the car, Leonard focused on them, recognising one of them, but he couldn't place him.

'Rude to stare, you know,' Weaver whispered.

The teenagers passed the car.

'Thought one of them looked familiar,' Leonard said.

'Let's go see what we can find out about this,' she said, holding up the memory stick.

'We'll have to hurry or we'll be late for the meeting. Byrd and Tanzy have enough on their plates without reminding us about being punctual.'

39

Thursday Early Evening
Police Station

The time was ticking on. Nearly six p.m..

Byrd was standing at the front of the meeting room with the small black remote in his hand, waiting for the others to sit down and feeling sad for himself. When his mother, Jackie, had asked Emma, the carer, who he was when he visited her, it hit home how bad she'd become, how damaged she was after the crash.

He'd lost his father physically, but now his mother was mentally decaying. The two people in the world he called his heroes. The person he'd become was because of them and the values they'd taught him. Twelve years ago Byrd had his sister and both parents, until his sister, Anna, had been brutally murdered. In Tanzy's opinion, and others, he'd say that was the turning point for Max Byrd. He used to be a bubbly, very-outgoing character, but the night when Anna was stabbed, four times in the stomach by a male drug addict in an alley in town, was the night that everything changed for DI Max Byrd. The new version of Byrd was more determined, more hard-working. For some it may have knocked them back, killed their ambitions and morals as an officer of the law, taught them the harsh lesson that this life is nothing short of cruel. His father always used to say to them both: 'Things will happen to you that don't seem fair. You want to know why? Because life just isn't fair. You have to deal with the cards that you've been dealt and play them to the best of your ability.' His words would stay in his head forever. Byrd was always looking to improve, looking at ways to mend this so-called broken system. He couldn't accept the reality that evil people seemed to have the free reign to roam the world and do whatever they liked. No, he would put it right. He would do his very best to prevent these things happening again. But life will be life, and as his father said, "Life just isn't fair."

DS Stockdale entered through the door, giving him a small apologetic wave for his lateness.

'We're missing a couple, but we better make a start,' Byrd said, looking towards Tanzy, who was standing to his left, nodding.

Behind them on the screen on the wall, there was a caption saying 'Daily Update' at the top, and underneath it, the day and date.

'Okay, so,' he started, 'we'll run a brief re-cap of yesterday before we move on the events of today.' Everyone nodded. 'Mark Greenwell was found at the Denes Park. As we know, forensics'—he pointed over to Tallow and Hope who were sitting towards the back of the room—'did a very good job and identified the cause the death which, as we know, was a knife attack to the throat. After Mark was taken to the pathology department and underwent an examination, we found whip marks on his back. So far, we are no further forward identifying the cause of this. Some of the masks were dated two years prior to his death and some of them were new. I assume he'd suffered in the past at the hands of, possibly, the same person. I'll update you guys later with any further findings. I spoke with Mac in DFU about his phone which gave us some vital information. He was able to show us the location of Mark's phone over the past few weeks and, apart from his home being a frequently visited location, there's another hotspot on Craig Street which we need to look into. I want to set up surveillance over the next few nights. When we can spare the manpower, of course. I know things are tight and there's a lot going on.' He looked around the room. 'Any thoughts?'

'Yeah, sounds good,' DC Cornty agreed from the right. 'Is this because of the drugs and money that was found on him?'

'That's right,' Byrd confirmed. 'We think he was a part of something bigger and we need to find out what. I also need to add something which the forensic team found too. There was a drop of blood found near Mark Greenwell. Tallow took it back to the lab for DNA testing and I've just been informed that the blood belongs to Lyle Wilson.'

The name was familiar to some of them. Byrd could see the cogs turning.

DC Cornty said, 'Is that the son of your friend, Keith?'

Byrd nodded sadly.

'Have you spoken with Lyle? Brought him in yet?'

'I've been to his house, but Lyle wasn't there. His father, Keith, said he hasn't seen him since Tuesday night.'

'The same night Mark Greenwell was murdered?'

'That's correct,' Byrd said. 'At the moment, although he's missing, he's our number one suspect.'

'Why are we finding this out now?' Cornty asked.

'Because I've just received the DNA match from the blood sample,' he lied.

Cornty turned to Tallow who was sitting behind him and watched Tallow nod to confirm Byrd's statement.

'So, we are looking for Lyle Wilson. As I know Keith and Lyle well, I'll come up with a profile for him as soon as possible.'

Byrd paused for breath, and clamped his eyes shut for a moment, bringing his left hand up to his temple in reaction to a sharp pain that ran across it.

Silence filled the room as everyone stared at him, wondering what the issue was. He squinted for a few seconds, and eventually it seemed to pass. Then he opened his eyes. 'Sorry about that...' He leaned to his left, handing Tanzy the remote. 'Can you do the next slide?'

'No problem,' Tanzy said, eyeing him with concern.

Worried stares lingered on Byrd as he padded a few steps over to the nearest chair and sat down into it.

'You okay, Max?' Tanzy asked him.

Byrd waved it away. 'I'll be fine, Ori, thanks. Go on.'

Tanzy didn't believe him but moved on, pressing the button on the small remote, bringing an image up of Sheena Edwards lying dead in the alley between Brougham Street and Zetland Street. 'This morning,' he said, turning back to the room, 'the body of this elderly lady, Sheena Edwards, was found by two young boys on their way to school. They phoned our operator who dispatched services there as soon as possible. Turns out, according to her husband, Malcolm, who lived with her on Brougham Street, she had gone to the shop and hadn't come home. He'd noticed the crowds gathering down at the bottom of his street and went out to see what all the commotion was about.

'Again, we had our best team on it'—he pointed to the senior forensics, who gave a brief nod—'and they found out she'd also been stabbed in the throat. Then she'd dropped her walking stick and stumbled a few feet before falling to the ground.'

Tanzy clicked the button and, on the screen, flashed an image of Sheena Edwards from a closer view. She was on her front, her arms awkwardly bent, with a pool of blood surrounding her. 'Max, could you tell the team anything that was found at the post-mortem?'

Byrd coughed, and slowly stood back up. 'Yeah, the lead Pathologist, Arnold and his assistant, Laura, didn't find anything other than the cut to her throat. They told me she was attacked with a very sharp blade. One which he thinks couldn't be purchased from an ordinary shop, indicating a specialist kind of knife.'

DC Cornty raised his hand.

'Yes, Phil?' Byrd said.

'Are there similarities between the knife attack on Sheena Edwards and the knife attack on Mark Green-well?'

'From what Arnold says, no.'

Cornty nodded his understanding.

'Good point though, Phil,' Tanzy said, then angled his body towards the screen again, and pressed the button. An image of a nine-year-old boy appeared, standing in a small kitchen, wearing a smile on his face and a school uniform, with a book bag gripped in his hand.

'Who's that, Sir?' DC Anne Tiffin asked.

'This is Damien Spencer. The receptionist from Rise Carr College, which is the school he attends, phoned his mother, Mandy, around nine-thirty this morning to inform her that Damien hadn't turned up for school. She told the receptionist that Damien had, like any other morning, set off to school in the direction he'd normally walk. She obviously worried where he'd gone. However, when Jacob and Emily were in the alley at the crime scene of Sheena Edwards, they found a small pencil case with the name Damien on it and a small yellow keyring with a smiley face on it. We spoke to Mandy Spencer and she confirmed that they belonged to her son, but she couldn't understand why he would walk that way, as that would be in a direction away from his school.'

'They must be linked,' Cornty said confidently, leaning forward.

'That's what we are assuming.' Tanzy looked to Byrd, holding the remote out to him.

Byrd took it with a smile and clicked the button. The screen showed a picture of a nine-year-old girl. 'This is Melissa Clarke. The receptionist of the same school phoned her mother, Tracy Clarke, informing her that she hadn't turned up either.' Byrd angled his body again to the screen and pressed the button on the remote. 'And this is Eddy Long. Nine years old. Any guesses what happened to him this morning?'

'He didn't turn up at school?' Tiffin said.

Byrd and Tanzy both nodded in unison, and Byrd clicked the button again, the screen showing the same three pictures but much smaller, so they could all fit on one slide.

'Ori, tell them about Jerry?' Byrd said.

Tanzy nodded. 'When we were talking to Mandy Spencer at Brougham Street, there was a knock at the door. It was one of her friends who had heard about Damien going missing. She informed us about a man up the road who'd seen something very important. After speaking to him, we learned he'd spotted a red Mondeo parked down an alley opposite his house. He told us that he'd seen Damien Spencer walking back to the car with a tall thin man dressed in a thin brown jacket and black jeans. He also said there were two other children in the back of the car.' He turned, pointing to the screen. 'These children, Melissa and Eddy.'

'Do we have a reg plate?' Cornty asked.

'Yes. We ran it through. Plates are fake but PC Andrews and I went to the Town Hall to speak to Jennifer Lucas about the CCTV in the surrounding area. We narrowed down an area where the Mondeo may have gone but the area is vast.'

'Why haven't cameras picked it up?' Stockdale asked, frowning.

'Some don't work, some are waiting on maintenance,' Tanzy replied with the slightest of shrugs.

'Typical,' Stockdale sighed. 'Why don't we —'

The door opened quickly.

Byrd and Tanzy and everyone else started as DC Leonard and PC Weaver stepped through the door.

'Sorry, sir. Sorry we're late,' DC Leonard said.

Tanzy looked disappointed in them.

'There's something you need to see,' Leonard said, handing over the USB memory stick to Byrd. 'We need to watch this now.'

'What's on it?' Byrd asked, taking it from him, then turned, padded over to the shelf near the screen and pulled out a laptop. 'Ori, pass me that wire.'

Tanzy went over to the screen. Hanging from it was a HDMI cable which he unravelled and handed to Byrd, who carefully placed it into the side of the laptop, then inserted the USB stick that Leonard had given him.

Moments later the laptop was mirrored onto the screen in front of them. He opened the file and clicked play. They watched the footage that was taken from the camera above HSS Hire three times.

Byrd sighed heavily.

'What is it, Max?' Tanzy said.

'I know who the naked man is.'

'Who?'

'Lyle Wilson. Our missing number one suspect.'

'Maybe he's not a suspect anymore, Max. Maybe he's another victim,' Tanzy said.

40
Thursday Evening
Darlington

After Arthur had taken Damien, Melissa, and Eddy up to the large room on the first floor of the house earlier this morning, they had looked around the high-ceilinged room in both awe and fear. They'd never seen a room like it. The ceiling looked as high as the sky. The walls were painted white, and the carpet was black. There were six single beds in the room, three on the right and three on the left, the foot of each bed pointing to the centre of the room, leaving a huge gap down the centre of it. Each bed was spaced nearly two metres apart and had a small bed-side unit with a lamp on and a glass of water. Beyond the two lines of beds there was a wide bay window which was locked, giving a fantastic view of the long rear garden. In the bay window there were countless toys, boardgames, remote control cars and trucks. A hint of lavender lin-gered in the air and the room was hot.

When Arthur left them and locked the door, the chil-dren moved further into the room and, at the far end, be-low the bay window, they saw three other children down on their knees playing with toys.

'Hello,' Damien had said to the children. There was a young girl and two boys, all similar in age to Damien, Eddy and Melissa.

'Have you come to hurt us?' one of the boys said in a Scottish accent.

'No,' Damien said softly, shaking his head.

'You won't hurt us?' the girl asked them with fear in her face.

'No, we won't hurt anyone.'

Damien, Melissa, and Eddy shuffled forward down the centre of the room towards them.

'My name is Damien, what's yours?'

'I'm Joseph. This is Annie'—he motioned to the girl, then pointed to the other boy—'this is John. He's my twin. When did you get here?' he'd asked.

'Just now. The tall man brought us straight up. Why are you here?'

'We were walking to school, all of us, and the red car pulled up and the tall man told us he was the teacher for the day, and to get in to his car, and he would drive us to school,' Joseph went on. 'Then he brought us here. We were driving for a few hours.'

'Where are you from?'

'Just near Glasgow,' Joseph had said.

'In Scotland?' Damien frowned.

'Yeah. Then they made us wear these clothes.' They were all dressed in grey pyjamas, a two-piece set made from cotton. 'Where are you from?'

'We live in Darlington,' Damien had told him.

'Where is Darlington?' Joseph asked. 'I've never heard of it.'

'That is where we are now. I don't know what the road is called but we are still in Darlington.' Damien had a worried look on his face, wondering why three children from Scotland were in the same room as them. 'Do your parents know you are here?'

They all shrugged. 'We don't know.'

When it had got dark outside they heard footsteps outside the bedroom door. The Scottish children went quiet suddenly and jumped into bed quickly. Damien, Eddy, and Melissa froze, not really knowing what to do, their little hearts beating so quickly in their chests, it hurt.

The door had opened and in walked Arthur with a tray of food.

'This is your supper. Make it last,' he said, placing it down on a small table near the door. Then another man walked in who was much smaller than the tall man and much rounder. In his hands he had some grey pyjamas, which he handed to Arthur and left. 'And when you have finished you three need to put these on. Remember, if you need the toilet, just press this buzzer and someone will come up and take you.' He pointed to the button on the wall near the door.

As Arthur turned to leave, Damien had said, 'When do we get to go home?'

He stopped and turned to the young man. 'Very soon, Damien, very soon. Just eat your food and put these on.'

Once they had eaten, and put their pyjamas on, they played with the toys for a while.

Then Damien asked the question which both Eddy and Melissa also wanted to know.

'Why do you all have no hair? Are you all poorly?'

'They shaved it off,' Joseph explained, sadly. He looked to his left at his twin, who was quietly playing with some small racing cars. 'How many times has it been, John?'

'Six times now,' John confirmed, not taking his eyes from the racetrack imprinted on the square mat below him. He then looked up at Damien, Melissa, and Eddy. 'They cut it when it gets too long.'

An alarm went off somewhere in the room. Joseph, John, and Annie stood up, leaving the toys where they were and got into their individual beds.

'What's going on?' Damien asked.

'It's bedtime. Put your pyjamas on.'

Damien climbed into one of the beds, pulling the covers up over him. In the next few moments the lights in the room went off, leaving it in total darkness, causing Eddy and Melissa to gasp in panic.

'It goes off the same time every night,' Joseph informed them.

Damien didn't understand, staring into the darkness. 'How long – how long have you been here?'

'I've counted fifty-nine days,' Joseph said, slowly. 'We haven't left this room since we got here.'

41

Thursday Evening
Low Coniscliffe

Byrd took a left into Gate Lane, driving a steady twenty miles-an-hour down the road until he reached the bend. The street was dark and quiet. There were no oncoming headlights and there was no movement anywhere. It was a well-respected, pleasant street in general which was one of the main reasons he'd moved here.

Slowing his X5, he noticed Claire's Renault Clio on the drive so pulled up onto the kerb. He lifted the handbrake and turned the engine off. As he was about to open the door his phone rang. He pulled it out and saw the name Keith Wilson.

'Ah, shit...'

He answered, 'Hi, Keith.'

'Hey, Max, how's the head?'

'A little sore, mate, but nothing that won't fix. What do I owe the pleasure?'

Byrd felt a little strange. Phoning each other was something they did three or four times a week. But this was different. Byrd was sure the naked man in the CCTV from HSS Hire was Lyle, and he didn't know what to do about it.

'I'm getting worried, Max,' Keith said, his tone dull. 'I haven't seen Lyle yet. It's been two days. He spends a lot of his time doing his own thing but I have never known him to be away for so long and not be in touch. He's a big lad now, but I'd be lying if I said I wasn't concerned.'

Byrd stayed silent.

'Max, you there?'

'Yeah, Keith, sorry. Well, we haven't heard anything yet or seen him around. So, I'm sorry I can't shed any light on it just yet. I've filed a report for him so things should develop.'

'Thanks. It's just I've never known him do this.'

'Is he seeing someone? A girlfriend maybe?' Byrd asked.

'No, well, not that I know of. If he is, he hasn't mentioned anything to me, but that's what they're like, Max. They don't tell you anything. That's why I wasn't concerned for him up until now. I've tried phoning and texting him, but I've heard nothing back. It's not like him. This thing that happened to Mark Greenwell has me shaken.'

Byrd was close to telling him about the CCTV footage but that would only panic him. There was no real evidence to suggest that the naked man on the screen was definitely Lyle Wilson. Perhaps it was someone else who highly resembled him, although Byrd was close to confident it *was* him. The best option, in Byrd's mind, was for Keith to believe that Lyle was ignoring his dad and that he'd come home soon, until he was sure.

Byrd stepped out of the car and closed the door, holding the phone to his ear, then used the fob in his free hand to lock it. The bright orange sidelights flashed twice, momentarily illuminating the immediate space around him. As he made his way up the driveway, he noticed the bathroom and bedroom windows were open. He'd learned that was one of Claire's foibles, regardless of how cold it was outside.

'Keith, I'll update you as soon as I hear —'

A blood-curdling scream rang out, startling Byrd as he paused in his stride. It took a fraction of a second for his brain to realise the sound was coming from the open window of the bathroom upstairs directly above him, the sound disturbing the silent street.

He wasn't fully certain but it didn't sound like Claire.

It was someone else, he was sure. Someone else was in his house.

'I need to go,' he said quickly and hung up, then dashed up the driveway towards his front door. Using his keys, he tried to open the door, but the other set of keys were in the opposite side of the cylinder and the keys wouldn't turn.

'Shit!' he shouted.

Then he heard the scream again. This time louder.

42

Thursday Evening
Low Coniscliffe

Byrd wrestled with the lock until, finally, the pins inside the cylinders aligned and he managed to turn it. As it clicked open loudly, he pushed down the handle, barging the door open into the warm hallway.

The scream inside was louder.

From the living room doorway, Claire raced out, and darted up the stairs two at a time. Byrd watched with wide eyes, wondering what the hell was going on. He left the front door open and followed her.

At the top of the stairs, he took a left and saw Claire standing at the bathroom doorway, staring at something inside. He stopped by her side and glared in. Standing in the bath, shaking, with her arms bent into her trembling body and her face screwed up with fear, was Claire's friend, Alice.

'Alice, what's going on?' Claire demanded to know.

'What's happening?' Byrd asked, concerned why she was screaming like that. He'd been so busy with work that he'd forgot that Claire had told him that Alice was coming tonight.

Shaking, Alice managed to point into the corner of the bathroom with her right hand, then dragged her hand back into her body, as if it would keep her safe. She was shaking. 'Over there. Please, help me.'

Claire leaned in cautiously, but Byrd held her back. 'Hey, let me…' Claire accepted and edged back, letting

Byrd move in front of her. He cautiously entered the bath-room.

He didn't know who was going to be there.

'There,' she gasped, stabbing the air. 'There!'

Byrd couldn't see anyone and looked back at her in con-fusion, wondering if she'd seen a ghost or something. 'Al-ice, I don't understand? What is it?'

She screamed again and wriggled into the corner of the bath.

Byrd frowned, unsure what was happening.

A fist-sized spider ran from behind the sink pedestal. It was that big it took Byrd a second to register it was actu-ally a spider. 'Jesus,' he gasped, and edged back a fraction.

The mammoth spider shuddered along the floor to-wards the bath - towards Alice - who was cowering down inside the tub with her hands up to her face. 'Get it away from me,' she begged, over and over, in desperation.

'Max, what is it?' Claire asked from behind him.

'A spider,' Byrd told her. 'Probably the biggest spider I've ever seen. Here… look.'

Claire, whilst keeping hold of Byrd's brown jacket, leaned in and had a look.

'Wow,' she gasped.

Once it reached the side bath panel, it stopped. The overall size of it wasn't far off an orange. The body itself was probably something close to the size of a Malteser.

'What on earth is that?' Byrd said, staring at it, wonder-ing what he would do if it turned and came towards the door. He wasn't the biggest fan of spiders. He wasn't afraid of them but he wasn't going to calmly pick it up and start petting it, he knew that for sure.

'Where did it come from?' Claire said, wondering if there was a brick missing from the wall somewhere.

'Probably from outside. You keep leaving the window open.'

He'd previously asked, even before she'd moved in, when she used to come over, why she always left them open.

Claire didn't reply, knowing it was a dig at her.

'Get it out, Max,' Alice begged, clamping her eyes closed.

'Just relax, Alice, it won't harm you.'

'Max, I'm not touching that, so you're doing it. I don't care if it got through the flipping window!' Claire told him.

Byrd turned around to the landing, remembering there was a Men's Health magazine that he'd placed there last night, and picked it up.

'Don't miss it…' Claire teased.

'I'll put it on your pillow for later when I catch it.'

She playfully punched him in the ribs.

'Right, Alice, it's only a spider. I'll kill it with this okay. Don't scream.' Byrd slowly entered the bathroom, taking small slow steps until he was three feet away. He noticed that Alice's trousers weren't fully up. She'd probably jumped off the toilet and dived into the bath.

Byrd raised the thick, rolled-up magazine into the air and waited. A few moments later the spider shifted back to the left and, under the modern spotlights of the bathroom, Byrd went for it. The hard slap of the magazine on the lino made everyone, including Byrd, wince. Slowly, he lifted up the magazine and relief washed over Alice's face when she saw the spider was crushed.

After she pulled her trousers up, she got out of the bath and they all went downstairs. She'd explained her fear of spiders, that it stemmed from an incident that occurred when she was a teenager in the bedroom of her parent's house. A spider had crawled on her wrist when she was lying on the bed and she'd felt a sharp prick then swotted it away. An hour later her wrist swelled and she started feeling dizzy and nauseous. The doctor at the hospital told her it could have been a bite from a false widow, which was rare but could happen.

'It's definitely dead?' Alice asked Byrd for the seventh time.

Sighing, he smiled and nodded to confirm. 'More chance seeing Santa and the tooth fairy walking through that door than the spider coming back to life. It's dead, Alice.'

As the worry physically seemed to leave her, she took a sip of wine and relaxed into the sofa in the living room. They were watching a film and having a catch up. On the table in front of them there were half full bowls filled with nuts, crisps, and pretzels. Next to them, were plates covered in thin layers of Korma and Masala sauce.

'We were talking about Mark Greenwell earlier, Max,' Claire said. 'We think it's drug related.'

Byrd, sitting on the two-seater sofa in the bay window with a whisky in his hand, took his eyes off the television and glanced over to his right. 'We're not sure,' he said, 'still trying to determine that. We have a few leads.'

He didn't mind speaking with Claire about things in a little more depth, but he didn't know Alice all that well, and wasn't at ease being as open with Claire when she had company. She was Claire's friend, had been for a while now, but some things were better told with some of the details missing.

'You don't know yet?' Claire asked.

'We're still looking into it,' Byrd told her, smiling.

'I bet it's so exciting,' Alice said.

'It can be… sometimes. A lot of it is paperwork. Overrated if you ask me.' Byrd grinned for a moment and faced the TV again. He wasn't in the best of moods this evening. After the day he'd had, especially after seeing his mother the way she was, it'd just made it ten times worse.

'I love Gerard Butler,' Alice said, pointing at the screen, 'Alex gets so jealous. I always seem to pick a film he's in.'

'I'm not surprised,' Claire said. Then they shared a loose giggle, fuelled with the alcohol they'd already drank.

Alice checked her watch. 'Is it that time already? Alex will be picking me up soon.'

'Where's he tonight?' Byrd asked.

'He's delivering Pizzas.'

Byrd frowned. 'Pizzas?'

'Yeah. And whatever else the good people of this town order,' she said. 'He has this friend he used to go to school with. He'd caught up with him a few months back. Hadn't seen him in years, and he told him he was looking for drivers. He wasn't desperate for money but does it once or twice a week. Gets him out of the house. As he works from home he says it makes a nice change.'

Byrd pondered what it would be like to work from home. Not that his job could ever really offer that option but a feeling of claustrophobia came over him at the thought of it.

'I don't blame him, to be honest,' Byrd admitted, 'I wouldn't fancy being stuck at home all day either.' He glanced over to Claire. 'Not that being stuck at home with you wouldn't be nice…'

Both Claire and Alice laughed.

'Oh, before I forget, Max, there's a letter from the DVLA. I've put it on the microwave,' Claire said.

'I'll have a look soon,' he told her.

'Right, I better get my things together,' Alice said, standing up. 'You want a hand clearing away?' she asked Claire, who was still seated, but told her she didn't. 'Okay, I'll go get my things. Do you guys have a downstairs toilet?'

'Just through the kitchen, at the end,' Byrd said.

Alice left the room as Claire rose and piled the empty plates and half-filled bowls on top of each other.

'Why didn't she use that toilet when she went before?' Byrd asked Claire, who paused and glanced his way.

'She needed a mirror to check her eyebrows or something. You know what she's like,' Claire explained, waving it off. She left the room and went to the kitchen. Byrd stayed on the sofa and finished the remaining whisky in his glass. The burning sensation in his throat was something he relished after days like this.

Byrd stood up, left the living room and stopped at the doorway where Claire and Alice were talking quietly. Alice noticed him and nodded. Then she told him she'd see him at the weekend for the meal they had planned for the three of them plus Alex. Another thing which had slipped his mind.

After a long hot shower, Byrd stepped out and, in his towel, he went downstairs, turned all the lights off, then came back upstairs. Claire was reading her kindle, slightly propped up with two pillows, the light from Byrd's lamp illuminating her pretty face. He took his towel off and climbed into bed.

'No underwear tonight, Max?' Her eyes never left her kindle screen.

'Nope…' he replied, pulling the covers up over him.

She smiled, placed her kindle down on her bedside table, and slipped under the covers.

Even the darkest clouds have silver linings.

43

Thursday Evening
Brougham Street, North Road

After three quick knocks at her front door, Mandy Spencer opened it. Standing on the path was Melissa Clarke's mother, Tracy, with a worried, anxious look on her face.

She stepped up and they hugged each other tightly.

'How you holding up, Trace?' Mandy asked, closing the door.

'I don't know what to do with myself, Mand. I'm climbing the walls,' she confessed quietly, trailing Mandy down the hallway into the dining room. The house was hot. Tracy took off her light blue Berghaus jacket, which she placed on the back of one of the dining room chairs.

'You want a coffee?' Mandy asked.

'I could do with a vodka...' she joked, fidgeting with her fingers.

Mandy stopped and turned. 'I do have Vodka if you want one?'

Tracy nodded several times. 'I need it, Mand. Don't judge me, I—'

'Believe me, there's no one judging you here. Come through to the kitchen. Henry's here, too.'

At the far end of the narrow kitchen, sitting on a high stool, was Eddy's Dad, Henry. They waved at each other before meeting in the middle to share a long hug.

'How you doing, Tracy?' he asked softly, rubbing her back.

Tracy pulled away, dabbing the tears from her eyes. 'I can't cope. I don't know what to do with myself.'

'Start by drinking this,' Mandy said, offering her a half pint glass of vodka and coke. She'd only asked for vodka but Mandy, after working with her for several years, knew her favourite drink was vodka and coke.

Tracy took it and had a big gulp, draining nearly half of it, then she padded over to the other free stool that was tucked under the breakfast bar and pulled it out.

'It's just awful,' Tracy struggled, the words clogging in her throat. She raised her hand to her eyes, where more tears had formed. 'Why has someone taken our babies?'

When DI Orion Tanzy had spoken to Jerry who lived up the street earlier, Mandy had been there when he confirmed he'd seen her son Damien get into the red Mondeo. Then she'd heard the part when he said there was a boy and a girl sitting in the back seat. When DI Tanzy returned to the station he phoned Mandy, telling her that there'd been missing reports about Eddy Long and Melissa Clarke. Mandy explained all three of them were in the same class and that Eddy was Henry's son and Melissa was Tracy's daughter, and that she found it very strange as she worked with both Henry and Tracy in the Planning Permission department at the Town Hall.

'Has it been on yet?' Henry asked, glancing down at his watch.

Mandy checked the time on the wall clock to the left and shook her head. 'It'll start soon. Come on, we'll go sit in the living room.'

Minutes later, they were sitting in front of the television. The lamp in the corner was on and the curtains were closed. After a car advert had finished on the screen, the local news started. A news reporter, sitting behind the low desk, dressed in a dark blue suit and blue tie with his hair gelled up to one side, told viewers that today was a day that would be remembered in Darlington for all the wrong reasons.

'Let's go to one of our reporters, who spoke to a local detective earlier at the crime scene,' the man said.

As the screen changed, the three of them saw a woman standing at the bottom of Brougham Street earlier that day, who introduced herself as Wendy Lynn, the local reporter for ITV News. 'The body of an elderly lady was found just behind me earlier this morning. Two young schoolboys, making their way to school like they did every morning came across the body, lying in a pool of blood. Local police were at the scene within minutes. The elderly female, now identified as Mrs Sheena Edwards, was pronounced dead at the scene. Mrs Edwards was the victim of a violent crime, a shock to everyone in the surrounding area and the town as a whole. We don't have any great details on what occurred or why, but as soon as we know, further information will be given. Forensics and the coroner have attended the scene and have gathered the evidence they feel is necessary to take back for analysis. They are currently in the process of doing that. This is Wendy Lynn, ITV news.'

'Bloody awful,' Mandy said, wiping her eyes, 'Sheena was lovely. Used to look after Damien when he was a little younger.'

Henry, who was seated at the end of the sofa, reached behind the back of Tracy and softly squeezed Mandy's shoulder.

The TV presenter offered his heartfelt feelings to the public and to the family of Sheena Edwards. Then he moved onto the next story.

'In the same street, earlier today, a further incident occurred. We go back to Brougham Street and once again speak to our reporter Wendy Lynn.'

Wendy Lynn was standing further up the street outside Jerry's house. Next to Wendy stood Jerry's cleaner, Jackie, who looked both sad and nervous about being on the camera.

'It's a very sad day in this street,' Wendy said. 'After the brutal murder just along this street, we learnt that three children appear to have been taken around the same time. I'm standing here with Jackie, who lives in the local area, who'll give us more information.' The lighting of the street was a little darker, clearly showing it was later in the afternoon. Jackie had changed out of her blue apron and was wearing a black jumper and had a little make-up on her face.

'I'm – I'm friends with Mandy Spencer,' Jackie started, 'I've known her for years. I was cleaning in the house behind me when Jerry, my client, had said that he hoped the little boy was okay. I asked him what he meant. He explained that Mandy's son, Damien, had been taken on his way to school earlier. I knocked on Mandy's door and spoke to her and the detectives that were in her house. One of the detectives asked me to take him to speak with Jerry. He'd confirmed the story about Damien getting into a red Mondeo, which was parked over there in the alley.' She pointed beyond the camera lens. The person behind the camera turned slowly and held its focus on the alley for a few seconds, then swivelled back to Jackie. 'Then he'd mentioned about the children in the back of the car. He said there was a little boy and a little girl too. It's just awful. I just hope they find them soon.'

'Thank you, Jackie, for your time,' Wendy said, facing the camera again. 'If anyone knows anything that can help us or the police with this investigation, please don't hesitate to get in touch by contacting the police one of the numbers below.'

At the bottom of the screen, there was a number for 'Missing Persons' and 'ITV News desk'.

'This is Wendy Lynn, on this very sad, dark day in Darlington. Back to the studio.'

Tracy leaned forward, bubbling with tears, her wet face soaked in the palms of her hands. Mandy, who was on her left, placed a trembling hand on her back to soothe her whilst she wept. Henry leaned over to comfort them both.

'They'll find them. They have their photographs. It's only a matter of time,' he told them, his eyes filling up.

'I just want to know why!' Tracy bawled. 'Why our children?'

Henry pulled her close and held her for a few minutes. 'We'll find... them, I... promise,' he whispered, his words clogging in his throat.

'The notes,' Mandy suddenly said.

Henry looked over the top of Tracy's head. 'Notes?'

'The notes and phone calls,' Mandy said. 'The notes on my car saying something bad will happen and the phone calls to the office number.'

'I thought you said it was a prank?'

'I – I didn't know what to think,' Mandy confessed, 'I thought it was, but maybe it was genuine. Maybe Mr Cairn was so pissed off about us not granting the permission, he's taken our children.'

'Like a ransom?' Henry asked, frowning.

Mandy shrugged. 'I don't know, Henry, I really don't...' she trailed off for a moment. 'I don't know what to think. It makes sense though. He wasn't very nice on the phone to me. He did say something bad would happen if the plans didn't go through.'

'If that's the case, we need to speak to the police right now.'

Mandy stood up and disappeared into the hallway. Henry comforted Tracy until Mandy returned a minute later with a small contact card in her hand. 'Here, ring this number. The detective gave me it earlier and said if there was anything at all, to ring him.'

Henry took it, glanced down at the card.

DI Orion Tanzy, Durham Constabulary.

He plucked the phone from his pocket, typed the number and pressed CALL.

Tanzy had just walked through the door of his home when the phone rang in his pocket. He would have arrived home earlier if not for a detour to the gym beforehand. It sometimes helped him relax after a hard day, and what a day it had been for them all.

'Hello?'

'Is this Detective Inspector Orion Tanzy?'

'Yeah... speaking. Who's this?' he asked, placing his gym bag down in the hallway.

'It's Henry Long. My son went missing earlier today. I'm with Mandy Spencer and Tracy Clarke.'

'How can I help you, Henry?'

'I think I know who took our children.'

44

Friday Morning
Police Station

Tanzy opened the email from Jennifer Lucas that she'd send late last night. He'd explained the situation and what'd happened to the naked man run over the previous night outside HSS Hire. Unfortunately, she'd already left the control room, but she'd passed it over to George Gavin, who was working nightshift. Instead of ignoring the message, she took the time to explain to George that a naked man had been running down Cleveland Street, sometime before midnight, and had been the victim of a driver knocking him down. Once she'd received the email containing the video file, she'd forwarded it on, adding 'Sorry about the quality, Ori. With regards, x'.

Tanzy took a sip of warm coffee, then clicked open the video file which filled the screen. The camera seemed to be positioned near the railway bridge, quite high-up, with a great view of the road below, going all the way down to the HSS Hire shop where the incident had occurred.

The quality of the video could've been better, hence her added message at the end of the email, but it was better than nothing and it was something they could hopefully work with. The time in the corner of the screen told Tanzy it was 11.43 p.m.. He focused hard until something caught his eye on the left. The naked man ran from Edward Street onto Cleveland Street, then sprinted as quickly as he could away from the camera.

A few moments later a 4x4 crept out and waited, the driver looking left and right until he decided to go left, accelerating down the road towards the running man.

Tanzy paused the video and rewound it back, then paused it when the car was at the end of Edward Street just before it turned left. He used the 'zoom in' button to see if he could get a better, more concise, image of the driver, but the nearby streetlights reflected off the slightly angled driver's window leaving nothing but a reflection.

He pressed play, then paused it again when he could see a clear view of the rear of the car. Zooming in once again, he couldn't determine the colour but he recognised the shape of it. He wasn't one-hundred percent sure but it looked like a Kia Sportage. Not the newest model. Perhaps the one before, dating back a couple of years. He tapped on the 'down' arrow and looked at the registration plate.

'Shit,' he said in frustration, seeing the plate had been removed. 'Brilliant.'

Pressing play, the Kia Sportage sped up away from the camera. In the distance Tanzy watched the naked man stop and turn, then start waving towards the oncoming car. Seconds later the Sportage drifted over to the left and knocked the man down. He disappeared from Tanzy's view somewhere in front of the car. Tanzy watched in awe as the brake lights came on, and the driver casually stepped out of the car, and went around the front of it. For a few seconds the man stood still, watching the naked man on the floor, then went out of sight.

Tanzy physically leaned closer to concentrate.

'What are you watching?' a voice said from his left, startling him.

'Morning, Max. The video from the CCTV that Jennifer sent me.' He leaned back and pointed to the screen. 'The naked man, who you believe could be Lyle Wilson, being run down on Cleveland Street late on Wednesday night.'

C. J. Grayson

Byrd's eyes widened as he placed his coffee down on his desk, grabbed his chair and sat down next to Tanzy. 'I'll take it back to the beginning,' Tanzy told him.

They watched it again. Byrd commented straight away about the car having no plates and agreed with Tanzy that it could be a Kia Sportage. 'Is it blue? Black?'

'It's hard to tell. I don't know,' Tanzy said.

Once the man disappeared from the camera view at the front of the car, he returned less than half a minute later with the naked man over his shoulder. He opened the boot of the car, threw the man inside, then shut it quickly. The camera on the video was so far away from the car but they could make out what was happening. After the man glanced up and down the street several times, he climbed inside the Sportage and drove away in the direction of North Road.

'And just like that, gone,' Byrd said, a hint of anger in his tone.

'I'll speak to Jennifer, see if any other cameras pick it up on North Road. This was put together by a guy called George, who works nightshift there. I'm sure if Jennifer had done it, she'd have found the car on a different camera somewhere else.'

'Yeah, good shout. Give her a ring soon,' Byrd agreed.

'Have you spoke with your friend, Keith?'

Byrd nodded twice. 'I have.'

'Have you told—'

Byrd shook his head, knowing what question Tanzy was going to ask him. 'I haven't told him, not yet.'

Tanzy narrowed his eyes. 'Why?'

'Just because the man looked like Lyle, doesn't mean it's him. The quality of the footage outside the hire place was good, but at the same time it was dark.' Byrd fell silent for a moment. 'It could have been one of a hundred people. There's no point in worrying him for nothing. The less he knows, the better. For now.'

Tanzy shrugged a little, leaving it with him to manage, then noticed the bags under his eyes. 'How'd you sleep last night? You look terrible, Max.'

Byrd raised his eyebrows. 'You do have a way with words, Mr Tanzy, I'll give you that.' He half-smiled towards him, but being honest, he loved how close they were and how they could be open with each other.

'I slept pretty shit to be honest. Had three whiskeys and still hardly slept. Claire had her friend Alice round for a takeaway and a few drinks. She left around ten when her boyfriend, Alex, picked her up.'

'That the one who plays football?'

Byrd nodded. 'Yeah, that's him. Plays seven-a-side over Longfield a few nights a week. Might see if I can get a game with him too. I'm feeling fit at the moment.'

'Still old and slow though, eh,' Tanzy said.

After Byrd gently jabbed his arm, he pulled himself closer to his own computer and logged on.

'Oh, I got a call last night from Henry Long,' Tanzy said.

'Father… of Eddy Long, the boy who went missing yesterday?' Byrd asked, frowning.

'Yeah, he—'

A sudden noise erupted from the office behind them, sounding like a phone being slammed down into the receiver, followed by several heavy steps, before the door swung open quickly.

'You two, in here…' DCI Fuller barked, then vanished back into his office, leaving the door open. A few of the other detectives and PCs in the office popped their heads over their desks to see what the commotion was about.

Tanzy and Byrd rose slowly, eyeing each other cautiously, then entered the office wondering why Fuller was in another one of his 'pleasant' moods.

It was cold in the office and Fuller was still wearing his coat, probably because he had just arrived when the phone on his desk rang.

'I would say good morning to you two, but it isn't a good morning. It's an absolutely shit morning.' His face was red, his breathing heavier than usual.

Byrd and Tanzy said nothing. Instead, they just sat down in the two chairs on the opposite side of the desk and waited.

Fuller took a heavy breath and clamped his eyes closed for a few seconds, then exhaled, his wide, round shoulders physically deflating. After he pulled his coat off and threw it on the floor, he took a seat, then looked up at Byrd and Tanzy, swapping his attention between them every few seconds. His eyes were tired. Dark puffy circles sat underneath them, as if he'd barely slept, which was probably not far from the truth considering the events of yesterday.

'I've had Eckles on the phone. He's playing war.'

This isn't good, Byrd thought.

'What happened?' Fuller demanded.

'What do you mean, what happened?' Tanzy asked.

'Yesterday. It was a day from hell,' Fuller shouted. 'What happened?'

Tanzy frowned at him, then angled his gaze towards Byrd, then back to the DCI. 'You know what happened. You received all of the reports from yesterday.'

Fuller leaned back, squinting at Tanzy, then he focused on Byrd. 'Max, can you enlighten me?'

Byrd tilted his head whilst he thought of an answer. 'I would but, as Orion has just mentioned, if you're referring to the crimes that happened yesterday, you will have already seen them if you read the reports that we all took the time to write up for you. Do you still require each individual to write the reports and send them at the end of the day?'

There was an uncomfortable silence between them. Although Tanzy seemed calmer than Byrd, he'd love the opportunity to dive over the desk and choke his superior if there was a chance of getting away with it.

'Yes,' Fuller finally said, his voice a little lower. He looked away from them towards the window, unsure what to say. The DIs waited, watching him, wondering what he was thinking.

'I read the reports last night,' he admitted, looking back to meet their eyes. 'I read each individual report. But I don't understand something...'

Neither Byrd nor Tanzy asked what it was he didn't understand.

'Why's it happening?' Fuller asked. 'Why is this shit happening in Darlington?'

Byrd and Tanzy stayed silent for a few moments, and when Tanzy didn't speak up, Byrd decided he would.

'Whether it's in Darlington, or whether it's in Middlesbrough, or York, or Newcastle, it doesn't matter,' Byrd started. 'Each individual has flaws. It's inside every one of us – that's including you sir, as well as Orion and myself – to self-destruct in some way. Doing something wrong often excites people in ways it shouldn't but it's just the way people are wired. Feelings of envy, anger, greed, power, being in control are often reasons, unjustifiable I may add, but reasons nevertheless why people behave, sometimes, in the way they do. The past few days are testament to this.'

Tanzy, with his mouth half open, listened to him intently. On the opposite side of the desk, Fuller held a similar expression to the DI.

Byrd went on: 'Mark Greenwell was found in the park with a knife wound to his throat. This, as we can see from the picture we are painting of it, was done out of anger. Where this anger came from is something we need to determine, but it could be linked to envy or greed. Sheena

Edwards was found in the back alley behind Brougham Street with a knife slice to her throat. Why her? Did her murderer feel so insecure he did it to feel a certain level of power by doing what he did? Did the man responsible have the desire to kill. Does killing, in general, give the individual responsible a feeling of self-worth under a crazy internal belief that by doing so they are in control and are capable of making their own choice?' Byrd shrugged. 'Then we were made aware of the three children who had been taken. Who took them? And why? Was this power? The ability to take and do whatever he or she likes without someone objecting their actions... at this moment, we don't know.'

Tanzy's mouth had open further as he listened to Byrd's words.

'So,'—he raised a finger in the air, as if emphasising the point—'this is why we are here, Martin. It's our job as a whole – and I don't just mean this team or this department, or me, or you, or Orion, but the force as a whole. Maybe even the whole group of good people out there – to ensure the world is mostly decent. It's a simple war of good vs evil. You can't have one without the other. It's inevitable that weeds will always grow in the nicest of gardens. And it's our job to keep the weeds at bay, find out why they've grown, and eliminate them the best way we possibly can, knowing at some point in the future they will grow back. So, when they do, we'll have the tools to be more effective.'

'Ever thought about becoming a Superintendent one day?' Fuller remarked.

'Maybe one day in the future, sir,' he said with an appreciative nod.

Nothing was said for a few moments, whilst the others digested the message Byrd was trying to make.

'Well,' DCI Fuller said softly, 'that's certainly put things in a way I've never heard of before.'

'I need to tell you something else, boss,' Tanzy said, leaning forward.

'Yeah?' he said, switching his focus to Tanzy.

'We may have a name for the weed responsible for taking the three children.'

45

Friday Morning
Duke Street, Town Centre

'Where is it?' Weaver asked as she slowed the car, shifting her focus left then right at the different business names and logos on the buildings on either side of the road.

'There…' said DC Leonard, pointing to the right.

Weaver slowed the Astra, flicked her indicator on, and pulled up at the side of the road. Once she'd turned the engine off, they looked to the building on the right. A sign was fixed on the wall next to a large blue door containing three business names.

One was Peter Main Graphic Design. The next name down was Annie's Flowers. The last one was the one they were looking for.

Cairnfield Developments.

After Henry had told Tanzy about the notes left on Mandy's car and the numerous phone calls from Mr Cairn, Tanzy ran a check on him, using the first name, which Henry had provided, being Andrew. According to PNC (Police National Computer) he didn't exist. However that didn't mean he wasn't an actual person. The PNC held approximately thirteen million names of people within the UK that have, in some form, committed a crime and have been arrested. These profiles often have further information about the individual including DNA and fingerprints. He then tried the PND (Police National Database), which is a large database of people that have done something that the police have previously investigated but from their findings, no arrests were made.

Andrew Cairn did not exist on either of those.

As soon as DC Leonard and PC Weaver were in the office, Tanzy had sent them on their first task of the day. They were to check out the Duke Street address that Henry had given him from the letters Mr Cairn had previously sent to the planning office.

They stepped out and shut their doors. Considering the time, Duke street was busy, people walking into town dressed smartly, presumably on their way into work.

Most of the parking spaces down the south side were taken up and would, no doubt, be filled before long. It was short stay parking, designed for people who were using the local businesses on that street, although Leonard didn't get a parking ticket.

The air was cold, just above freezing. Stepping onto the path, they felt a thin layer of frost under their feet and, carefully, made their way to the set of concrete steps up to the building. Leonard, who was wearing black trousers and a white shirt, covered by a dark blue padded fleece, took the lead, pushing open the main door and stepping inside, followed by Weaver, who was wearing her usual uniform.

The hallway was like any other hallway. There was a door to the left, a door beyond that, a door at the end of the hallway and a staircase to the right. Leonard took a few steps and stopped at the first door to the left, with its bright, colourful, funky sign fixed to it. Peter Main Graphic Design.

Leonard passed that, went a few metres down the hall and checked the next door. It had no sign on, so he continued towards the door at the end of the hallway. There was a sign on it.

Cairnfield Developments. Bingo!

He knocked on the door several times, then tried the handle, but it was locked.

A few seconds went by until he knocked again.

'Did Orion give you a number to call?' Weaver asked him.

Leonard nodded. 'Yeah. He said the planning office passed on the number they use to contact Mr Cairn. Apparently he's had a lot of involvement with them over the past few years in relation to various building work and property developments.' Leonard pulled out a small slip of paper that Tanzy had given him and punched the number from it into his phone. After pressing CALL, he put it to his ear. Weaver waited behind him.

'No answer,' he told her, then tried again. 'Hey, we'll ask in there. See if they know anything about them.'

Leonard knocked at the door with the jazzy sign and went inside. He was greeted by a modernised rectangular space, although it wasn't great in size. In the bay window, which looked out onto the street, there was a built-in desk with a computer sitting on top of it, the screen facing at an angle into the room. Whoever sat there, clearly enjoyed having a view.

To their left was a seating area with a plethora of samples of design work that the company had done. Behind the desk, on the opposite wall, there was a flatscreen television sitting in front of lime-green wallpaper with architectural shapes.

In the centre of the room there was a circular table, which had an array of business cards and leaflets, most of them offering the customers who walked in samples of their ideas and a taster of what type of work they dealt with.

Over to the right of the room, an area they couldn't quite see, they heard a sound. An almost inaudible humming which Leonard thought sounded familiar. A moment later, a teenager with a large mop of hair walked into view and noticed him.

'Jesus,' he gasped, raising a palm to his chest and taking a few steps back. 'I – I. Wow, Jesus. I never heard you come in.'

'Sorry to startle you,' Leonard said. 'Could I ask you a few questions?'

The boy, who appeared to be no older than twenty, nodded enthusiastically. 'Sure. Sit down at the table.' As Leonard moved, the young man noticed Weaver in her uniform behind and paused suddenly. 'Wait – what's this about?'

'No cause for concern,' Leonard assured him, pulling out a seat. 'Just need to ask you about Cairnfield Developments.'

The teenager sat down and placed his coffee on the table. 'Okay…'

'What's your name, Sir?' Weaver asked him as she took a seat.

'Danny, Danny Ledge.'

'Is this your business?' she said, glancing around briefly.

He shook his head and made a face, as if it would be a dream of his to own something like this. 'No, I'm an apprentice. In my second year. Peter owns it. He's out for the morning up in Newcastle. He'll be back after'—he frowned, looking up at the ceiling—'after lunch. Yeah, after lunch,' he confirmed with himself.

Weaver nodded. 'Do you know the owner of Cairnfield Developments, just down the hall?'

Danny shook his head. 'I've never seen him since I've been here. That's just over a year. I did a year full time at college then they found me a placement with an employer. I was lucky to be put with Peter. Some of the work we do are these business cards and flyers here.' He pointed to the various objects on the table in front of Leonard and Weaver.

'That's good work,' Leonard commented.

'This is my design,' he said, pointing to a red and black business card.

'Very good,' Weaver agreed, then smiled. 'So, you have never seen the owner, or anyone, go into that office?'

'No, sorry. Peter has been here a while, so he might know, but I'm not sure.'

'Okay. We'll pop back a little later this afternoon, hopefully speak to him then.'

'I'd say go and ask Annie who had the flower shop upstairs, but she moved to Spain a few months ago. I kind of miss her. She made these amazing hot chocolates with marshmallows.'

Weaver stood up, as did Leonard, and they both stepped out into the hallway. 'Thanks for your time,' Weaver said to him.

The geeky-looking young man waved at her and carried his coffee over towards the computer at the window.

'Who are you calling?' Weaver asked Leonard as he took his phone from his pocket.

'Orion. To let him know.' A few seconds of silence passed. 'Boss, it's James. We've just spoken to a lad who works at the office in the front of the building. He said he's never seen anyone go into the Cairnfield Development office in the year or so that he's been here. The office upstairs belongs to a woman called Annie who hasn't been here for a few months.'

'Is the door to Cairnfield Developments locked?' Tanzy asked.

'Yeah. We've knocked a few times without response.'

'Have you got your tools with you?' Tanzy asked.

'In the car,' Leonard said. 'You want me to...'

'Yeah. If there's a slim chance no one will turn up, do it. We need a lead on this. Eckles is on Fuller's case, which means he's on ours, which means—'

'You're on ours?' said Leonard, finishing his trail of thought.

'You're getting good at this detective thing, Jim.'

'Give me a few minutes. I'll ring you back.' Leonard ended the call and put his phone away. 'Two seconds,' he told Weaver.

'We aren't…?' she sighed, knowing what he was getting from the car and what he was planning to do.

'We are.' He opened the building's front door and stepped out into the cold. A moment later, he returned with a small rectangular box in his hand. Weaver moved out of the way and watched Leonard lower to his knees, so the lock of the door to Cairnfield Developments was eye level. It took him around two minutes to get in – it had been a while since he'd done it.

'Bingo,' he said, standing. He pushed the door open to see the long rectangular room was empty, not a single piece of furniture inside it. Disheartened, he plucked the phone from his pocket and phoned Tanzy to tell him the office was empty.

Tanzy thanked him and asked them to return to the station.

Leonard and Weaver were very competent individuals, but they had missed something. Above the door to Cairnfield Developments, a small video camera was recording twenty-four seven.

Across town, sitting at a desk, in a dark office, a man had been watching them on his computer screen.

Immediately, he picked up his phone and dialled a number.

When the call was answered, he said, 'Mr Darchem, we have a problem.'

46

Friday Morning
Claxton Avenue, Mowden

A dark blue Kia Sportage pulled up against the frosty curb and came to a gradual halt, the tyres quietly crunching on the wafer-thin layer of ice on the damp road. The man inside smiled to himself and leaned to the left, picking up the thin pile of paperwork from the front passenger seat. A moment later, after checking the information printed on it, he folded it in half and placed it inside his fleece pocket and zipped it up. In the footwell of the passenger seat, there was a square box, roughly a foot by a foot in size.

He picked it up, rested it on his knee for a moment, then stared to his right out of his window at the semi-detached house. It appeared to be a small house but the front of it was appealing. He could see the man through the window sitting at the table quite far back into the house, as if the wall between the living room and dining room had been removed.

Glancing away from the house briefly, he leaned to the left and opened the latch of the glovebox, allowing it to drop slowly. From inside, he picked a photograph up and held it against the steering wheel.

It was of him, his wife, and his two children, taken when they were in Disneyland Paris three years ago. As he stared into the eyes of his children, his heart felt heavy as the memories flooded back to him in sharp waves, as if he'd been stabbed in the chest multiple times. What an amazing holiday it was – probably one of the best ever.

Their infectious smiles made him do the same, as if nothing in the world mattered and everything was good again. Just like it had been in that perfect moment. If only he could have stopped time then.

But those days were gone. Long gone.

He carefully placed the photograph back into the open glovebox, closed it, then opened the driver's door, stepping down onto the path with the box in his hand. He carefully padded down the slightly inclined driveway and knocked on the front door. He was just over six feet with narrow but muscular shoulders. On top of the dark-coloured fleece and jeans, he wore a hi-viz vest.

It was all a part of the image.

The disguise.

After he knocked, it wasn't long before the man sitting at the table opened the front door, wearing a curious smile, the kind people used for a stranger at their door.

The man with the box held up his badge that hung from a green lanyard around his neck. 'Hey, I'm Paul. Got a delivery for you.'

The man standing inside the house frowned. 'You have?'

'Yup.'

'I haven't ordered anything,' he said, his frown deepening.

'It has your wife's name on it,' the man said, turning and showing him.

'Let me ring her first. I've told her about ordering things without telling me.' He plucked his phone from his pocket and put it to his ear. 'Ahh, she isn't answering,' he said in frustration. 'What's inside?'

The man in the vest shrugged. 'Not sure, Mr Cornforth. I'm just the driver.'

'Okay, I'll take it.'

'Don't suppose I could be cheeky and ask to use your toilet?' the man asked. 'I didn't have time this morning and I don't know if I'll get a chance soon. I feel bad for asking but—'

Cornforth waved him in. 'Yeah, no worries. Just here on the left.' He went back into the dining room and placed the package on the table next to his open laptop whilst the delivery man closed the small toilet door under the stairs.

As Brian Cornforth looked at the reports for the last quarter of 2019, he felt someone behind him. He could feel the carpet near his chair dip slightly. The way the still air had changed around him. He was sure—

By then it was too late.

He gasped when something very, very tight wrapped around his throat. Whatever it was, it dug into his skin fiercely and only got tighter. He pushed up off the chair backwards and stumbled, grabbing at his throat, trying to free whatever it was. It felt like a very thin wire. It was so tight he couldn't get his fingertips between his skin and the wire to free it.

The oxygen supply being cut off to his brain made him delirious as he was dragged back onto the floor, his heart pounding in his chest. A moment later, he dropped his arms beside him, and his world went black.

When Brian Cornforth's body went still, the man holding the wire loosened his grip and let Brian fall onto his side, then climbed to his feet. He knew he wouldn't have long before Brian gained consciousness but there'd be enough time to do what he needed to do.

Enough time to make him suffer.

47

Friday Morning
Greenbank Road

After Byrd knocked on the door, he took a few steps back, so he was level with DC Anne Tiffin. The curtains to the right moved a little, then became still.

A car passed behind them and someone shouted something inaudible, but neither Byrd nor Tiffin could decipher what it was, nor did they really care.

The white, faded front door opened and, standing there, was Mark Greenwell's mother, Anna.

'Hi, Anna,' Byrd said with a kind smile.

'Hi...' she said just above a whisper, unsure why they were there. Was it news about her son, Mark? Had they found the person responsible for his murder?

'Is it okay if we come in?'

She mulled over his words, then decided that would be okay, moving aside to allow them room to enter. The house was small and compact, the hallway narrow but decorated pleasantly. The living room was the first door on the right, then the stairs, then through the door at the end of the short hallway was the dining room, which led through to the kitchen.

'How you holding up, Mrs Greenwell?' Byrd asked softly, trailing her into the dining room. She appeared slimmer than she did a few days ago, her shoulders narrow, her movements frail as if she'd just woken up. Tiffin slowly followed them, glancing right into the living room as she passed the doorway, noticing two bed covers on the floor with pillows and empty sweet wrappers strewn around them.

Before she answered him, she asked them both if they'd like a drink. They both declined and stopped in the dining room.

'Sorry about the mess,' she confessed, 'I really need to get things cleaned up. Ethan stayed up late last night and we watched a film.'

Byrd eyed the bowls half-filled with sweets on the small table against the wall to the left. 'Don't worry about a thing, Mrs Greenwell, we're not here to see if you've hoovered every day.'

She let out a small smile and glanced to the floor.

'How you holding up?'

'I'm not, to be honest.' She raised her hand to her forehead, as if preventing an oncoming headache. 'I – I just don't know what to do anymore.'

Both detectives absorbed her words with sympathy. Tiffin had never felt a loss close to her but, with Byrd losing his sister in a similar kind of way, and his father very recently, he could relate to the feelings that Anna was experiencing.

'I know you don't think it will, Anna, but it'll get easier in time. Trust me, I've been through a similar thing in my life.'

Her eyebrows furrowed. 'Your own child?'

Byrd shook his head. 'No, sorry, I don't have children. My sister. Twelve years ago. And… my father two months ago.'

'Sorry for your loss,' she said quietly.

'The pain doesn't go away but you learn to cope with it,' Byrd assured her. 'It may feel like you won't be able to, but you will. You're a strong woman, I can see that.'

She nodded and looked back at the floor, unsure how to respond to the compliment.

'We were wondering,' Byrd said, 'would it be okay to have a quick look in Mark's room? See if there's anything that may be able to help us with our enquiry?' Byrd, before she responded, plucked the search warrant from his pocket. He didn't want to use it but once it had been signed he knew he had to act and leave the paperwork with Anna.

She managed a nod but didn't say anything.

'Thank you.' Byrd and Tiffin backed away and slowly made their way up the stairs. They recalled DC Leonard seeing the shoe boxes in Mark's wardrobe full of drugs on Wednesday morning and would take them back for evidence.

'It's just up on the left,' Anna said, appearing at the bottom.

'Thanks,' Tiffin said, turning back to her.

The door to the right was open, filled with a multitude of posters of sharks. Byrd didn't need to be a detective to work out that was Ethan's room. The door to the left was closed.

Taking a breath, Byrd grabbed the handle, wondering how long since it had been opened. Often, he found, when a family suffered the loss of a child, they didn't touch the room or didn't clean it. They left it exactly how it was when the child was there. That way they could feel them, could smell their scent. It's known that it often brought comfort to the parents. He pushed down the handle and edged the door open. The faintest smell of aftershave hung in the still, cold air. The bed to the left wasn't made, no doubt left as Mark had left it on Tuesday morning. There was a small pile of folded clean clothes at the base of the radiator under the window. They were mainly interested in was the contents of the wardrobe, so headed over to it. Byrd pulled the door open and peeked inside.

The shoe boxes were gone.

'Shit.' Byrd frowned and spend the next several minutes looking around the room, opening and closing drawers, checking through the things on the desk. There was nothing left in his room that could help them at all.

Back downstairs in the dining room they found Anna staring into space. Her hands were cupped around the mug that rested on the table surface in front of her, steam gently rising from it.

'Where's Ethan? At school?'

Anna nodded at Byrd. 'I'll pick him up at three.'

'How's he coping?'

'He – he seems fine for now. I don't think he really understands yet. You see, Mark spent a lot of his time out and about. He spent most of his time at his friend's house I think. Doesn't live far. Not sure what number but I'm sure some of them live on Craig Street.'

Byrd knew this from what Mac, the DFU guy, had said about the location of Mark's phone over the past few weeks. 'Do you know what number?'

'I'm sorry, I don't.'

Byrd pulled out a chair and slowly dropped into it. 'Anna, when we carried out the post-mortem of Mark, we found something unusual. Something which I need to ask you about?'

A look of concern washed over her face as her body seemed to tense. 'Wh – What?'

'The pathologist found marks on his back. They appeared to be whip marks. He had nine in total. He thinks some of them could date back more than two years. There's some that appear freshly done, probably done in the past few months. Do you know anything about them?'

She shook her head quickly and expressed a look of disgust. 'I – I don't know… marks? On his back?'

Byrd nodded. 'Nine in total.'

'He never mentioned anything to me about them.'

'Have you never seen them?'

'I haven't seen him without a t-shirt on for a few years. I – I never knew. God, what happened to him?' She raised a palm to her mouth, genuinely horrified by what Byrd was telling her.

'That's what we're trying to find out, Anna,' he said, smiling sadly.

'I don't know anything about them. God, who did that to him? I'll fuc—'

'We don't know, Anna, but we'll do our best to find out,' Byrd said, then paused a beat. 'How long ago, just out of interest, did Mark begin spending his time at his friend's house on Craig Street?'

She shrugged, thinking hard. 'At least three years. I don't… I don't know them that well. I mean I know a few of their names, ones that Mark has mentioned, but I wouldn't have thought they would have done that to him.'

'Anna, what I've learnt in this job, in over twenty years, is that people are capable of anything.'

They spoke for a few minutes more then Byrd stood and made his way to the door, followed by Tiffin. Once they were inside the car, he glared down the street, pointing.

'We need to find out what's going on in Craig Street.'

48

Friday Late Morning
Rise Carr College, Eldon Street

Tanzy stopped the Golf at the side of the road and applied the handbrake. Moments before he'd been on the phone to DC Leonard, getting an update about the office belonging to Cairnfield Developments on Duke Street. It pissed him off that it was empty, offering no information or leads on the whereabouts of the owner, Andrew Cairn, but he wouldn't let that distract him from the investigation. Often, life keeps knocking you back, but all you can do is get your head down, stay focused, and carry on.

So, unable to speak to Andrew Cairn, who Henry Long seemed to believe had something to do with the missing children, Damien, Eddy, and Melissa, he decided the next stop was at their school, Rise Carr College on Eldon Street, to speak to their teacher.

Tanzy opened the car door, stepping out into the chill. The sun had broken through the clouds, but it was still a long way off being warm. His long, grey parker jacket really came in handy on days like this. PC Andrews, on the other hand, had his standard black uniform on, topped with a padded jacket that the police classed as their alternative jacket for the colder weather. It offered little extra warmth and made Andrews look forward to getting home and getting in a hot shower after his shift. He closed the door, made his way around the front of Tanzy's bonnet and waited for a rusty-looking white transit van to pass. The driver, a man aged between fifty and sixty with a thin face, scowled at them both, realising that Andrews was police.

They both crossed Eldon street then through the two bricked pillars into the rectangular car park. They made their way over to the right bottom corner, where they saw a sign above the sliding glass doors, stating 'Rise Carr College.'

The glass doors slid open on their approach and, as they padded across the wooden floor towards the desk, their focus fell on a middle-aged lady with short blonde hair sitting behind it on a swivel chair. She wore thin-framed glasses and had something about her, something elegant. She was thin, tanned and carried herself well, her posture straight and solid. She heard their footsteps and looked up over the computer screen.

'Good afternoon, how can I help?' she asked professionally.

'Detective Inspector Orion Tanzy. This is PC Josh Andrews. We're here to speak to the headmaster about the disappearance of three of your students yesterday?'

'Have they been found?' she asked with eagerness in her voice.

'Unfortunately, not yet,' Tanzy replied, sadly.

'Okay, I'll call him now.' She picked up the phone to her right, dialled a few digits, and put it to her ear. 'Hello, Mr Heslop. We have the police here to speak with you about Damien, Melissa, and Eddy… okay… yes, I will. I'll let her know, too.' She hung up the phone. 'He's coming right now. I'm just going to contact their teacher as well, as she'd no doubt like to speak to you.'

'Okay,' Tanzy replied, giving a brief smile. He turned away from her and glanced around at the reception area. It looked new, as if recent money had been spent on it to make it look modern and fresh, a total contradiction to its appearance on the outside. One wall was covered in children's paintings, evidently starting from the lower years on the left, through to the older children on the right. Another wall featured a large – almost too big – photograph of the whole of the school, taken from a height somewhere in the playground, either by a drone or some mad man on the roof.

A minute later, a small, round man appeared in front of them, offering them both a firm handshake. He had a thinning bald head, and bright green eyes. 'I'm Jack Heslop, headteacher here at Rise Carr College. Thank you for coming in. Should we take a seat?' He motioned to their right towards a small table which was surrounded by low, deep, soft, blue chairs. They all sat down and sunk into the foam.

'It's awful what has happened to the children,' the headteacher started. 'When they didn't turn up for class, their teacher, Mrs Cornforth, checked and counted the children again. At first she assumed they were ill, or maybe running late. But at half nine, she went to check with Alison'—he motioned towards the short blonde-haired receptionist sitting at the desk behind them—'who confirmed that there had been no phone calls from any of their parents indicating they wouldn't be in.'

Tanzy frowned at the headteacher. 'Damien, Melissa, and Eddy are all in the same class?'

The small, round man nodded. 'Yes.' He then looked over to Alison, and shouted, 'Is Mrs Cornforth on her way?'

She gazed over. 'I've let her know the police are here.'

He glanced down at his watch. 'She won't be a moment… I hope.'

'So, do you think this has anything to do with the…' Mr Heslop fell silent.

'Murder of Sheena Edwards?' Tanzy said, finishing the sentence.

'Yes,' Mr Heslop said, the word almost clogging in his throat.

'We don't know, we are piecing things together,' explained Tanzy.

'I just think —'

There was a sound of spinning tyres coming from the car park, the sudden high-screeched noise coming through the closed glass entrance door.

'Give me a sec,' the headteacher said. He stood and dashed over to the door. Everyone knew there was a five mile-an-hour limit in the school car park. He'd made that clear on several occasions. Heslop arrived at the door to see what the noise was. A blue Peugeot 307 was heading sharply for the exit, taking a left, then disappearing.

Tanzy and Andrews appeared at the open glass doors just behind him.

'What was that?' Tanzy asked, studying the car park but not seeing anything.

'The sound of a car leaving the car park quickly.'

'Whose car?'

'The children's teacher, Jane Cornforth.'

49

Friday Late Morning
Rise Carr College, Eldon Street

'Try her again,' Tanzy asked Jack Heslop, the headteacher of Rise Carr College.

'I have. That's seven times I've rang her. She's not picking up,' he explained with a shrug, lowering his phone to his side. 'I can't keep trying all day.' He glanced beyond Tanzy and Andrews, grabbing the attention of the receptionist, who was sitting behind the desk with a worried frown on her face wondering why Jane Cornforth, the teacher of the missing children, had suddenly left. 'Alison, please try Jane again.'

She nodded, picked up the phone, and dialled the number again. Tanzy watched her, absorbing the worry on her face, realising that she too, thought it was a strange thing for Jane Cornforth to do under the circumstances.

'Why would she do that?' Andrews said. 'She knows we're here. Why would she go before speaking to us?'

'I – I… I don't know,' Heslop said. It was clear he didn't know. As far as he was aware, she'd been in her class when Alison had informed her that the police were here to speak to her about the disappearance of Damien, Melissa, and Eddy.

Then she left suddenly.

No explanation.

No reason for her actions.

Gone.

'It's going to her answering machine, she's not picking up,' Alison said from behind the reception desk, sighing heavily.

Jack Heslop huffed, his shoulders dropping an inch. 'I'll have to go to her classroom. She must have just left the students.' Then he shrugged at Tanzy. 'I don't understand this, Detective.'

Nearly a mile away, in the blue Peugeot 307, Jane Cornforth was hitting almost fifty miles-an-hour as she approached the bottom of North Road. The limit was thirty, but she needed to get out of that school and return home as quickly as possible. There had been no time to explain, she had to leave. After she'd spoken to emergency services asking for an ambulance, she placed the phone down on the passenger seat and both hands on the steering wheel.

She took a right at the large roundabout at the bottom of North Road, the tyres barely gripping the road as the rubber glided across the wet tarmac. A car beeped to her left, the elderly driver, who'd pulled out as she approached, thinking he had more time than he did, showing his annoyance. He probably didn't appreciate the two fingers she'd stuck up at him before she pulled onto St Augustine's Way towards Woodland Road.

She swung a right at the roundabout and put her foot to the floor. In front of her, a yellow Vauxhall Corsa slowed as the lights up ahead went from amber to red. There was no time to waste, so instead of braking, she put her foot down, heading straight over the busy crossroads.

The DHL van coming from the left, from Portland Place, didn't see her and ploughed straight into the side of the Peugeot, rolling the car twice until it came to rest, the roof of the car hard up against the now-bent metal barrier that bordered the footpath near the large block of flats. A woman nearby screamed and picked up her five-year-old son as they watched in horror.

All of the traffic on the crossroads came to a sudden halt, drivers' eyes wide and mouths open in shock. It wasn't long before several drivers got out of their cars, making their way over to the damaged blue Peugeot lay-ing on its side. A man who was walking by himself had stopped when he heard the collision. The car had rolled in his direction but crashed to a halt against the metal railing just in front of him. Through the smashed front wind-screen, he could see a woman in the driver's seat with her head tipped sideways, gravity pulling her long black hair towards the floor. He could see her face, covered in blood.

She didn't move.

The sharp realisation of what he'd witnessed had kicked in.

'Jesus!' he gasped, jumping over the barrier and climb-ing up onto the car to open the passenger door but it wouldn't budge.

'Just hold on, Mrs!' he yelled through the cracked win-dow. Then he looked around at the people who had started to circle the car. 'Someone help me, I can't open the door. She's unconscious. Someone...' The people around started to panic a little. One man jumped up and tried to assist but the door wouldn't move. It felt like it was welded shut.

Then they heard a sound.

A ringtone.

Both men glanced wearily at each other.

'Not mine,' one of them said.

'Not mine, either.'

They both looked through the cracked side passenger window. On the floor of the passenger footwell, there was an iPhone, the screen facing up in their direction.

'It's there,' one of them said, pointing.

The screen was flashing, the phone itself vibrating, making tiny arcs of movement in the shallow sea of glass at the bottom of the car. The caller ID was Jack Heslop. Seconds afterwards, the call stopped. Then a text message appeared. It was from her husband, Brian.

They lowered their faces closer to the glass. It read: **I'm so sorry, Jane. You're too late.**

50
Friday Early Afternoon
Darlington

The six children were all sitting on the floor, near the bay window of the huge bedroom. Melissa was next to Eddy, shaking, her face tucked into the middle of her bony knees, not quite believing that the other three had been there for fifty-nine days. Neither Melissa, Damien, nor Eddy had slept well last night, for obvious reasons.

'They haven't let you out, not once?' Damien asked Joseph as he was occupied building a ramp for the toy cars on the floor in front of him.

Joseph shook his head but showed no sadness. 'Only to go to the toilet and to brush our teeth.'

'Your parents must think...' he trailed off, not wanting to say it out loud.

'That I'm dead? Yup.' He looked away from Damien, tilting his head back, observing the all-too-familiar white ceiling above them. His face was emotionless, as if he'd been in the room for so long, he'd stopped worrying, stopped panicking, stopped feeling sad about it and accepted their situation.

'Have you tried to escape?' Eddy said, sitting under the window, watching him play so calmly.

'Twice. I won't try it again.'

He was terrified to ask, but he did anyway. 'Why? What happened?'

'Once, when the door opened at dinnertime, which is half twelve every day, without fail, I waited next to it. Annie and John had agreed to sit on the floor against this wall and I packed my bed with their pillows making it look like I was sleeping. When the man came in with a tray of food, I snuck out onto the landing. I got five steps until an alarm went off. A loud siren. I panicked and, suddenly, the man who came in with the food was behind me. He was so angry. As he pulled me back into the room, I saw a camera outside the door. That must have tripped the alarm.'

'When was the other time?' Damien asked. 'You said you'd tried twice.'

'I climbed out of the window,' he explained. Damien, Melissa, and Eddy tilted their gazes at the window. It was square, with a lock mechanism at the bottom of it. The window opened from the top, with hinges that allowed it to swivel inwards.

'What happened?'

'We tied the bedsheets together so I could climb down. It's pretty high. Before my feet touched the floor outside, another loud alarm went off. The same sound as when I tried it the first time. I dropped to the floor and ran, but I'd hurt my ankle when I landed, so I didn't get far.'

'How far did you get?' Damien said.

'Halfway down the driveway. I shouted but the traffic on the road was busy. No one heard me. Then someone grabbed me from behind and carried me back to the room.'

Melissa started to cry again. Eddy stared at the floor vacantly. Damien absorbed this information but tried his best to think of something, as he too, glanced away from Joseph.

'Has anyone else been in this room other than you three?' Damien asked.

'Yes. You're the third set of three to come here.'

'Where – where did the others go?'

Joseph shrugged. 'We don't know. The men sometimes come in and choose one of us. Sometimes two. We'—he motioned himself, John, and Annie with his hand — 'all arrived at the same time. We haven't gone anywhere, yet.'

He went on: 'As far as I know, we are safe in this room. We get food and water. We have a bed to sleep in and we have toys. When we get picked. I don't know where we'll go, so without knowing what will happen, I want to stay here.'

'How many—'

Damien's question fizzled out when he heard something on the other side of the door.

Footsteps.

All six of them focused on the door. Twelve watching eyes, wide and alert.

Then a buzzing sound was heard. Damien frowned at the door. It was almost like a hive of angry bees.

'Say goodbye to your hair,' John whispered.

Damien glanced his way. 'My hair?'

'Yeah…' Joseph said, 'just before they cut your hair, a man stands on the other side of the door for a minute with the sheers turned on. Then he comes in and shaves off your hair. Like I said, I've had mine done six times now.'

After the minute passed, the sound of the hair clippers stopped outside the door. Damien, Eddy, and Melissa glared with anticipation.

The door creaked open. Standing there, with a set of clippers, was a small stocky man with a greasy face and tanned skin. He entered the room, staring at them all.

'Who's first then?'

Melissa dug her head deeper between her knees and started to cry.

The man holding the clippers started to laugh and went over to her first.

51

Friday Early Afternoon
Claxton Avenue, Mowden

After getting Jane Cornforth's address from the headteacher at Rise Carr College, Tanzy and Andrews made their way over to the west end of town. A little while later they turned into Claxton Avenue.

'What number is it?' Andrews asked, squinting to see the signs along the street.

He told him.

Andrews pointed. 'There it is, small porch, white front door, wide window.'

Tanzy checked the rear-view mirror and angled over, slowing the car and pulling up onto the vacant kerb. There was a black Fiat Punto sitting on the driveway. Tanzy recalled it wasn't the same car that Jane Cornforth had left the school in less than half an hour before. It could be her husbands if she was married. Tanzy assumed she was as the headteacher at the school had referred to her as 'Mrs'. He opened the car door, the cold air fresh on his bald head. He reached up, scratching his throat for a second, a faint rash lingering from a shave earlier that morning.

Tanzy and Andrews met at the front of the car and stopped at the edge of the drive, assessing the house for a moment, quickly scanning the windows for any movement. They both moved down the side of the Punto and Tanzy, who was in front, placed his palm on the bonnet of the car. It was ice cold. The car hadn't moved for a while. 'Let's go see—'

A loud siren came from the left, cutting him off. They turned curiously at the noise, growing louder by the second.

An ambulance roared down the road towards them, coming to a stop in front of the house they were standing at. When it had stopped completely, the paramedic in the passenger seat, a small, but muscular, fit-looking woman, stepped out and glared at them.

'Is he okay?' she shouted, rushing to the side door and swinging it open. She grabbed a medical bag, slammed the door and turned. 'Is he okay?' she asked them again.

Tanzy frowned at the paramedic. 'Who?'

'Her husband?' she said, stopping in front of them. 'Is he okay?'

Tanzy frowned.

'Who are you two?' she asked, noticing Andrews in a uniform.

'Detective Inspector Orion Tanzy. This is PC Andrews. Why – why are you here? What's happened?'

'I'm Jessie. He's Paul.' She pointed towards the ambulance. 'We received an emergency call not long ago. An individual at this address required immediate assistance,' she said, panting. From the back of the ambulance appeared another paramedic, who they assumed was Paul. He was average height, quite stocky, with a kind face but hardened. Proof of years of experience involving these types of situations. He stepped down onto the driveway.

'You the police?' Paul asked. 'Can you get us inside?'

Tanzy went to reply but Jessie, with the medical bag over her shoulder, stepped around him.

'We've just got here. We're looking for a woman called Jane,' Tanzy explained. 'She was—'

'That's who made the call,' the man replied. 'We're here for her husband.'

Jessie used her hands as a visor and looked through the cold glass of the wide living room window. Her mouth opened in horror.

'What is it?' Tanzy said quickly, noticing her change in expression.

'You need to get us in there, now!'

52

Friday Afternoon
Claxton Avenue, Mowden

Tanzy took a step back, lifted his right foot, then with everything he had, he lunged forward into the white door. There was a loud crack as the lock snapped but the door didn't fully open. The metallic parts of the lock had bent. He sighed, tried again, and this time the door flung open, the door pounding into the wall inside the hallway.

Jessie, the female paramedic, moved past Tanzy into the house.

'Hey, wait!' Tanzy gasped, trying to grab her shoulder to hold her back but missing. 'Wait, we don't know who's in there.'

She dashed down the hallway but abruptly came to a halt at the doorway to the living room, staring into it.

Tanzy caught her up, Andrews just behind. Shoulder to shoulder, Tanzy and Jessie with wide eyes, glared in horror at what was on the floor in front of them.

Blood. Plenty of blood.

'Jesus!' Tanzy gasped, absorbing the scene before him.

Jessie stepped into the hot living room and stood over the man, who was lying on his back, carefully minding her footing near the blood surrounding him. The man's still eyes were wide open staring vacantly at the low ceiling above. There was a smell in the air that was familiar to Tanzy. Pastry or croissants, something like that. There was also a faint smell of lavender. Fabric softener he assumed, possibly coming from the nearby radiators drying damp clothes.

Paul entered the room, stepping around Tanzy and Andrews, to see Jessie down on her knees, looking over the man.

'Good God...' he puffed.

'I – I think this is a scene for you guys and forensics,' Jessie said, slowly standing. Paul agreed.

Tanzy turned to Andrews. 'Call it in, get the team down here immediately.'

Andrews nodded, pulled the radio from his belt, and stepped back into the hallway.

'What you think happened?' Jessie asked Tanzy, who was methodically analysing the scene and everything around it. The man's head was almost a metre from the door. His feet were pointing in the direction of the corner just left of the window, where a flat screen television sat neatly on a thick, expensive-looking wooden unit. The floor was a light wood, bordered by low stylish skirting boards that ran around the outside of the room, and the walls were a light blue. Two light-brown three-seater leather sofas sat perpendicular to each other, one on the left-side of the room facing the window, and the other on the right, facing the fire, which was just behind the man on the floor.

'Well,' Tanzy started, 'judging by that knife in his hand, chances are it could be self-inflicted. Could have severed his own femoral artery. The blood would have nearly gushed out, which would explain why there's so much of it.' Tanzy paused a beat, then faced Jessie. 'What was the nature of the call?'

'His wife rang for an ambulance, told the operator that he needed emergency assistance. Whatever assistance it was, as you can tell, we're past that point now.' She gave a sad smile, looking down at him.

'Yes, we are,' Tanzy sighed. He peeled his focus away from Jessie and glared back down at the floor. 'Maybe she had contact with him before this happened. Maybe that's why she left the school so suddenly.' He studied the knife on the floor. 'In your opinion, standard kitchen knife?'

Jessie, after a few moments, nodded. 'Looks that way.'

In the doorway, PC Andrews appeared, his complexion pale.

'They on their way?' Tanzy asked him.

'Coming now,' he confirmed, leaning to one side for support.

'You okay? You look like you've lost a little colour?' Tanzy commented, and, without making it obvious, both paramedics glanced his way, both understanding the situation.

'Think it was something I ate earlier. Stomach isn't right. I'll be okay soon.'

Tanzy nodded. 'Go outside. Have a breather if you want?'

Andrews, who didn't take much persuading, nodded and silently made his way to the door, stepping out into the cold, crisp afternoon. The skies above were still grey, the sun nowhere to be seen. It wouldn't be long until darkness was upon them and the frost would set in. They'd use portable lamps and UV equipment anyway, so Tanzy wasn't worried about it getting dark.

'Hey, what's that?' Tanzy said, pointing down at the front of the sofa, seeing something black on the floor, just next to the man's right hand. He tilted his head, aiding him to identify the object. Half of it seemed to be underneath the bottom of the sofa. 'Is it a mobile phone?'

'It could be, yeah,' Paul said, leaning over.

'We'll collect that soon. Forensics won't be too much longer.'

'There's something else,' Paul said, his finger angled further along the sofa. Another object. This was large and longer. He edged around the bloody body and lowered himself to his knees and bent forward. 'Looks like a laptop, maybe?'

'A laptop?' Tanzy repeated.

'Yeah – have you got a torch or a light? There's something white on top of it. Looks like paper?'

Tanzy reached inside his grey Parker jacket and pulled out a thin, silver Maglite, then bent down and handed it to him. 'Here.'

Paul turned on the light and lowered himself to the floor again, careful not to touch the feet of the man, and shone it under the sofa into the three-inch space. 'It's an envelope.'

'Okay, we'll wait for forensics to check for prints first before we touch it. Good spot.'

Paul shuffled back from the body and stood up, handing the torch back to Tanzy.

'Really think it was self-inflicted?' Jessie asked, frowning down at the man.

'It could be. It would have been difficult, though. I wouldn't fancy doing it,' Tanzy admitted, wincing.

'Where are his clothes?' Jessie asked, looking around carefully.

Tanzy shrugged.

'Never mind his clothes,' Paul said, 'where is his penis?'

53

Friday Afternoon
Claxton Avenue, Mowden

By the time that the forensic team had turned up, the afternoon sun was fading. Tanzy had turned on the lights inside the house and stood back, whilst Tallow, Hope, and Forrest, all dressed in white plastic coveralls and white face masks, stood around the body. Andrews was still in the hallway, struggling with the nausea he'd felt ever since he'd entered the living room.

Tanzy, standing at the far wall, now in overshoes and acting as first responder, with a A4 clipboard, had the job of signing team members in and out. Not a job he usually did, but Andrews, usually very capable, didn't seem on the top of his game today.

'Where the hell is his dick?' Tallow said, slowly shaking his head at Tanzy in amazement.

'I haven't seen it if you're actually asking me,' Tanzy replied. Then, to his right, he heard people enter the house, their footsteps echoing on the wooden floor in the hallway. It was Byrd, followed by DC Anne Tiffin.

'Welcome to the party, Max, what took you so long?'

'Reports and traffic. Usual shit. Is it bad?' he asked, joining him in the doorway to the living room.

'Bad enough,' Tanzy replied, moving a little to the left, allowing Byrd to see into the room. The naked man was still in the exact position he'd been discovered. Forensics hadn't moved the body yet.

Tallow briefly smiled at Byrd before focusing back on his camera, taking some more shots, the brilliant flash lighting up the room like stabs of lightning.

Amanda Forrest was on her knees, next to the laptop, envelope, and phone. Tanzy had mentioned seeing it under the sofa so, very carefully, without touching the pool of blood or the body, they'd lifted the sofa upright onto its side, leaning it against the small space of the wall next to the window, giving them better access. Under the light of the temporary lamps situated around the room, Forrest noticed a name written on the envelope.

Tanzy, watching her from a distance, noticed her frown, and asked, 'What does it say?'

'Jane.'

'Jane? That's the name of his wife,' Tanzy said. 'Likely suicide note.' He then turned his attention to the right of the room, noticing Tallow duck under the archway leading into the rear dining room. There was an old-fashioned dining room table with a polished sheen finish which reflected the glare of the temporary lighting they'd set up. On the far wall, there was a set of French doors that led out to a patio and garden. The left wall was filled with a brown unit with several shelves on. One was lined with four small six by four photo frames, the top two were filled with paperback books, all different colours, all different heights, a mixture of well-known and not so well known authors.

'See anything?' Tanzy asked Tallow, watching him near the French doors.

Tallow paused, angled his gaze upwards. 'Come see this.'

Both Tanzy and Byrd frowned, and then left their position near the chimney breast, stepping under the archway into the dining room. 'What is it?'

'Look,' Tallow said. They moved around the table to where he was standing.

'Jesus… is that…?'

Byrd saw it too. 'God…'

Tallow leaned over and, with gloved hands, picked up the object, then studied it for a few seconds. Stunned, he shook his head. 'Not often you find one of these at a crime scene.'

Tanzy padded over and stopped before them. 'He was blessed, wasn't he?'

'Seems that way,' Tallow replied, then looked into the living room. 'Hey, Hope.' She glanced his way. Holding the object for her to see, he said, 'I found the penis.'

'I don't want to see it,' she shouted, turning away. 'Bag it up. You can deal with that shit,' she replied, continuing to focus on what she was doing. Tallow gave Tanzy a half smile and moved around the table towards the forensics kit, which had been left under the archway. He picked up a bag and carefully dropped the penis into it, running his thumb and index finger across the top to seal it.

'How are you doing, Amanda? Tallow asked her.

She glanced up, half-smiled at Tallow and Tanzy. 'Erm… okay. Should we… should we open this?' She held the envelope in her hands, aiming the question at either Tanzy or Byrd, hoping one of them would answer.

'Yes, open it. We need to see what's inside,' Tanzy decided.

Judiciously, she turned the envelope and peeled away the seal, then pulled out the paper inside. All eyes were on her. She unfolded the paper, read the words, then said out loud: 'Jane, I'm sorry for the person I've become, I can't do this any longer.'

'Maybe Jane can help us with what this means exactly,' Tanzy commented. 'We need to speak with her as soon as possible.'

'Sir,' Andrews said, appearing in the doorway, his face still pale. 'Just had a call through. There's been a serious RTC on Woodland Road near town. A woman has been badly hurt, currently unresponsive. Ambulance and police are there.'

Tanzy nodded, waiting for him to go on, wondering why he was eager to tell him.

'According to the driving license in her purse she's been identified as Jane Cornforth.'

54

Friday Night
Darlington

In a very spacious study on the first floor of the mansion, Jonny Darchem was sitting at his desk looking through old photographs, reminiscing about the past. He was looking at a photo of his mother and father. They were at Redcar, standing on the beach. The flat, dull sea was placid behind them, the sky pleasant but dotted with clouds.

Footsteps came from the landing. Darchem looked up, seeing Jamie appear in the open doorway.

'Got a minute, boss?'

'Yeah, sure, come in,' Darchem told him.

Jamie sauntered into his office and stood before him. The office was rectangular with a large window at the end of it. Darchem's desk was on the left-hand side, catering a computer screen and an array of folders and paperwork upon it. Above the desk, there were photographs of Darchem's mother and father from years ago. The happy times. Behind him, on the right wall, were several head-high bookcases filled with paperbacks and hardbacks. Jamie didn't know whether Darchem read a lot of books or if they were just for show. He had never asked.

'What's happening with the next batch?' Jamie asked, looking down on him.

'It's being delivered tonight. I'll send some of the boys to go pick it up. We're going to try something different.'

Jamie frowned. 'Changing the supplier?'

Darchem shook his head. 'No. He's cheap and the product is good. So no, we're not changing the supplier.'

'What about what happened last year? Did it come from him?'

Darchem shrugged. 'These things happen, Jamie. If people want to risk having a good time and doing drugs, they have to accept the responsibility that sometimes there are consequences. Sometimes things go bad.'

'But it was our product.'

'I don't care. That young lass is no concern to me. As long as we get paid, I'm not bothered. Neither should you be. Why the sudden concern, Jamie?' Darchem swivelled fully towards him, curious to know.

Jamie noticed Darchem's undivided attention on him. It made him nervous.

'Well?' Darchem insisted.

'I – I think if we supply someone a service, that service should be a certain standard. I remember reading the report in the newspaper when the police found the girl. There was rat poison in the powder. I know we didn't put rat poison in. Why would we?'

Darchem shrugged, raising a finger, expressing a point. 'Exactly, Jamie, why would we? We wouldn't. We send the product out there. People buy it. People like it. Then people come back for more. It's a simple process which has worked for longer than I've been in the game. Whatever happened to the girl was nothing to do with us.'

'But she bought it from one of us,' Jamie said.

Darchem's face became more serious. 'Jamie, my boy, I need you to drop this. Whatever it is that you're thinking about, nothing will come of it.'

Just over a year ago, there had been a 999 call from someone at a party on Swinburne Avenue. A seventeen-year-old male had phoned emergency services when his friend had gone missing just after midnight. He, and several others, went looking for her. Over two hours later the girl had been found in Stanhope Park naked in a pool of her own sick. The cocaine she had taken, according to medical reports, had contained rat poison. The amount of alcohol she'd consumed, which had thinned her blood, allowed the poison to hit her bloodstream quicker than normal.

'Please drop it, boy,' Darchem told him.

Jamie nodded slowly, unsure. 'I feel bad because I was there at that party, boss. I'm the one who sold her the product.'

Darchem slammed his palm onto the desk quickly, the sudden bang echoing around the room making Jamie tense.

'Drop it, now. I'm not telling you again,' Darchem said, coldly. 'Do. You. Understand?'

Jamie sheepishly nodded and backed away out of the room.

Darchem sighed heavily after he'd gone. In hindsight, the girl wouldn't have died that night if Darchem didn't hand out the product when he did. His supplier had told him there could be an issue with it, that he'd had the powder out on his table at home the same time he'd had an infestation of rats, and that he'd kept rat poison nearby. He admitted to Darchem he'd spilled some rat poison on the table where the cocaine was and that it was unsafe to sell. Most of it would be fine but there was still a risk, the supplier had told him. Darchem wanted the product anyway at half the usual price. The supplier didn't want to lose money on the product and had agreed.

Then a day later, the seventeen-year-old girl died.

Darchem read it in the paper the following day.

And smiled.

55

Friday Night
Darlington

A few hours later, Darchem was down in the living room, sitting with Arthur. The huge television was on in the corner, but they were discussing what to do with the children upstairs.

'Damien isn't well,' Arthur told him, looking at a folder of Damien on his knee. There were five other folders just like it, closed on the seat next to him, piled on top of each other. They were profiles of Melissa, Eddy, Joseph, John, and Annie.

'Not well? How do you mean?' Darchem asked.

'He keeps saying his heart hurts. That he needs medication.'

Darchem stood up. 'Show me.'

A few minutes later they entered the bedroom on the first floor at the back of the house and switched on the light. Annie, John and Joseph were sound asleep. Melissa and Eddy were sitting next to Damien's bed, holding his hand filled with worry.

Darchem stopped next to the bed as Melissa and Eddy backed away quickly, returning to their own beds. 'What's up, Damien?'

'I have a pain in my chest and I feel sick. Really sick.' His voice was weak, his body frail and curled up. His face was as white as the bed sheet. 'I have a heart condition. I need my medication.'

Darchem turned to Arthur. 'He doesn't look well at all, does he?'

Arthur shook his head, a serious look in his eye. 'Can I have a word outside?'

Darchem agreed, leaving Damien, then closed the bedroom door. 'What's up?'

'Listen, Jonny,' Arthur started, 'no one is going to want him like this. We don't know how serious his heart condition is. He was fine a few hours ago. Last thing we want is a dead kid in this house.'

Darchem mulled over his words for a few moments. 'But we have a buyer for him. A guy from Manchester is coming in the morning. He liked the look of his picture.'

'In my opinion if you sell him like this your reputation will suffer. He needs to go home, back to his mother, before he dies. I'm no doctor but, if he continues to worsen, he'll be dead during the night.'

'Are you getting soft, Arthur?' Darchem asked, frowning.

'Jonny, you know me.' They focused on each other. 'You know me well. I couldn't care less what happens to the kid but, what I do know, is that we can't sell him like this. As I said, your reputation will suffer. I'm not telling you how to do business but you can't sell him. Why not offer Eddy plus one of the other kids?'

Darchem's face hardened. The thought of one of his employees suggesting something angered him. Then his face softened as he understood Arthur's point of view, realising it could affect his reputation.

'Tell you what,' Darchem said, 'I have an idea. Take the kid away. Tell the other kids you're taking him to get some medicine and that he'll be back soon. Do what you like with him. Throw him in the River Tees if you have to. Just get rid of him.'

'I understand,' Arthur said.

'Good.' Darchem turned and went back downstairs, leaving the problem in Arthur's hands.

Arthur returned to the bedroom with a smile on his face and stopped at the side of Damien's bed. 'Hey, Damien, we're going to take you to get some medicine. Okay?'

Damien half-smiled and managed a weak nod.

'Come on, let's get you up,' Arthur said, holding his arm and supporting his weight. Arthur went to where his possessions were and grabbed his shoes. He knew which were Damien's because he was the one who had taken them off. Bending down, he spread the empty shoe apart and placed it before Damien.

'Right foot,' he told him.

With a struggle, Damien raised his right leg, placing his bare foot into the cold shoe, then Arthur did the same with the other. From their beds, Melissa and Eddy were watching Arthur. Then Arthur put Damien's coat on over his grey pyjamas and led him out of the room, down the stairs, through the kitchen, onto the gravel outside.

The security light flashed on, illuminating the garden and garage space. Arthur's red Mondeo was parked in front of the garage. With an arm over the young man's shoulder he guided him across to the car, opened the door for him, and put him inside.

'Am I going home?' Damien asked once Arthur had climbed into the driver's seat and closed the door.

'Yes. But we need to get you some medication first. I know someone who can help.'

Arthur started the Mondeo, then guided the car down the side of the house onto the main road. Instead of going left, towards Damien's house, Arthur took a right instead.

Damien, crouched on the back seat behind him, was staring up through the passenger window in pain, watching the glare of the streetlights they passed every few seconds. Then the sound of classical music started playing from the front of the car. Damien stiffened slightly, remembering that the man had played it yesterday morning when he had brought them to the house.

It wasn't long before the car took a right and the view out of the window changed, as if the streetlights were set back a little from the road. Damien, using all of his strength, shuffled up and looked outside. They were on Coniscliffe Road heading in the direction of Broken Scar. Damien recognised it but didn't know the name of the road.

'Where are we going?' Damien whispered, slumping back down into the seat.

'To get you some medicine, Damien.'

A few minutes later Arthur slowed the Mondeo, took a left into Broken Scar, crawled up the steady incline, then down into the carpark at the bottom. He applied the hand-brake and switched off the engine.

'Where – where are we?' Damien asked, seeing nothing but darkness outside his window. He was terrified of the situation he was in, but he was too weak, too disorientated to care.

'The person who is giving us the medicine is going to meet us here. You'll be fixed up in no time,' Arthur told him, opening the driver's door and getting out. He then opened the back door and picked the nine-year-old up with ease.

In the darkness, with Damien in his arms, Arthur walked through the metal gate at the end of the car park and headed towards where he could faintly see the dams and the river in the light of the full moon above. He took a left and walked along the man-made footpath for a few minutes. The river to his right under the moonlight almost looked picturesque. There were no sounds around them, apart from Arthur's shoes and the soft flow of passing water. It would be almost impossible to see if not for the moonlight, but Arthur knew where he was going. He'd been here before, doing this exact same thing.

'I don't feel well,' Damien managed, as Arthur made his way carefully down to the riverbank.

'I know, young man, I know,' he whispered.

'Where are we going?' Damien asked, suddenly feeling Arthur manoeuvring down the muddy bank towards the water.

'To fix you.'

Arthur stopped at the side of the river, watching the flow of water before them. Then without a second thought, he threw Damien into the river.

56

'Shhhhh,' one of them said, raising a palm. 'Did you hear that?'

'Hear what?'

'Shhh.' The lad stared upriver, frowning.

His three friends, who were all drunk, glared at him as if he had three heads.

'What are you—'

'Shh, listen…' Jake said quickly.

'Jake, hear what?' a lad in a red jacket said.

'A splash. Just up there,' he said, pointing.

The four of them were sitting up in a tree, listening to songs on their phones and drinking beer. Jake had an infection and was on antibiotics for the next four days at least so he was sober and alert. He was just about to choose the next song when he heard the splash upstream.

'Hearing things, mate,' one of them said, laughing. The others laughed too.

Jake moved off the thick branch he was sitting on and made his way down the tree until he reached the floor.

'Where are you going, Jake?'

'You wait here,' Jake said. Using the light from his phone, he cautiously stepped down the muddy bank. He flashed his light on the river, glaring at the water flowing downstream, from right to left, staring intently into the limited light. The sound he thought he had heard sounded like someone jumping in. He found it odd as they'd been the only ones down here for a while now, and the water wasn't exactly warm.

If someone had jumped in or fell in, they wouldn't last very long.

'Jake, get back up here, dude!' one of the lads in the tree shouted from behind him.

Jake watched the river for a moment. He couldn't see it, so turned—

'Whoa…' he gasped. 'What is that?'

Something floated downstream, but he couldn't work it out. Then he saw an arm move. It was a body. A child? He moved closer to the water's edge. Whatever it was, it was level with him now. Then it rapidly passed him. The speed of the current was frightening.

'Shit, shit,' he said, panicking. 'It's – it's a… ah shit.' He placed his phone on the floor and quickly took off his coat, then took a step towards the water.

'What the hell are you doing?' someone slurred behind him.

'There's someone in the river. I'm going in.'

Without saying anything else, Jake jumped into the river and went after the moving body. Within a few seconds, he felt the current drag him to the centre of the river and, for a moment, he started to panic but tried to look downstream for any sign of the child. Just ahead, he could just about make him out, ten metres in front of him, his arms flailing side to side as he bobbed helplessly.

Knowing he didn't have long Jake leaned forward and started swimming front stroke. The speed of the water helped him along, until he banged his knee on a rock sending a hot pain up his body and he roared out in pain. He was sure he'd cut something and he wanted to stop but he needed to get the boy, needed to help him, so he powered on, his arms propelling him through the ice-cold moving water.

When he reached of the boy he grabbed the hood of his coat and pulled him back, causing the boy to moan.

'Hey, I got you, I got you!'

Jake wasn't sure what he was going to do now. The water was too deep to stand with a quick under current. He tried to steady his frantic breathing and keep both their heads above the water. To their left, he saw the river bank. He needed to get over there, get them to safety.

Starting to feel his own body tiring, he used his left hand to move toward the bank and pulled on the boy's hood with his right hand. After a few tries he realised he hadn't got far and the currents were very strong. Panic set in but he tried even harder, battling against the relentless power of the water, the lactic acid starting to build up in his muscles, clawing at his stamina and will to survive.

'Come on!' he screamed, dragging the boy as best he could to get to the bank. His left foot scraped the bottom of the river, and he felt the pull of the current lessen, a colossal feeling of hope growing inside. The idea of living almost overwhelmed him. In a tremendous amount of pain, he managed to pull the boy to safety, dragging him out of the river and placing him down on the stones. He stared down at him in the dark, hunched over himself, panting for a decent breath of air. He was freezing. The icy water had had a massive effect on him, so he understood why the boy was shivering profusely.

It felt like a lifetime but ten minutes later, his friends found them. Jake asked two of them for their coats whilst he took off the boy's clothes, leaving his pants on He laid him down on one coat and placed the other one over the top of him. He then told them to ring an ambulance.

It wasn't long before the sirens were heard in the distance.

Damien was still and unresponsive. Jake leaned over and whispered in his ear, 'Hold on, little man. Help is coming now.'

57

Saturday Morning
Darlington Memorial Hospital

Tallow and Hope had just arrived in the examination room of the pathology department. Arnold, with his assistant, Laura Thompson, had already taken Brian Cornforth's body out of the body bag ready for the examination. In the time they'd spent waiting, they'd taken a blood sample, a urine sample and strands of hair.

Byrd, Tanzy, the coroner Peter Gibbs, and PC Weaver were watching from a few feet away.

'We know what happened here,' Arnold started. 'From what you guys found at Claxton Avenue yesterday, it's clear he's received very disturbing injuries. The first one, as we can see'—he moved to his right towards Brian's head—'is major bruising around his throat.' He leaned in closer, picking up a magnifying glass from the trolley full of apparatus, and used it to inspect the injury. 'It looks like a wire of some sort has caused this.'

After a moment, he went to the second obvious injury that Brian had sustained. 'Here we can clearly see the penis has been severed. It has been cut off close to the base of it. We're left with a bloody pubic area. This will have to be surgically cleaned and examined to determine the type of cut and what instrument had caused it. We ran blood tests and toxicology, and we're waiting on results from them.'

'What was the official cause of death?' Byrd asked.

Arnold raised his finger, as if expecting the question. 'Good point. It appears from the bruising and the line around his throat that he was strangled by some type of wire, but he didn't die from that. Because of the amount of blood, in my opinion, when his penis was removed, the heart was still pumping and pushed a large proportion of blood out of the wound. Then, if we look closely'—he pointed to the throat. Byrd, Tanzy and the senior forensics leaned in. 'You can see a different kind of bruising. It was caused by two hands squeezing the throat. I think that was the official cause of death.'

Byrd and Tanzy nodded, mulling over his words. 'What else can you tell us from the short time in which he's been here?'

Arnold turned to his assistant, Laura, and said, 'Shall we?'

She nodded at him and moved further down so she was level with his knees. Arnold grabbed the nearest arm and pulled him towards the edge of the trolley, then both of them turned Brian onto his front.

On his back the detectives saw a mark that appeared to have been done by a whip.

'How old is that?' Tanzy asked, wincing at it.

'Only a few weeks old at the most,' Arnold informed them.

Byrd's phone rang inside his pocket, disturbing the silence of the room. He apologised and stepped back a few paces and answered it.

'Boss,' PC Weaver said. 'Mac has been through Brian Cornforth's laptop. I think it's obvious why the penis was cut off.'

58

Saturday Morning
Police Station

Byrd and Tanzy returned to the station, going straight into the office to speak to PC Weaver about Brian Cornforth's laptop.

She was tucked in under her desk to the right side of the room, her attention on the computer screen in front of her.

'Hey, Amy,' Tanzy said, pulling a chair out and sitting down next to her. Byrd took a chair from the next desk which was vacant, dragged it over, and dropped into it.

'Morning, boss,' she replied to Tanzy, then angled her gaze to Byrd and smiled.

'What do we have?' Byrd asked, wasting no time.

'Mac went through his PC. There was a substantial amount of child porn on there. Very disturbing images.'

'Jesus,' Tanzy said, shaking his head in disgust.

'I understand what the letter to Jane might have meant now.' He recalled the words on the paper found under the sofa at Claxton Avenue: *Jane, I'm sorry for the person I've become, I can't do this any longer.* 'She may have known about it,' he added.

Tanzy frowned at Byrd. 'It's unlikely.'

'Why?' Byrd asked, curious about his comment.

'The people who watch this stuff aren't quite wired properly. If she knew about it, with her being a teacher, she'd not only be disgusted by him but, if she took her job seriously, she'd have him arrested. If I was in that situation, that's what I'd do.'

'It's never that simple, Ori, and you know it.'

Weaver picked up on their disagreement and said, 'We don't know either way. We'll find out when she wakes up from her coma.' Her words distracted the detectives, bringing them back to what was important.

'What else did Mac find on the laptop?' Byrd enquired.

'It seemed there were documents about Cairnfield Developments. Planning ideas and drawing designs. There were also documents containing costs and a folder containing photos from previous jobs. I also came across a folder which was named 'The Team' which contained around thirty individual word documents. I haven't been through all of them but, from the first six or seven I opened, from what I can see, they contained information on individuals in the business trade. Two of them were plumbers, two others were electricians, one a plasterer… you get the picture.'

Tanzy and Byrd both nodded. Then Tanzy brought his hand up to scratch his chin for a moment. 'Was he a construction manager?'

Weaver shrugged. 'It's possible he could've been.'

'Okay.' Byrd straightened his posture in the chair. 'We'll wait for forensics to get back about the house on Claxton Avenue to see if there's any signs left by the intruder. In the meantime we need to speak to the doctors at the hospital, see how Jane is doing. We need to speak to her about the missing children and of course, about her husband, Brian.'

Tanzy nodded and stood up, ready for the day. He wasn't planning on being in all day because Pip had wanted to go somewhere with the kids. Eric wanted to go to soft play at some point over the weekend and Tanzy had agreed they'd all go. The last thing he needed was attitude and earache off Eric. In recent months, they hadn't done much as a family but he'd decided things would change.

As Tanzy went to leave PC Weaver's work area, DC Leonard appeared in the aisle before him, halting him in his stride.

'Boss, we got a call.'

'What is it, Jim?'

'Remember when we were knocking on doors in Claxton Avenue earlier, to see if anyone had seen someone enter the property of Brian and Jane Cornforth?'

Tanzy nodded, waiting.

'And there was a house opposite that didn't answer the door. The house with an old red Rover and old fashioned curtains.'

'I remember…' Tanzy said, wishing he'd get to the point sooner.

'Well, we've had a call from her. Her name is Margaret Dawson. She was out at the time but, after getting home and seeing the police van outside the house, she'd spoken to one of her neighbours who told her what'd happened to Brian. She has a camera on the front of her house that looks down on the driveway.'

'Okay…'

'She claims the angle of the camera can pick up the road and the house opposite, too.'

'Does it show what car it is?'

'Apparently it does more than that. It shows the man getting out of the car and walking into the house.'

Tanzy suddenly felt exhilarated. 'Come on, Jim, you're coming with me.' He patted his shoulder and walked around him, heading straight to the door and out into the car park.

59

Saturday Morning
Claxton Avenue

Less than ten minutes later, Tanzy and Leonard pulled up to the house. The woman, who'd made the call, watched them through the wide living room window as Tanzy brought his Golf to a halt. Tanzy glanced towards the house, noticing her behind the glass. She appeared to be in her sixties and a little plump, with short, silver hair. Behind her large, square glasses, Tanzy matched her gaze for a moment until she backed away and turned out of sight.

Before Tanzy had even stepped on her driveway the front door opened. Margaret Dawson waved at them, telling them to come inside, then courteously asked them both if they would like a cup of coffee. Not wanting to use any more valuable time, they both declined her offer, wanting only to see the CCTV footage.

'Please, come this way,' she said, her voice a little croaky.

Tanzy and Leonard followed her along the hall, then into the dining room where they walked through a haze of hanging cigarette smoke. Tanzy winced a little, noticing an ashtray full of cigarette butts on a large circular table surrounded by six chairs in the centre of the room. On the wall to the right, in the right alcove, there were several shelves, all jammed full of photographs. Some of them were black and white and some were in colour; some were small, and some were large. In the alcove to the left, there was an old, battered desk which had seen better days, which supported a large, thick computer screen, no doubt a modern piece of technology back in the year 2000. Wires trailed from the back of it down behind the desk, connecting to an ancient CPU unit and the electrical socket down to the left.

Margaret apologised for the mess and took a seat down in front of the screen. The chair looked weak, creaking under her weight, but she didn't seem concerned it would crumble under her.

Tanzy and Leonard stood behind her waiting for the screen to load up. To their left there was a set of wooden French doors which led out to a small decking area then, beyond that, an overgrown garden several weeks beyond needing a cut.

'I came back and noticed the people in the white suits. There was a tall man who was carrying a black case to the van. I asked him what had happened but he ignored me,' she said. 'That's when I knocked on Mary next door. She told me what had happened. Just awful. Poor Brian. How's Jane taking it?'

'We haven't spoken with Jane yet, so we don't know that information,' Tanzy replied with a thin smile, not wanting to speak about Jane or the crash on Woodland Road earlier. It was hard not to notice the CPU unit below them whirring away, the fan doing overtime until, finally, the desktop background appeared.

She nodded and clicked on one of the folders. There were hundreds of files, all with names that meant nothing to the detectives. 'Let me see,' she whispered, hovering the mouse over the colossal list. 'This one,' she said, finally settling on one then clicking on it.

The video file opened.

From the bar at the bottom, Tanzy noticed it was an hour long, and watched as the camera stared out onto the street. The primary focus of the camera was the old red

Rover on the driveway and the path beside it, but the road and the house opposite were clear and that excited Tanzy.

'Let me see,' she said again, using the mouse to scroll the time indicator forward until she stopped on seven minutes. 'This is it,' she told them, pointing to the screen.

Tanzy and Leonard watched intently.

At the top right part of the screen, a dark blue 4x4 appeared and stopped outside the house directly opposite. Tanzy knew it was a Kia Sportage, no doubt the same 4x4 as the one on the CCTV footage that had ran down the naked man on Cleveland Street.

For around five minutes the man in the driver's seat remained inside the car, his focus on something down on his lap. Then he leaned to his left, disappearing for a few seconds to grab something from the glovebox. The details of his face were okay, but not brilliant. It was clear the man had short dark hair, and that he was Caucasian. It was difficult to tell his age from this view. Also they recognised he was slim.

'Does he look familiar to you?' Tanzy asked Leonard, who shook his head.

'But you got him though, he's right there,' Margaret told them, stabbing the air in front of the screen, as if merely by seeing him on a camera they would put him straight into prison.

'I wish it was that easy,' humoured Tanzy.

The man stepped out of the car holding a box. He walked along the path a few paces then headed down the driveway to the front door. To the detectives he moved like someone would if they were between thirty and fifty. He didn't have that youthful bounce, nor was he slow and measured, just naturally relaxed going about his business. The door opened and there were a few words exchanged with Brian Cornforth before Brian nodded and the man stepped inside.

'If he's just delivering, then why's he going in?' Leonard said, scratching the side of his forehead.

Tanzy sat deep in thought but said nothing.

The time bar at the bottom of the screen indicated he'd been inside the Cornforth house for twenty-seven minutes before he opened the door and stepped down onto the path. He returned to the car and drove off, the car leaving the left side of the screen.

'And again, no plates,' Tanzy said in frustration. The camera was positioned so the car had come in from the right and out of shot to the left, not allowing them to see any of the front or rear plate.

'Would you mind if we put this video on a memory stick and take it back for analysis?' Leonard asked Margaret.

'Please, help yourself,' she insisted.

Leonard pulled a USB stick from the inside of his black fleece and lowered himself to the CPU to plug it in. Once retrieved, they thanked her and left the property, heading back to the Golf. Glancing over to the Cornforth house, now cordoned off by temporary plastic tape, Leonard said, 'Hopefully we can zoom in on the video. It's clear enough, just too far away.'

Tanzy agreed with him, and they headed back to the station.

C. J. Grayson

60

Saturday Morning
Police Station

The office was quiet.

Just the way Byrd liked it.

There were a few in, but it was far off full capacity. Usually it was quiet on a Saturday morning, but DCI Fuller had offered an open chequebook when it came to weekend overtime. Barry Eckles had increased funds to do whatever it took to clamp down on recent events.

Byrd sipped on his coffee, then placed it down on his desk. He was writing up his report from Brian Cornforth's house yesterday. It was difficult to write about the child pornography that Mac had found on his laptop and harder to consider that his wife, Jane, knew anything about it. When she's well enough to speak to him, he's hoping to find out she didn't know anything at all.

His phone to the right pinged with a text message. He moved it closer to him and opened it. It was from Claire. *Love you. Have a good day. Can't wait for our meal tonight x*

He'd completely forgotten they were going for a meal with her friend Alice and her husband Alex. She'd booked a table at Uno Momento for 7 p.m.. He placed his phone to the side and went back to his report. A few moments later he was disrupted by a ringing sound coming from Tanzy's desk phone.

'Hello, DI Orion Tanzy's phone, DI Byrd speaking.'

'Ahh... is this Orion Tanzy?' the voice asked. It was male, well educated and local.

'No, but it's his phone. I'm a work colleague of his. Who's calling?'

'My name is Peter Main. I have a graphic design office on Duke Street. Some of your colleagues came to my office asking for Andrew Cairn of Cairnfield Developments?'

Byrd thought quickly. Yesterday morning. DC Leonard had gone there with PC Weaver. 'Yeah, go on, Sir.'

'I was out at the time, but my assistant told me what your colleagues were looking for. They'd asked him to ring this number if I could help. The name on the card was DI Orion Tanzy.'

'Okay, go on,' Byrd encouraged him, taking his eyes of his screen. 'I can pass on the message when he returns to the office.'

'Okay. Well I haven't seen Andrew Cairn since I've been there so I can't help you with any information about what he does when he's here.'

Byrd felt a 'but' coming on.

'But,' Peter Main said, 'I remember I opened up one morning last year and there was a note in our personal letterbox. I'm assuming it was from him but there was no name on it.'

'Have you still got the note?' Byrd said.

'Yeah, hold on.' Byrd heard him shuffle and let out a slight groan, as if he was leaning to the side awkwardly. 'Yeah. It says if anyone comes in asking for me, give me a text on this number.'

'That's all it said?' Byrd asked, unsure of the relevance.

'Why do you want to speak to him?'

'It's an urgent matter. We need to ask him some questions. What is the number?'

'The number is turned off now,' Peter told him. 'Has been for a while now. But…' he trailed off.

'But what, Peter?'

'There was a package that was delivered here for him. It was too large to go in his letter box so the delivery driver knocked on my door and I took it in for him. I then rang the number. When I explained what it was, he told me to post the package to an address and that he'd pay me the postage and for my trouble. I couldn't argue with that.'

'What did he pay you?'

'After I posted it, the following day when I opened our letter box, there was a cheque for one hundred pounds. I rang him, saying there was no need but, as a thanks for my inconvenience, he insisted. So, I cashed the cheque. He told me to ring in the future if it ever happened again. But I think his number has changed or the line is disconnected because I haven't heard anything since.'

'Has there been any other packages?'

Peter said there hadn't been.

'Have you got the address you sent the package to? It's really important we get hold of him?'

'Is he in some kind of trouble?' Peter asked, now starting to annoy Byrd.

'No, sir. We need to ask him something which could be fundamental to helping us find a missing boy.'

'Okay, hold on.' Peter went silent for a little while, then said, 'Here it is.'

He told him the address and Byrd quickly pulled a sheet of paper from the printer nearby, scribbling down what Peter had said.

'Thank you, Peter, this will help in our investigation.'

'My pleasure,' he replied before hanging up.

Byrd pushed his chair out, stood up, and grabbed his coat. Across the office he stopped at PC Andrews' desk.

'You busy?' he asked him.

Andrews glanced away from his computer screen and pushed his lips out for a second. 'Just the report and a few phone calls I need to make.'

'Good,' Byrd said, 'you're coming with me.'

They left the office and headed across the car park to Byrd's X5.

61

Saturday Afternoon
Carmel Road, Darlington

The house was situated on Carmel Road North, roughly sixty metres up from the small roundabout at the end of Staindrop Road. It was colossal in size and had plenty of character. Byrd wasn't a property expert, but it was obvious it had been built before many of the properties in Darlington. He pulled up on the road, parking well onto the kerb to avoid disrupting the flow of traffic as Carmel Road was always busy. It was one of the main roads in Darlington.

On their way over, Byrd had told Andrews the story and the reason why they were there. He mentioned that Mandy Spencer, the mother of Damien Spencer, who had gone missing with Eddy Long and Melissa Clarke, had received threatening phone calls and notes left on her car, insisting that if the planning permission didn't go through, there would be consequences. According to Mandy, she'd rejected permission for a plot which Cairnfield Developments wanted to buy.

They wandered down the driveway, watching the house carefully, eyeing the windows, looking for movement. It was a semi-detached property, three levels high, with a high-pitched peak at the top of the house. The brickwork was old but well kept, aged perfectly in time, and stood solid, as if it had been there for two hundred years and would stand for two hundred more. To the left of the house, there was a wide, double, brown front door, which looked like it had been painted recently. The paint-work around the windows and windowsills also looked fresh.

Byrd noticed the driveway to the left continued down the side of the house to the rear of the property. Parked in front of a garage, he could see a Silver Bentley, the registration D2RCHM. Byrd knew who it belonged to but took out his notepad and jotted it down, then put it back in the inside pocket of his long coat. He could see no other cars, but there could have been more around the back out of sight.

Byrd stepped up onto the extravagant semi-circular shaped step and knocked on the door three times, his knuckles feeling the cold against the solid oak.

They seemed to wait forever until it slowly creaked open and, standing there, was a man who appeared to be in his forties. He was smaller than both Byrd and Andrews and sported a scruffy beard. His hair was thinning, greasy, in desperate need of a shower.

'Can – can I help you?' he asked, eyeing up the detectives.

'Good afternoon. I am Detective Inspector Max Byrd. This is my colleague PC Josh Andrews. Would it be possible to speak to Andrew Cairn?'

The small man frowned for a moment, his hand still holding the door, and then said, 'Mr Cairn isn't at home at the moment.'

'You sure?' Byrd asked.

He frowned hard. 'That's what I said.'

'Where is he?'

The man shrugged. 'I don't know. I'm not his babysitter.'

'Then who are you?'

'Sorry?'

'Who are you, what's your name?'

'Andy,' the man said.

'Andy?'

'Just Andy…'

'Not Andrew Cairn?'

Just Andy shook his head.

Byrd smiled. 'Well, *Just Andy*, do you know when Andrew will be home?'

The man shrugged again. 'I don't. I'm sorry. What is this about?'

'I need to ask him a few questions about his business. That's all, nothing major,' Byrd told him, then he looked beyond Andy, into the huge hallway.

Andy edged the door closed a little. 'Well, like I said, he isn't here.'

'Would it be okay if we come in?' Byrd asked.

The man narrowed his eyes. 'Do you have a warrant, Detective?'

Byrd shook his head.

'Then no, it isn't okay for you to come in.'

A few seconds of awkward silence passed before Byrd said, 'Let Mr Cairn know we've been, and that we'll be back real soon. Okay?'

Andy gave a smile and nodded his head. 'Sure thing.' Then he took obvious pleasure in slamming the door closed.

Byrd and Andrews turned, stepped down onto the driveway and made their way slowly back to the car parked at the side of the road.

As they climbed in, Byrd pulled out his phone and found the number he needed.

'Who you ringing?' Andrews asked.

Byrd ignored him, listening to the ringing in his ear until it was answered by DC Anne Tiffin.

'Anne, are you near a computer?'

'Erm… I'm not but I can be in a minute.'

'Please.'

A moment of silent passed.

'Right, I'm back at my desk. What is it you need?'

Byrd heard her tapping on the keyboard through the phone. 'I need you to run a check on a registration plate for me. It belongs to a Bentley.'

'Okay, go ahead.'

'D. 2. R. C. H. M.'

'Hold on, sir.'

Byrd waited, staring out onto Carmel Road at the gentle flow of passing traffic.

'Got it. It belongs to a Jonathon Darchem.'

'Jonathon Darchem?'

'Yeah,' she confirmed.

Byrd sighed heavily. 'Thank you, Anne. Thanks for checking that. How's it going at the office? Has Orion got back yet?'

'Just got back now. He mentioned the footage from across the road at Claxton Avenue. The quality isn't very good so were going to speak to Mac to see if he can adjust it. You heading back?'

'Yeah. Mention to Orion about the registration and who it belongs to. I'll see you soon,' he said, hanging up, putting the phone back into his pocket.

'Who is Jonathon Darchem?' Andrews asked, eyeing him suspiciously, then glancing back to the house wearily.

'Jonny Darchem is one of the most dangerous men in this town. His name has been whispered amongst people for years. He supplies drugs and deals in violence. In fact he supplies most of the drugs in the area and has an extensive number of people working for him. We know what he's up to, but we've never got anything on him. I've certainly never known where he lived.'

Andrews looked back at the house. 'Seems to be doing okay for himself, doesn't he?'

'He does.' Byrd turned on the engine and glanced in the side mirror before he pulled out. 'Chances are, there's no such person as Andrew Cairn, and he's using it as a front for a legitimate business.'

'Crafty bugger.'

'Come on…' Byrd said, annoyed with the constant flow of traffic, looking for a gap to pull out.

'What are we going to do about Darchem?'

Byrd's phone rang in his pocket. 'Hold on, Josh.' He pressed a button on the dash to transfer it to the car and pressed answer on the central console. 'Hello?'

'Is this Detective Inspector Max Byrd?'

Byrd didn't recognise the voice. 'It is, who's calling?'

'My name is Doctor Ian Donald from Darlington Memorial Hospital. I have some good news and bad news for you.'

Byrd absorbed his words, and replied with, 'Go on, Doctor…'

'The body of Damien Spencer was pulled out of a river last night by a seventeen-year-old male.'

'Jesus,' Byrd gasped. 'What – what happened?' Byrd took a right at the small roundabout and clicked on his indicator, pulling over to the side of the road so he could concentrate.

'It's unclear. According to the boy who saved him, who was there with his friends at the time, he heard a splash and saw Damien floating down the river. He dived in and went after him. A very, very brave thing to do.'

'Absolutely,' Byrd agreed. 'How did Damien get into the water?'

'We don't know that yet, neither does the young man who saved him. He just heard the splash, but it was too dark.'

'How's the young man doing?'

'We brought him in with Damien last night to check him over. The river water was close to freezing. He was okay though, no damage done. We took a statement and let him go earlier. We checked on the missing persons in and around Darlington, and the young lad fit the description of Damien. We called his mother straight away and she rushed down to see him.'

'How is Damien? We will need to speak to him as soon as possible. Get an idea what happened leading up to this.'

'Well that's the bad news, I'm afraid.'

Byrd said nothing, waiting for the doctor to tell him.

'He's in an induced coma. It was clear to paramedics he was not only suffering from hypothermia, but he was medically unstable. He has an issue with his heart and hasn't been getting his daily intake of medications.'

Byrd felt a pang of guilt he hadn't found out until now. 'Okay, Doctor, thanks for letting me know. We'll be in soon.'

62

Saturday Afternoon
Darlington Memorial Hospital

Opening her eyes, Jane Cornforth felt groggy, as if her mind wasn't completely in sync with her body. Her vision was blurred, but she vaguely noticed the lights above her. Two of them. They looked like flying saucers, moving side to side every time she blinked.

'Jane?' she heard a voice say. 'Jane, dear, are you awake?'

Her eyes fluttered and her vision returned. In front of her was a female nurse with short blonde hair, somewhere between fifty and sixty. She was thin and a little on the frail side but had kind eyes behind the thin glasses she wore at the end of her pointy nose.

'Jane, can you hear me? Nod if you can hear me, dear,' asked the nurse.

Jane Cornforth, dressed in the white nightie that the nurses had changed her into, nodded weakly.

'Good, Jane, that's brilliant. Are – are you able to sit up a little? There's some people who want to ask you some questions?'

'Could I...' she trailed off, her voice weak.

'Sorry, honey, could you say that again,' the nurse asked, patiently.

'Water?' Jane managed.

'Of course. Let's get you up and I'll get you a drink.' The nurse propped her up and placed a pillow behind her, then leaned over to the bedside table and poured a glass of water. 'Here you go.'

Jane's trembling hand took it, and she managed a sip before handing it back to the nurse.

'There's some people here that would like to speak to you. Would that be okay?'

Jane wearily nodded.

'Okay,' the nurse said, turning to the door. 'She says it's okay.' Then she turned back to Jane. 'If it gets too much for you or you feel unwell, press this button' — she lifted up a piece of plastic with a button at the top connected to a thin wire that ran along the bed towards a machine behind her — 'and I'll be straight back in, okay?'

'Okay.'

The nurse left the small room. DI Tanzy and PC Weaver sauntered in.

'Good afternoon, Jane,' DI Tanzy said quietly, stopping by the side of the bed. 'How you holding up?'

'I feel – I feel sore.' She tried to move up a little and winced.

'Hey, let me,' Tanzy insisted, getting her more comfortable.

'Thank you,' she whispered in pain. 'I feel like I've been hit by a wall.'

Tanzy took a few steps back, giving her some space. 'Can you remember what happened?'

She narrowed her eyes in thought. 'I was at the school. My husband texted me… he… he needed help.' She glanced to the window, piecing the story together in her mind. 'Then I left.'

Tanzy nodded, realising her memory was a little foggy about what had actually happened. He'd spoken to one of the doctors before he came in to see her who'd confirmed that there might be a possibility she would be confused. Tanzy was also aware she didn't know about her husband's death and he would have to break the news the best way he could.

'Can you remember driving on Woodland Road?' Tanzy asked.

'I – I don't… what happened?' Her eyebrows furrowed in confusion.

'You were involved in a car crash. A vehicle hit the side of your car, flipping you twice and you landed on the side. The fire brigade had to break into the car to get you out. Thankfully, the only damage is that broken arm you have there.'

She only noticed the pot on her arm. She looked down, placing her right hand on top of it. Her face went blank. 'I don't understand…'

'We came to see you at Rise Carr about the disappearance of the missing children. We were waiting in the reception area for you, but you got into your car and sped away, heading for home.'

Her memories flooded back.

'Oh, God…' She raised a hand to her mouth. 'Brian. I was going home to Brian. He needed help. Is he okay?'

'Why did he need help, Jane?'

'He – he erm…' she sighed, unsure how to say it, then collected her thoughts and tried again. 'Brian hadn't been feeling well in recent weeks. Not physically, but mentally. He's had it before but not as bad as this.'

Tanzy frowned.

'Depression,' Jane said weakly, filling in the blanks for him. 'He's on tablets for it. They're helping but he's not quite himself.'

Tanzy let her trail off and waited a few moments. 'What does he do as a job, your husband?'

'He's a project manager. Works for a company called Cairnfield Developments. They build houses, sometimes apartments. He works from home a lot and travels to various sites.'

'Does he spend a lot of time on his laptop?'

Jane nodded twice but frowned. 'Every day. If he's working away, he'll take it away with him, to watch films on a night, he tells me. He's probably gambling or doing something else, for all I know.'

Tanzy and Leonard nodded, knowing what Mac had found earlier.

'Has he gambled before?' Leonard asked.

She glanced beyond Tanzy, and said, 'God, what man doesn't!' Laughing, she looked back at Tanzy and became serious. 'So, is he okay, is Brian okay, I was so worried about him?'

'Were you the one who phoned an ambulance for him?'

'Yes. Yes, that was me.'

'Why?'

'Like I said, he hasn't been feeling himself recently and he did mention, God I shouldn't be telling you this, but he'd been talking about his father a lot and about how he committed suicide. Then, for some reason, he was talking about the worst ways to die. I asked him to stop talking about it, but when he texted me saying he might do something bad, that's the first thought that came into my head.' She paused a beat. 'That's when I left the school, I had to check on him.'

'Has Brian ever self-harmed before?'

'He…' she fell silent.

Tanzy said, '*He* what, Jane?'

'He tried to commit suicide a few years back. After his mother passed away, he couldn't cope living without her. They were close, you see. Cancer took her in the end.' She glanced away vacantly towards the window, going back to the sad time in her head.

'Jane,' Tanzy said, grabbing her attention again. 'We have some bad news, I'm afraid.'

Jane frowned.

'It's your husband, Brian. He's dead.'

63

'God, that was hard work,' Leonard said, standing outside the paediatric ward with Tanzy. Jane Cornforth had broken down in floods of tears and attempted to get out of her bed. She'd tried to walk out the door but, in the weakened state she was in, had fallen and had done something to her ankle. The two nurses who were at the desk, outside in the hallway, heard the commotion and had come in, helping her back to her bed. Tanzy and Leonard had no further questions for her and left her alone, with her grief.

Leonard hung around until Byrd showed up and told both of his superiors he was heading back to the station to do some work before he knocked off for the day. He knew Byrd and Tanzy were going in to see Damien Spencer. Even if he wanted to, two people in there was enough.

Byrd stopped near Tanzy and asked, 'How'd it go with Jane?'

'Tough. Very tough. She's absolutely devastated.'

Byrd said nothing, expecting as much.

'How'd it go at Andrew Cairn's house?' Tanzy asked, scratching his goatee.

'Interesting,' Byrd said. 'Turns out he wasn't in, according to the bloke who answered the door. But'—he raised a finger—'I did see a Bentley down the side of the house and checked the reg.'

Tanzy smiled. 'I know. The infamous Mr Darchem.'

Byrd smiled briefly. '*There's* a name we haven't heard for a while.'

'I haven't missed it.'

Byrd agreed and told him that the man at the door had denied them access and told them to come back with a warrant. 'We walked away. We'll get the warrant and have a look around. If Andrew Cairn doesn't exist, then Darchem is using the business for his own reasons.'

'And make a shit load of money elsewhere.'

'Exactly,' Byrd replied, shrugging. 'The man is like Teflon. Nothing will stick to him.'

'See what Damien says. Might give us enough to get a warrant if he's the man responsible for this.'

They both waited at the locked double door, peering through the glass. It didn't take long for one of the nurses to notice and approach them with a curious smile. Smiling, she went into the room next to the doors the detectives were waiting behind and leaned into the microphone on the desk. 'Can I help you?'

'Detective Inspector Max Byrd with Detective Inspector Orion Tanzy,' Byrd said, showing his ID. 'We're here to see Damien Spencer.'

'Can I see your ID too?' she said, nodding at Tanzy.

Tanzy complied, pulling his badge from his coat, and holding it up to the glass. She was satisfied and pressed the button down to her right. The doors gave a loud continual buzz until Byrd took the handle and pulled it open.

The nurse, who appeared to be around the age of forty, with slim with dark long hair and blue eyes, stepped out of the office. 'Damien is down the hall, room sixteen. His mother is there with him. He's currently being treated with medication but is unresponsive. So if you're here to ask him questions, it won't be much use, but you can speak to his mother if you'd like.'

Tanzy nodded his thanks, and he and Byrd drifted down the corridor towards room sixteen, passing several open doorways where they could see patients, some awake, some asleep, some with family with them, whilst others were alone.

The door to the room Damien was in was open a few inches.

Tanzy knocked twice, and said a quiet, 'Hello.'

Inside the small room there was a bed to the right. On the far side were machines and a cluster of complex wiring, some attached to Damien. On the closest side of the bed to the detectives, Mandy Spencer was sitting, her body half turned to them, her face puffy and her eyes red, full of tears.

'Hey, Mandy,' Tanzy said, approaching her with a sad smile.

'Hi,' she replied, her voice flat.

'How's he doing?' Byrd asked, stopping at the foot of his bed. He had a mouthpiece over his face which had a long flexible grey hose trailing from the bottom to the right of the bed.

'He's alive,' Mandy said, 'and that's all that matters right now.'

Byrd smiled, feeling a lump forming in his throat.

After a few moments of uncomfortable silence, they had asked her how she was doing and then had left. They spoke to one of the doctors in the corridor. He'd eyed them suspiciously, wondering who they were until they had explained. He told them he would contact them as soon as Damien woke up but was unsure how long that would be. According to the doctor, Damien's body had some repairing to do and, in his opinion, it would be a few days before he'd be well enough to speak to anyone. They thanked him and left.

'Much planned for tonight?' Tanzy asked him on their way back to the car.

'Going for a meal with Claire and some friends.'

'Oh, very nice. Where?'

'Uno Momento. Can't be bothered with it really. All I want to do is go home, lay down and go to sleep. Too much going on.'

'Might do you good, chance to take your mind off things.'

'Maybe. You doing much?'

'Nothing special. Told the kids we'd go to soft play this afternoon, and they want to watch a film tonight.'

Byrd glanced his way. 'Sounds good.'

'Yeah. They choose a film after an hour of arguing about which one and then we order pizza and stuff our faces with sweets.'

'Think I'd rather come to yours then,' Byrd said, smiling.

'They're hard work, Max, but honestly, it's the best. When you have kids, you'll see.' Tanzy slowed as he approached his car.

Byrd waved the idea away. 'Too old now, I think.'

'Never too old. If that's what Claire wants, go for it.'

'I'll be forty-two next year,' he protested.

'And forty-three the year after, then forty-four, forty-five,' Tanzy laughed. 'It's only a number, mate.' Tanzy took a few steps away from him towards the Golf. 'How's your mam?'

'I'm going to see her today. She forgot who I was last time I was there.'

Tanzy gave him a sad smile, seeing his body physically deflate when he told him. 'Send her my best when you see her.'

'I will do.' Byrd drifted towards the X5. 'Enjoy film night.'

'Always do.'

They went to their own cars and both set off home. Neither was aware that one of them would be covered in blood later.

64

Saturday Night
Uno Memento, Darlington Town Centre

'What time did they say they were getting here?' Byrd asked, a few minutes after they sat down.

Claire, who was dressed in a white tight-fitting dress, her hair down by her shoulders, told him less than five minutes. 'They are dropping Callum off at Alice's parents before they come,' she added. 'They should be here any minute now.'

'You look stunning tonight,' he said, watching her closely, how her lips reflected the soft lighting coming from all areas of the room.

'You're not too shabby yourself, Mr Byrd,' she said. He was wearing a dark blue suit jacket over a light blue, thin jumper, dark slim-fitting jeans and the brown shoes which Claire had bought him a few weeks before. After telling him he needed some new clothes and reminding him continually without success, she had bought him some herself, along with a few jumpers and several pairs of jeans. The half decent clothes he had didn't fit him anymore and he looked utterly ridiculous because of the two stone he'd lost.

Byrd smiled, then glanced down at his wristwatch. It was nearly quarter past seven. 'By the way, where did you put the letter you mentioned from the DVLA? On the microwave?'

'Yeah. Just on top of your car magazines.'

'I couldn't see it the other night,' he said, shrugging.

'I'll find it tomorrow,' she reassured him.

He glanced around him, absorbing the scene. The noisy restaurant was filled to the brim.

Their table, which was set out for four people, was positioned towards the back of the restaurant, on a higher level than the front of the place. The lower level had the till, bar area and front entrance door and window. Byrd was sitting with his back to the door, facing the back of the room, towards the toilets. He did a quick sweep of the place. Instinctive, nothing more. Something he did when he entered a room out of habit.

'Who you looking for?' Claire asked him, frowning.

He met her gaze and smiled. 'No one.'

'Max, you're not on duty now. Relax, okay.' She placed her hand over his.

'Hold on a sec,' he said, pulling his phone from his pocket.

'You're not going to be on that all night, are you?'

She was half-joking, half-serious.

'Of course not, just checking something before—'

'Hey, Claire,' an excited voice said behind them, followed by a clatter of high heels.

Claire recognised the voice, turned, stood up and gave Alice a firm hug. She appeared so different to when Byrd had seen her a few nights ago. Her hair was curled, her make-up was perfect; dark mascara made her green eyes shine like glowing emeralds, grabbing the attention of every man in there.

She released herself from Claire and, as Byrd stood up, she placed her arms around him and squeezed. 'Hi, Max. Thanks for coming out.'

'I didn't have a choice really,' he said, grinning. The playful joke was followed by a gentle slap on the side of his arm. Then she moved to the opposite side of the table, took her coat off, and put it on the back of the wooden chair. 'Max, meet Alex,' she said, her palm facing towards the man at the edge of the table. He smiled at Byrd and held out a hand.

'Detective… nice to meet you.'

'Please, call me Max,' he said, taking his firm grip. 'Hey, I like that shirt.'

It was black, slim-fitting and appeared to be made from silk.

'The boss' choice,' Alex replied, nodding towards Alice.

Byrd laughed. 'I know exactly what you mean. Please take a seat. Actually'—before Byrd sat down, he pointed to the chair opposite. 'Alex, would you mind if I sat there?'

Alex frowned, glancing at the chair he was about to sit on. 'Yeah… if you like.'

'Thanks.' Byrd grabbed his jacket and went to the opposite side.

'Why?' Claire asked, confused.

'It's a better way to get to know each other,' Byrd told her, then smiled to his right, where Alice was looking strangely at him. 'You don't mind?'

She shook her head. 'No, as long as I like your aftershave.'

'You'll have to ask Claire. She chose that too.'

They all laughed and settled in. It wasn't long before a waiter came to take their drink orders then, a minute later, returned with some menus. The real reason Byrd wanted to sit there was because it would give him a good view of the front of the restaurant. He wanted to see who came in and who came out.

There wasn't a particular reason why, it was just the way he was wired.

A minute later the waiter came back with the drinks and placed them down on the table. He then told them their food would be coming soon and to enjoy their drinks. They talked about their days so far, Byrd, obviously, missing out some of the parts so they could enjoy their meals without feeling queasy.

The conversation they were having was drowned out by a noise behind Byrd, coming from the back of the restaurant. He turned slightly, frowning at the disturbance. At the back of the room, four men were arguing about something. Byrd couldn't quite hear what the conversation was about but he could tell it was getting tense. He heard one of them talking about money and another calling one of the other men a liar. The people around them stopped their conversations to also look their way. The men, aged between thirty and forty, didn't realise they were the focus of the restaurant, until a waiter passed by Byrd and approached their table.

One of them looked at the waiter, frowning in anger.

'Excuse me, Sir,' the waiter said quietly. 'Would it be possible just to turn the volume down a little? There are other people who I'm sure would like to enjoy their meals with a little less noise.'

The man sitting on the right-hand side at the back stared at the waiter, then the expression on his face softened as he raised his palm. 'Yeah, no problem, we apologise.' He glanced around the tables near him and apologised once more.

'Thank you,' the waiter said, turning and making his way back down to the front of the restaurant.

'Some people just don't give a shit,' Alex whispered, making sure only their table heard. Then he glanced at Byrd. 'So, Max, how long have you been in the police?'

Byrd puffed his cheeks out for a moment. 'Nearly twenty-three years. Went in when I was eighteen.'

'Good effort that.'

'It pays the bills,' he replied, picking up his pint of lager.

'Is it exciting?' Alex asked, picking up his drink, taking a sip, then placing it down.

'Sometimes. There's a lot of paperwork involved but that comes with most jobs now I guess.'

Alex nodded, knowing what he meant.

'What is it you do, Alex?'

'I'm a business analyst.'

'That sounds… interesting,' Byrd said, but it was more of a question.

'It can be, depends how much you like facts, figures, and formulas. It can get boring sometimes but it's all part and parcel of the job.'

Byrd took another swig. 'Been doing it long?'

Alex shook his head. 'Officially, only a year but I've done things like it in the past.'

'What were you doing before?'

'Army. Was in there for over ten years,' he confessed.

'Why the change?'

'I missed home too much. I missed Alice.' He glanced over and she paused her conversation with Claire and smiled at him. 'I missed the kids, too. Only being off for a few weeks at a time and then back for six months stints was too much. I know a lot of people do it, but I couldn't cope any longer. I'd been doing business analysis before I went in and wanted to test myself again to see if I could make something from it.'

'That's fair enough,' Byrd commented. 'How many kids you got?'

'Two. Boy and a girl. Callum who's twelve and knows everything and Lisa who's eighteen and knows even more.'

'Where are they tonight?'

'Callum is at Alice's mother's and Lisa is doing her own thing.' He took another swig. 'Do you have kids?'

Byrd shook his head. 'No…' He felt Claire's gaze drift over to him. 'Not yet anyway…' She returned her attention back to Alice.

'Even at forty-one, there's always time.'

Byrd didn't respond to him. He was glaring at the window at the front of the restaurant. A man was standing up against the glass staring right at him. Byrd held the gaze and, after a few seconds, even Claire had noticed his strange behaviour. 'Max?'

He looked her way and smiled. 'What?'

'Why are you staring over there?'

He focused back on the window, but the man had gone.

Byrd frowned. 'Sorry, I was lost there.' He picked up his drink, took a long swig, then placed it back down. 'How do you know my age?'

Alex smiled at him. 'You said you'd been in the force nearly twenty-three years and went in when you were eighteen. Simple mathematics.'

Byrd pointed. 'Very good. Must be that analytical thinking of yours kicking in.'

They shared a laugh and both picked up their drinks. Moments later the meals arrived. Byrd had ordered pizza and Claire had chosen lasagne. 'Looks amazing, thank you,' Claire told the waiter, who bowed his head at them and walked away.

'Here mate, fuck you!' a voice shouted from the back of the room.

The noise in the restaurant came to an abrupt halt, and everyone looked at the four men sitting at the table at the back. One of them stood up, knocking his chair back with the hind of his knees and threw his white fabric napkin down on his chair. He then headed into the toilet, leaving the three men at the table.

Coming up the steps that separated the lower and upper level, two waiters appeared, staring towards the back of the room. Byrd didn't really want to get involved tonight. The past week had been one of the most hectic in his life. If he could have just one night off that would be brilliant.

The level of noise returned to normal soon enough and everyone carried on with their meals.

'Excuse me,' Alex said, pushing himself out from the table and standing up. 'Quick toilet break, two minutes.'

Byrd, Claire, and Alice continued eating. Byrd joined in with their conversation about a building development somewhere on the edge of town.

Alex pushed open the door that led to a small corridor. The door to the left was the men's, the door to the right was the women's and the door straight ahead along the small corridor led to a door marked Exit. He pushed open the door to the left and stepped inside the toilet. It was a small space: a sink to the left, a urinal to the right and, next to that, a cubicle in front of him.

The man from the back of the restaurant was standing at the urinal. He didn't look around or acknowledge Alex as he walked in, passed him, went into the cubicle, and edged the door closed. He wanted to stay out of the way, let the man cool off.

A moment later Alex heard someone else enter the toilet.

'What the fuck are you looking at?' he heard someone say. 'If you don't get out of my face, I'll rearrange it for you.' The voice was slurred, probably too much alcohol.

'You should have done the deal, bro,' another voice said. Then there was sound of footsteps and then a loud sigh, followed by a thud against the side of the cubicle.

Alex froze, wondering what was happening, then heard the toilet door shutting followed by a loud bang.

'What the...' Alex muttered. It was silent in the toilet. 'Hello?' he said, creeping slowly out of the cubicle. No one replied. He popped his head around the edge of the cubicle door and, on the floor, was a knife, soaked in blood. He gasped, edging back a little.

A groan came from near the urinal. Hunched against the wall was the man he'd passed moments earlier.

'Are you okay, mate?' Alex asked, keeping his distance.

The man roared in agony, stood upright and stumbled towards Alex, who backed away quickly, hitting his lower back against the sink. The man collided into him, rubbing blood over his hands and shirt, then fell to the right, collapsing on the floor near the door of the cubicle.

'Jesus,' Alex whispered, looking down at the blood pooling beneath the man and at his own bloody hands, wondering what to do. He left the toilet, took a right, then opened the door back into the restaurant.

Byrd was laughing at something that Claire had said.

'Help me, please,' Alex said behind them.

Byrd stood and took a few steps towards Alex. There wasn't another sound in the upper floor of the restaurant.

'Alex?' Byrd said softly.

Alex stared vacantly at the floor, not responding to Byrd.

'Alex, what happened?' Byrd was in front of him, watching him carefully, quickly taking in his bloody hands and the wet patch of blood on his black silk shirt.

Alex put his hands out and grabbed Byrd, then fell forward into him, his legs buckling as he collapsed to the floor.

'Ring the police and an ambulance now,' Byrd shouted to anyone that was listening.

65

Saturday Night
Uno Memento, Darlington Town Centre

'Alex? Alex? ALEX!' Byrd shouted, tapping the side of his face with his hand. 'Alex?'

Alex's eyes flickered for a few moments, then opened fully. He stared up at Byrd who was kneeling over him. Most of the customers who had been sitting in the upper half of the restaurant had been moved to the lower part.

'Alex, are you okay?' Byrd said.

Alex nodded. 'I – I think so. What happened?'

'You passed out.'

He frowned. 'I've never done that before.'

Byrd heard footsteps behind him and turned to see PC Weaver and DC Leonard appear together. Neither was wearing their uniform.

'Sir,' Leonard said, focusing down on Alex.

'You two got here fast. They've only just called it in.'

Leonard, glancing at Weaver for a split second too long for Byrd not to notice, said, 'We were passing. What's happened?'

Byrd told them both what he knew. Leonard glanced to the table where Claire was sitting comforting Alice, who'd got upset after seeing Alex collapse.

A few moments later, two paramedics arrived. They lowered to Alex's side and asked Byrd what had happened. He told them, then moved aside, letting them take over. He stood and faced Leonard and Weaver. 'Something happened in the toilet. Come on.'

They were all off duty, so they were without a baton or pepper spray in case of trouble. They approached the door to the toilet and Byrd went first. 'Stay close,' he told them. Inside the small corridor, he noticed the door in front of him was wide open, cold, moist air coming in.

He looked out into the darkness. Heavy rain pounded the ground. He edged back inside and pushed open the door to the men's toilet. Inside he saw a man lying flat on his front, his head near the entrance to the cubicle with both his arms trapped underneath him. A circle of blood, roughly a metre in size, had pooled on the tiled floor underneath him.

'Jesus,' Byrd gasped. He recognised from the man's clothing it was one of the men who had been sat at the table arguing.

As Byrd visually checked the rest of the toilet, he noticed the knife on the floor.

'We need forensics ASAP.'

Weaver pulled out her phone and found the number for the operator.

Leonard peered inside the toilet. 'God,' there's never a dull moment in this town.'

'You've been spending too much time with Orion. He says that every day,' Byrd said, still focused on the man.

'Did you see anyone else go in?' Leonard asked Byrd.

Byrd thought hard and realised he hadn't. As it stood, Alex was their number one suspect.

66

Saturday Night
Police Station

DI Max Byrd was looking through the one-way mirror in one of the interrogation rooms at the station. Standing next to him was the smartly-dressed DC Leonard, arms folded, leaning against a filing cabinet a few feet to Byrd's right.

'What do you think?' Leonard said, turning his head to Byrd.

Byrd shrugged. 'I don't know what to think to be honest.'

On the other side of the glass, sitting at a table, positioned in the centre of the square room, was Alex Richards. After arriving in Byrd's car, he had been told to take off all of his clothes apart from his underwear and given a plain white t-shirt, a black jumper, some grey jogging bottoms and some spare trainers to wear, whilst forensics were taking samples of the blood. Amanda Forrest, the only forensic officer in the lab, had also taken a swab of the blood on his hands to make sure it matched with the blood on the shirt. Tallow and Hope were at the restaurant, working the crime scene and would be busy for a few hours at least.

Sitting across from Richards was DC Anne Tiffin. She'd volunteered to work late to cover a few PCs who'd had holidays booked in from last year. She digested the story he'd given. That he had walked into the toilets, passed a man standing at the urinal, entered the cubicle, heard someone else enter the toilet, a very short conversation, what sounded like a struggle, then a bang into the side of the cubicle. That he had then found the man hunched over in pain and then he'd stumbled into him. That was why the blood was on his shirt and hands.

'Did you get a look at the man who walked in?'

Alex sighed. 'I've already said I didn't. How many more times do I need to say it. By the time I came out of the cubicle, he'd gone. There was only the man who was attacked. He stumbled into me and I had nowhere to go.'

Tiffin nodded several times, making notes.

'Can I go home now?' he asked. 'My wife is waiting for me.'

In fact, his wife Alice *was* waiting for him, but not at the station or at home. Byrd had told Claire to take Alice back to their house and wait. He didn't think Alex was responsible, but it was a formality they had to check, a process which needed to be done right.

There was a knock at the door.

'Come in,' Tiffin said loudly.

PC Andrews entered. In his hand, there was a small fingerprint scanner, which he placed on the table.

Tiffin thanked him before he turned and left.

'Here, we have a fingerprint scanner.'

'I don't even know why I'm here,' he said, slamming his palm onto the table. 'I'm innocent.'

The words and sudden change in movement took Byrd by surprise.

'Then you won't mind me taking your fingerprints so we can eliminate you from the suspects?'

He stared hard at the fingerprint scanner and sighed heavily. 'Am I under arrest?'

Tiffin shook her head. 'No, you know you're not. But regardless of that, you can't argue how the situation looks.'

Alex thought about what she'd said and nodded a few times in understanding. 'As the law states, don't I need to be under arrest before you to take my prints?'

On the other side of the glass, Byrd sighed. 'Come on, Alex, don't go down this road.' Byrd knew, if he chose not to give his prints, then he may have to be arrested.

'Why is he being awkward?' Leonard asked Byrd.

'I don't know...'

Leonard looked back through the glass.

'That's true, Mr Richards. I see you're familiar with the laws,' Tiffin said.

Alex smiled.

'If you won't voluntarily give your prints, I'm going to have to arrest you.'

He laughed for a few moments. 'This is so stupid.'

Tiffin stared at him. 'What's it going to be?'

'Fine, I'll give you the prints.'

Tiffin turned on the printer and asked him to place each finger and thumb on it one at a time. Reluctantly, he did so.

'Thank you,' Tiffin said, pulling the scanner back to her side of the table.

Alex nodded. 'Can I go now?'

'Not just yet,' she said, finding her feet. 'I need to check something.' She left the room and closed the door, leaving him alone.

A minute later, the door to the room that Byrd and Leonard were in, opened.

'Got there with the prints eventually?' Byrd mused, smiling.

'Awkward one, your friend,' she noted, stepping inside and stopping at the glass to have a look at Alex.

'It wasn't him,' Byrd said.

'How can you be so sure?' Tiffin asked, frowning.

'Because whilst you were in there, I got a phone call from the manager of Uno Momento. Earlier, before I left earlier, I'd spoken to him and asked him to check the camera in the corridor outside the toilets. It shows Alex going into the toilet, followed by another man who appeared tense. Less than a minute later, the man ran out, took a left and went out the door that led to outside.'

'What was outside?' Tiffin asked.

'There's a yard with the bins and access to a back alley.'

'Okay. I'll tell him he can go.'

Byrd agreed. 'I'll take him back to mine. That's where his wife is.'

'So, chances are,' DC Leonard said, 'all the prints taken at the scene will be useless if the guy ran out the back?'

Byrd shrugged. 'Yup.'

When Byrd had seen Alex walk out the toilet and collapse on the floor, he'd told everyone sitting in the top part of the restaurant to move away but that they needed to stay, as they'd need to be questioned. As soon as PC Andrews arrived, he'd taken people's prints and contact information. That way, if there was a match with the prints on the handle of the knife, there would be confirmation.

'You mentioned the four men on the back table?' Tiffin asked.

'Yes. One of them was the victim. When Alex collapsed I scanned the room and there were only two people at that table. The third man was missing. My guess is that he's our guy.'

'We need to find out who was sitting there.'

'Already did,' said Byrd. 'The manager confirmed the booking was under the name of Carrington. Anne, look into males, aged thirty to forty with the surname of Carrington?'

'No problem. How long will forensics be at the restaurant?'

'A few hours at least. Tallow and Hope should be able to confirm Alex's story from what they find. They'll be able to decipher the blood spatter.'

The restaurant video is being emailed over. I'll take a look first thing tomorrow when I do my report.' Byrd yawned. 'There was me thinking I'd be able to go for a quiet meal and relax for a change. I should've known better.' They all shared a smile. 'Right, I'll take him away. Thanks for dropping in. Go and enjoy the remainder of your evening… whatever you two were up to.'

As Byrd made his way back to his X5, in the freezing cold with Alex Richards, his phoned beeped in his pocket. A text message from Keith. It read: *Still no sign of Lyle, mate. I'm getting very worried now. Have you seen him?*

'Not yet, old friend, not yet,' Byrd said to himself, as he turned the engine on and headed for home with Alex.

67

Sunday Morning
Police Station

Tanzy had enjoyed his night off. After they returned home from soft play, the kids had a bath, put their pyjamas on and watched Toy Story 4 together in Eric's room.

Tanzy and Pip decided to get a takeaway. Nothing fancy or flash, just a pizza box with chips and donner meat from one of the local shops. They'd decided to watch 'The Equalizer' with Denzel Washington, which was one of Tanzy's favourites. He couldn't believe that Pip had never seen it, but she was more of a romcom type. They rarely watched films together, as when they did, they usually bickered long enough for Tanzy just to agree with what Pip wanted.

A little later, in bed, he had stared at Pip, watching the way her hair fell to one side and the way she breathed. She was a beautiful woman and Tanzy seldom stopped to admire her. Normally he was too hung up on what was going on at work, or something with the kids, but, in that very moment, he felt all the love in the world for her. He was proud of her too. He'd never been dependant on drugs or alcohol but, in his line of work, he'd seen hundreds of people that were. Many of them failed when they tried changing things but Pip had gone over two months now free of alcohol, and he was proud of her achievement.

Now, back at the station, he watched the footage of the man getting out of the dark blue Kia Sportage. He felt like he knew him, that he looked familiar in some way, but he couldn't place it. Mac had done a great job altering the image quality but the quality of the camera let it down, so, unfortunately, it wasn't as clear as he'd hoped. It would be very unlikely to get facial recognition from it.

'Why did you go inside?' Tanzy asked himself.

He'd rang Byrd earlier, apologising if he'd woken him and for not replying to the text message Byrd had sent him last night, about what had happened at the restaurant. Tanzy had woken at two in the morning and went straight up to bed, without checking his phone. Byrd had confirmed that Tallow and Hope's reports should have been sent to Tanzy for him to look at, along with the video footage from the restaurant manager.

He played back the video again from Claxton Avenue, watching the man in the green Hi-Viz vest go inside.

'If I was getting something delivered, what reason would someone give to come in,' he whispered. Then he realised it could only be one thing. He picked up his phone, found the number and pressed CALL.

'Orion, you do know what time it is, don't you?' Jacob Tallow, the senior forensic, asked.

Tanzy glanced down at his wrist. 'I do. Twenty-to-nine.'

'Exactly. It's a Sunday morning!'

'Hey, sorry I woke you, I—'

'It's all good man, I'm awake,' Tallow said. 'What—'

'Who's that calling?' Tanzy heard faintly through the phone who sounded close to him.

'Someone from work,' Tallow explained, presumably to his wife. 'What do I owe the pleasure, mate?'

'Erm… it isn't about what happened at the restaurant. It's about Claxton Avenue.'

'Go on.'

'I was wondering why Brian Cornforth let the guy in. There's only one thing I can think of.'

'Which is?' Tallow said groggily.

'To use the toilet,' Tanzy said.

'And you're going to ask me if I dusted the toilet handle door for prints aren't you?'

'I am,' Tanzy said.

'Shit…'

Tanzy fell silent for a moment, surprised by that. 'Would it be possible at some point today to get the prints off the door handle? I can get the key and meet you there.'

'Give me an hour, Ori, I'll see you there.'

'You're a good man.'

'I know,' he said, hanging up.

Tanzy finished his coffee, stood up, grabbed his coat and headed out into the cold.

An hour later Tallow turned up in his own car, a black Volvo XC60. He pulled up behind Tanzy's Golf and stepped out with a small briefcase. The air was fresh, clear and still. There wasn't a cloud in the sky.

Tanzy met him at the end of the driveway. 'Jacob, thanks for coming.'

'Anything for you, Ori, you know that.'

They walked down the slight slope, careful of their footing on the icy paving slabs and stopped at the door. Tanzy pulled a key from his coat, placed it in the keyhole, turned it and edged the door open slowly.

Inside the hallway it felt colder than it had outside. Tanzy padded along the hall, and on his left, was the closed toilet door.

'Did either you or Hope go in the toilet?'

He nodded. 'I did. I remember opening the door to see what it was. I checked for any signs or prints. But, for some reason, I didn't check the handle.' A tinge of embarrassment crossed his face.

'Happens to the best of us, don't worry about it,' Tanzy reassured him. 'The saving grace is that everyone will have worn gloves yesterday so, if the man's prints are there, they still will be.'

Tallow moved in front of Tanzy and lowered himself to his knees in front of the closed door. He opened the lid of his black case, pulled out a small tub of powder, opened the lid and, with a brush, dabbed it into the powder then, slowly and carefully, applied it to the brass handle of the door.

'From the video, he didn't wear gloves when he entered,' Tanzy said, 'so if he did ask to go to the toilet, hopefully this door was shut and he had to use the handle to open it.'

Tallow carefully brushed the powder into the handle, revealing several thumb. He placed the brush down on the lid of his kit and picked up a roll of special clear tape. He delicately pressed down on the print, then peeled it away. He repeated the process for the underside of the handle where he would expect to find fingerprints. In total he managed to get eight prints.

'Brilliant, Jacob,' Tanzy said, standing a few metres back watching him.

'Chances are that some of these will belong to Brian and his wife Jane.'

'But there's always a chance they're won't.'

'There's always a chance,' Tallow confirmed, standing up, his head almost catching the ceiling pendant above him. 'I'll take these back to the lab and run them. The missus wants to go out today, but I've told her I'll be back in time.'

'Appreciate that, thanks man.'

68

Sunday Evening
Craig Street, Darlington

'Which one do you think it is?' Weaver asked Leonard.

'I haven't got a clue. Just keep your eyes peeled.'

They'd been instructed by Tanzy to sit in Craig Street and keep an eye on any suspicious activity. They knew, from the location tracker on Mark Greenwell's phone, that he spent a lot of his time on this part of the street. The problem was that they didn't know which house. Mac, from DFU, had done his best but sitting there was their best option for now.

'Hey, look...' said Leonard, pointing.

Weaver followed Leonard's finger across the street.

Two teenagers strutted down the path and stopped at a house, then knocked on the door. A moment later, it opened, and they disappeared inside. Ten minutes later they watched another male with his hood up, approach from the direction of Greenbank Road, and stop at the house. He also knocked on the door, waited until it opened, then went inside.

'Think we've found the house,' Weaver commented.

Leonard agreed. 'We'll sit a little longer, see what happens and report back.'

Almost twenty minutes later, after several teenagers had come and gone, they saw car headlights in their wing mirror. The car passed them, then slowed, pulled over and stopped directly in front of the house.

'You seeing what I'm seeing?'

Weaver nodded. 'A red Mondeo.'

Shortly afterwards, another car passed them. It was a dark blue Kia Sportage, but neither Weaver nor Leonard noticed it as their attention was on the red Mondeo. The Mondeo's lights went off. The driver stepped out. He was tall and thin, wearing a long coat that draped down to his knees.

'You getting this?'

Weaver said, 'Yeah,' as she captured the image on her camera.

The tall man made his way around the front of the car and knocked on the door.

The driver of the dark blue Kia Sportage had passed the red Mondeo, reached the end of the street, and had taken a right into Greenbank Road. He'd grabbed the object from the passenger seat, opened the door, and stepped out into the cold. He made his way back to the corner of Craig Street and watched from there. The object was small enough to be concealed in his pocket so anyone watching wouldn't suspect anything.

He ambled down the street, stopped at the red Mondeo and bent down by the side of the car. He pulled the object from his pocket and placed it under the wheel arch. He then stood and carried on walking until made his way around the block back to where he'd parked.

'Who's this guy?' Leonard asked.

Weaver was still clicking away. 'Not sure. I've got him on camera though.'

'What's he doing?' Leonard said, noticing the man behind the Mondeo.

'Doing his shoelace? I don't think he's one of them. He didn't even acknowledge the house.'

Leonard picked up his phone and called Tanzy's number.

'Yeah, we're just at Craig Street, boss. Seems to be a lot of activity at a particular house. Several people coming and going. Thought I'd let you know that a red Mondeo pulled up and the driver went into the house too. Can you remember the registration plate that the old guy on Brougham Street gave? The red Mondeo that took the kids?'

'Hold on,' Tanzy told him. 'Yeah, it's NA66 CFD.'

'Just confirm that again please?' Leonard asked, frowning.

'NA66 CFD,' Tanzy confirmed through the phone.

'We got it, that's the one. It's parked right here,' Leonard told him.

'Sit tight. I'll ring it in, and we'll get a warrant on that property immediately. What's the number?'

Leonard glanced to his left, across the road, and noted the house number, then counted the houses down until he reached the one they were watching and told him.

'Okay, good. Melissa Clarke and Eddy Long could be in there. Stay where you are and don't leave the car, okay. Back up is on the way.'

'You got it, boss,' Leonard said hanging up.

Just as Leonard put down the phone, the door to the house opened. The tall man who had arrived in the Mondeo was at the door telling one of the teenagers something. Whatever it was, it seemed more of an order, as the boy nodded several times.

The tall man returned to the car and got in, turned on the engine and edged out onto the road.

'Do we wait for back up, or...' Weaver was unsure.

'No, we follow the car,' Leonard said, turning the key.

69

Sunday Evening
Craig Street, Darlington

'Here, phone Orion back,' Leonard said, throwing his phone onto Weaver's lap. 'He'll be the last caller.'

Leonard veered the car onto the road and put his foot down, accelerating up to forty MPH. He noticed the red Mondeo take a right and so did the same.

'Hey, Orion,' Weaver spoke into the phone. 'The red Mondeo has moved We're currently in pursuit. Going up Greenbank Road in the direction of town.'

'Okay, stay with it, don't do anything too rash. Keep a safe distance and don't lose it. The driver should be considered very dangerous.'

'Okay, we understand.'

'Just to update you, I've called dispatch. They're arranging an armed response vehicle to go to Craig Street and they will be there within twenty minutes.'

'Should we continue to follow the Mondeo?'

'Yeah, stay with him. Make sure you have his description noted down as well.'

'Already done, Sir.'

'Good work,' Tanzy praised her. 'I'm leaving the house. Should be in Darlington within ten minutes. Anything happens, just ring me.'

'Understood,' she said before ending the call.

The Mondeo reached the cross-junction traffic lights at the end of Greenbank Road where it met Woodland Road. When the lights turned green, the Mondeo went right and accelerated onwards. Leonard just made the green light in time to make the turn and maintained a steady gap behind the car. The road was busy for a Sunday night, so they hoped the driver wouldn't get too suspicious of them trailing him. He passed the hospital and continued driving down Woodland Road, passing the petrol station on the left. It wasn't long before he hit the small roundabout at the end of Woodland Road and took a left, then another left at the next roundabout.

'Where's he going?' Weaver said.

The Mondeo accelerated up the bank, then slowed a little, and pulled over to the side of the road. The hazard lights came on.

'What's he doing?'

'He knows we're following him. He wants us to overtake him.' Leonard was in two minds. 'Orion told us not to lose him.'

'What are you doing?' Weaver asked, as he slowed the Insignia and pulled over behind the Mondeo. 'James, what – what are you doing?'

'If this is the guy who's responsible for taking those kids and killing Sheena Edwards, he isn't getting away with it. We need to bring him down. Ring Orion now. Tell him the car has pulled over and we're approaching the vehicle.'

The Insignia came to a halt behind the Mondeo and Leonard put the handbrake on firmly to prevent it falling back down the inclined road.

Weaver glanced his way nervously and shook her head. 'He's not answering.'

'Come on,' Leonard said, 'let's go.'

Both Leonard and Weaver opened the door and stepped out. It was bitterly cold now. As they approached the Mondeo, there was classical music coming from inside.

'You hear that?' Weaver asked, frowning. Leonard nodded, approaching the driver's side but, before he got there, the door was flung open and the tall man got out. He was six or seven inches taller than Leonard who glared up at him.

Arthur stared down at Leonard. 'You seem to be following me?'

'I need to ask you some questions down at the station,' Leonard said.

'We aren't at the station,' Arthur said. 'We're standing on Carmel Road. You can ask me questions here.' His voice was cold and flat. He wasn't intimidated by either Leonard or Weaver, who was keeping her distance at the opposite side of the car.

'No can do, Sir,' Leonard advised, 'we're taking you to the station.'

Weaver pulled out a set of handcuffs and held them for a moment so Arthur could see them but all he did was smile at her.

'Sir, we need to take you in!'

'Are you arresting me?'

'I am.'

'On what grounds?' Arthur said, frowning.

Leonard took a few steps towards Arthur and placed his hands out for Weaver to throw over the set of cuffs, which she did. 'You're coming with me.'

Arthur reached inside his jacket and pulled out a gun.

Leonard froze to the spot, unable to take his eyes off it. He raised it to Leonard and pulled the trigger. The bullet hit him in the side of the chest and he fell onto the floor, wailing in pain.

Weaver threw her hands to her mouth and gasped.

Arthur very casually placed the gun back into his long coat, turned around and got into the car. A moment later the Mondeo pulled away up Carmel Road and out of sight. Weaver rushed over to Leonard, pulled her radio from her belt and pressed the red button on the top of it, then requested immediate medical attention. The red button was known as Code Red. This blocked all other police radio's in the area and left hers open, so everyone was aware of what had happened.

70

Sunday Evening
Carmel Road, Darlington

Tanzy was there within minutes of Weaver phoning him to tell him that Leonard had been shot and that the Mondeo had gone.

On his way there he'd contacted dispatch telling them to send a unit in the direction of Carmel Road south and to request air support. He knew that the closest NPAS (National Police Air Service) centre was near Newcastle but as this man was linked to the kidnapping of three children and the murder of an elderly lady and shooting of DC Leonard, it should be treated as a priority.

Tanzy pulled over at the side of the road behind Leonard's car. He couldn't see Leonard or Weaver. He turned off the engine and jumped out.

'Just hang in there, Jim, hang in there,' Weaver cried, tears streaming down her face. She was hunched over him, holding his head off the floor. There was a pool of blood underneath him and his black fleece was saturated.

Tanzy rounded the car and saw them a few metres in front of the bonnet.

'Jesus,' Tanzy gasped. 'Amy, is he okay?' He lowered himself down, noticing Leonard's gaze faintly switch to him. 'Where's he shot, Amy?'

'I don't know,' Weaver confessed. 'I—'

'Just try and relax Amy, an ambulance is coming.' Tanzy lifted Leonard's arm an inch to get a better look at the amount of blood he'd lost. 'Is he wearing a vest?'

Amy shrugged, not knowing.

He looked into Leonard's vacant eyes. 'James, are you wearing a vest, buddy?'

Leonard struggled to maintain eye contact with Tanzy and looked into the dark sky above. His chest was rising and falling rapidly as he struggled for breath.

'Where did it hit you?' he asked him. Leonard couldn't answer. Then to Weaver: 'It can't have penetrated the vest, so it must be his arm or arm pit. Help me lift him and take off his jacket.'

'We should wait for—'

'Amy, he's losing blood too quickly. We need to find out where it's coming from and stop it the best we can. Help me.'

They pulled him up slightly and Tanzy carefully peeled his arms out of his jacket and managed to pull it off. Leonard winced in pain. Underneath the jacket he was wearing a black t-shirt, and underneath that, his stab vest. 'We need this off too,' he said, referring to the t-shirt. It took a little longer as it was tighter, but they managed it.

'You got your light?'

Weaver found her torch from her belt and passed it to Tanzy. 'Here.'

'We need to turn him onto his side a little,' he told her. 'To get a better look at this.'

After they turned him over, Tanzy shone the light down onto his left side. 'This might hurt, Jim. Just bear with me, mate.' Tanzy took hold of his left forearm and, very slowly, started to raise it a little, causing Leonard to scream out in pain. 'Sorry, sorry, mate, just hold on – where's that fucking ambulance at!' The light from the torch showed Tanzy a bullet hole just under Leonard's arm pit. 'I'm going to put your arm across your body,' Tanzy said, guiding Leonard's arm across and placing it on the middle of his vest. 'It'll give the paramedics a better look when they get here.' He turned his attention to Weaver. 'Amy, how many times did the guy shoot?'

She seemed flustered, trying to think. 'Erm... once I think.'

'He didn't shoot at you?'

She shook her head quickly. 'No, no.'

'Okay.'

The wail of distant sirens ripped through the air. 'Will he be okay?' Weaver asked.

Tanzy nodded. 'Yeah, looks like the bullet went straight through. I don't know why he's being so dramatic to be honest.'

Weaver gave a short laugh and placed her hand on top of Leonards. 'Hang in there, Jim, help is coming now,' said Weaver. 'Can you hear the sirens?'

When the ambulance arrived, two paramedics, a man and a woman, jumped out the back with a stretcher, and placed it down near Leonard.

'What happened?' asked the male paramedic.

Tanzy explained the best he could from what Weaver had told him. She was quiet, watching the paramedics check him out. After a few minutes, they lifted him onto the stretcher and put him in the back of the ambulance.

'I'm going with him,' Weaver told Tanzy.

Tanzy watched her climb into the back and the female paramedic leaned out, grabbed the handle and pulled the door closed. Then the ambulance disappeared down the road, taking a right at the roundabout and down Woodland Road towards the hospital.

Tanzy took a deep breath and returned to his car. On his way to the incident, he'd spoken with Sergeant Jack Tunstall, the sergeant on shift, about the raid at the house on Craig Street. Tanzy had suggested an armed tactical unit to handle it as he considered these were dangerous people they were dealing with. Tunstall agreed and informed Tanzy that he was getting straight on it.

As Tanzy turned the key to start the engine, his phone rang. It was PC Josh Andrews. He knew Andrews was on shift and was heading to Craig Street.

'Josh, what's happening there?'

'Ori, you need to see this,' Andrews said. 'I've seen nothing like it in my life.'

'I'll be straight over. Sit tight.'

71

Sunday Evening
Craig Street, Darlington

Tanzy pulled up near the house on Craig Street. Light shone brightly from every window. There were two police vans parked directly in front of the house, and two police cars parked across the middle of the road. The street was full of police officers, some in tactical gear holding weapons and other PCs milling around, taking notes and speaking with neighbours. Most of the neighbours were either out on their doorsteps watching or peering through their windows to see what all the fuss was about.

Through the windscreen of the Golf he noticed PC Josh Andrews standing a few feet from the front door. He turned the engine off and opened his door, a rush of cold air seeping in, and got out. He moved around the car and stepped onto the path, making his way towards the house.

'Hey, Orion,' PC Donny Grearer said, hearing his approach.

'How's it going?'

'I'll let *you* decide that one. Go have a look in there,' he said, smiling. 'We've hit the jackpot.'

Tanzy nodded and drifted past him, approaching Andrews.

'Josh,' Tanzy said.

Andrews had finished a conversation with one of the neighbours and turned to face him. 'Hey, boss.'

To their right, they heard shouting, screaming, and swearing. 'They in there?'

Andrews nodded to the police vans. 'Both are full, as well as the cars.'

'Jesus,' he gasped. 'What did you find?'

Andrews waved him on. 'Come on, I'll show you.'

Tanzy followed Andrews into the terraced house, stepping up into a narrow hallway lined with grubby cream wallpaper that used to be white, and a dark brown carpet clotted with stains. The stairs were straight ahead, and there was a door to the left leading to the living room and a door beyond that leading to the small dining room. They passed the first door and took the second, Tanzy noticing it had a few holes in the base of it, as if it had been subject to a good kicking in the past. In the dining room, on a square table that was placed against the chimney breast, there must have been over two hundred bricks of white powder, roughly six inches by four, all solid.

Tanzy froze on the spot. 'Jesus fucking wept!'

Andrews smiled at him. 'Jackpot.'

Tanzy exhaled as he padded closer to the contents on the table.

'How much you reckon it's worth?' Andrews asked him.

'No idea at all.'

They heard footsteps behind them. Tanzy turned to see Sergeant Jack Tunstall walk in. He was short, but wide, with a scar on the side of his cheek from a knife attack during the last week of his initial ten-week training as a constable. It hadn't improved his looks, that's for sure.

Tanzy shook his hand, matching his equally firm grip. 'Hey, Jack. Hit the jackpot I think.'

'About time these fuckers were found out. I reckon they were running the whole town's drug supply. We'll take them all down the station and question them. Good tip off from Mac in DFU. I heard what he did with Mark Greenwell's phone.'

Tanzy nodded. 'He knows his stuff.'

'Right, we better go. We've checked everywhere. There were a few drugs and bits knocking around, but it's all been collected for evidence.' He turned to PC Andrews. 'Can you take more photos of this and start bagging it up please. I'll send someone else in to help.'

Andrews, who had been temporarily seconded over to CID for a few months, nodded to his Sergeant and took out his phone. Before he started taking photos, he turned to Tanzy. 'I'll be back on days this week, so I'll catch up with you then.'

Tanzy nodded and patted him on the back. 'Good work, Josh.' Then Tanzy followed Sergeant Tunstall out into the hallway. 'He's a good lad,' he said to the sergeant.

'He is. One of our best, is Josh.'

They both stepped outside into the cold and noticed the street was busier than before. Tanzy glanced to his left, seeing a news van and, just next to it, a female reporter, standing in front of a camera with her back to the house.

He wanted to go home, get a shower and go to bed. He decided to ring Weaver when he got home and check up on Leonard. He was sure, from his own experience, that Leonard would pull through no problem.

Despite Leonard's injury, it had been a successful day for the police. Tomorrow might be different.

C. J. Grayson

72

Monday Morning
High Row, Darlington Town Centre

Two men dressed in suits were walking side by side along High Row, talking about the meeting which they had planned for 9 a.m.. One of the directors was coming into the bank for an urgent meeting about cyber security. There'd been a breach.

'Graham, the thing is,' the taller of them said, 'if we tell him the things we've missed, we'll be gone. You know that as well as I do.'

Graham nodded. 'It's a tough one, Pete. He might already have evidence about what we haven't done. He knows the regs inside out, that's why he's the boss.'

'We'll see what he says. We could always plead ignorance?'

'Always an option.'

They continued walking along the top of High Row, passing Greggs on their left. The time on the town clock showed them it was just before seven. If they got there with plenty of time, they could prepare for the director's arrival and attempt to cover all bases.

They angled their walk and took the steps down onto the path opposite Burger King, heading towards their bank. Up ahead they saw something at the bottom of the Joseph Pease statue.

Pete pointed, laughing. 'Looks like he's had a good night, doesn't it?'

Graham was focused on the window of Waterstones to his right, then glanced up ahead. 'Who?'

'The guy up there, look.'

They drew a little closer. There was a man sitting on the floor with his back against the thick concrete block at the base of the statue.

'What's he doing?' Pete said, squinting to see better.

'Is he naked?'

'I – I think he is,' Pete said. 'It's bloody freezing. What's he playing at?'

'Why is he sitting like that?'

They were roughly forty metres away now but angled their walk over to the statue to get a closer look.

'We should check if he's okay, Pete. He'll freeze to death.'

Pete agreed. 'Must have had some wild…' he trailed off and stopped, as did Graham, when the scene at the base of the statue finally became clear.

'What. The. Actual. Fuck.' Pete stared, trying to make sense of it. 'Graham, why's he like that?'

Graham couldn't take his eyes off him and stayed silent.

In front of them, sitting at the base of the statue, was a naked man, with his arms tied out to the side and fixed there somehow. His face and hair were white, as if covered completely in powder, so much so, they couldn't see his features very well. There was something around his neck, too.

'What is this?' Pete whispered. As they drew nearer, they noticed his wrists were bound by rope. The rope was tied around both sides of the statue base, probably knotted together at the opposite side to keep his arms pinned where they were. The man's face was completely still and covered in what looked like talcum powder.

'Is this real?'

What was around his neck was clearer now. It was barbed wire. Beneath the wire, they could see his throat was red raw and there was a very thin but deep line across

318

it, as if the skin had been sliced with a knife. From his mouth, foam leaked and had hardened on his chin.

'Is this a fucking wind up?' Pete shouted, then looked around.

'This is for real,' Graham said. 'We need to ring the police now.'

73

Monday Morning
High Row, Darlington Town Centre

The first PCs to arrive on the scene were Weaver and Grearer, who parked up on the flat area outside the Vodafone store. Their arrival was followed by further PCs, CID, forensics, and an ambulance, although it was clear the person at the base of the statue was beyond the help of paramedics.

It was an early start for them, but what better way to start a fresh Monday morning than being thrown in at the deep end.

They'd set up a huge perimeter with tape, preventing access for dozens of workers who'd joined the growing crowd, asking questions about what was stopping them getting through. It was PC Weaver's duty to take charge as first responder to the scene. It was also her job to sign everyone in and out for the duration of the process.

Tallow and Hope decided, because of the location of the naked body and openness of the scene, they would set up a tent around the body. That way, it would give them a little privacy and at least preserve the body if the heavens started to open which, according to the days forecast, was imminent.

Very soon afterwards, as if they'd timed it to perfection, Byrd pulled up in his X5 and Tanzy in his Golf. They parked up on the footpath opposite Burger King and got out at the same time.

'Just what we need. Perfect start to our Monday morning.' Tanzy shook his head, making his way across the concrete with Byrd.

Standing at the tape, on the side closest to Burger King, was Weaver. 'Morning,' she said to both of them.

'What do we have, Amy?'

'I can't really describe it,' she explained, frowning. 'Think it's better for you to see for yourself. Here, put these on.' She handed them some blue overshoes.

The tent that the forensics had set up resembled a gazebo, but with only two sides to it. Four lots of barrier tape had been set up in the area, preventing people seeing into it.

Byrd and Tanzy heard talking inside the tent.

'What do you think that is?' Hope was asking Tallow.

Tallow was taking photos, the flash of the camera hitting the plastic sheeting like a stabs of lightning before they faded away.

'Could be talc... could be cocaine... could be fake snow,' he said.

Byrd and Tanzy stopped at the side opening of the tent. 'Safe to come in?' Byrd asked.

'Not just yet, unless you have overshoes on. I need to check for prints,' Tallow replied.

'Jesus Christ, what happened to him?' Tanzy said, scratching the side of his head. They couldn't see the man on their approach due to how the tent had been set up.

Hope, who was standing a few metres from them, dressed in her disposable plastic suit and white face mask, shrugged. 'What's your opinion on this one, Orion?'

Tanzy sighed a little, absorbing the scene for a moment then looked back to Hope. 'I have nothing yet. What's your thoughts?'

'Jacob doesn't agree, but I think it's spiritual,' she said, glancing Tallow's way.

'It's not that I don't agree, I'm just not sure. The scene isn't speaking to me yet.'

Hope rolled her eyes at him then smiled at Tanzy. 'Okay Mystic Meg, well let me know…'

Byrd and Tanzy, despite the forensic team moving around and occasionally stepping in their line of sight, considered the naked man for a long time.

'Do you think it's him? Lyle Wilson?' Tanzy said, glancing Byrd's way.

'No idea.' He looked at Tallow. 'It's clear he hasn't been here for long, but how long's he been dead?'

The man's face was covered with white powder but the rest of his body was clear to see. Tallow lowered himself, looking at the skin, how it had bloated and the odd skin colour. 'Almost three days?'

'Emily, what would you say?' Byrd asked.

She put the hair sample she'd cut from the man's head into a small, clear bag, then moved back a little, analysing him. After a few moments, she said, 'I'd have to agree with Jacob. It's also obvious that he wasn't killed here.'

Byrd nodded, then looked at Tallow. 'Would it be possible to clean his face a little? I want to know if it's Lyle Wilson or not.'

'Sure.' Tallow let the camera hang from a lanyard around his neck, shuffled outside the tent to where their kit was and pulled out a small brush.

Byrd frowned at the naked man as he waited for Tallow.

'What's up?' Tanzy asked, noticing his expression.

'If this is the guy who was knocked over, I'm just wondering why he's turned up now and not yesterday, or the day before, or the night he was knocked down on Cleveland Street.'

'Think it's the same person who killed the others?' Tanzy asked.

'I... I assume so. Lyle Wilson was clearly associated with Mark Greenwell and spent much of his time around the Denes park. There's also a common link with Brian Cornforth as both were strangled. I think the killer is responsible for all three deaths.'

'What's their link?' Tanzy asked, his eyebrows furrowing.

'Mark and Lyle, if this is Lyle, are similar in age. The anomaly is Brian Cornforth and how he fits into it. But if Mark and Lyle had spent a lot of time at the house on Craig Street and were a part of that drug operation, then chances are they were working for Jonny Darchem.'

'It's a shame we have nothing to nail the bastard with,' Tanzy sighed.

Byrd raised a finger. 'But we will, don't worry. We need to speak to Damien to see how the Mondeo fits into this and to locate the house he was taken to. We're still looking for Melissa and Eddy so, as soon as he's well enough, we'll head over there.'

'If this is linked to Jonny Darchem, the question is why is someone doing this to his men?' Tanzy said. 'An enemy? Someone he's pissed off in the past?'

'Maybe,' Byrd replied, looking down at the body. 'What's your first impression here, mate?'

'I think someone hung him up by a wire, killed him that way, then brought him here. Then he put him in that position, tied his hands up like that, placed barb wire around his neck and poured the powder on him.'

Byrd nodded. 'Okay.'

'You?'

'Yeah, the barbed wire is just for show. He wasn't strangled with it because it doesn't match the mark on his throat.' He looked at Tallow, who'd returned to the tent and was now bent over the body. 'You think it's cocaine?'

Before Tallow brushed away the white powder, he pinched a little of it from the man's hair and rubbed it between his index finger and thumb. 'Same consistency with cocaine, Max. We've already got a sample of it and we'll test it at the lab later.'

Tallow carefully started brushing away the powder from the face and the features became clearer.

Byrd knew straight away it was Lyle Wilson and felt sick to the pit of his stomach. The thought of telling his friend, Keith, made him physically sick.

Byrd took a few steps back until he was outside the tent and bent over slightly. Tanzy came out and placed a palm on his back. 'You alright, Max?'

Byrd took a lung full of icy air, closed his eyes and eventually breathed out. 'I *fucking* love this job.'

Tanzy gave a sad smile, then glanced around the area while Byrd had a moment to himself. After he'd done a slow three-sixty sweep, he counted four cameras that might help them with had happened. He'd have to pay Jennifer Lucas at the Town Hall control room a visit to check them out.

'You okay, Max?'

Byrd nodded. 'Feel a little light-headed but I'll survive.'

Tanzy patted him on the back again and they both moved back to the tent. When they got there, Tallow had finished dusting the powder off the man's face. It was now clear to all of them that the man was Lyle Wilson. Byrd imagined the conversation he'd have to have with Keith later this afternoon. He was dreading it.

'What is left to do?' Byrd asked Tallow and Hope.

'Plenty, Max,' Tallow answered, a little frustrated.

Byrd noticed it. 'Everything okay mate?' he asked him.

Tallow took a deep breath. 'Yeah, fine, sorry. It's just the last thing we need first thing on a Monday morning.'

'I know,' Byrd replied, shuffling his feet. 'Other than the obvious cut around his neck, do you think he's sustained any other injuries? Not including obviously any possible injuries when he was run over?'

'I know what you're thinking, Max. You're wondering about the whip marks, aren't you?'

Byrd nodded at Tanzy.

'Peter is on his way,' Tallow said, glancing down at his watch. 'I don't want to move him until he's here. Then we can remove the rope and have a closer look.'

Almost twenty minutes passed before Peter Gibbs, the coroner, turned up. PC Weaver had signed him in at the tape and provided him with some overshoes to enter. He stopped a few feet into the tent and glared down at Lyle Wilson. There was a vacant expression on his face, as if he had other things on his mind, or maybe drank too much wine the night before.

'Do we know him?' Gibbs asked no one in particular.

'We do,' Byrd said. Gibbs gave Byrd his attention as he went on: 'I know him. It's one of my friend's sons. I've known him for years. He went missing three nights ago. His phone was found at the scene where Mark Greenwell was found in the Denes park.' He paused for a moment to collect his thoughts. 'It's definitely Lyle Wilson.'

Tallow and Hope moved back to allow Gibbs to have a closer look. He made some notes and took several photographs. 'We'll take the body to pathology, see what Arnold and Laura come up with.'

Byrd and Tanzy nodded.

'Are we okay undoing the rope tying him to the statue?' Tallow asked Gibbs.

'If you have everything you need, I don't see why not.'

'We need to get a look at his back,' Tanzy said.

Tallow went around the back of the monument and released the single knot in the rope. 'Undoing it now. Catch him if he drops forward.'

Hope was holding up his weight around the other side. 'Go on – got him.'

Lyle's body flopped forward a little and Hope gently lowered him to the ground, turning him over as she did so they could see his bare back. 'Come and see this,' she told the detectives, who stepped forward eagerly.

On his back, there were seven whip marks: some faded, some fresh. They all ran from the rear of his right shoulder all the way down to his left hip.

'We need to stop this fucker ASAP,' Byrd shouted.

Tanzy nodded. 'I'll go see Jennifer Lucas to check those cameras. I'll meet you guys later at the hospital for the post-mortem.'

Gibbs nodded. 'I need to prepare some paperwork for this.' Then he looked at Tallow and Hope. 'You guys do what you need to do and give the paramedics a shout when you're done, then we'll take over.'

Byrd and Tanzy left the scene, ducked under the tape, and headed back to their cars.

'I heard what happened to Leonard last night,' Byrd said. 'How's he doing?'

'I spoke with Amy last night. She went to the hospital with him. He's still there but is doing okay. Amy stayed with him for a few hours until the doctors told her he needed to rest so she went home.' They stopped at the cars. 'The bullet went straight through, just missing his vest by'—he raised his hand, making a very small gap between his thumb and finger—'he was unlucky, but it isn't life threatening.'

'Good,' Byrd said. 'I heard you had air support. Did they, or any of the ground units, pick up on the Mondeo?'

Tanzy shook his head. 'I felt bad for using them.'

'That's why they're there.' Byrd looked back at the scene. He could see Tallow bending over his kit beside the tent. Then he focused back on Tanzy. 'You heading over to see Jennifer?'

'Yeah. If any of the cameras can tell us something, she's the one who'll make it happen.'

'Okay, I'll catch up with you soon. I need to contact Keith before this gets out.'

Tanzy's face softened. 'Good luck, Max.'

'Thanks, I'll need it.'

74

Monday Morning
Town Hall, Darlington Town Centre

Tanzy signed in and was told to go upstairs. He knocked on the control door and stepped inside. As usual, the room was dark, the majority of the light coming from the cluster of screens to the left of the room. The chair which Jennifer usually sat in was vacant, and, for a second, he glanced around wondering where she was. Over to the right, he heard something.

'Hello, Orion,' she said, reaching up to one of the shelves, placing something back. She turned to him and smiled. 'What do I owe the pleasure today?'

'I need your skills,' he said, watching her elegantly move across the room and sit down on her usual chair.

She nodded. 'Go on…'

Tanzy explained the crime scene at the statue and that, whoever had put the man there, would have done so in the last twelve hours.

Jennifer took hold of the mouse and navigated the cursor where she needed to. 'There's six cameras on High Row. From where you're saying, at least three of them should see what you're after.'

'I counted four,' Tanzy said.

'Well aren't you clever?' she said, focusing back to the screen.

He smiled, looking up. On the screen, furthest to the right, on the bottom row, the image changed.

'From what you have described this is probably going to be the best one, but I can change it depending on what we see.' The angle appeared to be above Burger King facing north. The Joseph Pease monument was in darkness and there was no sign of Lyle Wilson's body at the base of it. The time at the bottom corner of the screen was 9.01 p.m. last night.

'Whoever put it there, will have done so in the early hours, so no one would be around. Scroll forward to two in the morning, please,' Tanzy said.

As she scrolled along the time bar at the bottom of the screen, Tanzy glanced down at her. Her hair, her skin, the slight arching of her lips.

Stop it, he told himself, focusing back on the screen.

'Okay, this is two in the morning,' she said.

A mirror image from earlier. There was still no body.

'Go to four in the morning.'

On the screen, they saw the body at the base of the monument, exactly the same way it was half an hour ago when he was there. 'Go back maybe an hour, please, Jen.'

'Sure.'

At three a.m., the body wasn't there. 'Can you fast forward it?'

'Yeah.' She tapped on the fast forward icon. At 3.07 a.m., a dark blue Kia Sportage came in the shot from the right bottom corner of the screen. She pressed play, watching in real time as it slowly crawled across the screen until it stopped in front of the monument.

'Pause it there.' They could see the outline of the man inside the car. Tanzy squinted, then pointed. 'Can you zoom in on the registration?'

'Should be able to.' She zoomed in and dragged the rear of the car into focus. The letters and numbers were very clear. Tanzy took out his phone, found the number he needed and put it to his ear.

'Yeah, it's Detective Inspector Orion Tanzy, can you run a plate check please?'

'Go ahead,' said the operator.

'N. U. 1. 3. P. T. X.'

'Hold on.'

After a few moments, the operator said, 'Mr Tanzy, are you sure that's correct?'

Tanzy frowned, looking towards Jennifer. 'Can you zoom in more, or maybe enhance it?'

She zoomed in more and pressed a button which altered the pixels of the still shot.

'Yeah, I confirm it's NU13PTX.'

'I'm sorry, sir, but that plate doesn't exist on the DVLA database.'

'Okay, thanks for your time,' Tanzy said, hanging up before the operator could respond. He turned to Jennifer. 'It's a fake.'

She gave a sad smile and looked up at the screen, pressing play. The driver of the car got out. The camera picked his head and shoulders up over the roof of the Sportage but there was something odd about him.

'Pause it. Zoom in on his face.'

She did.

'What's he wearing?' Tanzy asked, unsure what he was looking at, then it made sense. 'Is that a balaclava?'

Jennifer tilted her head. 'Looks like it.'

'Great...' Tanzy sighed. 'Play it. See what he does.'

The man went to the back of the car and opened the boot. He leaned in and pulled something out. It was a naked body. He carried it around the side of the car which was, unfortunately, out of the camera angle.

'Is there a camera that can see the other side?' Tanzy enquired.

Jennifer moved the cursor on the large screen and found a camera that was fixed to Next. She was sure it was facing south, in the direction of High Row. If so, it should show them what they needed to see. 'Hold on, let me...' she made a ticking sound with her tongue for a moment. 'Ahh, here we go.' She was right. She scrolled to a similar time: 3.07 a.m., and pressed play. This time, they saw the Kia Sportage crawl into view from the top left of the screen and come to a halt. The driver got out, already wearing the mask, and went to the back of the car. After opening the boot, he dragged out the body and carried it over to the monument. He slowly placed it down into a slumped sitting position. He returned to the boot of the car and grabbed a bag and some rope. He lowered himself to the naked man and tied the rope around one of his hands, then walked around the base of the statue until he was back where he started. He took a step back and admired his own work, coming back into view of the camera.

He then bent down to the bag and picked up what seemed to be the ring of barbed wire and placed it around Lyle's neck.

'What is this guy doing?' Jennifer asked, her palm over her mouth.

Again, he stood back to observe the man.

Although the man was wearing a balaclava, at least Tanzy could see his physique. He was tall, at least six foot. And he was slim. Not skinny, but athletic and strong. After a few moments, he took a few paces to the right and lowered himself back down to the bag.

He pulled out another bag, similar in size to a carrier bag. It was full. He then lifted the bag above the man's head and poured its contents over his head and face.

'What – what on earth is that?'

'We think it's cocaine,' Tanzy told her. Then at 3.22 a.m., the man put the bag in the back of the car, climbed into the driver's seat, and drove off, out of camera shot.

'Can we try and see where the car goes?'

She nodded, manoeuvring the mouse until she found a north-facing camera near the town clock. She scrolled the time along to 3.21 a.m.. A minute later, the Kia Sportage came into view and casually rounded the ninety degree bend down towards St. Cuthbert's Way.

Tanzy shook his head and smiled.

'What's funny?'

'He isn't even speeding or rushing to get away. It's as if he has all the time in the world.'

Jennifer could hear the tension in his words and found the next camera. They watched the Sportage pass and disappear at the bottom of the screen.

'Where did he go? He either went left onto Crown Street or straight over,' Tanzy told her.

She found the camera at the end of Crown street, fixed to the side of the library.

'Let's see if he comes this way,' she said, carefully watching the screen.

The car turned and drove towards it, passing the William Steads pub then, strangely, it slowed and pulled up behind a black Jaguar that was parked on the corner of The Northern Echo building.

The Kia Sportage flashed its headlights at the Jaguar. Then the driver of the Sportage stepped out and waited. The driver's door of the Jaguar opened and another man stepped out, dressed exactly the same as the man from the Sportage. He was the same height and build. He was like a clone. He was also wearing a balaclava.

At the same time, they looked directly up at the camera and waved for nearly a minute, their movements mirroring each other.

It was the strangest thing Tanzy had ever seen.

Then both men walked towards each other, high-fived as they crossed and got into the other's car. Seconds later, they were gone.

'What the hell has just happened?' Tanzy gasped in astonishment.

'Hold on, we can see the plate of the jag,' Jennifer noticed, pointing at the edge of the screen. 'See?'

Tanzy leaned closer to the screen. 'Yeah, just. Hold on, I'll call it in and get a check on the plate.' He pulled his phone back from his pocket and called PC Weaver this time.

She answered in a couple of rings. 'Orion.'

'Amy, are you back in the office? I need a favour.'

'No not yet. I'm still in town, forensics are just clearing up. What's up?'

'It's alright, I'll try Cornty,' he told her and hung up.

He found Cornty's number and pressed CALL.

'Sir?' he answered.

'Phil, are you at the station near a computer?'

'Yeah, I'm at my desk now. How can I help?'

'I need you to check a plate for me?'

'Go on…'

'Right, it's S. B. 1. 3. M. T. P. Got that?'

'Yeah, hang on.' There was some background noise. 'Why are we checking this plate, sir?'

'It belongs to a car that's possibly owned by someone responsible for the murder of Lyle Wilson. Anything?'

'Erm… I'm not sure how to tell you this.'

'Is it a fake plate?'

'No, it's registered to someone.'

'Come on, Phil, who's it registered to?'

'It's registered to Detective Inspector Max Byrd.'

75

Monday Morning
Town Hall, Darlington Town Centre

'Can you *say* that again, Phil?

'The Jaguar is registered to Max Byrd.'

Tanzy was stunned. So much so that Jennifer glared up wondering what he'd been told.

'I – I don't – I don't understand,' he muttered. 'He doesn't have a Jaguar. How long has he had the car?'

'The date of registration for the ownership of that vehicle was just over three weeks ago. It matches up with his address too. He's the owner.'

'Okay, thanks. Say nothing, Phil, leave it with me.'

'But shouldn't we—'

Tanzy hung up, placed the phone on the desk, and dropped his face into his palms.

'Orion, what's happened?' Jennifer asked softly, taking a gentle grip of his forearm.

'I need to go. Thanks for your help.' He pulled himself away from the table and made his way to the door quickly, his head swimming with this new information. Within two minutes he was sitting in his Golf, rubbing his hands together and breathing heavily. He considered the men on the CCTV screen. Could one of them be Byrd? He had lost weight and could fit the image, but who was the other man?

Was he working with someone?

He pulled his phone out and decided to call Byrd, to give him a chance to explain what was going on. There

334

had to be a reason. There had to be. Tanzy was shaking as he found Byrd's number and pressed CALL.

The phone rang twice then Byrd cancelled the call.

He tried again.

It went straight to voicemail. Byrd had turned his phone off.

'Max, what are you playing at?'

He threw his phone onto the passenger seat so hard it bounced up and hit the inside of the passenger door. Sighing, he banged on his steering wheel so hard that the horn sounded in the car park and people passing by frowned at him.

He leaned over, picked up his phone and found PC Josh Andrew's number.

As soon as it was answered, he said, 'Have you seen Max? I need to speak with him immediately.'

'I'm at the office, boss. Cornty has just told me about a car being registered to him.'

Tanzy clamped his eyes shut and tipped his head back onto the head rest. 'Listen, keep this under wraps. DCI Fuller does not find out about this yet. Tell Phil that he needs to keep his big mouth shut. Who else has he told?'

'A few of us,' Andrews admitted.

Tanzy sighed. 'Find him right now and hand the phone to him. I need to speak to him.'

'Okay, hold on, he's on his way to Fuller's office.'

'Get to him before he gets there, quick!'

Andrews started to pant a little. 'Phil, Phil. Here, Orion is on the phone, he needs to speak with you.'

'Yeah?' Cornty said into the phone.

'Phil, what are you playing at?' said Tanzy.

'I – I don't know—'

'You *do* fucking know,' Tanzy barked. 'You need to keep this quiet until I've spoken to Max, okay. Stay away from Fuller's office. That, DC Phillip Cornty, is an order from me, your superior. Do you understand that?'

Cornty gulped. 'I understand.'

'Let me speak to Max first, okay,' Tanzy told him. 'There must be a reason for this.'

'Okay.'

'Pass the phone back to Josh, please.'

Andrews came back to the phone.

'Sir?'

'There's another problem, Josh,' Tanzy said. 'It isn't only one guy we're looking for, it's two.'

'Jesus.'

'Yeah. Listen, keep it quiet. I need to speak to Max first. I owe him that.'

They disconnected and Tanzy tried calling Byrd again.

Straight to answerphone.

'Where are you, Max?' he whispered.

76

Monday Afternoon
Carmel Road, Darlington

Jonny Darchem was sitting at his kitchen table when Andy rushed in, carrying a laptop under his arm. He pulled out the chair next to Darchem and dropped into it, opening the laptop.

'You need to see this, boss.'

'What is it?'

Darchem had been watching the footage sent to him a few days earlier, of the camera above his office on Duke Street picking up a man and a woman breaking in. Fortunately, he didn't keep anything in there because it was a front for this legitimate business and was under a different name, Cairnfield Developments. Work regarding his property developments was carried out at home, so his identity was kept a secret. He's used his contacts to obtain a passport in the name of Andrew Cairn, then set up bank accounts and insurance under that name. According to the bank and insurance companies, and anyone else who did business with him, the office on Duke Street was the only address registered. Outside the door to the office, was a secure letterbox, so that items or letters posted to him, could be picked up at night by Jamie. In that way, nobody from the design company next door would ever see anything.

He'd also watched the news headlines about the police hitting his property on Craig Street and seizing a substantial quantity of drugs. It was a setback but it wasn't the end of the world. He had other properties, and he wasn't stupid enough to keep all of his merchandise in just one place. He'd been in this game long enough to know that these things could potentially happen. He'd just redirect things for a while before setting up something else. He was a businessman, and he considered himself very good at what he did.

'What is it?' Darchem asked Andy, noticing him fidgeting.

'Just watch,' Andy said, opening a video file. 'I remotely hacked Brian Cornforth's laptop to transfer all of the business documents and information and found this...' He pointed at the screen. 'Just watch.'

For the next three minutes, Darchem and Andy watched the footage closely, Andy keeping an eye on his boss' reaction.

'Play that again,' Darchem said, coldly.

On the video feed, they watched Brian come back to the laptop and settle into his chair, then a moment later, a man entered from his hallway, wearing a Hi-Viz vest, and crept up behind him. The man placed a wire over Brian's head, pulled it tight around his throat, and dragged him back off the chair onto the floor. For a minute, no one was on the screen, until the man stood up.

'How are we watching this? Was it recorded?'

'All of our laptops are set up with an internal recording device. While the user is logged in, there's a camera recording what's in front of it permanently. I had a look back to the day he was murdered.'

'Very useful, indeed.' Darchem looked at the man from the still shot on the screen. 'I know him. He's familiar.'

'Who is he?'

Darchem opened up the internet on his own laptop and typed something in the search bar, then pressed ENTER. A huge list of results quickly came up. He clicked on the first result, which took him to the website of the local newspaper, The Northern Echo. He scrolled down a few pages and stopped.

'That's him,' Darchem said. 'That fucker's just made the biggest mistake of his life.'

77

Monday Evening
Stonedale Crescent, Darlington

Alice Richards had finished washing the dishes when her phone rang. She dried her hands, placed the folded tea towel neatly on the drainer and picked it up.

'Hey, Alex.'

'Hey yourself. You alright?'

'Yeah, just finished washing up.' She left the kitchen, and turned off the light, heading to the stairs.

'How's Callum doing? He didn't seem very happy when he got in from school. Sorry I didn't get chance to see him, I needed to finish an important report.'

'He's okay. He said one of the boys at school was calling him names or something. I told him that I'd speak to his teacher tomorrow morning. You busy?'

'Got loads of deliveries. The last one will be cold by the time I've dropped it off.'

'Might get more tips though,' she laughed.

'Here's hoping.' He fell silent for a moment. 'What's Cal up to now?'

'Just in his room, playing on the PlayStation.' She started climbing the stairs. 'It was mad what happened on Saturday at the restaurant, wasn't it? I was thinking about it earlier. It was a nightmare.'

'I know, I know. When the guy stumbled into me, I shit myself,' he confessed. 'Well, not literally.'

'Can't believe they thought you had anything to do with it.'

'I can't blame them. They're just doing their jobs.'

'Where are you now?'

'At the top end of Yarm Road. Got a few deliveries around here. They try and make it easier by getting the order drop offs as close as possible.'

'Makes sense,' she said. 'Hey, I was thinking...'

'Thinking what?'

'Hold on,' she said.

'What?'

'Shh... I think I heard something,' she said.

'It'll be just Cal—'

'Shh...'

Alex turned left at the roundabout onto McMullen Road, waiting for her to speak.

'There's someone outside,' she whispered.

'There's what?'

'Someone outside the back door.' Alice froze on the landing, glancing over the handrail down into the well-lit hallway. Behind her, she could hear Callum on his PlayStation through his closed bedroom door.

'Alice, is this a joke?'

She didn't reply.

'Alice, are you being—'

There was a loud crack, then a bang, through the phone.

'The back door in the kitchen is being smashed in, Alex! Alex, the back door...' she trailed off, moving quickly into Callum's room and closing the door immediately. 'Callum, Callum, get up, get up off the bed now!'

Callum looked at her strangely, wondering what on earth she was doing.

'Callum, up now!' She threw the phone onto the floor and, using all the strength she had, pulled Callum's bed towards the closed door.

'Alice, what the hell is going on?' Alex shouted down the phone.

'Mam, what is—'

'Help me move this. Quick,' she begged Callum.

He pulled his headset off, threw it down onto the floor, and dashed over to help her.

They could hear heavy footsteps on the stairs.

'Alice!' Alex cried. 'Hold on, I'm coming home!'

Footsteps pounded on the landing outside the door and, just as she was about to push the bed against the closed door, the door was kicked open.

A man walked in, dressed in black and wearing a smile from ear to ear. There was a knife in his hand.

'Hello, Alice,' he said.

Alice grabbed Callum and backed into the furthest corner from the doorway. Both of them started to cry.

78

Tanzy hadn't wanted to do it, but he felt he had no other choice. He'd tracked the location of Byrd's phone and the technology he was using told him that it was at Byrd's home. He'd tried calling throughout the day, but Byrd's phone had been turned off.

Byrd hadn't turned up for the post-mortem of Lyle Wilson. Tanzy had made an excuse for him, telling forensics and the pathologists he was busy attending something else. From the post-mortem, it was clear Lyle had been strangled with a very thin, sharp wire. Consistent with the other victims, Lyle Wilson had seven marks on his back, most likely done with a thin whip. Two of them were fresh, and in the opinion of the senior Pathologist, Arnold, they'd been done within the last two weeks ago. The hardest part of Tanzy's day was speaking with Fuller, who had asked him what was happening on the case. Tanzy didn't tell him about seeing two men on the CCTV and about the black Jaguar that was registered to Byrd.

Tanzy pulled up outside Byrd's house, purposefully blocking Byrd's X5 which was on the driveway. The street was quiet and dark.

He got out of the car and closed his door gently, taking a lung full of cold air. He stared at Byrd's house for a moment. There was light coming through the curtains in the living room and through the bathroom blinds just above the front door.

There was no Jaguar in sight as he looked up and down the street.

He wasn't sure how he was going to approach this one. It was a situation he'd never been in, but he figured if things got physical, although Max had undergone hand-to-hand combat training, Tanzy's Judo training would give him the upper hand.

He walked up the driveway and knocked twice on the door.

He heard footsteps, then Claire opened the door, smiling.

'Hi, Claire. Is Max in?'

'Yes, please come in,' she said, standing back, holding the door for him. 'It's been a while, how you keeping?'

Tanzy stepped into the warm hallway. 'It *has* been a while, Claire. And I'm fine thank you.'

Claire closed the door. 'How's Pip doing? And the kids?'

Tanzy looked down the hall, then glanced back at her. 'All good. Where's Max?'

'Oh, he's just in the kitchen. He'll be happy you called,' she told him, pointing down the hall.

Tanzy frowned, then strolled down the hallway into the kitchen. At the table, there was an empty glass with a half-full bottle of whisky next to it.

'Max?' Tanzy said into the empty kitchen.

Claire followed Tanzy into the kitchen but couldn't see Byrd. 'Max, you in here?'

'In the garage. Just a second,' they heard him say from the door off the kitchen. 'Is that you, Ori?'

'Yeah,' Tanzy replied, shouting loud enough to be heard.

'Can I make you a tea or a coffee, Orion?' Claire asked, slowly passing him, heading for the kettle.

'No, it's fine, I'm okay, thank you.'

A minute later, Byrd stepped through the door from the garage, then closed and locked it. He placed the key on a key hook fixed to the wall and walked towards Tanzy.

Tanzy watched him carefully.

'How you doing, Ori?' he said, holding out his hand. 'Thanks for dropping by.'

Tanzy frowned at the man he'd known for as long as he had been in the police force and didn't shake it.

Byrd narrowed his gaze. 'What's the matter, Ori?'

'Are you being serious, Max?'

Claire glanced his way, wondering what was going on, a worried look on her face. 'What's going on?'

'I'll let Max tell you.'

Byrd said, 'I'm sorry, I don't understand. What's happened?'

Tanzy smiled and tilted his head. 'Come on, Max... don't play games.'

'Ori, I'm confused, mate,' he muttered, sharing confused stares with Claire who was standing at the kettle. 'Ori, what is this?'

'Did you kill Mark Greenwell?'

Byrd frowned.

'What about Brian Cornforth?' Tanzy added.

Byrd, a perplexed look on his face, was lost for words.

'Well, did you?' Tanzy persisted.

'Now listen, son, I don't know what you're getting at but, if you ask me that again, you're going on your arse. You hear me?'

Tanzy smiled and shrugged. 'Really? Think you could take me on?'

'You can count on it.'

'Go on then, give me your best shot...'

79

Monday Evening
Stonedale Crescent, Darlington

Alex Richards slammed the brakes on outside his house, bringing his car to a screeching stop in front of his driveway. The phone call with Alice had ended seconds after he'd heard her and Callum screaming.

He jumped out and ran as fast as he could to the front door. He unlocked the door and barged it open with a shoulder.

'Alice!' he shouted. 'Alice!'

The house was quiet and pitch black. He pressed the switch to his right, the hallway erupting in cold harsh light.

'Callum!'

The house was silent.

He raced up the stairs, taking the steps two at a time until he reached the landing and froze. Through the open bathroom door he could see something written on the mirror.

Too Late.

His heart missed a beat, his stomach turning as he backed out of the bathroom and ran to Callum's bedroom. His door opened halfway until it bounced off the side of Callum's bed.

He stepped over the bed and turned on the switch on the wall.

The room filled with light.

There was blood all over the white carpet.

He looked around the room. It was a mess. Callum's chair was tipped over next to his broken desk. His wardrobe door was barely hanging on by one hinge, the other door had come off and was against the wall to the left. Callum's clothes were all over, small piles scattered around.

He saw the body slumped against the wall in the corner and, immediately, knew it was Alice. There was a pool of blood underneath her, the bottom of her dressing gown was saturated in it.

'Alice?' Alex said quietly.

Cautiously he went over to her, placing his hand on her shoulder then pulling her back to see her face. He screamed and threw his hands to his mouth. Letting her go too quickly, she dropped to the floor with a thud, her body twisting, glaring up at him with wide, vacant bloodshot eyes.

Her dressing gown was pierced in several places from a violent knife attack. He took a few steps back, stumbling on the floor. The tears fell as he shook with anger.

He turned his attention to the landing but, after carefully checking the house, he couldn't find Callum. He had to assume he'd been taken.

He moved to the kitchen, opened up a cupboard, grabbed a bag from the bottom, and went out the back door towards to his car, determined to settle the score with the man responsible for this.

80

Monday Evening
Low Coniscliffe, Darlington

'Don't be shy, Max, take your best shot,' Tanzy said, adjusting his stance a little. 'Or do you need me to ask you again if you killed Mark Greenwell?'

Byrd lunged forward with a straight jab to Tanzy's nose. Tanzy was quick, but not quite quick enough as Byrd's knuckles caught the side of his nose. He stumbled back a step, surprised at the speed which Byrd had delivered it.

'Not bad,' Tanzy said, nodding his head.

'Not just a slow old man after all, eh?' Byrd shouted with his fists raised high.

'Please, just stop!' screamed Claire, only metres away from them.

'You only had one shot and you messed up,' Tanzy told him.

Byrd lunged forward again with the same jab but Tanzy saw it coming a mile away, ducked and drove a right hand into his kidneys. Byrd slumped over in pain.

'Why did you do it, Max?' Tanzy shouted.

Byrd didn't answer. Instead, he straightened up and threw himself at Tanzy, trying to grab him. Byrd almost had his grip on Tanzy's throat, but Tanzy used his hands to deflect his attempt, turning Byrd side on. It opened up an opportunity for Tanzy to come in from his side and place his right hand over his arms and bring it under his chin. He moved to the back of him, bringing his left hand around to the opposite side and he got him in a choke hold, then squeezed. Byrd was tough, Tanzy realised, his strength took him by surprise but, he'd choked much bigger men in the same position and knew it would be only a matter of time.

Byrd struggled until his body became limp. Tanzy lowered him to the floor slowly and grabbed his handcuffs from his belt. He turned him over, grabbing both of his hands.

'Max Byrd, I'm arresting you on the—'

Tanzy felt an excruciating pain to his head before he lost consciousness and passed out on the floor next to Byrd.

Claire stepped back, her hand shaking, and dropped the frying pan on the floor.

His eyes fluttered open. He didn't know where he was. The floor underneath felt harder than his bed. It was much colder too. The pain in his head made him feel sick. Lying on his side, he brought his hand up and touched the top of his head, feeling the hard lump rising, and winced.

'What the f…' he whispered, looking up, his eyes focusing on the light above him. As the dizziness faded, he turned onto his front, pushing himself up to look around.

'Where – where…' he tried to say, then fell silent.

And then he remembered what had happened.

To his left, sitting at the table with his chair facing towards him, was Byrd. His hand was on a baseball bat ready to use it if necessary. Claire was sitting opposite him, watching Tanzy in anticipation.

'Orion, first of all, keep calm,' Byrd said, 'because I genuinely don't understand why you came here tonight or why you asked me the questions you did. I've had a pretty shitty day too, so' — Byrd shuffled slightly in his seat — 'for the benefit of the friendship we've had for nearly twenty years, I need you to stay calm and relax. Come and sit down and explain to me what is going on.'

Tanzy smiled at him, and very slowly stood up, a rush of blood finding his head. He looked at Claire. 'What did you hit me with? A hammer?'

She pointed to the frying pan on the worktop to her right.

'Nice,' Tanzy sighed, steadying himself.

'Please, come and sit down. No more fucking around and fighting. Talk to me,' Byrd insisted.

Tanzy padded over to the table, disorientated, and dropped into the seat next to Byrd.

'Would you like some water, Orion?' Claire asked.

He nodded to her. She grabbed a glass from the cupboard and filled it at the sink.

'Ori... what's happened?'

'You *really* don't know?'

Byrd shook his head. 'Enlighten me...'

'Do you own a black Jaguar? Registration plate S. B. 1. 3. M. T. P.'

Byrd frowned at him. 'You know what car I drive, I—'

'Just answer the question,' Tanzy told him.

'No, I do not own that vehicle.'

'Okay.'

'What is so special about this vehicle?' Byrd asked.

Tanzy told him about the video where the Kia Sportage stopped behind the car. He mentioned the two men getting out and waving at the camera.

'Directly at the camera?' Byrd asked, frowning.

Tanzy nodded. 'I checked the registration plate with the DVLA. You're the owner. It's registered at this address, Max.'

Byrd scrunched up his face, then looked over to Claire who was similarly confused.

'What?' he said.

Tanzy shrugged. 'Any explanation how that is possible?'

'Honestly, Ori, I don't understand this. Have you got the video?'

Tanzy pulled out his phone, navigated to his video folder, pressed PLAY and turned it around so Byrd could see it. Claire craned over the table to watch it too.

'And… that car apparently is registered to me?'

'According to the DVLA, it does.'

'DVLA?' Claire said. 'The letter.'

They both glanced at her. 'What letter?' Tanzy asked.

Byrd remembered. 'I didn't read it. Where did you say you put it?'

She went over to the microwave and sifted through the random pile of envelopes, takeaway leaflets and magazines. 'I put it on here. Except… it isn't here. Where is it?'

'When did this letter come, Max?' Tanzy asked.

'Three days ago,' Claire replied, confidently. 'Yeah, one-hundred percent I put it on there.' She checked through the pile again. 'It's definitely not here.'

'If what you're saying is true, Max, and trust me, I want to believe you, then it seems someone has set you up. That letter from the DVLA could have been the logbook for the Jag. The date of the registration was less than three weeks ago.'

Byrd mulled over his words, trying to think of anyone who would do such a thing.

'I want to apologise for coming in like that and not giving you enough chance to explain,' Tanzy said. 'I've known you nearly twenty years. You're my best friend, for God's sake. I'm sorry.'

Byrd reached forward and patted Tanzy's hand. 'Don't worry about it. I won't go so easily on you next time,' he added, with a wink.

'Sorry for hitting you over the head, Ori,' Claire confessed, wincing. 'Instinct took over.'

'It's Max rubbing off on you.'

They shared a laugh.

'You said you've had a shit day,' said Tanzy. 'I haven't seen you all day. Where've you been?'

'After we left the scene this morning, I got a call from one of the carers at Ventress Care Home.' He fell silent for a moment, then he said, 'My mother died. I've been sorting that out all day.'

Tanzy, realising Byrd had lost one of the closest people to him, pushed out his chair and stood up. 'I'm so sorry, mate,' Tanzy whispered, tears in his eyes. Byrd stood up too, and they did something which they hadn't done in all the years they'd known each other.

They shared a hug and cried.

81

Angela turned around and faced Leah, shrugging, curling back a few strands of her long dark hair behind her ear. 'She's not answering. Try calling her again.'

Leah, sitting in the driver's seat in the yellow Renault Clio, pressed CALL for the sixth time. After a few moments, she shook her head. 'It rings then goes to answerphone,' she shouted from the car.

'Where is she?'

Angela stepped back onto the driveway and peered down the side of the house. The side gate was open. She didn't know Alice all that well, but she was worried. They'd agreed to pick her up at 9 a.m. and, on previous occasions, she'd been waiting at the door with her coat on.

'The side gate is open,' Angela shouted back to Leah. 'I'm going in.'

'Hold on, 'I'll come with you,' Leah said. 'I want to have a look inside. See this décor she keeps bragging about.' Leah sauntered over in heels, light jeans, and a tight fitting leather jacket. She'd been to the hairdressers yesterday and not only got her hair cut shockingly short, but she'd dyed it blonde. Once she was level with Angela, they gingerly made their way down the side. When they were through the gate, Angela saw that the back door was open and badly damaged.

'Alice?' she said, then again louder, 'Alice!' There was no sound coming from the house.

'Should we go in?' Leah asked, unsure.

Angela stepped into the cold kitchen. The night chill had filled the whole of the house, making it feel colder than outside.

'Alice!' Leah shouted.

Nothing.

'We should ring the police,' Angela said.

'Unless she's taken Callum to school?'

'Alex takes him. She told us, remember?'

They went into the hallway and checked all the rooms downstairs.

'She might be still asleep,' said Leah as she started climbing the stairs. 'Alice!'

At the top of the stairs, they noticed the bathroom door was open.

'Hold up. What's that say on the mirror?'

Angela stood next to her and looked inside. 'Too late?'

'What does that mean?'

They both turned, heading along the landing. There was a door to the left that was half open. Angela pushed the door, but it was jammed against something. 'Alice, you in here?'

She peered inside and saw the mess. 'What the hell went on in here? It's as if a bomb has gone off.'

'Let me see,' Leah said, poking her head in. 'Jesus, someone must have broken in. We need to ring the police.'

Angela looked around the room and saw the blood. The carpet was soaked with it. 'Al – Alice?'

She let out a blood-curdling scream.

82

Within half an hour DI Max Byrd and DI Orion Tanzy, along with forensics and a small team of PCs, were at the Richards' house.

Byrd and Tanzy were standing in the doorway to Callum's bedroom.

Byrd shook his head. 'Well, this makes sense.'

'What does?'

'Why Claire said she'd tried calling Alice last night but hadn't got an answer.' Byrd sighed and looked away for a moment. Tallow, Hope and Forrest were all in the room, dressed in their usual white disposable suits and face masks. Hope was crouched down near Alice, taking a sample of her blood. Tallow was standing back with his camera in his hand, looking at the photos he'd already taken. Forrest was to Hope's left, making notes on the blood spatter.

'Seems she was stabbed multiple times here,' Forrest said to Tallow, who put his camera down to give her his full attention. 'Can you see the thicker lumps there. And there.'

Tallow nodded.

'This is where she was wounded, then she stumbled into the corner. Can you see that pattern across there? It seems she put up a fight.'

Byrd looked over to the wall, where the plaster had been dented in various places. She looked at Byrd and Tanzy. 'I'm assuming this is one of her children's rooms?'

'He's called Callum,' Byrd said. 'He's twelve, I believe. And they have a teenage girl, Lisa, who's just turned eighteen. *This* is Alice Richards. She's a friend of my partner. Her husband was involved in the incident at Uno Momento on Saturday night.'

'Does your partner know about this yet?'

'No,' he said, then turned his attention to Hope. 'Emily, how long has she been dead?'

'At least twelve hours,' she said, confidently.

Once Hope had moved away from the body, Tallow took photos of the whole room, and then a short video. He placed his camera to one side and, with help from Hope, they pulled Alice away from the corner and placed her down on her back. They lifted up her soaked vest and counted six stab marks to her stomach.

Byrd clamped his eyes shut for a second, struggling to get the images of what had happened out of his head.

'Who the hell did this?' Tanzy said.

'Where's the husband? Any sign of him?' Tallow asked. They had checked the house briefly before returning to this room. There had been no sign of Callum, Lisa, or Alex. Byrd shook his head.

From the landing, DC Cornty called out, 'The media is here.'

Tanzy said, 'Keep them back. Make sure Weaver and Andrews stay at the tape. This is really going to piss Fuller off.' He sighed and looked at the floor. 'This town is going to shit.'

Byrd nodded in agreement but said nothing.

Cornty said, 'Do you think it's the same killer?'

'The brutality is definitely similar,' Tanzy said.

'But how is she linked to the others? Our speculation so far is that Mark Greenwell and Lyle Wilson were a part of a drug ring which, we know, Jonny Darchem has strong links to. Brian Cornforth worked for Cairnfield Developments which we know was registered to an empty office on Duke Street but the guy next door told us he forwarded the mail on to Carmel Road. That's where, apparently, Andrew Cairn, lives, although we suspect is Jonny Darchem. How does *she* play her part?'

Byrd gave a small smile and said, 'I need some air.'

Tanzy watched him walk slowly down the stairs, his body slumped and shoulders dipped. Turning back to the room, he watched Tallow put something in a plastic clear bag.

'What's that?'

'Saliva swab.'

Hope faced Tanzy. 'Where's the children and husband?'

'That's what we need to find out, because at the moment, despite Max knowing him, the number one suspect responsible for this is Alex Richards.'

Downstairs, Byrd had come to the same conclusion and had begun to think long and hard about what, and certainly why, this had happened.

83

Tuesday Late Morning
Beechwood Avenue, Darlington

Byrd first needed to find Alex Richards. From their meal on Saturday he'd got his number, just in case Alex ever needed a football player if they were short.

Sitting in his X5, he called it. Straight to answerphone.

PC Weaver was sat next to him, relaxed, her hands down on her lap. They'd spoken to one of the PCs at the station, who'd told them Alex's dad, Patrick, lived on Beechwood Avenue, just opposite St. Augustine's Primary School.

'Come on,' Byrd said, opening his door. Weaver did the same and made her way around the rear of the car. The chance that Alex was here was unlikely but they might learn something from his father or he might be able to contact him.

Byrd opened the metal gate, the rusty hinges creaking loudly, approached the door and knocked several times.

Weaver, standing behind him, shivered in her uniform. It was a few degrees lower than yesterday, but it was bright, the sun shining low to their right.

The front door opened and, standing on the mat over the threshold, was a man that appeared to be in his seventies. He was of average height, had long whispery hair and a beard that Santa would be proud of.

'Can I help you?' he asked.

Weaver asked him if he was Patrick Richards.

Patrick's eyes narrowed as he said, 'Yes?'

'Have you seen your son Alex?'

His eyes shot left, then right. 'Not in a few weeks, no. We had a falling out a few months ago. He only pops over when he needs something.'

Byrd nodded. 'Can we pop in for a moment? I have some bad news I'm afraid.'

Patrick, after digesting his words, nodded and moved aside. 'Sorry about the mess.'

Byrd and Weaver walked into the large, wide hallway. The décor needed some TLC, that was obvious. Everything about it told Byrd that a woman didn't live there.

'Is there a Mrs Richards here?'

Patrick shook his head sadly. 'Passed away three years ago. Cancer.'

Weaver gave him a sad smile and followed him down the hall.

'Please, sit in here,' he said, motioning to the living room. Inside the room, the ceiling was high, the walls were painted a faded duck-egg blue, and the carpet was black. There was a sofa to the left near an old fireplace which looked older than he did, and a television in the corner near the window, but not much else, leaving plenty of floor space to the right. 'I used to have another sofa, but I sold it,' he explained, pointing to where it used to be.

'We're okay standing,' Byrd said.

'What's this about, Detective?'

'Unfortunately, we have some very bad news. Your daughter-in-law, Alice Richards, has been murdered in her home.'

Patrick threw his hands up to his mouth in shock. 'What – what happened?'

'We're currently investigating that, but we need to speak to Alex. I've tried phoning him but there's no answer.'

'*You* have his number?' his father said, frowning.

'Yeah. My partner and I went for a meal with Alex and Alice on Saturday. Alice was a good friend of my partner.'

'I see...' Patrick said. 'Do you want me to call him?'

'If you could, yes please,' Byrd said, appreciatively.

Patrick went over to the mantel piece and grabbed his phone. It was an old model, Byrd could tell, but he didn't know the make. Patrick took his time finding his son's number, as if not quite sure how to use it, and finally put it to his ear.

'Just calling him,' he told Byrd and Weaver, who exchanged a quick glance towards each other because it stated the obvious.

'No answer. There's a voice that comes on saying to leave a message or something.' Confusion enveloped his face for a moment.

'Okay, thank you for trying,' Byrd said. 'Can you tell me about Alex. I know I went for a meal with him but I don't know him all that well. Anything about his military service or his current job that might help us find him? Any friends or places he might be?'

Patrick scrunched his face up, thinking what to say. 'He's thirty-eight and he was in the army for ten years.'

'What did he do in the army?'

'Everyone thinks he was front line personnel, even Alice did, and his kids. But he wasn't.'

'*He*... wasn't?'

'No,' he said, shaking his head. 'He was a part of an SAS unit. He'd go away spending months at a time wherever the government sent him. I think – I think I'm the only person in his family that knows the truth.'

Byrd didn't know what to say.

'Have you spoken with their daughter, Lisa?' Weaver asked.

Patrick frowned and shook his head. 'How is that possible?'

'She may have phoned you recently,' Weaver countered.

'Lisa is dead...'

Byrd and Weaver fell silent, then Byrd spoke: 'Alex was talking about her the other night, saying she was busy doing her own thing?'

'Alex can't accept what happened to her. That's why he came out of the army.'

'*What* happened to her?'

Over the next few minutes, Patrick explained the story.

Byrd thanked Patrick Richards, handing him a contact card. 'If you do see him or speak with him, tell him to call Max. He knows who I am.' Byrd went to turn and walk out the door when Patrick spoke:

'Detective…'

Byrd turned.

'Don't underestimate him. He's unlike anyone I know.'

Byrd gave him a long stare, processing his words, then turned and followed Weaver outside into the cold.

84

Tuesday Afternoon
Carmel Road, Darlington

In the huge living room, sitting on the wide sofa, Jonny Darchem was watching the television. He was taking a sip of coffee when the programme he was watching was interrupted by breaking news.

On the screen, was a reporter, standing at a semi-detached house in Stonedale Crescent, a cul-de-sac off Milbank Road in Darlington. Darchem picked up the remote and turned up the volume.

The blonde-haired reporter said, 'We're standing in a quiet cul-de-sac in front of a home where a woman, thirty-eight-year-old Alice Richards, has been found murdered. Two of her friends, who were meant to be picking her up, gained access to the house, behind me, by using the back door which had been left open. After becoming worried, they searched the house and found Mrs Richards dead in her son's bedroom. At the moment, the whereabouts of her husband, Alex Richards, and their son, Callum Richards, aged twelve, is unknown.'

'Don't worry,' Darchem said to the television, smiling, 'Callum's safe upstairs.'

The reporter went on: 'Police and detectives are very keen to speak to Alex Richards. He hasn't been seen since last night when he delivering pizzas around Darlington. Mr Richards has spent more than ten years in the army and if anyone knows his whereabouts, they are requested to contact the police immediately.'

C. J. Grayson

'Army eh?' Darchem said, looking to his left towards Arthur.

'This is Abigail Trent, ITV News,' the reporter said, before the camera cut off and returned to the studio.

'Army,' Darchem said again.

Arthur shrugged.

'And you killed his wife and brought his son here.'

He shrugged. 'Don't worry about it. I can handle him.'

'You see, Arthur, that's what I like about you. No task is too difficult.' Darchem stood up and looked out of the impressive bay window onto his front garden, then watched the passing cars. The sky above was clear blue; there wasn't a cloud in sight. 'It's a lovely day today.' He turned back to Arthur, whose dark eyes were watching him, and said, 'Do you think he knows his son is here?'

'I doubt it,' Arthur replied. 'What are you going to do with Callum? He's older than the children we normally deal with.'

'He is. But he's handsome, isn't he? There'll be someone out there who wants him. We'll just sell him for a reduced price.'

Darchem went back to the sofa and sat down with a worried expression.

'What's with the face?' Arthur asked.

'I keep thinking about something.' He fell silent for a moment. 'The night his daughter died was the night of that party, right?'

Arthur nodded.

'Mark Greenwell, Lyle Wilson, and Brian Cornforth were all there. Now they're all dead, Arthur. He knows what happened. He knows what happened to her. At first, I thought this could be the Farlans or the Haleys, but it's not gang or drug related, is it? It's pure revenge.'

'Who else was at the party that night?' Arthur asked.

'Jamie was there. He was talking about it a few days ago, feeling all sad about it for some fucking reason.'

'Who else? Were you there?'

Darchem shook his head. 'No. All the people who've been killed worked for me in some way. Why now? Why, a year after her death, are these things happening. Someone has been talking to him, someone has told him what happened.'

'Did you say Jamie was there?'

Darchem nodded. 'I suppose he's not dead yet.'

'Maybe Jamie is the one who's been talking?'

'That's ridiculous, Arthur, and you know it. Jamie is solid. I've practically raised him as my own. I've offered him a home, money, anything he wants.'

'Where is Jamie?' Arthur asked, standing up.

'I haven't seen him all day,' Darchem admitted, watching Arthur head for the door. 'Do you honestly think Richards knows where I live?'

Arthur smiled. 'Well, we'll soon find out if he turns up. How could he know, though? Unless he's put a tracker on one of our cars.'

85

Tuesday Afternoon
Darlington Memorial Hospital

Byrd met Tanzy at the entrance to the Paediatric ward. They explained to the nurse at reception that they'd received a call from Damien Spencer's mother, Mandy. He'd woken up and doctors had told her he was okay to speak to the police if they still needed to ask him questions about what happened to him.

'What's with the iPad?' Byrd asked, noticing it tucked under Tanzy's arm.

'You'll see,' he replied.

The nurse led them down the brightly lit corridor. It was lined with children's drawings and paintings of the nurses who had helped them. The children had signed their names and drawn smiley faces. It was a nice touch.

It wasn't long because the small, silver-haired nurse took a left through an open door. To the left-hand side of the room, sat up in the bed, was Damien Spencer. Mandy Spencer was sitting beside him, talking about something which was making him giggle. Byrd smiled inside, happy he was okay.

The nurse introduced the detectives to Damien and then left, telling them to let her know if they needed anything.

Mandy smiled at Tanzy.

'How you doing, Mandy?'

She nodded.

'It looks like you're feeling much better, Damien? Tanzy said, switching his attention to the bed.

Damien gave a big nod.

Byrd and Tanzy found two chairs nearby and sat down on the opposite side of the bed to where Mandy was sitting.

'How you feeling, mate?' Byrd said.

'I feel good.' Damien glanced at his mother to see if that was the right answer. She smiled proudly at him.

'Good, that's brilliant,' said Tanzy. 'Now, would it be okay if we asked you some questions? Would that be okay?'

Without looking towards his mother, he nodded confidently.

'Brilliant. Now if there's a question you don't understand or don't want to answer, it's okay, Damien.' Tanzy added, placing the iPad on the bed next to him.

Another nod. He glanced down at the tablet near him. 'I have one of those,' he told them.

'Really? Well lucky you,' replied Tanzy. 'Then I guess you'll know how they work and do just fine with this.'

Normally, when it came to speaking to children, Tanzy took charge. Byrd wasn't a father and didn't have a lot of experience of dealing with them.

'Okay, we know what happened to you. We know that you were taken to a house, weren't you?'

Damien bobbed his head.

'Good. What I would like to do is try and find that house. Do you think you can help us do that? Then maybe we can find your friends too.'

'I'll do my best,' he said, softly.

'That's great.' Tanzy looked at Mandy. 'That's okay, isn't it, Mum?'

She nodded. 'Of course, Detective.'

He smiled, then leaned in towards Damien, placing the iPad on his bed covers, on top of his legs. 'Have you heard of Google maps?'

His face lit up. 'Yeah, I've seen my house on there.'

'Have you? Well what I'd like to do is go to a place on Google maps, and from there try and find out where the man in the red car took you. Do you think we can try doing that?'

'Yeah, okay,' he said, smiling.

'Brill. I'm using something similar to Google maps, but it's called Instant Street View. Tanzy typed *Woodland Road, Darlington* into the search bar and tapped ENTER. The screen showed the roundabout at the end of Woodland Road, which happened to be exactly where Tanzy wanted it to be.

He lifted it up slightly, so Damien had a better view. 'Do you know this roundabout?'

He nodded.

'When you were in the car, which way did you go?'

'That way.' He pointed left. Tanzy tapped the arrows on the iPad, angling the focus of the 3-D virtual image to the left, where the screen appeared at the next small roundabout.

'Why are you starting there?' Mandy asked, confused, thinking it made more sense to start on the street they lived. Brougham Street.

'Through CCTV we tracked the red Mondeo to this spot then we lost it.'

She nodded.

'So, Damien, do you remember if the man went left or right?'

'He went left.'

Tanzy double-tapped the screen taking the screen up Carmel Road.

'Do I keep going?'

Damien leaned forward, taking over, double-tapping the screen, then again, then stopped. He dragged the focus of the screen ninety degrees to the right, so the screen faced a huge house with a long garden.

'Is that the house?' Tanzy asked him.

'Yes.'

Tanzy angled the screen and showed it to Byrd. He recognised it as the same house he'd gone to in an attempt to speak with Andrew Cairn of Cairnfield Developments.

Byrd pulled out his phone and rang PC Weaver. 'Amy, listen, we need a meeting in half an hour at the station. Round people up. Tell them Orion and I need to speak with them immediately. Get Fuller in there too. And get in touch with Sergeant Tunstall. I want him sitting in for this one as well. We won't be long.' Byrd ended the call and placed it back into his black trousers.

'Do – do you know who lives there?' Mandy asked from across the bed.

'We do,' Byrd confirmed. 'And believe me, the person responsible will be going straight to prison for this.'

Byrd and Tanzy thanked Mandy and Damien for their time and left the room, walked down the corridor, and signed out at the reception of the Paediatric ward. Within five minutes, they were back in their cars, heading for the station.

86

Tuesday Late Afternoon
Police Station

When Byrd and Tanzy entered, they realised that the room contained more people than they'd ever seen in there. PC Weaver had done a great job rounding people up.

Tanzy took hold of the small black remote, pressed the button, and the screen flickered on at the front of the room. 'Hey, everyone, thank you for coming.' He looked over to Jack Tunstall. 'Thank you, Jack. And your team.'

Several of them nodded back at him.

'Right, we've just been to the hospital to speak to Damien Spencer. As you may know, he was kidnapped last Thursday morning on Brougham Street. According to him, he was taken to Broken Scar and thrown in the river during the middle of the night and left to drown. Fortunately, for Damien, a brave teenager jumped in and saved him. Damien has been kept at the hospital until earlier today, he woke and was able to talk to us. He's just confirmed the address where he was held. The strongly suspect the house belongs to Jonny Darchem.'

Muttering swept across the room.

'I know, we can finally nail this piece of shit.'

Sergeant Tunstall joined Byrd and Tanzy at the front and, over the next five minutes, they came up with a plan of attack to take down Jonny Darchem at his property. The chance were Darchem was armed and that he wouldn't be alone. Baring in mind what Damien had told them they'd have to be careful to avoid harming any children that may still be inside. They stated three objectives.

One: arrest Jonny Darchem.

Two: rescue the children that were inside.

Three: carry out the first two objectives in the safest, most practical way possible.

'Before we all go,' DCI Fuller said, from the left, 'where are we on Alex Richards? Has anyone located him?'

'Nothing yet,' Tanzy replied. 'The media have an image of him and are showing it to the public across multiple networks and social media applications.'

'At the moment, Alex Richards remains the prime suspect to his own wife's murder, and the abduction of his son.'

DCI Fuller nodded. 'Anything else?'

Tanzy this time. 'We picked up a registration from the dark blue Kia Sportage which we caught on CCTV. The plates came back fake. Take a look.' He pulled a memory stick from his black jeans and placed it in the side of the laptop they used for their presentations. A moment later, after clicking through a few files, he clicked on an image which showed the Sportage's plate: NU13 PTX.

'We checked this plate,' Tanzy told them. 'Fake.'

DC Anne Tiffin raised her hand. 'Something isn't right with that, boss.'

'What's that, Anne?'

'That registration implies it's a 2013 model. That model Sportage is newer than that, I'm sure of it.'

She stood up and went over to one of the desks, grabbed a pen and notepad, then returned to her seat. She wrote down the reg: NU13 PTX and stared at it for a few moments.

'What you thinking, Anne?' Tanzy asked her.

'I think the real plate is NU18 BTX. He's altered the eight to make it look like a three and the B to make it look like a P. Can someone check this please?'

'I'll do it,' Byrd said, pulling a chair out in front of the laptop.

The door opened to their left and Tallow walked in.

He noticed everyone staring at him but focused solely on Tanzy. 'Ori, I finally finished running the prints from Saturday night at Uno Momento. One of them matches the prints I got from the handle on the toilet door at Brian Cornforth's house.'

'Who's our guy?'

'Alex Richards,' he said.

Tanzy nodded. 'Right, lets pack up and —'

'Hold on, Orion,' Byrd said. 'Just confirmed, the owner of a blue Kia Sportage with the registration NU18 BTX belongs to an Alison Richards.'

'Okay, thanks, Max.' Tanzy turned to face everyone. 'We execute this plan, we get Darchem, we find the children. Then we find Alex Richards. Any questions?'

Silence.

'Okay, good, let's get going.'

87

Alex Richards waited in the Kia Sportage on the corner of Thornberry Rise in the darkness. He could see the driveway of Jonny Darchem's house through the front passenger window. He had been there for nearly twenty minutes. On his phone the magnetic tracking device he'd placed under the wheel arch of the red Mondeo, was telling him that the car was at Darchem's house.

When Jamie had come to see him a few weeks ago, he'd told him everything. Everything about the night his daughter had died, everything about Darchem, including the men who worked for him.

'Why are you telling me this?' Richards had asked him nearly a month ago, when Jamie had appeared outside of his home after he returned from delivering pizzas.

'Because I'm sorry for what happened to your daughter. It wasn't my fault, but I was there. We were all doing drugs but hers had been contaminated with poison.' He had paused, unsure whether Alex was going to hit him. 'It's going too far now,' Jamie added. 'I can't take any more of it. What Darchem does to families is unforgiveable. He needs to be stopped.'

Alex stared at the tracking app he had open on his phone. The red Mondeo hadn't moved for a while now.

According to Jamie, Darchem's associate, Arthur, carried a gun on him at all times. If he saw him coming, he wouldn't hesitate to fire. He'd also informed Richards about the children, how they were taken and kept at the house until they were sold and shipped off to buyers across the country. What the buyers did with the children after they were sold was something Darchem wasn't interested in. All he cared about was the money.

Alex knew Callum was in there. He also knew, according to Jamie, that Callum wasn't in immediate danger.

His phone on the passenger seat lit up and vibrated. He picked it up and read the text message from Jamie. *Arthur is going out.*

'Good,' Alex said to himself, placing the phone on his knee and rubbing his hands together. Then he picked it back up and opened the tracking app. The Mondeo's location moved fractionally, until it hit Carmel Road and took a right in the direction away from him.

It was safe to go in.

Richards decided to leave his car. No one from inside the house would see it where it was, and he certainly didn't want any cameras picking it up if he went down the driveway.

He crossed the dark road, then slowed, glancing into Darchem's next door neighbour's driveway which sat in total darkness. He took a right through their neighbour's open gates and lightly made his way along the gravel to a tall row of hedging that separated the gardens. Any cameras that Darchem did have, wouldn't have seen him. Jamie had informed him this would be the safest way.

Richards approached the neighbour's house slowly, creeping along the gravel, his measured steps crunching lightly on the stones below. He stepped around a Black Volvo XC90, and kept low, making his way around the side of the house.

When he found himself in total darkness, he pulled a small torch from his pocket and shone it down at the floor. He stopped at the back corner of the huge house, poking his head around to look into the garden. There was a dim light on in the kitchen.

Keeping low he quietly passed the window until he reached the fence that divided the neighbour's property and Darchem's.

Very gently, he pushed against it. It was solid. He placed the torch back into his pocket and peered into Darchem's garden. It was in darkness, but he knew there was a security light and that he would have to stay as close as possible to the house to avoid setting it off and being seen by the camera.

He struggled over the top of the fence and quietly dropped down onto the other side. Keeping low again, he made his way under the number of windows until he reached Darchem's back door. He glanced up, noticing the camera fixed high on the wall, overlooking the gravel near him.

This would be the moment of truth. Had Jamie been honest with him or was this one big trick? Would a swarm of guys loaded with weapons appear from the darkness or would he get straight in undetected.

He grabbed the handle of the back door, very slowly pushed it down and edged the door open an inch. His heart rate was pumping so hard in his chest, it felt like it was going to explode. He opened the door further. Inside was the most extravagant kitchen he'd ever seen. Everything was brand new. The worktops were made from marble. The under cupboard lights were something you'd only see in a magazine.

'Thank you, Jamie,' he whispered to himself.

He quietly closed the door, then turned, keeping low until he found himself behind a huge island situated in the centre of the enormous space.

The phoned in his pocket vibrated twice. A text message. As quietly as he could, he pulled out his phone. It read: *JD Living room.*

How long will Arthur be? He replied
A while.

Sit tight. Act normal.

He placed his phone back in his pocket and peered over the island. The kitchen was empty. He heard faint music coming through the open doorway into the hallway, presumably from the living room.

He pulled out his phone and sent a text to Jamie: *How many in the house?*

Seconds later, it vibrated: *Darchem, me, Andy and Eric upstairs. And Children.*

Alex lowered himself behind the island and returned the text: *Get JD to come in kitchen.* He pressed SEND and waited.

Jamie was sitting on the sofa closest to the door with an empty bottle of beer in his hand. On the other sofa, Darchem took a last swig of his own, then lowered it down to his knee. They were watching some documentary about planes. Darchem was fascinated with them for some reason. The way the wings were shaped to keep them in the air so something. Jamie couldn't care less, but it was best to smile, agree, and go along with him.

The whip marks on his back were sore, the flesh was tender and open. In private he'd asked Andy to put some Vaseline on it and bandage it up, just like he had last month. If Darchem knew, there'd have been another mark alongside it. Darchem always said to his boys they had to take what they deserved and deal with it like men.

If you make a mistake, own it. Pay the price and face the consequences, were his words.

Darchem turned away from the television and looked at Jamie. 'You're quiet tonight, little Jamie?'

Jamie focused on the floor and didn't look up.

'Don't ignore me, son,' Darchem said, sternly.

'I'm – I'm tired, that's all,' he replied, glancing up briefly to meet his dark eyes.

Darchem nodded. 'You want another beer, son?'

Jamie bobbed his head, leaning forward to get up. 'Yeah, do you want one?'

'Sit down, I'll get you one,' Darchem insisted, standing up.

Jamie fell back into the sofa, watching Darchem wander across the rug towards the door. He sighed a little, the wounds on his back uncomfortable. This time, the whipping had been for the police raiding the house on Craig Street. Darchem had told him to manage the house, keeping the operation clean and simple, causing no suspicions or unusual activity. Darchem had lost a lot of product so he had vented his anger towards Jamie.

Jamie had heard the stories from the others about the whippings. Most of them hadn't believed it until it was too late, until they were in too deep to get out. They were threatened that their families would pay the ultimate price if they tried to leave and they all knew Darchem was capable of doing anything.

'Back in a minute,' Darchem said, walking through the doorway into the hall, heading for the kitchen.

88

Tuesday Early Evening
Carmel Road, Darlington

Alex Richards waited behind the island in the kitchen. He heard a voice say something coming from the direction of the hallway. His phone buzzed gently. *He's coming now*, the text from Jamie said.

He heard footsteps on the tiled floor of the kitchen, then the bright lights above came on. Richards' heart was beating quicker than it ever had. Finally, he was in the same room as the man responsible for his daughter's death.

From the sounds he figured Darchem had moved over to the side, then he heard a door open. As Richards had entered the kitchen, he noticed the double-doored fridge was over to the left side of the huge room so assumed that was the noise. After the fridge door closed, Darchem moved a few steps and pulled open a drawer, then one by one, opened the lids of the beer bottles.

'Bin open,' Darchem said.

Richards frowned, then a second later, to his right, the lid of the bin raised, with a quiet mechanical sound.

One bottle cap was thrown in. And then another, but the second one hit the rim and fell down on the tiled floor with a series of pings until it settled.

'Ahh, fuck,' Darchem said, placing the bottles on the side and making his way over.

It was only a matter of seconds before Darchem passed the island and picked up the cap. If Richards didn't move, Darchem would see him, and would be in a much better position to attack him down on the floor.

Richards knew Darchem was dangerous. He'd heard a story that Jamie had passed on, that he'd hit a man so hard in the face, he'd cartwheeled. He knew he'd have to be on his game, Darchem wouldn't go down easily.

As the footsteps were approaching to his right, Richards silently shuffled to the left, and moved around the side of the island. The size of it was roughly two metres by four, so there would be a lot of ground to cover to do what he planned in his head.

Darchem picked up the bottle cap, and stood, raising his hand in the air, like he was taking a shot with a basketball at a hoop, and threw it.

Richards, now at the opposite side of the island, tip toed around to the side Darchem was on.

The bottle cap hit the back of the bin and Darchem raised his arms in the air like he'd potted a three-pointer in an NBA game. 'He shoots and he scores.'

Then he stopped dead, staring at the back door

Richards was a metre behind him, keeping low, ready to pounce.

'What the...'

Darchem padded over to the back door. He noticed it wasn't fully closed. Frowning, he opened it and peered out, curiously checking around the gravel and across the garden, which sat in silent darkness. Richards, two feet behind him, was setting himself.

'No one would dare...' Darchem whispered, then edged back but, as he did, he saw a flash of movement. An arm came around him and dug under his chin against his throat. Then he felt another arm from the left. Darchem was extremely strong but even he couldn't get under the grip and release it.

His first thought was Jamie. He knew Andy and Eric were upstairs and he hadn't heard them come down in the time he'd been sitting in the living room with Jamie.

'Jay...' he coughed, saliva spurting from his mouth as he fiercely scratched at the forearms and hands of Richards. His windpipe was being crushed by the powerful force and, after a few more seconds, his world went dark.

Richards stumbled back a little, breathing heavily, and lowered him to the floor. He let out a heavy breath, then went over to the drawers near the cooker and pulled open the third drawer. Jamie had told him he had left him some thick cable ties there. Richards had made it clear he wanted to speak to Darchem first.

Killing him too soon would be too good for Darchem. Richards needed him to know it was him and why he was doing it. And he wanted the satisfaction of seeing Darchem's life drain from him.

He grabbed the pack of cable ties, closed the drawer, went back to Darchem, and turned him over onto his front. He brought his wrists together and put three of the cable ties around them, pulling them as tight as he could, so tight that the plastic dug into his skin.

Then he put his feet together and tied his ankles, restricting his movement for when he woke up, which Richards knew, wouldn't be long.

Darchem was sitting on his sofa in the living room when he opened his eyes. His head was pounding and his shoulders were screaming in pain. He realised his hands were somehow behind him, tied together.

He tried to separate his legs, but he couldn't. Then saw the cable tie around his ankles and realised why.

'The fuck is this?' he shouted, glaring around the room. 'That you, Jamie, fucking around?' The television was on in the corner and the fireplace in front of him was still burning away. He felt hot and uncomfortable. And angry.

'Jamie!' he shouted.

'Jamie won't help you, Jonathon.'

The voice came from behind him.

Darchem turned his head as best he could but his view was restricted. He certainly didn't recognise the voice. 'Who the fuck is that? Untie me now. I'll fucking kill you,' he spat.

Richards, before answering him, checked his phone and saw that Arthur's red Mondeo was now somewhere across town.

'You there, you coward? Attacking a man from behind. Must be proud of yourself?'

'And taking children away from their parents and selling them to desperate wierdos is one of your proudest moments?'

The question startled Darchem and he didn't reply.

'Where's my boy?' Richards asked, getting closer to him.

'If you've figured a way how to get in here and tie me up, I'm sure you're clever enough to find him.'

Richards moved out from behind the back of the sofa and stood before him, glaring down at Darchem. He then lowered himself to his knees and smiled.

'The fuck is funny?' Darchem spat.

'You've always been so careful, haven't you, Mr Darchem? Always been hiding in the shadows, carrying out your operations, ruining the lives of teenagers and addicts in this town. Everyone knows it's you, but the police can't do anything about it. But now…'

'Now… what?'

'Well, you see, you've fucked up three times in the past few weeks.'

'Really?'

Richards nodded confidently.

'Enlighten me...'

'Well, firstly, you took those three kids on their way to school. Sorry, it wasn't you, it was your handsome monkey. Arthur, is it? He—'

'I can't wait till he comes back. He'll rip your pretty little face off.'

'I'm sure he will. Now, as I was saying, you fucked up because Damien Spencer isn't dead.'

Darchem frowned. 'Of course he is! Arthur threw him in the river. He told me he did.'

Richards raised a finger and smiled. 'He was saved, then taken to hospital. No doubt, he's told the police everything, where you live, what you've done. It was kept out of the media, I'm assuming so you didn't find out. If you knew he'd survived, you'd have sent your chimp round to finish him off before he was well enough to talk to the police.'

'I don't hear any sirens,' Darchem said, smiling. 'Do you?'

'Not yet, Mr Darchem, not yet.'

'Go on then… what's the second thing?'

'The second thing is that you killed my wife.' Richards leaned in closer and stopped when he was within a few inches of his face.

'You have nice eyes, Alex,' Darchem commented, 'I think if—'

He stopped talking when Richards headbutted him hard, the momentum sending him into the back of the sofa with a loud groan. Instantly, blood poured from his nose, down his chin, onto his t-shirt.

'I do have nice eyes,' Richards replied, grinning, waiting for him to get over the blow.

'Where did you learn that - the school of fairies?' Darchem asked him, licking the blood around his mouth. 'Mmmm, tasty. What's the third thing? I have things to do.'

'Killing my daughter last year. Your product killed her. That means *you* killed her.'

'And what are you going to do about that?'

Richards was astounded at the audacity of the man. Then pulled the knife from his pocket, leaned forward and pushed it against his throat—

'Whoa whoa, it wasn't my product!' he said quickly. 'It's not my product, Alex. On that night, my supplier brought over the gear direct to the party. I had no idea it was poisoned.'

Richards held the knife hard against his throat, the tip of piercing the skin so a drop of blood appeared at the tip.

'You're talking shit,' Richards said.

'Alex, I'm not a liar. When your daughter died, I spoke to my supplier. He confirmed there could have been a chance the cocaine was contaminated. He told me the next five loads would be at half price as a sweetener if I didn't mention it. I'm a businessman, what can I say…'

'You're a waste of space.'

'Look around you, I don't seem to have done too bad for—'

Richards put more pressure on the knife, silencing him, a trickle of blood now running down the blade.

'Who was the supplier?'

Darchem didn't answer.

'I might let you live if I get a name.'

'You're killing me either way. I know what you're capable of, so you might as well just—'

Richard's knife was driven straight through his throat with such force that Darchem's body hit the back of the sofa. The blood sprayed from his throat. He looked Darchem in the eyes and watched his life ebb away.

It was one of the most satisfying things he'd ever done.

89

Tuesday Early Evening
Carmel Road, Darlington

Out in the hallway, Jamie was waiting for Richards. Although he hated Darchem he couldn't watch him die, although it was no less than he deserved in Jamie's opinion. He was a monster.

'All done?' Jamie asked, nervous in close proximity to Richards, the bloody knife still in his right hand.

Richards nodded. 'Where's my son?'

'I'll take you,' he said, 'follow me.'

Jamie led Richards up the huge, wide staircase. When they reached the top, he took a right, then another right until he arrived at a closed door. Jamie pulled out a set of keys and unlocked the door.

The room was in darkness and silent. Jamie went in first, flicked on the switch to the right, the room filling with a cold, harsh light. Richards followed him inside and noticed there were six beds, three on either side, with a walkway down the middle of the room.

The sudden bright light woke each child and they groggily sat up, rubbing their eyes. On the closest bed to the door, was Callum, his son.

He gasped and ran over to him, dropping the knife onto the floor. He picked Callum up, hugging and kissing him over and over. 'Are – are you okay?'

Callum started to cry but managed a nod before he dug his head into his father's shoulder. The other children watched in awe, unsure what was going on, exchanging glances with each other, and obviously wondering who this man was that they'd never seen before.

'Right, let's get out of here,' Richards said, turning towards the door.

Jamie was standing there holding the knife that Richards had dropped just before he picked up Callum. After a few moments, Jamie spun the knife around and offered the handle to him. 'You dropped this, Alex.'

Richards let out a small sigh and thankfully took the knife. 'Thank you, Jamie, for what you've done. You need to get out of here before the police come. Do a runner, start again somewhere.'

Jamie smiled, shaking his head. 'I've done too many bad things to make a fresh start anywhere. Like Darchem always told us, we must own our mistakes and face our consequences like men.'

'Darchem is gone...'

'Come on, I'll show you out,' Jamie offered.

Richards and Callum followed Jamie downstairs but, when they reached the bottom, the greasy-looking IT guy Andy stepped out from the kitchen, and all three of them stopped.

'Where on earth are they going?' he asked Jamie, frowning in confusion.

'They're going home.'

'Are you mad?'

Jamie shrugged.

'I – I can't let them leave,' he told him. 'Darchem will kill us.'

Jamie smiled and took a few steps towards him. 'Andy, go have a look in there. Go on.'

Andy moved back so he would have a clear view of the living room. On the sofa near the bay window, he saw Darchem, his hands tied behind his back and his face, neck and clothes covered in blood.

'Jesus!' Andy gasped, glaring back at Jamie.

'You see, he's gone now,' Jamie said. 'There's no reason for us to keep living like this. The monster is dead.'

'Just wait till Arthur finds out about this.'

Jamie turned and held his hand out to Richards for the knife. Jamie turned and took a step towards Andy, who burst out laughing.

'And what on earth are you going to do with that, little boy?'

Jamie, without answering the question, stabbed him several times in the chest. Richards put a hand over Callum's face and pulled him close to mask what was happening.

When Andy had slumped to the floor, Jamie turned and handed back the knife to Richards.

'Before you go,' Jamie said. 'Is it true what Darchem said about the supplier knowing the cocaine was poisoned.'

Richards mulled over his words. It seemed his revenge wasn't complete. 'You got a name?'

'I do,' Jamie replied, then told Richards the supplier's name.

Somewhere in the distance, they heard the sound of sirens heading in their direction.

'Go,' Jamie told him, then went back upstairs to the children's room.

On the hall floor, curled up behind the front door, Andy coughed up blood. He'd heard Jamie go back upstairs, and somehow, managed to grab his phone from his pocket. Every movement sent pain through his body, but he sluggishly brought it up to his face and unlocked it with his bloody fingers.

He found the number he needed and pressed CALL, then tapped on the speaker button.

'Yeah,' said the voice.

'Arthur, it's Andy… Darchem is dead. Richards has been here. He's took his kid back.'

'Where's Richards and the kid?' Arthur asked calmly.

Andy remembered overhearing what Jamie had told Richards a few moments before he left and, in his last breath, he told Arthur where they'd had gone.

90

Tuesday Early Evening
Carmel Road, Darlington

Armed response and an array of police vehicles were speeding down Carmel Road towards Darchem's house. The first vehicle turned in and drove down the driveway until it stopped before the front door. A second vehicle entered, followed by a third, then a fourth.

Byrd pulled up on Carmel Road, halfway up the pavement. Both Byrd and Tanzy got out and briskly walked down the driveway towards the house. A team of armed officers were entering through the open door, followed by a cluster of PCs, Amy Weaver and Josh Andrews being among them.

They heard a gunshot from inside the house causing Byrd and Tanzy to drop to their knees.

'Inside!' Tanzy shouted. 'Come on!'

Byrd and Tanzy stopped at the entrance of the house and peered into the hallway. Down to their right, they saw a man lying on his side, covered in blood. PC Andrews was kneeling down over him but, from the sea of blood beneath him, it was obvious he was dead.

Byrd and Tanzy stepped in and heard footsteps in the living room to their right. Slowly, they focused on the man on the sofa, awkwardly leaning back, blood covering the front of his body. The armed response member shouted, 'Clear,' before he left the room and went onto the next.

The detectives entered the room slowly.

'That's Darchem,' Byrd said, looking over to the sofa. Tanzy recognised him too, although it'd been a while since they'd both seen him. Six years before the police had been called when Darchem had allegedly punched someone, knocking several of their teeth out. However, several people in London had vouched that Darchem had been there when the fight had occurred so they'd had to remove him from their enquiries.

Now he stared vacantly up at the ceiling covered in his own blood.

There was a sound in the doorway behind them.

'Boss,' PC Weaver shouted. 'Upstairs. We found the children.'

Tanzy and Byrd left the living room and followed Weaver, climbing the stairs quickly. They passed several armed response personnel who were sweeping the rooms upstairs. They'd come across one of Darchem's men, a forty something guy who went by the name of Eric. He was claiming his innocence, that he'd done nothing wrong. PC Josh Andrews had cuffed him and was leading him out. Weaver and Byrd and Tanzy stepped aside, allowing them to pass on the landing.

They continued, stopping at an open door, where they saw several armed responders standing over the body of a young male lying on his back. There was a gun in his hand and blood covering his face. It was obvious he'd done it to himself and that this had been the gunshot they'd heard on their approach to the house.

'Have forensics been called?'

Weaver turned. 'Yes. And an ambulance too.'

'Good work,' Tanzy said to her.

'Come on,' Weaver told them, ignoring the praise, heading along the landing and taking a right, then another right. 'There's five of them.'

They arrived at the doorway to the children's room and stepped inside.

The five children were seated on the nearest bed side by side, holding each other's hands. A PC was kneeling down in front of them, making sure they were all okay. As Byrd and Tanzy came into their view, the children visibly tensed, obviously unsure who they were as they weren't wearing uniform.

Byrd raised his palms. 'It's okay, it's okay, we are with the police.'

'Yeah, don't worry,' PC Weaver assured them, 'they're our friends.'

'Are you all okay?' Byrd asked, kneeling down.

A collection of nods followed.

Tanzy looked down on them. They were dressed in grey pyjamas, their heads were shaved, and all of them had expressions of absolute relief that they were saved.

'Is one of you called Melissa Clarke?' Byrd asked. He knew which one was Melissa, but he wanted to see her smile with happiness when she heard her name being called.

Melissa, who was sitting to the far right of the bed, raised her hand. Byrd shuffled over to her. 'Your mother and father will be very excited to see you.' Smiling, he turned away and then asked, 'Do we have an Eddy Long here?'

The boy seated second from the left raised his hand quickly. 'I'm Eddy!'

'Good, it's nice to meet you!'

He looked at the other three but didn't recognise them. 'What are your names?'

'I'm Joseph Cameron,' the boy on the left said. Byrd picked up a Glaswegian accent straight away. He pointed to the boy on the other side of Eddy. 'This is my twin brother, John.'

'And what's your name?' Byrd asked the girl who hadn't spoken yet.

'I'm Annie Longstaff,' she said, her accent similar to the boys. 'What was the sound before?'

She was obviously referring to the gun shot, the detectives realised.

'It doesn't matter about that now. Everything is okay and you guys are all safe,' Byrd assured them confidently.

Tanzy took over. 'Well, it's very nice to meet you, Melissa, Eddy, Joseph, John, and Annie. Do you think it would be okay if you waited here while we got a doctor to come and check you are all okay? Then, after that, we can get you back home.'

They all nodded at him.

'Amy,' Byrd said to Weaver, grabbing her attention, 'can I have a private word?'

Weaver nodded and stood up, following Byrd out of the room to the landing. Byrd turned to face her.

'I need you to get in touch with the Greater Glasgow police. Ask them about children with those names that have been reported missing. Get straight on it.'

Weaver nodded and took out her phone to call the station for the number she needed.

Byrd turned back to the room but stopped when his phone pinged with a text message.

It was from Keith: *I really need to speak to you about something important, mate. As soon as possible.*

Byrd frowned, not knowing what it was or what it could be. He pressed the CALL button and put it to his ear. He was assuming it would be about their conversation yesterday when Byrd had told him they'd found Lyle.

'Keith, what's up, I'm busy…'

'Max, I need to tell you something important,' he said.

'I'm listening.'

'I need to tell you in person. You have to come to my house as soon as possible.'

'Listen, Keith, I'll be tied up for a little while. I'm at a crime scene…'

'I need to see you. I haven't been totally honest with you about things.'

Byrd glanced around. 'Can it wait?'

'No, Max, it can't. It's urgent. I'm in trouble,' he replied. 'I'll be waiting.' Keith hung up the phone and the line went dead.

Byrd wondered what on earth he was talking about. Whatever it was, it seemed important and Keith was obviously distressed. He *was* one of his best friends, after all.

Byrd headed back into the room and got Tanzy's attention, waving him over. 'Can you handle things here?' Byrd asked him when he joined him in the doorway.

Tanzy frowned. 'Why?'

'Keith Wilson says he's in trouble, he needs to speak with me now.'

'Can't it wait, we're busy here, Max.'

'I know but there's practically all of the station here, minus DCI Fuller,' Byrd explained. 'An ambulance is coming. Forensics are coming. There are three dead bodies who aren't going anywhere and five children that we've saved. One less old detective won't be missed.'

'Will you be long?'

'Doubt it, although I'm not sure what he has to say. I'll let you know when I'm coming back. Ring me if there's any updates.'

Tanzy nodded and watched Byrd turn, go down the stairs, and out of sight.

91

Tuesday Early Evening
Willow Road, Darlington

Alex Richards, once he'd dropped his son Callum off at his father's house, pulled up to the house in the dark-blue Kia Sportage. He turned off the engine, got out, and stepped up onto the path.

Standing at the gate of the house, he could see the number on the wall near the window. It was the same address Jamie had told him earlier, just before leaving Darchem's house. The living room curtains were closed but there was a light on behind them. The room directly above the living room was also lit, presumably the man's bedroom.

He opened the gate and walked to the front door, pushed down on the handle and was surprised when it opened. Once he was inside, he closed it gently, trying to keep as quiet as possible.

There was a light coming from the room at the end of the short hallway. He could see a table, then beyond that, a long narrow kitchen. To his right, there was an open door into the living room. He pulled out the bloody knife from his jacket and took a few steps inside. A television stood on a unit in the corner, switched on to some American police show. In the middle of the room, there was a black rug, located in front of a three-seater sofa against the far wall.

He slowly backed out and glanced up to his left, towards the stairs which were set in darkness. Heading towards the dining room at the end of the hall, he silently made his way towards the light and, peeping around the corner, saw a man sitting at the table on one of the chairs furthest away from him, focusing on the phone in his hand.

Next to the phone, was a block of white powder.

The man noticed Richards out of the corner of his eye and looked directly at him.

Richards walked in, holding the knife by his side.

'You?' the man said, an expression of shock over his face.

'You know who I am?' Richards asked.

'I – I saw you on the news. The police want to speak to you,' the man told him, his voice almost breaking.

'Apart from the news, do you recognise me?'

The man at the table nodded.

'So, you know why I'm here, then?' Richards asked him, padding closer to the table. He glanced around, trying to locate any weapons that the man might be able to reach before he got to him, but he saw nothing.

The man nodded. 'I'm genuinely sorry for what happened to your daughter. And your wife too. I saw that part on the news.'

'I don't need your sympathy. If you were that sympathetic and decent, you would have disposed of the poisoned product so that my daughter would have lived.'

The man dipped his head for a moment. 'I know.'

Alex Richards, knife in hand, slowly moved closer to him, cautious of what the man might do, but the man stayed where he was. He didn't try to move nor did he make Richards change his mind about what he intended to do.

As Richards stopped beside him, he glanced up, staring into Richards' black eyes.

Richards tightened his grip on the knife but froze when he heard someone enter the room behind him.

'Keith, what's going on?' Byrd said, absorbing the scene, seeing Alex Richards standing beside his friend with a knife in his hand. 'Alex…'

C. J. Grayson

92

Tuesday Early Evening
Carmel Road, Darlington

Tanzy watched the paramedics enter the room and check over the children. He smiled, happy they were now safe. PC Weaver entered, placing her phone back into her pocket and said, 'I've been in touch with a sergeant from the Greater Glasgow Division. I explained the situation and gave him names of the children. He confirmed the children were taken roughly two months ago. They'd suspended the investigation and limited their use of resources, assuming the children had gone for good.'

Tanzy knew, after twenty-four hours of a child or adult going missing, statistically they were usually found. However, after forty-eight to seventy-two hours, it was rare that a child would be found, and if they were, it would be in circumstances which were less than desirable.

'Darchem was a bastard,' Tanzy said, then glanced down to the floor.

'He was,' she agreed.

Tanzy looked away, frowning, in deep thought.

'What's up?' Weaver asked him.

'Max got a text from Keith Wilson, saying he needed to speak to him urgently. Max went to his house but said he'd be back soon.'

'When did he go?'

'Less than five minutes ago, but I have a bad feeling about it. Something isn't right.'

'Why, Orion?'

395

'It's – it's just a feeling I have,' he told her. He thought a little more. 'With Alex Richards still out there, the streets aren't safe. Not even for us. I want you to come with me. We'll go to Keith's house. Once I know things are okay, we'll come back here.'

Weaver nodded and followed him down the stairs. When they reached the bottom, they saw Tallow and Hope walking in, dressed in their usual white outfits, wearing face masks. They were directed to the right by Sergeant Jack Tunstall who was standing in the centre of the hallway.

'Busy night eh?' Tanzy said.

Tunstall sighed. 'No kidding. Where you guys off to?'

'I have a bad feeling about something. It could be nothing, but I need to check.'

'You need any help?'

'Amy and I should be fine,' Tanzy said, walking past him.

As they reached the open door, Tunstall shouted, 'Wait.' Tanzy and Weaver turned. Tunstall then leaned around the door in the kitchen and shouted, 'Jericho, here please mate.'

A large officer in tactical response gear, holding a gun down by his side, came into view. In a deep voice, he said, 'Boss?'

'Jericho, go with DI Tanzy and PC Weaver please. They need to check something out.'

Jericho nodded, then made his way to the door, stopping before Tanzy and Weaver. 'Let's go.'

The three of them left the house and got into a marked Astra, the one that Weaver had used to drive to the scene. Tanzy climbed into the driver's seat, turned on the engine, and reversed the vehicle off the driveway. As they turned left at the roundabout, heading into Cockerton, they noticed a red Mondeo coming from the opposite direction, turning left into Deneside Road.

'There!' Tanzy shouted.

Jericho, in the back seat, became alert. 'What?'

'Look, it's the red Mondeo!' Tanzy informed them.

Weaver caught a glimpse of the reg plate as it turned into the road and nodded her head. 'It's him, the man who shot Jim Leonard.'

'Okay, okay,' Tanzy said. 'Let's all keep calm. We'll follow him.' Tanzy, without signalling, took a right turn into Deneside Road, ending up roughly thirty metres behind the red Mondeo. It took the first left into Newlands Road and, for a moment, it went out of sight. As they turned, they saw the car halfway up the street, approaching Willow Road. At the junction, it went right. Tanzy accelerated to the junction and, glancing right, noticed the Mondeo had stopped a few houses down.

A tall man stepped out of the Mondeo holding a gun in his hand and went through the open gate of a house. Then he opened the front door and stepped inside.

Tanzy recognised the dark-blue Kia Sportage and Byrd's X5 on the road.

'What the hell is going on here?'

He stopped behind the Mondeo and climbed out, Jericho with his gun ready, moving them aside and going in first through the gate. Tanzy and Weaver followed.

That's when they heard the gunshot from inside the house.

93

Tuesday Early Evening
Willow Road, Darlington

Byrd reached the end of the hall and walked into the dining room. He saw Keith sitting at the table.

'Keith, what's going on?' Then he saw Alex Richards standing next to him with the knife in his hand. 'Alex…'

Richards stared at Byrd for a long time, until Byrd moved forward. 'Alex, I'm going to need you to put down that knife.'

Richards said, 'No fucking chance. He killed my daughter.'

Byrd frowned at his words, then glanced down at Keith. 'I – I don't understand?'

Richards glared down at Keith. 'You want to tell him?'

Keith told Byrd about the drugs, that he'd been having issues with rats and that he had accidently knocked over the tub of rat poison which had mixed with the cocaine.

'Cocaine?' Byrd shook his head. 'What Cocaine?'

'The cocaine I sold Darchem last year. The stuff he sent his boys out with, the same stuff that Lisa Richards used a few hours later.'

'What – what, wait on a minute,' Byrd said, unable to get his head around this. 'Keith, I don't understand?'

'I've been a dealer for years, Max,' he confessed. 'You see that plumbing van outside?'

Byrd nodded.

'I haven't touched a spanner in years. That's what I wanted to speak to you about. Alex found out from one of

398

Darchem's men that his daughter had died from the product I'd supplied, Max. All of this is my fault. Mark Greenwell, Brian Cornforth and my own son. I killed my own son.'

He dropped his face into his hands and started to cry.

'Fucking man up!' Richards screamed.

Byrd kept a close eye on the knife in Richards' hand, knowing that if Richards decided to cut Keith's throat, there'd be nothing he could do to stop him. Without a weapon Byrd tried a different approach.

Moving to his left, he pulled out a chair at the opposite end of the table and sat down. Both Keith and Richards watched him closely. He was about to say something when he heard a sound to his right. He looked.

Standing in the hallway, with a gun in his hand, was Arthur.

Byrd jumped up the same time as Arthur fired the gun at him.

94

Tuesday Early Evening
Willow Road, Darlington

Byrd instinctively threw himself forward, then dived to the left, behind the table.

The sound of the gunshot took Richards by surprise but he darted to the left, towards the wall for more protection, keeping his eye on the doorway, ready for whatever was coming through it. Arthur entered the room, holding the gun at arm's length and Richards threw his knife at him.

The knife hit Arthur in the arm, causing him to drop the gun. Richards charged towards him, going in low with his right shoulder into Arthur's midsection, driving him back and slamming him into the wall with a sickening thud.

Arthur pulled the knife from his arm, and let it fall to the floor, then began to hit Richards on the top of his head with his elbow. After the sixth strike, Richard's grip loosened and Arthur rolled him away, then crawled across the floor to reach for his gun.

Byrd, from Arthur's left, kicked him in the side of his face. It barely seemed to affect him, although Byrd felt like it should have taken his head off his shoulders. Byrd tried again, bringing his right leg up, but Arthur grabbed it, and stood up, lifting Byrd up with him. Then, with unbelievable strength, Arthur threw Byrd onto the table which collapsed, causing Byrd to hit the floor with a loud thump.

Arthur casually bent down and picked up the gun, then stood up straight, facing Keith Wilson. He raised the gun at Keith's chest—

The sound of a gunshot echoed loudly.

Arthur stumbled and turned to his right. Along the hall near the front door, Jericho had fired a shot at him. His first bullet had caught Arthur in the right arm. Arthur turned fully towards him with an outstretched arm, his gun levelled and Jericho's second bullet hit Arthur in the centre of the chest.

Arthur swayed a second, then keeled over, landing on the floor near Byrd.

Richards, recovering from Arthur's blows, pulled himself onto his hands and knees.

Jericho, Tanzy, and Weaver charged down the hall and entered the room.

Looking quickly around the room Jericho could see Byrd on the floor and Keith at the chair he was sitting on when Byrd had first entered the room. He hadn't moved a muscle and had watched the whole thing. Seeing no immediate threat, Jericho picked up the radio from his belt and called for back-up.

Tanzy lowered himself to Byrd, checked to see if he was okay. Byrd winced in pain.

'Where are you hurt?'

'My back,' Byrd said. 'I can barely move it.' Byrd attempted to get up.

'Just stay there!' Tanzy ordered him. 'Back up is on the way.'

Tanzy looked up to Jericho, who was standing over them. 'Call for medical attention, too, Max is injured.'

'What about Richards?' Byrd whispered.

'What about him?'

'He's over there on the floor,' said Byrd, pointing to his right.

Tanzy looked to where Byrd had pointed.

'There's no one else here, Max.'

95

Tuesday Early Evening
Willow Road, Darlington

'Then, where the fuck is he?' Byrd shouted in frustration, looking around the room as best he could.

Tanzy looked up at Jericho and signalled towards the back door. Jericho nodded, knowing what he meant, and dashed into the narrow kitchen with his gun raised high. There was no one there but felt the cold air when he saw the back door was open.

Alex Richards had escaped.

Byrd reached for Tanzy's hand and squeezed it. 'We did good, didn't we, Orion?'

'What do you mean, Max?'

'The kids from Glasgow, we found them,' Byrd said quietly. 'And – and…' he trailed off in pain.

'Hey, don't talk. Just try to relax, Max,' Tanzy said softly.

'Melissa Clarke. Eddy Long. Even Damien Spencer. We found them, Orion.'

'We did,' Tanzy said, squeezing his hand, grinning proudly. 'We got them.'

Tears formed in Byrd's eyes as he rested his head back to the floor and stared at the ceiling.

'Don't be getting all soft on me, Max. Tonight isn't over! We have a long night ahead of us. We need to find Alex Richards.'

Byrd told Tanzy to help him up to his feet.

'Careful, take it slow,' Tanzy told him, helping him up. 'You alright?'

C. J. Grayson

Byrd nodded, rubbing the back of his neck where he felt a little blood. 'Just a cut, I'll be fine.' He then turned to Arthur, dead on the floor. 'Tough one that guy!'

'They all go down eventually, Max, you know that,' Tanzy said, winking.

Then they both looked at Keith, who was still sat on the chair.

'Why did you come here, Max?' Tanzy asked. 'What did he want so badly?'

Byrd explained about the drugs, the rat poison, and the deaths it had caused. He turned to face Keith.

'Come on, Keith,' Byrd said. 'I'm taking you to the station. Out of respect for our past friendship, I'll take you in.'

Keith nodded in agreement, stood up slowly and, without hesitation, placed his wrists together in front of Byrd, who cuffed them. Then Byrd read him his rights and told him what was going to happen. He turned to Tanzy. 'I'll take him in my car. Back-up will be here any minute, but I'm not wasting any more time on this. We need to get back to Darchem's house – it's a mess over there. And we need to wrap things up.'

'Sure, I'll wait here. I'll report it. You guys go,' he told Byrd, then watched him lead Keith into the hallway and out the front door towards his X5. He then turned to Weaver, who looked tired. 'You okay, Amy?'

'What a day, Orion.' She sighed lightly. 'Ready for my bed.'

'You and me both.'

Weaver let out a tired sigh but smiled.

Byrd led Keith down the path to his car.

'In the back, Keith,' he told him. Keith complied, leaning in and swinging his legs inside. Byrd closed the back passenger door and climbed in the front, dropped into his seat and sighed heavily, rubbing his face with his palms.

'Thank you being honest with me,' Byrd said to him, glancing through the mirror.

Keith matched his stare. 'It was about time.'

They shared a smile together, then Byrd placed his key into the ignition, but froze when he saw something in the rear view mirror, in the boot of his car.

Alex Richards was behind Keith, and the knife's blade in his hand glistened in the nearby streetlights.

96

Tuesday Early Evening
Willow Road, Darlington

Alex Richards sliced Keith's throat with a thick, deep horizontal cut. Blood sprayed from his throat down the front of him, and onto the back seats of the car. There was a look of terror in his eyes.

Byrd hadn't seen anything like it.

'You fucker!' Byrd screamed at him, turning to face the back of the car. 'You – you – you fucker. Bastard!'

Keith's head dropped forward, then his body fell to the right until he was laid across the back seat.

Byrd turned quickly and pressed the LOCK button on the car's central locking, then turned back to him. 'Now you're fucked, Alex.'

'What makes you think I want to get away?' he said holding up a set of keys, smiling.

Byrd scowled at him. 'You have nowhere to go,' he told him.

'I don't want to go anywhere. I'm exactly where I need to be,' he said calmly.

'You're going to prison,' Byrd said, matter-of-factly.

'I don't think so.'

Byrd took a deep breath. 'Why, Alex? Why all this? Mark Greenwell, Lyle Wilson, Brian Cornforth. Jonny Darchem. Keith Wilson? Why?'

'Because they all played a part in my daughter's death. Each one of them. Weeks ago, someone admitted what had happened. For that, I let him live. He told me what happened at the party and who was there. Mark and Lyle gave her the drugs. Brian came onto her more than once, but the fat bastard wouldn't take no for an answer. Jonny Darchem was a bastard and you know, as well as I do, I've done you and everyone in this town a favour there.' He paused for a moment. 'And Keith was responsible for the poison in the cocaine. He said it himself. If it wasn't for him, we wouldn't be in this mess.'

'How long had you planned this?'

'A little while,' he told Byrd. 'Once I found out how my daughter had died, I kept hearing Alice talking about her friend's wonderful partner, the hotshot police detective. How she claimed you had life all figured out, how driven you were. So, I thought I'd fucking show you. I registered a Jaguar I bought in your name. I'm sure you saw the letter from the DVLA?'

Byrd nodded. 'We lost the letter, though.'

Richards smiled, shaking his head. 'No, Alice took it from the microwave in your kitchen when she was round. I knew the letter would come and we'd planned it perfectly. Once I told her what Jamie had said, she was happy for me to do this. She found your spare set of keys from a tin you kept in the cupboard above the microwave.' He paused a beat. 'What I hadn't planned was you turning up tonight and ruining it.'

'Well I apologise for doing my job.'

'You're such a superstar detective aren't you, DI Max Byrd?'

'I saw the video after you dumped the body of Lyle Wilson at the Joseph Pease statue. Who was the other man? There were two of you near the library.'

'Just an old friend. He played no part in this. I paid him a hundred pound to dress in the clothes I sent him and to get out of the Jaguar and wave at the camera when I signalled him.'

Byrd stared, waiting for more. Then, behind Richards, through the rear windscreen, he saw blue lights flying down Willow Road towards them, sirens piercing the cold, winter air.

'Your time is up, Alex.'

'Like I said, I'm not going to prison. My job here is done. It's been a pleasure, Max Byrd.'

Byrd watched Richards raise the knife to his own throat and, in one swift movement, he sliced across it, blood spurting as he fell back into the back of the boot.

'No, you fucking coward!' Byrd screamed at him. He opened the door quickly, dashed to the back of the car, and opened the boot. Richards' dead eyes stared vacantly up at Byrd as the blood pooled in the boot of the car.

Byrd sighed heavily and turned round to face the oncoming cars. To his right, he could see Tanzy in the doorway of Keith's house, obviously wondering why he wasn't on the way to the station.

He walked over to Byrd's car and saw Richards in the boot, his eyes gaping open staring up at the stars, the knife still in his hand.

'Where's Keith?'

'In the back.'

Tanzy went to look but Byrd grabbed his arm and shook his head.

'Richards waited in the boot for us, sliced Keith's throat. Then his own.'

'Are you hurt?' Tanzy asked.

Byrd shook his head slowly then looked down the road at the oncoming blue lights.

Tanzy stepped across to the rear of the car and sat on the edge of it, next to Byrd. The back-up cars slowed behind and came to a stop, followed by an ambulance.

'Well, at least we're still alive, Max,' Tanzy said, patting his shoulder.

'That's true.'

A paramedic came over to check if they were okay. Byrd told him they were and told a nearby PC that there was a dead body inside the house and the two bodies in the car just behind him.

Tanzy and Byrd waited at the back of the X5 for a few moments, knowing their night wasn't over just yet, watching the frantic activity in front of them.

'How you holding up, Max?'

'Never a dull day in this town,' Byrd replied.

'Hey, that's my line…'

Their eyes met, and they shared a tired smile.

'Someone once told me to count your rainbows, not your thunderstorms,' said Byrd.

Tanzy frowned at him. 'I like that. Who said that?'

Byrd smiled sadly. 'My mam. It was the last thing she said to me before she died.'

Epilogue

Jonny Darchem's house was searched thoroughly by the police. They found the DNA of numerous children who'd been held captive in the large bedroom on the first floor. Searches for the children would be carried out immediately and any potential leads would be followed up.

Melissa Clarke and Eddy Long were returned home the same day they were rescued and Tracy Clarke and Henry Long burst into tears when they saw them alive and well.

The children from Glasgow, Joseph and John Cameron, and Annie Longstaff were collected by members of the Greater Glasgow Police and taken safely home to their parents.

The man they arrested at Darchem's house, Eric, had confessed to the police how Darchem had kidnapped children and sold them on to people all over the country, and that he'd been doing it for years.

The man who stabbed the victim in the toilet of Uno Momento had been finally found after attempting to break into a jewellers in Queen Street in the middle of the night. He confessed to killing the man at the restaurant and was sentenced to life in prison.

Jake Anderson, the brave teenager who jumped into the River Tees to save Damien Spencer, was mentioned on the ITV News a few days after he saved Damien, standing with the Mayor of Darlington, who said he was very proud of him and what an amazing example he was for the people of Darlington.

Tanzy continued turning in every day, fighting the good fight, leading the team under him. He had booked a holiday for the summer with Pip and his children, Eric and Jasmine. They were all excited and looking forward to getting away. Pip was now six months sober and couldn't be happier with life. He continued with his Judo training and had started helping the tutor teach one of the beginner classes at the Dolphin Centre.

Claire had settled into her new home with Byrd and she'd re-decorated a few rooms. It was easier for Byrd to go along with it since he knew it made her happy. And, to her credit, it looked good. He'd slowly got over the fact his mother and father weren't going to be around anymore, and visited their graves twice a week, leaving flowers and telling them how much he loved them. On the 17th of April 2020, Claire had told Byrd she was pregnant. They found out several months later, they were going to have a boy and, after some thought, had decided to call him Alan, after Byrd's father.

Acknowledgements

I hope you enjoyed 'Never Came Home' as much as I did writing it. It took me around four months to write the first draft and a further two months to edit it, which was similar to the first book in the series, That Night. My debut novel, Someone's There (a standalone, not linked to the DI Byrd and DI Tanzy series), took me four years after changing the story several times. So, I'm happy I'm (sort of) getting the hang of the process.

A big thank you goes to my family and friends. Their support in my passion is a blessing. I really appreciate it. From my experience, as many writers will know, it's very hard finding the time to write when you work full time and have a family, not to mention day-to-day living, so a big thanks goes to them for their patience.

A special mention to several Facebook groups such as Crime Fiction Addict, Crime Book Club, Books on the Positive Side, Book Mark, and Skye's Mum and Books, for their support. There are many great individuals in these groups, some of those who are fellow writers and, almost every one of them, avid readers. In one way or another, they have supported me, whether it be friendship, light entertainment, or book recommendations. Feel free to check out their pages as they are always looking for new members to share their passions for reading and crime.

I have to be honest and say Never Came Home wouldn't have been published the way it was without the following three people.

James Leonard (who enjoys reading Linwood Barclay and Blake Crouch) took the time to go over this and, with his knowledge and skills on police procedures, he guided me where I was blind and picked up on several parts which didn't quite fit together. Thank you for doing that, Jim, and for the on-going support with my writing and, of course, our friendship.

Shez Barker (an avid reader who enjoys Chris Carter and Barbara Copperthwaite) connected with me via social media and, after plenty of social interactions, I now consider her a good friend. I know her job as a nurse is very time consuming and demanding, so for her to use much of her spare time to proofread this is massively appreciated. She picked up on some very valuable points which has sharpened this novel up so I want her to know I'm very grateful for that. Her support has stretched back before I published my debut novel and that's something I'll always remember.

Dave Peacock (a family friend who enjoys reading Bernard Cornwall and many others) is a very meticulous, avid reader, who picked up on the smallest of errors which I was too blind to see. He offered his advice on grammar and suggested ways to alter various parts which dramatically improved the pacing of the story. His editorial skills were second to none. Thanks to Dave for taking the time to do that and for his careful, valuable eye. He told me he wants to write a novel of his own in the future, which is something I seriously hope will happen.

Many people have helped me in some way during the last seven months whilst writing Never Come Home. I'd like to acknowledge the following individuals for their support: Leigh Lewis, Deepak Patrai, Shaun Lewis, Chris Strong, Keith Greer, David Hall, Judith Hall, Laura Thompson, and Ivan Gaskin. I could name many, many more.

My biggest thank you goes to my wife, Becky. An absolute superstar of a woman who holds our family together like glue, letting me hide away and write while she keeps the children busy. I'm surprised she hasn't packed her bags and left because I'm book-mad but she's still here supporting me.

My last thank you is to you, the reader. You make all of this possible. Some of you have read all of my books so far and have continually shown your support via my social media profiles (Facebook, Instagram etc.) with your kind likes, generous shares, and valuable comments. Without you, I wouldn't be typing this.

Thank you.

About the Author

C. J. Grayson has self-published his third novel six months after he released his second novel, That Night. Writing will always be hard (if you write, you'll know what's involved), but it's a passion he's always loved and he'll continue to do it for as long as he can. He loves reading crime thrillers, watching supernatural / horror films, and drinking gallons of coffee.

In his earlier days, he did an apprenticeship in Pipefitting and worked in Engineering and Construction. He completed his HND in Mechanical Engineering and a Level 6 Diploma in Business Management.

He's aged 31, lives in Darlington, in the North East of England, with his wife, Becky, and their three boys, Cameron, Jackson, and Grayson.

After this novel, he plans to write the third book in the DI Max Byrd and DI Orion Tanzy series, so he hopes you'll be looking forward to that. After that, who knows...

If you can spare a few minutes and enjoyed this book, he'd really appreciate some feedback on Amazon and / or Goodreads. Your thoughts and support are more valuable to him than you'll ever know. They keep him up till the early hours writing.

Keep up to date with his current work and updates regarding future novels through his website and following social profiles. You can also sign up to his Newsletter by going on www.cjgraysonauthor.com and filling in the very short form at the bottom of the page. You will get updates on progress, exclusive giveaways, and news before the rest of the world does, so feel free to sign up.

www.cjgraysonauthor.com

www.facebook.com/cjgraysonauthor/

www.goodreads.com/author/show/19642709.C_J_Grayson

www.instagram.com/cjgrayson_writer/

www.twitter.com/CJGrayson4

Thank you.

Printed in Great Britain
by Amazon